BLACKOUT!

"Thirty seconds to preflare," said Post, glancing at the bright green symbols on the space shuttle's Head Up Display. "One minute to landing."

Reynolds said, "You'd think we were approaching Edwards instead of some emergency field halfway around the world from it."

Through the last broken layers of clouds the dark shape of the island Mahé was clearly seen. Along most of the shoreline were clusters of light marking the locations of hotels.

Directly ahead of the shuttle lay the airport runway, a ribbon of illumination some two miles long. Rows of approach lights flashed at either end, and there were floodlights on its hangars and support buildings.

And then, without warning, they all started going out.

"Jesus Christ!" Reynolds said.

"Huh?" Post said, and looked up from the HUD's reflector plate just in time to see the runway's beckoning glow disappear.

"They've turned everything off!" Reynolds shouted.

PHOENIX CAGED

JOHN-ALLEN PRICE

ZEBRA BOOKS
KENSINGTON PUBLISHING CORP.

ZEBRA BOOKS are published by

Kensington Publishing Corp.
475 Park Avenue South
New York, NY 10016

First Printing: June, 1993
Printed in the United States of America

To G. Harry Stine (aka: Lee Correy)—
Rocketry expert, curmudgeon and fellow novelist.
Without whose assistance neither this book
or
THE PURSUIT OF THE *PHOENIX*
would have flown so high or so accurately.

Prologue

*****Break**Break**Break*****
COMSUBLANT SIGNIT Bulletin
TIME: March 30, 1992. 0800 hours.
FROM: COMSUBLANT Hq. Norfolk, Va.
TO: Holy Loch, Scotland
    U.S.S. John Marshall (SSN 611)
    Captain T.W. Carver, commanding.
With the completion of your refit and shore leave following the *Ocean Valkyrie* incident, you are ordered to return to home port, Norfolk Stop You are to weigh anchor by no later than 0700 hours, tomorrow Stop On your arrival at Norfolk you and SEAL Team Commander Glenn Allard are to report immediately to Vice Admiral Daniels office for reassignment STOP
END TRANSMISSION ********************

"Captain Carver . . . Commander Allard," Admiral Daniels acknowledged, when his secretary opened the office door and motioned the two officers in. "You needn't bother sitting, this won't take long."

The remark caught the lower-ranking officers by

surprise, and caused them to stop after they made their salutes. One of them, the black captain, already had his hand on a chair and was swinging it around so he could slide into it. He gave a sideways glance to his younger, white subordinate and then straightened up.

"I know that tone of voice," said Carver. "This isn't going to be pleasant. So let's get on with it, sir."

"You know it, mister. And you two thought you were going to be welcomed home as heroes," said Daniels, at first surprised by Carver's directness. "Well you're not going to get it in this office. The British and the Europeans have given you all the cheering you'll receive. The party's over, gentlemen, your day of reckoning is here."

"For what, Admiral?" said Allard, trying to look innocent. "We rescued the oil rig crew, and prevented the terrorists from carrying out their mission."

"Don't get smart with me, Mister Allard. You may be special forces, but I'm still your overall commander. Where his sub goes, you go. Not unless you'd like a transfer?"

"Sorry, sir. You're not going to split us up that way."

"Good, I'd prefer taking care of two problems with one order anyway," said Daniels. "And you're both guilty of the same offense."

"And which one is that?" Carver requested. "Success?"

"Disobeying my orders, Captain! On February fourth you were issued an order to return to Norfolk, after the cancellation of your commando exercise. But you chose to ignore it to pursue your own glory and self-promotion."

"If I may be allowed, Admiral. There was another COMSUBLANT order later in the day. It alerted us

8

to the taking of *Ocean Valkyrie,* and advised all Special Forces to pre-position their resources."

"Yes, Captain, I know the bulletin," said Daniels, waving his hand to dismiss it. "General orders don't outweigh specific orders. You should've returned here to await your assignment, and you should never have contacted the British on your own."

"Submarine captains have traditionally been allowed a great latitude in interpreting orders," said Carver.

"Yes, I know. That's the typical excuse all sub skippers cite for disobeying orders, and it won't help you here."

"What would you have preferred, Admiral? For the Libyans to have succeeded in their plan to destroy the North Sea oil fields? As it is we only just beat them out. If I had obeyed my 'specific' orders, they'd be celebrating their victory, and my sub would be scrapped."

"Victory? I don't exactly call sinking the oil rig and losing a half-dozen men a victory," Daniels snapped sarcastically. "And the only Libyan 'connection' I see in all this is that you sank one of their submarines. Which they're suing us for in the World Court."

"What the hell? What about all the information the Israelis gave us on this Blood Revenge group?" Allard asked.

"Commander, now really. Do you think I believe everything the Jews tell us? They'll say anything to improve their popularity and get still more weapons out of us."

"An anti-Semitic submarine officer. How the hell did you get past Hyman Rickover?"

"That will be enough, Mr. Allard!" said Daniels, letting his anger show more forcefully. "If I were

9

your superior you'd be facing a disciplinary board for that remark. As it is, I can only send a letter of complaint to the commander of Navy Special Forces. While I doubt such an action will have any effect on your attitude, I think your next assignment will. Your SEAL Team and the *John Marshall* are being reassigned to Diego Garcia, for an indefinite period."

"I know skippers who've been assigned there," Carver replied, and for a brief moment the shock registered on his face. "They call it Purgatory. I leave it to you, Admiral, to come up with an appropriately 'biblical' punishment for us."

"What would be more appropriate would be the scrapping of your submarine and your early retirement. But the Washington press and your protectors, especially Congresswoman Claudia Chalmers, would protest too much. If I put you at the end of the world, in a few months people will forget you're heroes. They'll forget you even exist and then, God willing, I can deal with you the way I want."

"Don't be so sure, Admiral. You'll have to haul my black ass off my command in chains before I'll let you scrap her."

"That will be enough from you, too, Mr. Carver," said Daniels, without the anger he directed at Allard, but with a hint of triumph in his voice. "I'll allow your crew to benefit from my Christian charity and give you sixty days for shore leave and preparations for departure. You have your orders, I suppose it's traditional to wish you luck. You're dismissed, Captain. Commander."

The Admiral pressed a button on his desk-top communications panel and almost immediately his secretary opened the door. Carver and Allard came to attention before being ushered out to collect their caps and raincoats. They said little to each other until they had left Daniels's offices; until they had even left the building the offices were located in. Outside an early spring rain was falling. Light, yet just enough to make the sidewalks and parking lot sloppy.

"Well, I hear at least the weather's nice at Diego Garcia," Allard finally spoke up. "We won't have to worry about freezing to death."

"No, just dying of boredom," said Carver, making a direct line to the staff car which had brought them to the building. "I've heard from other skippers who were stationed at Garcia. They've had men go stir crazy and try to swim back to the States, or steal their ships. I hope I can keep my men from doing anything like that. What about yours?"

"SEALs are already crazy, so you don't have to worry there. We can probably keep our men happy with shore leaves in Australia. I'll see if Allard Technologies can charter an airliner to fly our families there."

"Must be nice to belong to a family with real money." As Carver reached the staff car he almost beat out the driver to opening the passenger door; he and Allard only had to wait a moment before climbing inside. "And we may have to use it the way you mentioned to keep our crews together. Seaman, take us back to the *Marshall*. Might as well get the hard part over with and tell them the bad news first."

11

One

"CAP COM, this is *Phoenix*. We've completed preliminary systems tests, the bird is nominal. Julie's in the air lock and Major Glassner's doing his final EVA checks. Over."

"Roger, *Phoenix*. You are go for EVA. If everything checks out you'll be cleared for satellite deployment. Cochran's at lunch but he'd still like to know how his Lady's doing. Over."

"Tell Ed there aren't any stranded Russians for us to rescue," Reynolds observed. "But for her first time out since she made history the girl's doing just fine."

From his vantage point in the commander's seat, there was much for Clayton Reynolds to observe. Nearly two hundred miles in altitude, the space shuttle *Phoenix* was over the central Pacific and just south of the Hawaiian Islands. Ahead of him he could see the approaching landmasses of North and South America. Like the Pacific Ocean, they were partially hidden under a broken cloud cover which contained at least one cyclonic storm system.

Immediately behind Reynolds the shuttle's flight

13

deck had become quiet and less active with the departure of Rebecca Wheeler to the mid deck. There, she would help Allan Glassner complete preparations for his Extravehicular Activity (EVA) walk. For the moment Reynolds only shared the flight deck with Walter Post, the *Phoenix*'s pilot.

"Boss, the aft station flight controls check out just fine," said Post, locking the safeties on the two hand grips. "I'm coming forward."

Before he pushed off from the aft crew station, Post glanced through its observation windows. Nestled snugly in the spaceplane's huge cargo bay was the sole reason why it was now in orbit: a KH-12 Keyhole reconnaissance satellite. More than forty feet long and of the same general configuration as the Hubble space telescope, the KH-12 sat in a specially designed cradle. Its solar cell panels were folded against its sides; its aperture door closed tightly over its imaging systems.

"How does everything look back there?" asked Reynolds.

"From the payload status panels the bird is nominal," said Post, who stopped his glide forward by grabbing hold of the cockpit seat headrests. Then, he glanced down at the floor hatch to his left. "And it looks like Rebecca is helping Allan get his cooling garment on. What did Houston have to say?"

"We're go for EVA. And if the KH-12 passes all its tests during the space walk, we're go for deployment."

"Good, once we release it we can do a little sightseeing and finish those student experiments. Let's find out how Julie's doing."

"All right, you listen to Houston. I'll switch to the intercom," said Reynolds, hitting one of the toggles on the communications panel over his head. As he lowered his arm, his attention suddenly switched to outside the cockpit. "Walt, I think there's a . . ."

A white flash briefly illuminated the cockpit windows, as a sharp jolt rippled through the shuttle's airframe. It was far more powerful than the firing of its thrusters, or even the main engines. When the flash ended there was a flurry of small particles hitting the windows; all of them originating from a jagged hole in the nose thruster module.

"Meteor! Commander to crew, meteor strike! Nose RCS module. Check mid deck for penetration and damage. Walt, get up here and warn Houston. We have an in-orbit emergency."

"What the hell? Did I hear right?" Major Allan Glassner asked, speaking slowly and loudly so he could be heard through the face mask of his Portable Oxygen System.

"If you heard a 'meteor strike' you sure did," said Rebecca Wheeler. "Look!"

As she turned she let go of Glassner's ventilation and cooling garment, causing it to drift away instead of dropping to the floor. Rebecca pointed at what she had spotted from the corner of her eye; plumes of orange mist spiralling out one of the mid deck's storage lockers. It only took a moment for the two astronauts to realize what the mist was.

"Hydrazine!" Glassner shouted, pulling on the blue flightsuit he had been trying to slip off. "The meteor must've ruptured one of the RCS fuel tanks. Get outta here, Becky! Seal the roof hatch. Julie and I will take care of this!"

Pushing off from the floor, Rebecca sailed for the hole in the roof's port side. With some wiggling, she pulled her way through it, slamming the hatch cover

15

shut and locking it a few seconds later. By then Glassner had his flightsuit back on and was opening a floor panel to access the shuttle's life-support system. From there he would help isolate the mid deck's atmosphere from that on the flight deck.

"Houston, this is *Phoenix*. We've suffered a meteor strike," Post repeated, as Reynolds checked both manually and on the General Purpose Computer (GPC). "We confirm damage to the nose RCS module, we have a hydrazine fuel leak on the mid deck. We are declaring an in-orbit emergency and request an abort advisory."

"Roger, *Phoenix*. We copy," said Houston's Capsule Communicator, Caroline Ross. "We're switching to abort mode. Standby on advisory."

"Which means they're running around like chickens with their heads off," said Reynolds, clicking one last pair of toggle switches on his left-hand panels. "This has to be the only airplane in the world that can declare an emergency and have ground control panic, while we remain calm. Flight deck atmosphere is now isolated from the mid deck. We're operating on separate life supports. Rebecca, is that hatch sealed?"

"Yes, Commander," she answered. "Looks like we won't be doing any more flying between the decks. What shall I do next?"

"Go to the aft crew station and deactivate all satellite systems. This bird will have to fly on another mission. Walt, pressurize all RCS engines in the nose module. Then hit the cutoff valves to their fuel tanks. Flight deck to air lock, Julie, as soon as you're finished suiting up I want you to enter the mid deck and help Allan."

"Boss, are you sure we should close the fuel lines?" said Post, his hand poised to reach the Reaction Control System (RCS) panels over his head. "Shouldn't we try to leave them open as long as we can?"

"No, the hydrazine tank is venting its contents to a vacuum," said Reynolds. "If we don't close the lines now, everything will get sucked into space. Hopefully, we'll have enough propellants in the lines to do what little maneuvering we need. Flight deck to air lock, Julie, do you copy your instructions?"

"I copy, Clayton," said Julie Harrison, lowering her helmet onto her suit's neck ring and clicking it in place. "I'll be out as soon as my gear's ready."

With her glove and helmet seals locked, Julie tapped the oxygen control switch on her chestpack. In moments the black woman's space suit had inflated to the point where she could test it for leaks. Once she had finished, she disconnected her suit from its wall-mounted service umbilical, switching to internal power and its own oxygen supply.

Instead of depressurizing the air lock to begin her EVA, she reached for the mid deck hatch's handle and rotated it. Through the tiny observation window, Julie could see Glassner rushing to stow equipment before it was contaminated by the hydrazine mist. With a smooth clicking, the latches retracted, and Julie easily pushed the hatch cover out and then up to the right. She emerged from the air lock head first; taking care not to catch her backpack or chestpack on the hatch rim. When she finally stood upright she nearly collided with Glassner.

"Still want to tell me your second mission is going to be uneventful?" he asked, speaking loudly so they could hear each other.

17

"No, would you like to tell me you still want some excitement on this flight?" Julie replied. "Finish locking up the galley. I'm going forward for the med kit. You'll need some gloves to protect your hands from the fuel."

"Phoenix, this is Houston. Abort advisory completed," said Caroline. "The list is as follows. You are too late for a reentry attempt at any continental U.S. field. If you select one of them, you must wait until your next orbit. You are no-go for Kourou in French Guyana, Rota, Dakar and Ascension. Botswana is possible, but the political situation there is deteriorating. Your optimum abort fields are Mahé Island in the Seychelles and Yarmouth, Australia."

"Roger, Houston. We copy," said Post. "All right, Clay, which one will it be?"

"Well, the Seychelles aren't Australia," Reynolds observed, watching a visual display of the abort fields on the cockpit's middle CRT screen. Immediately below it was the center pedestal, with the computer keyboard he was using. "But the GPC says it's three thousand miles closer, and I've heard the weather's nice there even in January. Tell Houston we're go for Mahé Island. I'm dumping the flight programs and initiating emergency deorbit program load."

"Commander, the satellite's been deactivated," said Rebecca. "All systems are cold. What shall I do next?"

"Lock yourself into one of the aft station's foot restraints. We're coming up on our deorbit burn in two minutes, twenty-seven seconds. Mark. The event timer is on and running. OMS engines, armed. Abort program Six-Zero-Nine, loaded. Transferring

18

OMS system to GPC command. Rebecca, stand by to secure payload bay doors after deorbit burn. Reynolds to mid deck, we're going to reorientate the orbiter for the burn."

"Allan, did you hear? We're going to have to find something to hold onto," Julie warned, shoving the medical kit back inside its storage locker. "I went through this on my last flight."

"You mean your *first* flight," said Glassner, trying to be humorous. "One mission and the girl thinks she's a veteran. Let's have those gloves, I can already feel my skin tingling."

Pushing off from the forward bulkhead, Julie moved back to the galley with a package of surgical gloves in her hand. By the time she reached Glassner, he was standing near the center of the mid deck with his hands already raised. She ripped open the package and, allowing it to drift in front of her, easily removed the thin latex gloves.

She could see Glassner's hands were starting to turn red from exposure to the hydrazine drifting around them. Julie carefully slid first one glove, then the other, over his hands. In spite of her attempts to be gentle, Glassner still winced in pain as the latex rubbed against his skin and fitted tightly around his fingers.

"Now, no matter what you do don't start scratching," said Julie, snapping the glove ends around the cuff of each sleeve. "Until we can get you treated, it will only make things worse. Hold on."

Julie and Glassner grabbed hold of each other's arms when they sensed the cabin starting to rotate around them. Because of the gear they both wore, neither could hear the thruster engines firing, and

19

only Julie heard the flight deck chatter on her headset.

"May I have this dance?" Glassner asked.

"Watch it, my husband's a jealous man," said Julie. "From what Clay and Walt are saying, the deorbit burn will start right after they finish maneuvering. You can still use the vertical bunk, I'll have to brace myself against the front bulkhead. Let's hope monomethyl hydrazine isn't as corrosive as it is hypergolic."

Responding to the GPC-selected burns of its thruster engines, the *Phoenix* pivoted on its central, Z-axis until it was slowly coming around to a tail-first attitude. Afraid of exhausting their limited fuel supply in the nose module, Reynolds and Post took almost twice as long to reorientate the shuttle. They completed the maneuver with only a few seconds to spare.

"Walt, lock your flight controls," Reynolds ordered. "Switching RCS thrusters to GPC command. OMS engines are pressurizing, exhaust nozzles have completed their gimbaling. Deorbit burn in five seconds. Four seconds. Three, two . . ."

At zero seconds, the two Orbital Maneuvering System (OMS) engines fired simultaneously. With only six-thousand-pounds thrust apiece, they had just one percent of the available power from the three main engines they were mounted above. But the huge main engines were cold, their nine minutes of use had come at the start of the flight. Now, the flight would begin its end with a three-minute firing of the comparatively weak OMS motors.

The deceleration effects from the shuttle's orbital velocity of more than seventeen thousand miles an hour occurred immediately. Both Reynolds and Post felt themselves being lifted out of their seats and pulled against their restraint belts. The straps dug painfully into their shoulders and stomachs; to counter it they grabbed their inactive control sticks and pushed against them. At the aft crew station, Rebecca took hold of the manipulator arm pistol grips to prevent her from being jerked backwards. On the mid deck, Glassner was pressed into the side of the vertical bunk while Julie had the most comfortable ride of the entire crew. The thick insulation of her space suit made it feel as though she were being pushed into a body-shaped mattress.

"Houston, this is *Phoenix*. Deorbit burn, completed," Post informed, while Reynolds slid out of his commander's seat. "We are now in Preentry Coast. Rebecca will secure the cargo bay doors. Clay is putting on his G suit. I'll reorientate the orbiter and will initiate emergency APU start. Over."

"Roger, *Phoenix*," said Caroline. "What are conditions like on the mid deck? Over."

"It's still filling with hydrazine mist. Glassner's suffering from some exposure to it, and Julie's going to try stopping it from leaking onto the deck."

"We copy, *Phoenix*. You are eighteen minutes to reentry commit. We're alerting Seychelles Tracking, they'll have Mahé International ready for you. Advise us immediately of any changes. Houston, out."

"Walt, before we do anything else we better drink this," said Reynolds, producing a series of foil containers from a flight deck locker. He sailed one each to Post and Rebecca, then tore the cap off the one he kept for himself. "If we're to land in the next hour, we'll need our Gatorade."

"But what about Allan and Julie?" Rebecca asked, easily snatching her container out of the air.

21

"I'm afraid they'll have to suffer through the dizziness and weakness until after we land. There's nothing we can do for them, we'll have our hands full just flying the ship."

"Ray, I'm glad you got here so fast," said one of the few staff members manning the Seychelles tracking station. He jumped up from his console and met the newest, highest-ranking, NASA officer to appear in the operations center.

"Well, how far away do I live from here?" Ray Fernandez answered, shaking the younger man's hand. "Half a mile? Less? There isn't too far you can go on this rock. And what does Houston have for us to solve? For getting me up at this hour, it had better be big. You better change that display, Joel, it's now January twenty-first."

Fernandez motioned to the time and date display on the wall map that the instrument consoles all faced. While the clock had just moved past midnight, the card below it still showed the previous day's date. Beyond the local time, the map revealed little else except the positions of NASA's other tracking stations in its worldwide net. It was not an electronic, computer-controlled marvel with glowing lines depicting the shuttle's orbital tracks. In fact the only part of the map showing any information on the *Phoenix* was an LED readout giving its orbit number, velocity, and the latitude and longitude of its current position.

"Houston's on the Secure One channel," said Joel Lomberg, pointing to a lighted button on the main communications panel. "They switched from the normal command channels the moment the problem began."

22

"It's losing speed," said Fernandez. "It's gone below normal velocity. Has it made a deorbit burn?"

"I'll let Houston explain. But it is serious."

Fernandez lifted one of the com panel's telephone receivers to his ear and hit the flashing button. He barely got to identify himself when Houston started explaining the emergency. He didn't ask many questions, there was no need to. In less than a minute he had all the information he wanted.

"We copy, Houston. Keep the line open, I'm switching to a headset." Fernandez laid the receiver aside and accepted the lightweight microphone and earphones his assistant handed him. "Joel, we got about fifty minutes before the *Phoenix* lands. After all its success, why did this have to happen to Ed's Lady? Houston, this is Seychelles Tracking. I'm back. We are activating the Microwave Landing System. We will contact the Seychelles government and airport. We'll have a field advisory for you in a couple of minutes, and should have traffic restricted about a half-hour before the orbiter lands. Over."

"Roger, Seychelles. We copy," was Houston's reply, heard on both the headsets and the Operations Center loudspeakers. "We will need your field advisory soon. The orbiter will begin communications blackout at L-Minus twenty-five minutes. Over."

"Don't worry, Houston, you'll get it. This is Seychelles Tracking, out," said Fernandez, then he tapped another button on his com panel. "This is the station manager to all personnel. We have a Code Alpha alert. The *Phoenix* has to make an emergency reentry, and Seychelles International has been selected for the landing site. Security desk, contact all off-duty personnel on the Alpha One list. Orbiter Support, power up the MLS and run a systems check on it. Joel, contact the airport. Let's get their cooperation now and contact Independence House later."

"Yes, on the corner of Revolution Avenue and Karl Marx Street," said Lomberg, using an auxiliary com panel on the console to get an outside line. "We'd do better to call the Libyan and Cuban embassies. They're the real power in these islands. And need I remind you that the airport refused to cooperate in the last month's emergency landing test."

"Well they'll have to now. This isn't an exercise, this is the real thing. People's lives are at stake."

"At least this isn't happening in the middle of the night," Edward Cochran sighed, walking into Houston's Mission Control center and heading to the back row of command consoles. "So we don't have to be roused out of bed and dragged here. Bill, what's the latest news on my Lady?"

"It may be midday here, but it's after midnight on the Seychelles," said Bill Corrigan, the Flight Information Dynamics Officer. "They'll have to wake up a lot of people to help us. As for the *Phoenix,* Clay and Walt have managed to reorientate her for reentry. They may even have some fuel left in the nose thrusters."

"I hope they do. Maneuvering a shuttle without the nose module is like threading a needle with baseball mitts on. Caroline, how do they sound?"

"At first, scared. Then again who wouldn't be?" said Caroline, hitting the "receive only" button at her Capsule Communicator station. "They sound better now, but still nervous."

"Ed, who's been told about this?" Corrigan asked. "Since it was a military flight to begin with, the Pentagon already knows. But who else?"

"I contacted Engleberg the minute you got the

news to me," said Cochran. "He's telling the State Department and the White House. I also gave orders for Glavkosmos and CNES to be told."

"Good, at least the other space agencies don't have to wonder if this is part of our mission or not. What we're going to have to worry about is the landing site itself. We've just been going through this."

Corrigan handed a slim folder to NASA's Director of Manned Flight Operations. It was marked "Contingency Abort Fields: Seychelles International Airport, Mahé Island." Inside it were State Department and CIA updates on the island nation, a few NASA memos and even some newspaper and magazine articles. Cochran glanced through the reports and articles whose headlines attracted his attention—none of which reassured him.

"Christ, this sounds like Albania with palm trees," he said, laying the folder on the command console. "Does it get worse?"

"It does," Caroline Ross answered. "The Seychelles government has refused to renew its signing of the Astronaut Return Treaty."

"What the hell's wrong with these people? Haven't they heard the news for the last four years? Communism sucks."

"They're being bankrolled by the Cubans and the Libyans," said Corrigan. "Not to mention their tourist industry. With financing like that, communism can still work."

"Is it too late to switch the *Phoenix* to another landing site?" Cochran asked, glancing at one of Mission Control's side screens. The world map on it showed the spaceplane's current orbital track and the positions of all the abort fields. "How about Botswana? Or Yarmouth?"

"Sorry, Ed. Your Lady's too late for either. The

25

only thing her crew can do at this stage is return to orbit and wait another thirty minutes for a try at Edwards."

"I won't make Clay or Walt do that. It looks like we're stuck with the Seychelles . . . Caroline, what stage of their reentry are they in?"

"They've positioned the orbiter for entry," she said. "And are going through their preentry check-lists."

"Okay, contact them once they're finished," said Cochran. "We have to let our friends know what they're getting into."

"Better get up here, Walt," Reynolds advised. "I'm ready to finish our entry switch over lists."

"Sure thing, just as soon as I grab my lines," said Post.

Like Reynolds before him, Post was now wearing an orange antigravity suit and his launch/reentry helmet. The ribbed air bladders on his stomach and legs squeaked softly as he moved forward and slid back into the right-hand seat. Rebecca took the two air lines running from his suit and connected them to the oxygen ports at the base of the center instrument pedestal. The third, much larger, line she plugged into the portable breathing unit behind the pilot's seat.

"Walt, I've hooked up your G suit to the orbiter's oxygen supply," said Rebecca, standing between the two cockpit seats. "And your helmet line to your Personal Egress Air Pack."

"Thanks, Rebecca. Better get back to your work on the cargo bay," Post responded. "I'm ready, boss."

"Cabin relief systems A and B," said Reynolds, fixing the second reentry cue card to the velcro board

26

between the cockpit's forward windows. "Systems, enabled. Cabin vent isolation, enabled. Antiskid system, on. APUs?"

"Auxiliary Power Units One, Two and Three, on," said Post.

"Nosewheel steering?"

"Nosewheel steering, off."

"Entry roll mode?"

"Entry roll mode, off."

"Speed brake controls?" said Reynolds, grabbing the throttle/speed brake lever on the left side of the cockpit. And Post wrapped his hand around a similar lever on the center pedestal's right side. Bumped and jostled out of position during the mission by crew movements, both levers were pushed back to their forward stops.

"Speed brakes reset and locked down," Post answered.

"Good, SRB and External Tank separation systems?"

"SRB and ET systems on automatic."

"Air Data system?"

"Switching Air Data to Navigation mode."

"ADI system?"

"ADI rate, medium. ADI error, medium."

"Hydraulic Main Pump pressure switches?"

"Switches One, Two and Three on Normal. Hydraulic pressure indicators read High Green. Switch over checklist complete."

"Time to tell Houston," said Reynolds, changing his com panel to transmit/receive. "Mission Control, this is *Phoenix*. Reentry switch over checks completed. Ready to test orbiter flight surfaces and initiate propellant dump. Do you have anything new for us? Over."

"Roger, *Phoenix*. Our Seychelles Station is activating its Microwave Landing System," said Cochran, his deep voice catching the flight deck crew by surprise. "Clay, how's my Lady doing?"

"Ed, is that you? I thought you were baby-sitting some senators? Since when did you become CAP COM?"

"Don't worry about them, they're old enough to take care of themselves. Now, how about the *Phoenix?* Over."

"Crippled. But she'll get us down," Reynolds answered. "I almost didn't see the meteor that hit us. I hope we can find something of it, it would make an interesting souvenir. Will Mahé's airport be ready for us? Over."

"The Seychelles Tracking Station is preparing for you," said Cochran. "Cooperation with the Seychelles government will be more of a problem. They've been increasingly hardline, but they haven't responded to this crisis yet."

"Roger, CAP COM. When was the last time you heard that, Ed? Advise us when you get a response out of those people. We'll check in with you again after propellant dump. This is *Phoenix,* out."

"Roger, *Phoenix.* Just letting you know what you may be flying into. This is Houston, out."

"Clay, payload bay door radiators have been deactivated," said Rebecca, moving up from the aft crew station, where most of the control panels were either dark or showing red status lights. "The payload doors are closed. All bulkhead and centerline latches have been locked. Payload bay is secure.

"Good, now put on your helmet and take your seat," said Reynolds. "We're about fifteen minutes from atmospheric entry. Walt, ask Julie how they're doing on the mid deck. I'll start the flight surfaces test."

* * *

"Julie, this flightsuit isn't protecting me!" Glassner warned, after tapping Harrison on her shoulder. "My skin's starting to itch under it."

"Hold on, Allan. I have Walt on the line," she said, turning away from the forward lockers she'd been examining. "Yes, Walt. It's getting worse down here, and I haven't even opened the one locker where most of the hydrazine is leaking from. Allan's still being affected by it. I think he'll have to go in a rescue ball."

"Okay, Julie. Break out one and put him in it," Post answered. "Clay wants to know if we should depressurize the mid deck. Over."

"That would certainly clear out this buildup. And it'd be another reason to put Allan in a ball. How much time do I have?"

"You've got fourteen minutes, thirty seconds to atmospheric entry. Let me know when you're ready, and we'll begin."

"Roger and out. Allan, it's time to get 'stuffed,' " Julie ordered, motioning over Glassner's shoulder. "Locker B-Seven."

She pointed to an array of lockers next to the air lock, on the starboard side of the bulkhead. Larger though less numerous than the ones lining the forward bulkhead, they contained all the EVA-related supplies. Glassner popped the latches on the seventh locker and pulled out a compactly folded square of heavy fabric.

One of the shuttle's Personal Rescue Enclosures, the square was easily spread into a thirty-inch sphere. Glassner zipped the sphere open and sat on it, clutching his oxygen pack to his chest. Doubling up around the pack, Julie pulled the enveloping en-

29

closure over him. In minutes she had it zipped shut and was pulling the buoyant sphere over to the mid deck's tier of bunks.

"It's a tight fit, Allan, but it's the best place for you!" she shouted, getting a muffled response from the sphere. "Julie to Flight Deck, Allan is now inside the rescue ball. Over."

"Roger, Julie. Commencing mid deck emergency venting procedures," said Post.

She was still wedging the bright blue sphere into the lowermost bunk when a distant hissing caught her attention. Raising her head to look around, she immediately caught sight of the swirling vortices of orange mist at the port and starboard sides of the deck. In less than a minute the hissing stopped, though the tornado-like funnels continued to spiral. For a few moments Julie was transfixed by the sight; until she felt Glassner rolling against her legs and she returned to her work.

"Entering Item Three-Six Execute," said Reynolds, tapping out the commands on the GPC keyboard. "And the nose RCS is armed. Entering Item Three-Seven . . ."

The moment he hit the keyboard's "Execute" switch the nose thruster module started venting what remained of their propellants to space. There was only a thin, brief whisp of monomethyl hydrazine from its purge valve, while a much larger plume of nitrogen tetroxide spilled out from the module's opposite side. Fifty seconds later Reynolds entered another command to close the valves.

"Mission Control, this is *Phoenix*. Propellant dump completed," he informed. "We're approximately seven minutes to atmospheric entry. We are

L-minus thirty-six minutes, fifty-one seconds to landing. Do you have anything new for us? Over."

"We copy, *Phoenix*. We can only tell you that CNES and Glavkosmos have been notified and are ready to help," said Cochran, still assuming CAP COM duties. "Engleberg is talking to the White House and State Department. And you'll be happy to know you're interrupting all the networks."

"Have you anything new on the Seychelles? Over."

"Sorry, nothing new. Remember it's midnight there, they'll probably have to wake up the Prime Minister. Over."

"Roger, Mission Control. We'll advise when we hit the atmosphere," said Cochran. *"Phoenix,* out. Rebecca, how are you doing back there?"

Cochran looked over his right shoulder and found her still locking the buckles on her restraint belts. Rebecca's mission specialist seat was anchored behind Post's seat and to its right. From there she could monitor the heat sensors in the shuttle's Thermal Protection System (TPS), and the payload bay control panels.

"Everything looks nominal," she said, attaching the line from her Personal Egress AirPack (PEAP) breathing unit to her helmet. "The TPS has been activated, but I have no meaningful readings yet."

"Let me know when you do," Cochran responded. "Walt, check the APUs again. I'll inflate our G suits. When you're done, raise Julie and find out how she's doing."

When the hissing stopped so did all the other noises, except for Julie's own breathing. She didn't hear the sleeping bag straps rasp against the rescue sphere, or the buckles click when she finally secured

31

it inside the lower bunk. As she stood up she caught sight of an erratic movement in the middle one.

The marshmallows Rebecca had smuggled aboard the shuttle had since exploded out of their bag. They were five times normal size and had orange stains from hydrazine contamination. Before they could float out onto the mid deck, and from there into the cabin air vents, Julie slid the bunk's panel shut.

For the first time since she emerged from the air lock, the deck was reasonably clear. Apart from the marshmallows' reaction, the lack of an atmosphere had little effect. The vortices were gone, though the hydrazine still dribbled out of the locker in streams of droplets which drifted toward the cabin vents.

Julie moved toward the front bulkhead and flipped up the thumb latches on the damaged locker. After lowering its cover plate, she pulled out the drawer and opened it. Inside was most of the shuttle's camera equipment, now thoroughly contaminated by the propellant. As Julie searched its contents, some of the smaller pieces started floating away. She paid them scant attention, concentrating instead on finding the one object she normally would not expect to find in the drawer.

When she found its entrance hole, it didn't take her long to discover the meteor embedded in the back of a camera body. She pried it out of its resting place and examined it as she resealed the drawer.

"I should've known it would be an iron-nickel meteor," said Julie, turning the angular, marble-sized piece of space metal in her hand. "A stony one would've broken up as it went through the heat tiles."

"Julie, this is Walt. What's going on?" Post asked. "Did you discover the meteor? Over."

"Yes, I got what's left of it in my hand."

"Good, don't let go of it. We'll need to show it

after we land. You better strap yourself in, we're about two minutes from atmospheric entry."

"Roger," said Julie, sliding the meteor inside a pouch on the flap covering her space suit's waist ring. "So far as I can tell, Allan's doing all right. Let me know when we hit the blackout layer. Mid deck, out."

The mission specialist seat Julie and Glassner had anchored to the cabin floor had not been designed to be used by an astronaut wearing a space suit. After reclosing the locker, Julie backed into the chair as best she could. Though she had removed all its cushions, and tilted it aft by ten degrees, she still found it impossible to sit without her backpack pushing her forward.

Almost as difficult was reaching for the shoulder straps, then pulling them forward and trying to lock them over her chestpack. She had just started to fumble with the lap belt when Julie noticed the drifting film rolls she had allowed to escape drop suddenly to the floor.

After skirting above it for more than a day, the *Phoenix* had returned to earth's atmosphere. It was back in a gravity environment; Julie could already feel her arms getting heavy and became dizzy when she moved her head rapidly. She gave up trying to connect her lap belt when she could not even get her fingers to obey her commands. Instead she decided to hold the ends of her belt, and hoped that would keep her in her seat.

"Mission Control, this is *Phoenix*. We are at entry interface," Reynolds announced. "We're changing orbiter body flap control to Automatic and we'll need our altitude readings in feet, over. Walt, tell Julie we're ending mid deck depressurization. Rebecca, you have any temperature readings?"

Reynolds already knew there would be something to report. Visible in the lower corners of the cockpit windows was a glow ranging from dull red to orange. The shuttle was plowing through the boundary layer between space and the Earth's atmosphere. Its velocity was now dropping rapidly, and it was picking up the effects of atmospheric friction. A plasma sheath of ionized, electrically charged particles had begun to envelop the spacecraft.

"Orbiter nose and wing leading edges are at eight hundred degrees," said Rebecca, glancing down the display of thermal sensor readouts. "Rudder's leading edge is seven hundred degrees. Lower forward fuselage, mid fuselage and wing undersides are in the four-hundred-degree range. The aft fuselage is under three hundred degrees."

"*Phoenix,* your altitude is three hundred and ninety thousand feet," Cochran informed. "Your velocity is seventeen thousand miles an hour and decelerating. You're approximately four minutes to Loss-Of-Signal. Over."

"Roger, four minutes to LOS," Reynolds repeated. "Walt, hold the nose at thirty-four degrees. What did Julie say?"

"That she wished she had taken her Gatorade," said Post, as he kept his eyes focused on his instrument displays. "And she wants Houston to know that their seats weren't designed for space suits."

"I'll let them know. Begin repressurizing the mid deck, we got plenty of O-Two on board and I don't want to lose Allan if his rescue ball fails. This is the first time we've ever had to use one of them."

Reynolds glanced out the port cockpit windows while he gave his latest set of orders. In just a few minutes the ionization glow had climbed halfway up the windows. The color had also changed to bright red and varying shades of orange. Even through the forward windows the glow could be seen; when it reached the overhead skylights the blackout would begin.

"Orbiter nose and wing leading edges are at eight hundred and seventy degrees," said Rebecca, knowing almost by instinct the next question Reynolds would ask. "Rudder leading edge is eight hundred degrees. Other readings are lower."

"*Phoenix,* this is Houston. You are two minutes to LOS," said Cochran. "Have you anything to tell us before blackout begins? Over."

"Roger. Julie wants you to know you can't wear a space suit and sit in a mission specialist seat at the same time," Reynolds answered. "Everything appears nominal. You got anything new to tell us about our landing site? Over."

"Latest update from Seychelles Tracking is they may have to use our ambassador to contact its government. I wish we could have something better to tell you, but I doubt we will before blackout time. Over."

"We understand. Just make sure you have something for us when we come out of LOS."

"Roger, *Phoenix.* We promise we will," said Cochran. "Take good care of my Lady, Clay. You are seventy seconds to LOS. This is Houston, out."

Just over a minute later the plasma sheath could be seen in the flight deck's skylight windows; it had completely encased the spaceplane. For the next twelve minutes all radio communications with the outside world would be impossible. It was now over Africa's Atlantic coast, just above South Africa. By the time the *Phoenix* emerged from the blackout

35

layer, it would be over the Indian Ocean, less than six hundred miles from the principal island group in the Seychelles.

"This is Orbiter Support to Operations Control, the Microwave Landing System is up and nominal," said a technician at one of the center's few manned consoles.

"I copy your status," said Fernandez, double checking a row of lights on his own command console. Then, he caught sight of the main entrance doors opening behind him. "This is the station manager to all incoming personnel. We have a Code Alpha alert. The *Phoenix* is making an emergency reentry, and we're the landing site. We are L-minus twenty-three minutes, twenty-one seconds to touchdown. Joel, has Benoit Aubin called back yet?"

"No, all incoming calls have been from our people," Lomberg responded. "The line we left open for him hasn't flashed yet."

"Well he has to be back at the airport by now. I'll try him again. You find out who the new arrivals are."

While another influx of returning staff entered the operations center, Fernandez picked up a telephone receiver and dialed the same number he had tried nearly twenty minutes ago. Though he got through to Seychelles International Airport in moments, he had to wait several minutes for its manager to finally answer him.

"I hope you know it is well past midnight, Mr. Fernandez," said the lyrical, though clearly agitated, voice at the other end of the line. "What is your problem that I had to return to work at this hour?"

"The *Phoenix* has suffered damage from a meteor

36

hit, and she's making an emergency reentry," Fernandez answered. "The crew's picked the Seychelles as their landing site, and we need your help bringing them in. What's your traffic like?"

"At this hour we have only one flight inbound. I'm sorry for your spacecraft, but as an unscheduled flight it needs government permission to land. You've been told this before."

"But this is an emergency, Benoit. The shuttle is about twenty minutes away from landing, and your government offices are closed. There's no way we can get permission. That wasn't part of our emergency procedures."

"We will not be dictated to in our own country!" Aubin stormed, his agitation immediately blowing into anger. "Don't try hiding your naked imperialism behind a crisis! If you want our cooperation I suggest you have your ambassador respectfully contact our Prime Minister. Good morning, Mr. Fernandez."

Before he could offer another argument, Fernandez could hear the line go dead at the other end. In his own frustration he slammed the telephone receiver back on its cradle.

"Ray, we got enough personnel to man a convoy of service vehicles," Lomberg managed to say, before the phone call was noisily ended. "Provided we don't get shot by the airport guards. What happened?"

"Aubin's thin skin," said Fernandez. "This needs a diplomat's touch. Someone more 'respectful.' I'm contacting Ambassador Griffen's residence. She can handle this government better than I can, and I hope she can do it quickly."

Fernandez grabbed a notebook always kept on the command console and thumbed it open to the section on U.S. embassy personnel. He picked up the receiver he had recently slammed down and punched

37

in a new number on the telephone's keypad. This time he hoped for a faster, friendlier response.

"RCS pitch thrusters deactivated," said Reynolds, tapping a row of buttons on the cockpit's instrument pedestal. As he released each button, its glowing status light flicked out. "Elevons now control pitch. How does she feel?"

"A little stiff," said Post, trying to get his diminutive control stick to change the indicated positions of the elevons. "But since we're still doing fifteen thousand miles an hour, what wouldn't be? It's going to make the roll reversals interesting."

"Let me know if you need help, I'll activate my controls. Rebecca, what are the new readings?"

"We're now at maximum heating conditions," she reported. "Nose and wing leading edges have just passed fifteen hundred degrees centigrade. Rudder leading edge and forward fuselage are at eleven hundred degrees. Outer wing sensors show the same levels. Mid and aft fuselage readings are under one thousand degrees, except for the body flap."

"That always gets hotter than the rest of the tail structure," said Reynolds. "Don't worry about it. We're coming up on our first roll reversal. Changing ADI rate switches to High. Roll and Yaw Switch to CSS."

Control Stick Steering (CSS)—for the first time since it reentered the atmosphere, the shuttle was flying entirely under human command. Less than four minutes later Post was forcing his control stick over to the left; beginning a long, snaking S-turn designed to bleed off the spaceplane's still considerable velocity. To properly execute the maneuver, he had to rely on what his instruments showed him.

Outside the cockpit there were no visual reference points or landmarks for him to use. The plasma sheath still surrounded the *Phoenix,* making Post feel like he was flying inside a neon tube. If he and Reynolds could have seen outside, they would just be able to spot the island of Madagascar, lying under a partial cloud cover. Ahead of them, some seventeen hundred miles farther to the east and deeper into the night, lay their destination. Mahé Island, the Seychelles.

"Thank you for taking my call at this time, Mrs. Griffen," said Fernandez, nervously eyeing a mission event timer on his console. It was now winding below fifteen minutes. "We have a Code Alpha alert. The shuttle is making an emergency reentry and will be landing at Seychelles International."

"The shuttle? You mean the *Phoenix?*" Ambassador Lynn Griffen interrupted, the tone of her voice changing immediately from irritation to concern. "What caused the crisis, and when are they due in?"

"A meteor damaged its nose thrusters and caused a fuel leak. It will land here in fourteen minutes, forty-four seconds. I've been trying to get the airport staff to cooperate with us, but Benoit Aubin is refusing to follow our emergency procedures. He demands that you contact the Prime Minister for permission for the shuttle to land."

"Well this is certainly more important than a damn cocktail party. I wish you'd have phoned me earlier."

"I would have," said Fernandez. "Had I known what Aubin's demands were. Like the rest of this government, they seem to change from one day to the next. Can you help us, Lynn? I'd sure hate to see the *Phoenix* greeted on touchdown by the Seychelles

39

People's Security goons, instead of our support trucks."

"You haven't given me much time but I'll do what I can. Fortunately, the British ambassador hasn't left the party yet; he has more influence with Albert René than I do. Leave a line open for me, Ray."

"Will do, phone extension three-three-seven. Good luck, Lynn." More gently this time, Fernandez laid the receiver back on its cradle and then punched in a command on his com panel. "Leave a line open for me. Set aside one for Aubin. This keeps up and soon we won't have anything left for our people to call in on. How many do we have?"

"So far, thirty-eight," Lomberg answered. "What are we going to do with our support convoy?"

"Keep it here," Fernandez admitted. "We have trucks and vans, the People's Defense Forces have armored cars. We'd never get past the airport main gate. Tell the convoy commander to put some lookouts on our roof. If we can't be at the airport, at least we can see what's going on there. When you're through with him, tell Communications to contact that inbound airliner. I'm contacting Houston, we have about twelve minutes before the shuttle's handed over to us."

"We're less than one minute to blackout layer exit," said Reynolds, glancing at the cockpit's event timer. "Walt, how are the APUs doing?"

"APUs are nominal," said Post, shifting his attention to one of his side panels. "I don't think cold-starting them did any damage. Becky, when's the temperature going to go down in here?"

"Ambient cabin air temperature is ninety-four degrees, *and* it is falling," Rebecca noted, checking the

40

environmental sensor panel. "The reason it's been so high is we're isolated from mid deck and we can't circulate air from it."

"It's starting to break up," said Reynolds. "Rebecca, keep your eye on it. I'm going to start transmitting."

Reynolds motioned over his shoulder at the skylight windows; where the orange-red plasma sheath could be seen thinning out. For the moment it was only an occasional patch of darkness. But within seconds, tears appeared in it, permitting Rebecca to see the night sky and for radio broadcasts to make their way out.

"Mission Control, this is *Phoenix*. Mission Control, this is *Phoenix*. Do you read? Over," Reynolds began, then paused for a moment to listen for any reply in the static. "Mission . . ."

"Roger, *Phoenix*. We read you five by five," said Cochran, interrupting Reynolds in mid-sentence. "We're getting your flight telemetry again. You're looking good. Over."

"Ed, you're still CAP COM? Why haven't you given that job to someone else? Over."

"Because right here and now, this is the best place for me. What do you need, Clay? Over."

"A field advisory on the Seychelles," Reynolds asked. "Have you guys cleared up your problems with them?"

"Frankly, the situation there is still 'confused,' " said Cochran. "The airport is refusing to follow the emergency procedures we agreed to, so our ambassador is trying to reach their Prime Minister. We'll get you permission to land, hopefully before you arrive there. Over."

"Well, you have twelve minutes to do it in."

"No, we have eleven minutes, forty-two seconds to

work with. *Phoenix,* your altitude is one hundred and eighty thousand feet. Your speed is eighty-three hundred miles an hour, and you're five hundred miles from Mahé Island. Over."

"Roger, CAP COM. Keep us advised on our landing field," said Cochran. "We're beginning our second roll reversal. *Phoenix,* out."

It only took seconds after emerging from the blackout layer for the plasma envelop to finish dissipating around the shuttle. Still hot enough for its undersides to glow, the airliner-sized vehicle shot through the upper atmosphere at more than four times the speed of an artillery shell.

Gently, Post eased the *Phoenix* into a long starboard S-turn to use up more of its velocity. Though they could now look out their cockpit windows, there was little for him or Reynolds to see except for the stars they once had been a little closer to. Even from an altitude of thirty-four miles, the main island group of the Seychelles was still over the horizon. What few islands passed under them now were either uninhabited or too sparsely populated for any signs of civilization.

"Captain . . . Captain, you must wake up," said the officer who entered his commander's quarters. "Anatoli Pavlovich, we have a crisis."

Captain Anatoli Pavlovich Raina turned over in his bunk, and fumbled for the switch to his reading light. When it snapped on, he squinted in its glare until his eyes adjusted to the sudden burst of light. He glanced at the wristwatch lying on his desk, before looking up at the figure standing over him.

"It's nearly one in the morning," he croaked, his voice cracking from dryness. "This had better be

42

good, Yegorov. I hear no alarms, so what is our 'crisis'?"

"It isn't us. It's the Americans," said Major Sergi Alekseevich Yegorov. "There's been increased activity at their tracking station. Most of it on their secure channels, and they just activated their Microwave Landing System."

"Landing system? Is something wrong with their shuttle?"

"I think so, but I'm not sure. Baikonur hasn't fully responded to my questions. They still don't like the KGB. . . . We could just ask the Americans?"

"That would be too easy," said Raina, sitting up in his bed. "We're supposed to *work* at gathering intelligence. Have our radars spotted the shuttle yet?"

"No, and if it was still in orbit we should have by now," Yegorov answered. "For whatever reason, I believe the *Phoenix* is making an emergency landing. I would like to call up more of our crew, but I need your permission . . ."

"It's granted. Wake up everyone you need, including general ship's crew. Get back to your surveillance center, I'll meet you there."

As Yegorov turned to leave, Raina grabbed his pants off a nearby chair and pulled them on. Next it was his shoes, then a new shirt and finally his cap. Partway through his dressing, he heard Yegorov's voice on the ship's intercom, ordering more of her crew to report for duty and for the rest of her boilers to be fired up. The moment he was finished, Raina left his cabin and, instead of heading for the bridge, turned down the passageway for his ship's true heart.

The intelligence gatherer *Navarin,* officially registered as an oceanographic research ship, carried in fact only the most cosmetic of ocean research equipment. Almost everything else—her radar and satellite

43

dishes, and an imposing array of radio aerials — were for the surveillance of NASA's tracking station on Mahé. It was now anchored approximately a mile off the island instead of in Victoria harbor. In direct line-of-sight with the tracking station, the best position for its true mission.

"All right, Sergi Alekseevich, what do you have to show me?" said Raina, upon entering the surveillance control center, and approaching the KGB Major.

"As you can see on the monitor readouts, the NASA-installed Microwave Landing System at Seychelles International has been operating for the last five minutes," said Yegorov, tapping one of the TV screens at his console. "For about twenty minutes before that, NASA was running the usual diagnostic and calibration tests. On this monitor, the station's radio traffic with Houston has increased, and switched entirely over to secure channels."

"Yes . . . I also see the *Phoenix* is more than eleven minutes late in its flypast. Something is happening."

"However, there is an anomaly. The airport hasn't changed its operations. It hasn't declared an emergency, and there's still a commercial flight inbound. Our lookouts report some activity at the tracking station, but no convoy of support vehicles has left it. This is most strange."

"No. Unfortunately, it is not strange," Raina sighed. "Our Seychelles 'comrades' are being difficult again. If the shuttle does have an emergency, then they're making the situation even more dangerous for it. Send this information immediately to Baikonur, Sergi, then join me on the bridge. We may witness something very unique."

"Communications, do you have the airliner?" Fernandez requested, when he noticed the operators at that console talking actively.

"Yes, sir. It's Air France flight fifteen-ten," said one of the men. "They're about forty miles out and beginning their initial descent. So far, Seychelles Approach Control hasn't told them of the emergency."

"Transfer it to me, I'll handle them." Fernandez switched his headset to the channel set aside for commercial aviation frequencies. He heard the communications team advise the French pilots then, after an electronic tone, they were switched over to him. "Air France Fifteen-Ten, this is Ray Fernandez. I'm station manager, NASA Seychelles Tracking."

"Yes, Mr. Fernandez. What is the reason for your staff contacting us?" asked a neat, clipped voice on the earphones. "What is this, 'crisis'? Over."

"The space shuttle *Phoenix* is making an emergency reentry and is now less than ten minutes away from landing at Seychelles International."

"Mon Dieu, les idiots . . . I'm sorry. The idiots told us nothing. Would you wish for us to hold until your spacecraft lands? Over."

"Thank God he thought of it instead of me asking him," said Fernandez, briefly wrapping his hand around his microphone. "Yes, Air France. If you could hold north of Mahé, over Praslin Island, it would help us greatly. Over."

"It was the *Phoenix* that my country's greatest pilot flew into history last year. Of course, we'll help you. We have the lights of Praslin in sight, and enough fuel to orbit for ninety minutes. We won't land until we hear specifically from you. This is Air France Fifteen-Ten, out."

"Thank you, Air France. If you'll listen to the international distress frequency, you'll catch the landing. This is Seychelles Tracking, out." Fernandez switched the channel back to the communications team before turning to Lomberg. "If only all our problems could be that easily handled. Now, what do the lookouts have to report?"

"Moving speed brake to one hundred percent," said Post, pulling the throttle lever to its back stop.

The *Phoenix*'s rudder hinged open, spreading into its hypersonic slipstream and creating enough drag to dramatically cut its velocity. In the first seconds, it shed several hundred miles an hour, causing everyone to be pulled against their restraint belts until the deceleration became continuous. The spaceplane was now some three hundred miles from Mahé Island, and preparing to drop below one hundred thousand feet. Mahé and the other main islands were still too distant to be seen directly, though a slight glow on the eastern horizon could now be seen.

"Just like popping the speed brake on an F-18," Post added, adjusting his shoulder straps so they would not dig into his collarbones. "And just as painful."

"We're about two minutes from our next roll reversal," said Reynolds. "Check with the mid deck and see how Julie and Allan are doing."

By turning her head as far as she could, Julie was just able to look past the mid deck's galley and catch a glimpse of the outside world through the entry hatch's window. Only ten inches in diameter, it allowed her a limited view of the night; whereas a few minutes before all she could see was the orange-red glow of the ionization envelope.

"Julie, this is Walt. How's it going down there?"

46

"Just . . . just fine," she stammered. "Wish I could have a better view though."

"Next time, we'll install a picture window. How's Allan?"

"Still with us. I can hear him moving around in the bunk. We still have a slow hydrazine leak into the cabin, and it's building up again."

"Christ, where's that stuff coming from? All right, we'll depressurize the mid deck again," said Post. "Activating cabin purge vents A and B."

Being slightly heavier than air, the monomethyl hydrazine was settling to the floor and forming a layer of thick orange fog, unlike the suspended mist it created in zero gravity. When the port and starboard vents were opened, it took several moments for the fog to swirl up the walls to them.

While there was not enough air at a hundred thousand feet for a human to breathe, there was just enough for sound transmission. After the initial, loud outrush of the cabin's atmosphere, the noise slowly fell to a soft hissing Julie could just barely hear through her helmet.

"Mid deck air pressure down to less than one pound per square inch," Reynolds noted, watching a gage on one of his side panels.

"Shall I close the vents and repressurize?" asked Post.

"No, we're coming up on our third roll reversal. We'll repressurize before we hit our Heading Alignment Cylinders. Deploying air data probes, now."

Reynolds tapped a pair of buttons on the cockpit's center pedestal, opening two small hatches in the shuttle's nose, just above the damaged thruster module. The instruments he activated would give the

47

Phoenix its own airspeed readings, and also operate many of its conventional flight instruments. Half a minute later it began another velocity-shedding S-turn; this time to the left.

"Guess who this is?" said Lomberg, holding out the telephone receiver he had just picked up. "Benoit Aubin."

"I suppose we finally did something that caught his attention," said Fernandez, slipping the headset plug out of his left ear before taking the receiver. "Yes, Mr. Aubin. What can we do for you?"

"You can stop interfering with airport operations and violating our national sovereignty," Aubin demanded, his anger rising and his creole cadence diminishing. "Control of commercial airliners is *our* business, Mr. Fernandez. Not NASA's! If you persist in your interference, we'll report you to the international aviation authorities and the appropriate United Nations' agencies!"

"I'm sorry but we had to in order to maintain shuttle safety procedures. I think if you'll check the U.N.'s Astronaut Return Treaty, you'll find we are entitled to."

"Our Prime Minister has given us orders not to co-operate with you. We will not be dictated to."

"This isn't a matter of national sovereignty. It's about international cooperation," said Fernandez.

"Tell your shuttle to land somewhere else," said Aubin, ignoring all the arguments. "Tell it to land at your naval base in Diego Garcia."

"Are you kidding? That's more than a thousand miles away. The *Phoenix* has reentered, and it's committed to the Seychelles. By now you should be picking it up on your radar. It's less than six minutes from landing."

48

"Phoenix, this is Houston. You are L-minus five minutes, twenty-five seconds to landing," said Cochran. "Have you acquired Seychelles MLS? Over."

"Roger, Houston. We're getting MLS telemetry and we're ready to begin Terminal Area Energy Management," Reynolds answered. "Have you anything new on our landing site? Over."

"I'm afraid so, Clay. And frankly, it isn't good. Apparently the Seychelles government will not cooperate with us. The airport is active and our tracking station is warning off the airliners. At least you'll be able to land safely, but I can't tell you what you'll find once you're down. Over."

"Okay, Ed, we'll handle one crisis at a time. We're ending our fourth roll reversal and on track for the Heading Alignment Cylinders. We'll advise you after we hit Waypoint One, Houston. This is *Phoenix,* out."

For the last time, the shuttle S-turned and swung on course for the first element of the Microwave Landing System. The Heading Alignment Cylinders were two, eighteen-thousand-foot diameter columns standing side by side about seven miles from the end of Seychelles International's runway.

"Here we go," said Post, watching an electronic representation of the cylinders on his CRT screen, and glancing at the flight information being projected on his Head Up Display. "We're at Waypoint One and I'm taking the port cylinder. Commencing TAEM interface."

Sliding to the left, the *Phoenix* began spiralling down an invisible column that reached from sea level to its current altitude of over eighty thousand feet. Now only some sixty miles from its landing site, the spaceplane's crew could at last see the Seychelles main island group through the broken layers of clouds below them.

Nineteen miles long, Mahé was by far the largest and most heavily illuminated of the islands. Countless lights flickered over it, from its North Point to Police Bay at its southern end. By far the largest concentration was at the neck of Mahé's northern finger, its capital of Victoria. The other islands were, by comparison, much less conspicuous. To the east, Frégate Island and to the north, Praslin and La Digue Islands showed only a few clusters of light. And to the west, just fifteen miles off of Mahé, Silhouette Island lay dark and undetectable to the astronauts.

"I warn you, Fernandez, if you attempt to talk with your spacecraft we'll jam the frequencies," Aubin threatened. "The People's Defense Forces have the capabilities."

"We're using the International Aviation Distress channel," said Fernandez, his own anger heating up. "You jam it and you better believe there'll be a major incident, mister!"

"Ray . . . Ray, it's Houston," Lomberg said tentatively. "They're getting ready to hand her over."

"Be right with them. Aubin, the shuttle is landing in five minutes. If you're not going to cooperate then don't interfere!" Fernandez slapped the receiver back on its cradle, and slid the headset plug into his ear in one clean motion. By the time he pressed the transmit/receive switch he had managed to calm down a little. "Yes. Yes, Houston. We're ready for the hand over."

"I know you are," Cochran answered. "But what about the airport? Is the government going to cooperate with us?"

"Sorry, Ed, I'm afraid not. I haven't heard yet from our ambassador, but I doubt she got past the Prime Minister's Libyan advisors. However, I can verify that the runway is clear and the inbound airliner is in a holding pattern."

"Then that will have to do. Get ready to take control of the *Phoenix*. We'll be handing her over at L-minus two minutes."

"We are one minute to autoland guidance," said Post, the instant a flashing symbol appeared on his HUD. "Our airspeed is Mach One. Our altitude is fifty thousand feet. Deactivating RCS yaw thrusters. We now have full rudder control."

To test what his instruments showed him, Post tapped his rudder pedals, and the *Phoenix* responded by slewing its nose a few degrees to the right, then left. A few seconds later, and for the first time since the opening minutes of its lift-off, the shuttle was travelling slower than the speed of sound.

It continued to spiral down the Heading Alignment Cylinder, it was now at fifty thousand feet and beginning to enter the broken cloud layers which covered the area. At first the clouds were thin and wispy. The thick mountains of cumulus began a mile below the spacecraft and would continue to the cloud deck's fifteen-hundred-foot base.

"Mid deck has completed repressurization," said Reynolds, watching his side panel gages. "Better let Julie know she has a new atmosphere, until she opens the side hatch. Mission Control, this is *Phoenix*. We're thirty seconds to hand over, and we're getting autoland telemetry from Seychelles MLS. Over."

"Roger, *Phoenix*. The only field advisory we can give you is the runway's clear and all traffic's been diverted," Cochran responded. "Take care of my Lady, Clay, and good luck. Houston, out."

"I will, Ed. We're switching over to the distress channel. *Phoenix,* out." Reynolds was silent for only a moment as he hit the channel selector toggle on his overhead com panel. "Seychelles Tracking, this is *Phoenix*. Do you read? Over."

"Roger, we read you five by five," said Fernandez, his voice coming in sharp and clear. "Your altitude is fifteen thousand feet. Your airspeed is four hundred and thirty miles an hour. And you are eight miles from runway threshold."

"We copy, Seychelles Tracking. We're ready to intercept autoland glideslope," said Reynolds.

"Roger, *Phoenix*. Once you begin guidance interface you need not acknowledge any further transmissions. You're L-minus two minutes to landing."

"Speed brake, fifty percent," said Post, sliding its lever to the halfway mark. "Runway entry point coming up."

The shuttle made one last turn around the three-mile diameter cylinder and broke away from it exactly at the location shown on the cockpit CRT screens. And after holding the spaceplane's nose up for the last fifty minutes, Post dropped it below the horizon line, assuming the glideslope angle indicated on his HUD.

"Seychelles Tracking, we have acquired autoland guidance," said Reynolds. "We can see Mahé's lights ahead of us."

"Roger, *Phoenix*. They may be the friendliest reception you'll get here," Fernandez answered. "We can only promise you a clear runway. Over."

From thirteen thousand feet, the lights of Victoria

and the rest of the island glowed brightly, even reflecting off the lowest layer of clouds. Beyond them there was little other illumination on the Indian Ocean's velvety black mantle. Only a few of the other islands and some ships near Victoria's harbor could be seen.

"So, you finally decided to join us," said Raina, turning to the back of the bridge when he heard boots stamping up the passageway.

"Yes, the *Phoenix* is less than two minutes from landing," Yegorov replied, as he tried to catch his breath. "The NASA tracking station is talking to her on the aviation emergency channel. . . . They also talked directly to the inbound flight, and it is now circling Praslin Island."

"NASA did? Not the airport tower? Our former comrades *are* being difficult. They're listening too much to their Libyan and Cuban friends. These next two minutes are going to be very dangerous."

"Apart from shooting down the spacecraft, what can they do? They're not cooperating, but they're certainly not interfering."

Yegorov pointed out the bridge windows, to the bright glow of Seychelles International Airport on Point Cascade. Its control tower and a few of its other buildings were visible. Even more noticeable were its outer marker and rows of approach lights; some of which extended out into the bay and were only a few miles from *Navarin's* bow.

"I don't know what they could do," Raina said finally, staring down the bow of his ship to the approach lights. "But if I did, I'd warn the Americans about it."

"He's back," Lomberg warned, seconds after putting a telephone receiver to his ear. "And he wants to talk to you."

"I'll take it," said Fernandez. "He probably won't talk to anyone else. Watch the shuttle for me. Yes, Benoit. What can I do for you now?"

"You can call off your invasion," said Aubin in a surprisingly calm, cadenced voice.

"What? You mean you're going to give up without a fight?"

"No, we will fight for our country and our socialist revolution." What had momentarily been calm grew strident, and the old anger returned to Aubin's voice. "We've been tracking your spacecraft on radar, Mr. Fernandez. And I warn you, we shall resist this act of aggression."

"Act of aggression?" Fernandez repeated. "What have you been inhaling in the last few minutes? I don't have time for this, Aubin, talk to me after the *Phoenix* has landed. In about ninety seconds."

"What the hell was that?" Lomberg asked, once the phone was hung up.

"Aubin's idea of a joke. What's happening now?"

"The orbiter's gone below eight thousand feet and it's in the groove. The crew hasn't deviated yet from the optimum trajectory on the MLS."

"Thank God we got Post," said Fernandez, putting his headset on again and pressing the transmit/receive button on his com panel. "He can make a plane fly like it was on a set of rails."

"Thirty seconds to preflare. One minute to landing," said Post, glancing repeatedly between the bright green symbols on his Head Up Display and the flight path trajectory on the CRT screen below it.

"And we are nominal."

"Damn near perfect," Reynolds corrected. "You'd think we were approaching Edwards, instead of some emergency field halfway around the world from it."

"I learned from my last flight to keep myself current on all abort sites. This is just like the simulator."

While Post had little time to stare at anything in the cockpit windows except his HUD, Reynolds could afford a few seconds to enjoy the view. Through the last broken layers of clouds, the island of Mahé was clearly seen.

No longer a glow on the horizon or a dark silhouette outlined in lights, Mahé's terrain had become visible. Its capital was still the most dominant feature, though the city's illumination brought out the mountains backing it up and the white sand beaches stretching to either side. Along most of the shoreline were clusters of light marking the locations of hotels, with the largest concentration just across the island's mountain spine from Victoria.

Directly ahead of the shuttle lay a ribbon of illumination some two miles long. Rows of approach lights flashed at either end, there were perimeter spots for its taxiways and floodlights on its terminal, hangars, and support buildings. And without warning, they all started going out.

"Jesus Christ, they're turning everything off!" Reynolds shouted.

"Huh? What?" said Post, looking up. And for the first time in several minutes, he looked beyond his HUD's reflector plate to see the runway's beckoning glow finish shutting down. On the CRT screen below it, the shuttle symbol dropped under its ideal trajectory line.

"I don't believe this," said Yegorov. "They can't be

so stupid."

"Believe it," Raina said grimly. "And if the American cosmonauts aren't good, the shuttle could easily crash. Lieutenant, the microphone . . . Captain to crew! All rescue details are to activate searchlights immediately and train them forward."

One by one, powerful blue-white beams flickered on along the *Navarin's* superstructure and swung toward its bow. The searchlights on its bridge wings, and those immediately behind them, lined up perfectly on the outer rows of approach light towers. Though they could not penetrate far enough into the night to reach the runway's threshold, wherever their arcs fell they washed away the darkness.

"Do the lookouts confirm it?" Fernandez asked.

"I'm afraid they do," said Lomberg, his face growing pale. "The airport's completely dark. Even the rotating beacon on the control tower is off. What the hell are we going to do?"

"Operations Control to Orbiter Support, keep your eye on the Microwave System. The bastards may try to sabotage that next. Seychelles Tracking to—"

"Ray, the lookouts have something new to report. That Soviet spy ship, the *Navarin?* They say it's turning on all its searchlights! And pointing them at the runway!"

"You're kidding," said Fernandez, his mouth dropping open. *"Phoenix,* this is Seychelles Tracking. Can you spot a large ship about a mile from the runway? Over."

"You bet we can," Reynolds answered. "And

whoever those guys are, we'd like you to thank them for us. Right now we're going to be busy. Initiating preflare. L-minus thirty-two seconds to landing. Over."

"Speed brakes, seventy-five percent," said Post, slapping his lever closer to its backstops. "Here we go, the home stretch."

As he eased his control stick to a neutral position he reduced the glideslope angle from twenty-two degrees to one and a half. By the time he was finished, the shuttle had broken through the cloud base. The runway and blacked-out airport were now in clear view. And in spite of extinguishing almost all their lights, the glow from Victoria and the *Navarin*'s powerful beams made them still dimly visible.

The *Phoenix* whistled over the darkened approach light towers, which stood out starkly in the searchlights' glare. Though its speed was reducing constantly, it was still doing better than three hundred miles an hour as it neared the runway threshold. Still too fast to lower landing gear or use the elevons as flaps.

"Landing gear systems, armed," said Reynolds, lifting a cover plate on his forward panel and flipping the switch under it.

"Phoenix, your altitude is one hundred and thirty-five feet," Fernandez abruptly added. "You are twenty-five hundred feet to runway."

"Preflare ended," said Post. "Initiating flareout."

From a near-level attitude the shuttle pitched its nose up, by some thirty degrees. The maneuver slowed it dramatically and put its still-retracted main gear in the proper touchdown position.

"Phoenix, your altitude is ninety feet. You are eleven hundred feet to runway."

"Deploying landing gear." Reynolds lifted a cover

plate next to the first and pressed the switch it protected. Immediately above it, a trio of lights changed color. "And we have three green."

"Gear down and locked," said Post, feeling the vibrations ripple through the airframe; he almost didn't need to check the indicator lights. "Now to land this brick before I stall her."

The spaceplane crossed the threshold doing just over two hundred miles an hour. For the first thousand feet down the runway it bobbed gently and drifted to the left, until Post corrected. All the while Fernandez kept reading off its altitude in ten foot increments, until the last ten feet.

"Main gear, twenty feet," he reported. "Ten feet. Nine feet. Eight feet. Seven . . ."

Post continued to hold the *Phoenix* in its nose-high attitude until a solid jolt shook it. Then he pushed his control stick forward to bring the nose gear down, and finished slapping the speed brake lever to its backstops.

"Hit the pedals lightly," said Reynolds. "We still have about a mile of asphalt to use."

Nearly invisible in the dim illumination were the puffs of smoke from the shuttle's main gear with each application of its brakes. Dark and over a thousand feet away, the airport's control tower, terminal, and hangars all flashed by its starboard wingtip. Unnoticed except for a line of headlights snapping on.

"I think we're down to the last thousand feet of runway, boss," Post warned, after the latest distance marker came briefly into view. "Plus whatever overrun it has."

"Which probably isn't much," said Reynolds. "Time to see if it was worth paying Goodrich all the money we did."

In unison, Post and Reynolds jumped on their foot pedals and held them down. Still travelling at nearly a hundred miles an hour, the *Phoenix* emitted sharp squeals and continuous trails of smoke from its main wheels as its brakes were applied. For the final time, the crew was pulled against their restraint belts. Not as painfully as earlier times, yet everyone held their breath until it ended. With less than a hundred feet of usable asphalt left, the airliner-sized spacecraft ground to a halt.

"Seychelles Tracking, this is *Phoenix*. We are down," Reynolds sighed. "Wheels stop at L-plus two minutes, nine seconds. Over."

"Roger, *Phoenix*. Wheels stop," said Fernandez. "We have no convoy on the field to meet you. Is anyone approaching the orbiter? Over."

"Affirmative. We got someone and they don't look friendly. We're going to hurry our shut down procedures. Maybe we'll get them done before we're arrested. Over. Walt, let Julie know she can release Glassner. And tell her we're going to have visitors. Real soon."

"I'm way ahead of you," said Julie, in response to Post's order. "I'll have him out in minutes."

Releasing her straps and lap belt, she eased out of her seat and turned slowly for the bunks. In spite of her cautious movements, Julie could feel herself becoming dizzy as she bent down to the lowest one. She found the rescue ball had shifted position and quickly released its straps to roll it out.

The canvas sphere moved on its own and gave a series of muffled noises, only some of which sounded like speech to Julie. She pulled open its zipper, causing Glassner to spill out of it backwards.

After being trapped in it for some forty minutes, he had difficulty straightening out and needed help to stand up.

"Rub my back. Please!" he begged, bracing himself against the tier of bunks. "It hurts worse than my arms or legs."

"I bet it does," said Julie, starting at his shoulders and working her way down. "I don't think they built the sphere to ride out reentry in."

"Push harder, that's better. I don't see any hydrazine floating around. . . . Can we go off our personal systems?"

"Not yet, there's still some hydrazine residue in here. And we may have to keep wearing our systems in order to post-flight the orbiter."

Because of her padded gloves, Julie had trouble rubbing any life into Glassner's back. She had to push and stroke vigorously in order to give him any satisfaction. When she got to the base of his spine, she reached up for his shoulders to begin the process all over again. It was then they both noticed the flickering of blue light through the external hatch's window.

"What's going on out there?" Glassner asked.

"It's our welcoming committee," said Julie, who had to turn her whole body to look directly at the window. "Yes, Walt. Will do. I got our orders, Allan. We're to welcome our visitors. We'll have to reschedule your massage for later."

Julie finished turning around and squeezed past her seat, then the mid deck's galley to reach the side entry hatch. She first peered through its center window before unfastening its sealing lever and pulling it back. With a loud hiss the pressure seal was broken, followed by a soft clicking as the latches were undone. Glassner joined her on the last ones, then together they pushed the three-hundred-pound hatch out and lowered it.

With their view no longer restricted to a ten-inch diameter window, they could see that their spacecraft was being surrounded by a convoy of police cars, airport crash trucks, military jeeps, and even a few armored cars; their squat, angular silhouettes backlit by the newly reactivated perimeter lights.

The moment the hatch had started to move, spotlights from several vehicles were trained on it. In response, Julie switched on her helmet-mounted spots and swung them down upon a squad-sized group approaching the *Phoenix*. Most of the squad wore the silvery asbestos suits of rescue personnel. Only one wore what appeared to be a military uniform, and was also the only member to be armed.

"Your names and ranks!" he barked, pulling an automatic from his holster and waving it at the astronauts.

"Major Allan Glassner! United States Air Force!" Glassner shouted back, pacing his words so they would not be garbled by his oxygen mask.

"Mrs. Julie Harrison! Mission Specialist! National Aeronautics and Space Administration!" said Julie, using the same cadence so she could be heard.

"What? A woman?" said the official, momentarily surprised. "No matter. I am Lazare Sampras, Minister for People's Security. Tell your captain I am boarding your spacecraft."

"No, we can't let you!"

"What? You're refusing to let me aboard? I'm the head of the People's Security Forces. You cannot refuse."

"We still have a hydrazine fuel leak!" Julie warned. "It's very dangerous! Only your crash crew can come on board. You must wear protective clothing!"

"Very well," said Sampras, reholstering his automatic. "Inform your captain and the rest of your crew to disembark immediately! I am placing you under arrest for violation of flight safety rules and illegal invasion. Your spacecraft will be seized as property of the Seychelles People."

Two

Crisis Management
A Second Chance

"Ahoy, *Simpson*. Ahoy, *Simpson*. This is Marge, we are preparing to land. Stand by to be boarded. Howard, activate the hover lamps."

The ghost-grey Sikorsky Seahawk had been circling the U.S. Navy frigate for almost twenty minutes, waiting for its wingman to show up, waiting for the warship to answer its calls or put back into Diego Garcia. Now, with the second SH-60 on the horizon and closing rapidly, the first one broke out of its holding pattern.

Approaching the ship from dead astern, the helicopter dropped to one hundred feet and slowed until it was almost matching its speed. An *Oliver Hazard Perry*-class frigate, the USS *Simpson* had a bulky, truncated superstructure which ended in a large set of hangar doors and a flight deck for the last ninety-odd feet of its hull length. Normally, one of the doors would be open, a landing detail waiting inside it, the Air Traffic Control Center manned and the deck awash in low-visibility red light. Now, however, everything was dark and no one had appeared to receive the helicopter.

"Commander, your men ready to disembark?" asked the pilot, Lieutenant J.G. Dean Marron, glancing quickly over his shoulder.

"Everyone's ready, even the bobbies," said Glenn Allard, crouching between the two pilots' seats. "Will you wait for orders from your captain?"

"You mean Homer? No way. And don't you tell him I called him that."

"Don't worry, your secret's safe with me. Just give us the jump signal when you get her stabilized, and we'll do the rest."

Seconds later Marron ordered his crew chief to open the SH-60's side hatch; it was the last verbal command he gave. The muted thumping of the rotor blades and turbine whine jumped to deafening levels the moment the helicopter's starboard hatch was cracked open. Gale-like winds blasted its interior as the crew chief finished sliding the door forward.

By then Allard had rejoined the other five men of his command, and the two British Constables who would make the actual arrest. Normally outfitted for AntiSubmarine Warfare (ASW), the Seahawk's main cabin had lost its ASW consoles, system operator's seats, and sonobuoy racks. All were stripped out to make room for the Sea-Air-Land Team (SEALs) and policemen.

The helicopter dropped another fifty feet in a gentle glide toward the *Simpson*'s flight deck. When it swept over the end of the frigate's transom stern, the glide stopped, the rest of its descent would be vertical. The hover lights in the SH-60's nose were angled down to keep the landing marks on the deck illuminated. Now the machine bounced and yawed as it edged closer. Without minute-by-minute knowledge of how sea conditions were making the ship behave, Marron refused to actually touch down on it.

When he finally matched its cruise speed, and smoothed out his maneuvers to a steady hover, he extinguished the few cabin lights he had left on. Almost at once the helicopter rolled from side to side as Allard and his chief petty officer initiated the assault on the frigate.

They landed feetfirst on the gently heaving deck and stumbled until they regained their balance. They crouched low, to avoid possibly being hit by rotor blades, and unslung the shotguns they carried on their backs. The rest of the SEALs jumped within seconds of Allard, taking up the same defensive stance as he did to cover the landing. Last to arrive were the two policemen, who lost their footing and rolled across the flight deck until the SEALs stopped them.

Lighter by over a thousand pounds, the Seahawk lifted rapidly away from the warship, swinging to the left and climbing back to its original altitude. Suddenly the hurricane of rotor wash ended; along with the blades' rhythmic slapping and the roar of turbine engines. For the first time in minutes the assault team could speak to each other.

"Christ, this feels like a ghost ship," said the chief petty officer, training his shotgun on the hangar doors.

"It should. We're only going to find nineteen men here out of a crew of one eighty-five," Allard replied. "You ready to go, Stony?"

"Just lead the way, Commander," said the mountain of a man wearing a constable's uniform. He pulled a wheel cap from under his raincoat and set it on his head, at last he didn't have to worry about it being blown off.

"Good. John, take the point. Those of you with riot loads are to stay with me. Those with Ferret rounds are to put on your gas masks and hang back until you're needed. We don't know how many are responsible for taking this ship, if it's everyone we'll need the gas."

Allard waited until the two SEALs whose Ithacas were loaded with CS gas rounds had their masks on before signalling his group to advance. He selected the port hangar and had his men cluster at either side of it as he activated the exterior controls. The moment the hangar's door started to rise, a harsh light spilled out across the flight deck. In seconds, when it had risen to chest height, the SEALs started ducking under it.

Inside they found the cavernous hangar empty and unoccupied; the Rapid Haul Down and Traversing gear strewn about the deck. Allard had the Air Traffic Control station between the two hangars checked to make sure it was empty; then moved his group onto broadway.

The central passage that ran virtually the entire length of the ship's superstructure was also empty, and the SEALs advanced down it cautiously. They stopped at each hatch to make sure no one was hiding behind one of them. Not until they were nearing the Combat Information Center (CIC) did they finally come across someone else.

"Freeze, sailor! Hands in the air!" John Landham shouted, pointing his shotgun at a seaman the moment he emerged from an open hatch.

"Christ, don't shoot!" was the startled reply, a tray load of sandwiches, glasses, and coffee mugs crashing to the deck. "You're the SEALs from that submarine, aren't you?"

"Damn right we are," said Allard, advancing to

join his point man. "Who the hell's in charge of this joyride?"

"Captain . . . I mean Chief Petty Officer Jerry Brody," said the enlisted man, his eyes frozen on the shotgun in Allard's hands. "He told us we were on a secret mission. And that we'd rendezvous with Commander Homer . . . I mean Commander Correy, after we left Diego Garcia."

"Jesus, you brought that crap?" Landham asked.

"Yes, sir. Mr. Brody's had eighteen years in the Navy, I've had two. When someone like that tells you to jump, you jump."

"I understand," said Allard, though he didn't lower his weapon. "Where's everyone else on this ship?"

"There's two guys in CIC." The sailor pointed up broadway to a hatch on its starboard side. "There's four or five more on the bridge, I was bringing chow to them."

"Where else?"

"There's some more in the enlisted men's mess, and the rest are in the engine room."

"You did good, sailor," Allard replied. "The Brits will take care of you. John."

Allard motioned to the Combat Information Center's entrance, and seconds later he and Landham were flanking it; their compact Ithaca shotguns poking inside.

"I was wondering when someone like you would show up?" said the petty officer at the command console, as the SEALs rushed the darkened room. "We've been watching our helos on radar for the last half-hour."

"Reggie, check the weapon systems," said Allard. "Safety everything. If you were watching us, why didn't you contact us?"

67

"Brody told us to maintain M-com silence, and since he has ten years on me I do what I'm told. On the other hand, I didn't tell him you were making a landing attempt. So he didn't order evasive action."

"Thanks for the assist. I'd wondered why this one was going so easy. Where's Brody now?"

"On the bridge," said the petty officer, smiling. "And he's sailing higher than a kite."

Broadway ended a few feet past the CIC's entrance with a steep flight of stairs leading to the bridge. Emerging from the center, Allard and the senior constable ascended the stairs together. Stopping just short of its top, they were able to see or hear everyone on the *Simpson*'s bridge.

Two men sat in the center, contoured seats for the ship's helmsman and telegraphist. To their right, a third man leaned against the captain's chair while a fourth worked at the chart table and the fifth had just exited onto the starboard bridge wing. With a nod from Allard, the constable was the first to reach the top of the stairs.

"And just what the bloody hell is going on here?" he questioned, his deep Scottish burr making almost everyone who heard it jump.

"I'm Bart Simpson, who the hell are you?" said the chief petty officer in the helmsman's seat.

"Senior Constable Baxter, Scotland Yard. I'm here to arrest the man responsible for stealing this ship."

"You motherfucker, you told us this was a secret mission!" said the black man who jumped out of the telegraphist's seat. "I knew there was something screwy about this from the start!"

"That's all right, lad. We know," said Baxter, stepping onto the bridge, and up to the contoured seats. "And just where the hell do you think you were going?"

"Bayonne," said Jerry Brody, turning so far in his seat he started to slide out. "Alice is going to marry my brother. I can't let her do that. I love her better than he ever could."

"What, a girlfriend?" the black seaman responded. "All this is over a girlfriend? I oughta pull your dick off."

"No one's going to do any dick pulling here," said Allard, finally stepping onto the bridge. "Brody, you are relieved of command. Under the terms of the British Indian Ocean Treaty and Naval Party Twenty-Zero-Two, Constable Baxter will take you into custody. Put the cuffs on 'im, Stony."

"Arrested? What the hell am I being arrested for?" Brody protested, as Baxter grabbed him by his right arm and slipped a handcuff link around his wrist.

"Grand theft, warship. We'll get the other charges later. Sailor, I want you to take over the helmsman's chair and slow this ship to permit a landing. Your second helicopter is inbound with some of your officers."

"Commander. Commander, it's already down," said one of the SEALs coming up the stairs behind Allard. "And we have a casualty."

"What? I didn't authorize it to land," said Allard. "Did it crash? And who got injured?"

"Ship's captain ordered the helo to land. And he's the one who got injured. He jumped too soon and broke his ankle."

"That's Homer for you," said Brody, now he was standing against the bridge's row of windows, with Baxter finishing up his cuffing.

"From now on it's Commander Correy to you," snapped one of the other seamen he had deceived. "Brody, you'll get the 'Bart-of-the-month' award for sure."

"Is everyone from the second helo on board?" Allard asked, ignoring the comments.

"Yes, sir. And she's still sitting on the pad," said the first SEAL. "Ship's officers should be here in a few moments, and Mr. Cusano's team is helping with Commander Correy. The ship's CIC has also received an urgent message from the Rock. They want you to return immediately."

"What? This operation isn't finished yet and they want me for another? Are we getting two of these 'drunken sailor' calls in one night?"

"I don't know, Commander. But the order for your return was sent by Admiral Nicolson himself on a secure channel."

"The brass ashore must really want me," said Allard, still confused. "For what, I'm going to have to find out on my own. Take your orders from Larry Cusano, and Larry only. The ship's officers can only give you 'suggestions,' not orders. Remember, you're my SEALs. Not theirs. Stony, it looks like I'm going to have to leave you this time."

"Don't worry, Commander. I've done this often enough to know what happens next," Baxter answered. "I'll find a convenient nick to put our thief in until we make port, and I'll watch out for your lads. Good luck, Commander. See you ashore."

Safetying his Ithaca and reslinging it, Allard took the stairs back down to broadway. Stopping for a moment at the CIC, to confirm his orders and talk with Cusano, he made his way aft to the hangars. He found the Air Traffic Control station manned by one of the *Simpson*'s officers and a furiously buzzing helicopter sitting on the flight deck.

The Seahawk was empty, except for its pilots and crew chief, even the injured Correy had been moved inside. Once Allard had climbed aboard it, the helicopter's rotor blades began slapping louder. It rocked on its landing gear before lifting off and allowing the frigate to sail out from under it. Setting course due east, it climbed to the altitude of the first SH-60, and together departed for Diego Garcia.

"Thank you for getting here so quickly," said Cochran, when the last officials he had been expecting entered the conference room. "It's ironic that we met here only two weeks ago to discuss contingencies for just such a crisis. Ladies and gentlemen, be seated. Mrs. Kosinski, what does the State Department report?"

"Our ambassador still hasn't spoken directly to Prime Minister Albert René," said the State Department representative, taking her seat at the room's table. "Only to his advisors."

"The Libyan ones or the Cuban ones?" injected the CIA official.

"Probably both groups. Ambassador Griffen has had better luck with the Seychelles Foreign Minister. She confirms that our astronauts have indeed been arrested, and the space shuttle confiscated as 'property of the people.' She was told that a more definitive and official statement will be issued in the morning, Seychelles time. Which will be early evening here."

"I guess we can all wait for it," said Cochran. "I may still be in Houston around then anyway. What does the ambassador have to say about my crew? Has she seen them? Does she know where they are?"

"She thinks they're somewhere in the airport, and has persuaded the Foreign Minister to let her visit them," said Kosinski, smiling. "If she does, she'll be the first American official to visit them."

"A small victory for us. What about the Astronaut Return Treaty? Can't we enforce it on them?"

"The UN treaty was originally signed when the Seychelle Islands were a British colony. Since becoming independent, they have not renewed the treaty. Though they privately assured us they would honor it."

"Private assurances aren't worth the paper they're not written on," Cochran replied. "Mr. Horner, what have you heard from Langley?"

"A lot of 'we told you so,' " said Horner, pulling a folder out of his attaché case and displaying the printout sheets stuffed in it. "These are reports from our Seychelles field office since early 'ninety-one. They show the Marxist government turning increasingly hardline, the result of increasing Cuban and Libyan influence, and waning Soviet influence. Since there's no more East Germany, there are no more East German advisors to the government. Czechoslovakia and Hungary have withdrawn all their advisors because of human rights abuses. Now, Cuba's DGI trains the People's Security Force and Libya's military, the People's Defense Forces. There's been a recent infusion of military equipment, trainers, helicopters, and more armored cars."

"Does the CIA have any 'connections' in the Seychelles government?"

"Once we had, but not anymore. Nor do the French and British services. The DGI has been very good in rooting out pro-Western members of the secret police and military. Most were forced into early retirement, and a few of the stubborn ones have disappeared. We have no connections left. It's been rumored for months that a secret pact was signed between Libya and the Seychelles. However, we don't have the human resources to confirm it and until

72

three hours ago that wasn't a priority for us."

"I'm certain the White House and the Pentagon will tell you it is now," said Cochran, before turning to the only uniformed individual in the room. "Which leads us to you, Commander. As Department of Defense liaison, can you tell us what your service and the others have in the central Indian Ocean?"

"Apart from a few Marine guards at the embassy, there are no American forces on the Seychelles," the naval officer responded. Like the CIA representative before him, he also produced a folder and started leafing through it. "But as you all know, a thousand miles to the east is our base at Diego Garcia. Almost all the resources there are Navy or Marine Corps, which will make any operation an all-Navy show. We have a dozen supply ships and attack transports assigned to U.S. Central Command, the hospital ship *Comfort* and the command ship *LaSalle*."

"Most of which is useless to us because the Marines who are needed to run their equipment are in Okinawa or Hawaii," said Horner. "We don't want to invade the Seychelles, just get our shuttle back."

"From what you and Kosinski are saying, we may have to. For more immediate use, there's VP-44, a patrol squadron with P-3 Orions. We also have several warships and submarines docked at Garcia, many of them will be sailing soon for strategic pre-positioning while the State Department negotiates with the Seychelles government. For heavier firepower there's a battle group in the Arabian Sea with the carrier *Eisenhower* and the *Belleau Wood* with a Marine battalion landing team."

"Strategic pre-positioning? What do you think these ships have to be pre-positioned for?" Kosinski asked.

"Evacuation, blockade, and possible offensive operations," said the commander. "You in the State Department can negotiate and see the rosy side of things all you want. Grenada, Panama, Libya, and Iraq have taught us to prepare for any contingency."

"I agree," said Cochran. "My recent experience tells me we must be ready for any event. And the more I hear about the Seychelles, the less I like it."

"I remain confident that we can find a negotiated end to this crisis," said Kosinski. "I can just guess what the military is doing. Can you tell us what NASA is preparing for?"

"We're getting our 747 carrier ready. It was at Edwards for the return of the *Phoenix,* and should be fully prepared for departure by tomorrow morning. It and a C-5 we're borrowing from the Air Force will leave for the nearest available field to the Seychelles, probably Diego Garcia. I'll find out how they're doing real soon, I'll be flying to Edwards tonight."

"What do you mean you are?" Horner responded. "You're the director of manned flight operations. You should be here to coordinate NASA's part in this crisis."

"The *assistant* director of flight ops can do this just as well as I can," said Cochran, starting to glance at his wristwatch. "And you've met with Phil almost as many times as you've met with me."

"What does Mr. Engleberg have to say about this?" Kosinski asked.

"If last year taught Bob Engleberg and the rest of NASA's management anything, it's not to get in my way. My friends and my ship are in danger, and where I can do the most good for them is at the closest possible base. Not sitting in a comfortable room halfway around the world. Now, let's come up with a list of positions and options for Phil before I leave for my flight."

In just under an hour and a half's worth of steaming, the *Simpson* had managed to sail forty miles from Diego Garcia. On their return flight, the two Seahawks covered the same distance in less than fifteen minutes. From their cruise altitude of three thousand feet, they could see the brightly illuminated coral atoll within minutes after leaving the frigate.

Twenty miles south of the Great Chagos Bank, and the most southern of the island archipelagoes associated with it, Diego Garcia was a footprint-shaped outline of coral sand. Its dark center was Eclipse Bay, open to the sea at the north end and filled with the glowing deck and riding lights of nearly two dozen ships. On the atoll's western arm was the principal base, its runway a gleaming three-mile ribbon of sodium vapor lamps extending out into the bay. The rest of Garcia's scattered facilities (water towers, satellite dishes, administrative buildings, barracks, and piers) were bathed in soft light from the floodlamps.

Allard's Seahawk dropped behind the leader as they entered the field's landing pattern and clattered over the bay. They both settled in front of the control tower, where the balance of the *Simpson*'s crew was waiting for them. Most went to the first helicopter; there were just two men to greet the second.

"Admiral! Terry, what's going on? And whatever it is, it's not my fault!" Allard shouted, until they had moved far enough away from the SH-60s to speak in more normal, conversational levels.

"Your informal nature is always 'refreshing,' Commander," said Rear Admiral Adam Nicolson, irri-

75

tated but he returned the salute Allard gave him. "A major crisis has come up, virtually in our own backyard. We'll explain it better when we're inside."

While the helicopters were being loaded with some of the frigate's crew, the naval officers entered the administration building next to the control tower. Away from the sounds of rotary and fixed-wing aircraft being prepared for flight, and in an area where security matters could be discussed openly, Allard discovered why he had been recalled so urgently.

"You're kidding. . . . When did the shuttle land?" he said, taking a seat in a briefing room where most of the island's senior ranking officers had been gathered.

"About two hours ago," said Terence Carver, taking the seat next to him. "And it took NASA more than an hour after the meteor strike just to land the ship."

"The orbiters are pretty sophisticated flying machines, I know that from Allard Technologies' subcontract work on them. So the reentry time doesn't surprise me. What does is their decision to land the *Phoenix* in the Seychelles. Don't they know what's going on out here?"

"Compared to what's happening in Botswana and the rest of Southern Africa, the Seychelles must've seemed idyllic," Nicolson answered, stepping up to the seat at the head of the table. In response, the assembled officers rose quickly to attention. "Gentlemen, thank you all for reporting at this hour. Emergencies never seem to occur at reasonable times. You've heard the reason why we're here, the space shuttle *Phoenix* has crash-landed on Mahé Island and has been seized by the Marxist government there. We're the closest and best-equipped Allied base to the crisis point. What we do here now will

76

help shape our government's response to it. Please be seated."

"To echo Mr. Allard's remark, why on earth did NASA choose the Seychelles?" said a Royal Navy lieutenant-commander, the only British officer in the briefing room.

"The decision wasn't made on the Earth. It was made by the astronauts themselves," said Nicolson. "And in the middle of a dangerous situation. They selected the landing site which would allow them the fastest reentry. And it's a sad commentary on this world that they couldn't make the right decision based on their emergency alone. Wishing the situation were different won't make it so. We're going to have to deal with it as it is. What about our pre-positioned stores? Can we use any of them?"

"All I have here are maintenance and security personnel," said a Marine Corps colonel. "It would take at least two days to start bringing in the combat troops we'd need. Frankly, the Army's Eighty-Second Airborne can get its alert force here faster. And we do have the Marine battalion already mated to its combat gear on the *Belleau Wood.*"

"Yes, it and the *Eisenhower* are about three-days sailing from Mahé. How soon can the rest of you weigh anchor?"

"Speaking for the other ships' captains, we can set sail in twenty-four to forty-eight hours," said a U.S. Navy commander, with a nodding agreement from most other officers of the same rank. "Of course for the sub skippers, it's different."

"We already have our reactors going through systems checks," Carver responded, as he glanced at the captain of a nuclear attack sub. "Both our boats are fully provisioned and I have Glenn's exec rounding up his SEALs. We'll be ready to cast off in an hour."

77

"I knew you would be," said Nicolson, smiling slyly. "If the State Department can't negotiate an end to it, this crisis could be perfect for your sub and its capabilities. Admiral Daniels's plan to deep-six it and your career could be backfiring. I know you're eager to go but, before I let you do so, I'd like to have a damn good idea of what your plans are. Unlike surface ships, I know once a submarine leaves the harbor its skipper 'traditionally assumes a great latitude in interpreting orders.' "

"Even after all these months, I'm still famous for that defense."

"I wouldn't exactly say 'famous,' Terry. Now what are your plans? Sailing direct to the Seychelles?"

"Not directly," said Carver. "But eventually we will. If you'll look at the map, I'll explain what I want to do."

While one of the briefing room's side walls was lined with windows overlooking the airfield's flight line, the other had a map of the Indian Ocean hung on it. Well illuminated, the map's plastic surface was covered with cryptic grease pencil marks denoting American, Soviet, and other naval force's activities—from the Persian Gulf and Red Sea on its left side, to the Australian continent on the other. The moment Carver mentioned it, all eyes swung toward it.

"My boat had been scheduled to leave soon for Reunion Island," he continued. "To carry out maneuvers with the French forces based there. I'd like to depart now, do a Subscape run to Reunion, and link up with the French before heading to the Seychelles."

"How far away is that island?" Nicolson asked, sliding the eyeglasses back and forth on his nose to get the best focus on the map.

"Twelve hundred miles due south of Mahé. It's about the same distance from here to Reunion. If this space shuttle crisis develops the way I think it might, then Diego Garcia will become very busy and very well-known. Even more so than during the Iraq War. At Reunion, I can operate in relative secrecy and deploy quickly from it."

"We could also make use of the tactical forces the French have there," said Allard, speaking up for the first time since the meeting began. "They got C.160 transports, some patrol boats and a *Rubis*-class nuclear sub. Ironically, they have more useful equipment there than we have on this rock."

"And they have people who can operate all of it," said Nicolson. "All we have are our ships and Commander Fuller's Orions. Who, you'll notice, is not here. He's flying the first recon sortie to Mahé."

The deep, omnipresent buzzing grew a few notches louder, causing some of the men to glance out the windows. In the flight line's floodlights, a lone patrol bomber rolled out to a taxiway. In a few moments the ghost grey aircraft became a dark silhouette, framed only by its anticollision and landing lamps after it moved beyond the floods.

"Is there any way we can speed up the sailing times?" asked Nicolson. "I'd like to have something under way by first light."

"Beyond the nuclear subs, the only boats that'll move out of this lagoon by dawn are the tugs," said another of the ship captains. "The only fully fueled and provisioned warship we had was stolen by a CPO."

"Then why not use it?" said Allard, blurting it out. "The *Simpson*'s already at sea, and we can use the helicopters to ferry the rest of its crew out to it."

"I heard its captain broke his leg and the *Simpson*

is now being commanded by its executive officer. Hardly what I'd send into a crisis."

"Yes, it's unconventional," said Nicolson. "And coming from Mr. Allard it's not unexpected. But in this situation it may just be what we need. Remember, gentlemen, even if a ship were to leave within the hour it would still take almost two days to reach the Seychelles. We need to get something there as fast as possible. If the *Simpson*'s XO feels his ship is up to it, they're going. Mr. Smythe, what about this visit we were supposed to get from the Royal Navy?"

"The frigate *Alacrity* has departed the Persian Gulf task force," Smythe answered. "I'll see if the Admiralty can arrange to have it rendezvous with your ship."

"Good, I'll let the Pentagon and NASA know we're getting multinational help. Gentlemen, what I need from those of you who are ship captains is a timetable as to when your ships can sail. Mr. Carver, Mr. Allard, I suggest you get back to your submarine. You'll probably get orders to sail by the time you're ready to do so."

"How do you feel, Allan?" Reynolds asked.

"Like someone's finally killing the fire ants that are crawling over my skin," said Glassner, his voice light with the sounds of relief. "I hope you got more bottles of this lotion."

Stripped down to his NASA-issued briefs, Glassner stood with his legs spread apart and his arms held out from his sides. His skin was a mottle of red splotches, ranging from deep red on his hands and around his neck to a bright pink on his upper arms and torso. Uniquely, his face was clear of any such irritations, saved by the face mask of his Portable Oxygen System. Starting with his hands and working their way in, Julie and Rebecca were rubbing him down with a bottle of white lotion from the shuttle's medical kit.

"Don't worry," said Julie, rubbing his left arm. "We got one bottle for each of us in our med kit. We're lucky these shitheads let us take it off the orbiter."

"We're lucky they're keeping us together," Post remarked, walking up to the holding cell's door and back again. "I would've split us up. And I definitely wouldn't hold us here in the airport jail."

He had just turned away from the door to start another trip when it clanked loudly. The crew jumped at the sounds, then clustered around Reynolds when the door swung out and a heavyset black officer strode in.

"Well, Roger? Do the interrogations begin now?" he asked.

"Not yet, spaceman," said the officer, Captain Roger Lifesay of the Seychelles Police Force. "At least not by my men. You'll be happy to know one of your demands has been met. You're going to meet with your embassy staff. Ambassador Griffen . . ."

The commander of the airport police unit stepped away from the cell's entrance and motioned for the people behind him to come in. First to appear was an attractive, auburn-haired woman in her forties, followed by a U.S. Army major who appeared to have spent most of his time on the beach. The moment they were inside, Lifesay bid his goodbye, squeezed past them, and shut the cell door behind him.

"I'm Lynn Grif. . . . My God, what happened to you?" said Griffen, when she noticed the astronaut standing at the center of the group. "I wasn't told anyone had been injured."

"I'm the new superhero for the nineties," said Glassner. "I'm Pizza Boy."

"Better not let any radioactive adolescent turtles find you," Post added. "I think all they eat is pizza."

"You're both wrong, the X-Men are the new heroes," said Reynolds. "Argue it with Marvel Comics later. Ambassador, I'm Commander Clayton Reynolds. Major Allan Glassner was poisoned by the hydrazine fuel leak. Since we landed, the only medical treatment he's received is what we're now giving him."

"That's something we should've expected," said the Army officer. "Commander Reynolds. Major Glassner. I'm Major Ron Goldman, Military Attaché. Will you need to be hospitalized?"

"Not so long as I have this lotion," Glassner replied, nodding at the plastic bottle Julie held in her hands. "Ladies, let's not let ceremony stand in the way of relief."

"Ambassador, what's happened to the *Phoenix?*" Reynolds asked. "We've heard nothing about her since we were dragged away."

"Your spaceship is still surrounded by emergency crews," said Griffen. "And it's still sitting at the end of the runway. From what your tracking station can see, the crews have made no attempt to move the ship, not even when the French airliner finally landed."

"Did Ray's staff see anyone board the orbiter?"

"They did. And they think something was taken off, but they couldn't tell what."

"This is just fine. We weren't finished post-flighting the *Phoenix* when they jerked us off it," said Post. "If they're not careful these assholes could still turn a safe landing into a disaster. We have to go back and properly deactivate the systems while there's still power to do so."

"Don't worry. You will," Griffen informed him. "I was able to convince government officials to let you back aboard the shuttle for just those reasons."

"Thank you, Mrs. Griffen," said Reynolds, verbalizing the sigh which spread through his crew. "Do you know when we're going? The orbiter won't have power for much longer."

"Soon. I'm told we will all be taken in an airport security van. Will you need to wear your breathing systems?"

"Yes, until everything is secured and the mid deck washed down, no one can board the shuttle unprotected. Have you been told what we're being charged with? Captain Lifesay wouldn't even tell us that."

"You've been charged with violating flight safety rules," said Griffen, pulling a sheet of paper from her jacket pocket. "Making an unscheduled landing, refusing orders from Seychelles authorities, flying an unlicensed aircraft, creating a toxic chemical hazard, and something called 'crimes of imperialism.' "

"What? Those are bullshit charges," Post snapped.

"I know they are, don't worry about them. We'll get these matters cleared up soon. There are other things you have to worry about. Ron wants to ask you a question."

"What do you have aboard the shuttle that's sensitive?" Goldman requested, lowering his voice. Even though he could still be clearly heard in the holding cell.

"Our main payload is pretty sensitive," said Reynolds. "Nothing we can do about that. However, there is some material of a 'soft' nature we can deal with effectively."

"We can also deal with our payload," Rebecca advised, while she continued to rub lotion over Glassner's right arm. "The payload bay doors do have payload bay door motors."

"Good thinking. I hope we all know what to do when we get back to the *Phoenix*. Before we go, Ambassador, there's something we want you to have. Excuse me, Julie."

Allowing Julie to keep working on Glassner, Reynolds moved behind her and reached into the pouch on her waist ring flap. He pulled out an angular, marble-sized piece of iron and nickel. Holding it gingerly between his thumb and forefinger, Reynolds turned and motioned for the handkerchief in Griffen's breast pocket. Once he had it, Reynolds placed the meteor in the center of the linen cloth and carefully folded it over.

"This is what caused our emergency," he said, handing the handkerchief back. "It still has hydrazine residue on it so be careful. We didn't want to show it to our jailers, we thought they'd toss it into the nearest ocean."

"Don't worry. We'll take good care of it," said Griffen. "Ron, your case . . ."

The moment she had the meteor in her hand, she was passing it over to Goldman. The attaché case he had been carrying snapped open in an instant and remained open just long enough for the meteor to be stuffed in its lid flap.

"We'll take it to the tracking station staff after we leave here," Griffen added. "And don't worry, as bad as this now looks, it will be over soon. When the public reaction hits this government, they'll change their minds."

"Bridge, this is Nucleonics. System checks completed. Reactor is on line, all power settings are available."

"Roger, Dominic. I'll let you know when we need you," said Carver, holding down the toggle on his bitch box. "Bridge, out. I never knew rounding up sixty men and seven officers on one little island could be so much trouble."

From his position in the *John Marshall*'s flying bridge, Carver could see most of Eclipse Bay and had a commanding view of the narrow pier leading out to his submarine. At the pier's shore end, a truck had just come to a stop and was off-loading men from both its cab and tailgate. They marched down the pier with everyone carrying a heavy pack, except for the leader.

"Glenn, where did you find this group?" Carver asked, using the bridge loudspeakers instead of the bitch box.

"Body surfing on that stretch of beach near Minni Minni!" Allard shouted. "Is my exec back?"

"Yes, Jaskula returned less than ten minutes ago. He found his stragglers at Barton Point. He commandeered a liberty boat and brought them across the lagoon. There were three men with him. Is this the last of your team?"

"The last, Terry. We're set to go."

"Then hurry it up. We don't have all night," said Carver, holding his fingers over the buttons on the intercom panel. "Deck crew, stand by to cast off. Radio Room, warn the tug we're readying to depart. Engineering, give me maneuvering speed on my command. Helm, stand by to take her out."

As the last of Allard's men stepped through the conning tower hatch, the gangplank was retracted onto the pier, and the bow and stern lines were slipped off the cleats. Almost at once the huge submarine started drifting away from the pier, causing the tug which had been hovering on its starboard side to move in closer.

"Deck crew, retract the cleats and secure your safety lines," said Carver, bringing the hand mike up to his mouth again. "Radio Room, tell the tug we need a nudge starboard aft. Engineering, I want maneuvering speed. Glenn, did the stragglers give you any trouble?"

"No, in fact they gave me less trouble than the men I left on the *Simpson*," said Allard, climbing through the bridge's floor hatch. "They wanted to return with the ship, until I told them what we may be facing."

"I hope they won't be upset if nothing comes of this. After so many dry runs they should expect it."

As Allard finished stepping out of the floor hatch he felt the submarine jar slightly. Nearly two hundred feet behind its conning tower, the tugboat rubbed up against its starboard flank. Pushing its stern toward the shore, and swinging its bow out into the lagoon.

"Helm, ahead slow," Carver ordered. "Is she answering?"

"Helm, aye. She's answering, Captain," responded a familiar voice on the intercom speaker. "Ahead slow."

Even in the highly illuminated waters of Eclipse Bay the *John Marshall* was little more than a black silhouette, more than four hundred feet long. Only the flashlights used by its deck crew and its tiny handful of running lights gave it any detail. After nudging it once, the tug backed off and let the submarine move out on its own.

"All these ships lit up like casinos," said Allard. "And we're the only one ready to leave."

86

"That's usually the way it is," said Carver, taking a moment to glance at the supply ships and other vessels scattered around the bay. "Remember how the Brits were caught flat-footed by the Falklands War? The Iraq Crisis was unique in that we had a few days' notice. Lieutenant, watch our stern. Just in case somebody slips off. Helm, make ready for one-third speed."

Near the deep center of the lagoon, the sub could maneuver on its own, though the tug would continue to escort it until they reached the entrance. Briefly, it was illuminated as it passed the runway's southern threshold. Built on squat, massive stilts, the runway extended nearly half a mile into the dark waters. Its sodium vapor lamps washed the night away from the *Marshall* revealing a smooth black hull. It was featureless except for the squared-off hump behind its conning tower, where the Polaris missile tubes were once housed. Off its starboard bow was another black silhouette riding low in the water, more rounded and not quite as long as the former missile boat.

"There's the *Hammerhead*," said Allard, pointing to the attack sub. "What did you and her skipper decide? I take it she won't escort us."

"Correct. She's not equipped with the Subscape system," Carver answered. "Most *Sturgeon*-class boats were considered too old for it. Only the *Los Angeles*-class and the boomers were outfitted. She'll head north of the Seychelles, where she'll either be a decoy for us or join the *Eisenhower*'s battle group. Helm, ahead one-third. Bridge to deck crew leader, secure your detail."

As the *Marshall* increased its speed to eight knots, its ride became rougher in the lagoon's confined waters. The chief petty officer commanding the deck crew gathered in his men, and after a few minutes the only personnel remaining topside were in the flying bridge. All too quickly the submarine was reenveloped by the night as it passed the glowing runway.

"Radio Room, make message to Harbor Control," said Carver, rolling his sleeve back to glance at his wristwatch. "Departing Diego Garcia. Zero-Four-Forty-Five hours, local time."

With the entrance channel well-marked by automated lighthouses, the *Marshall* did not slow when it passed Eclipse Point and Spur Reef. The tug trailed it into the Indian Ocean for another twenty minutes before putting back. Once alone, the sub extinguished its running lights and the last detail secured the bridge for diving. The eight-thousand-ton warship filled its ballast tanks with water and slid unnoticed beneath the waves.

Three

Reconnaissance
Outside Influence

"Tac-Co to Pilot, we've crossed the international time line. Resetting clock to Zero-Five hundred hours, Seychelles time."

"Roger, Tac-Co. We copy," answered Commander Raymond Fuller, watching the digital clock on his front instrument panel drop back an hour. "God, you know you're dealing with a long-range target when you have to cross time zones. Pilot to Radar, you have any contacts?"

"Radar here. No airborne or surface contacts," said one of the sensor operators in the main cabin behind the cockpit. "But we'll probably be picking up some fishing boats soon."

"Roger, let me know the moment you get anything. Pilot to ESM, what are you detecting?"

"Some surface radars and a little radio traffic, most of it civilian. The radars appear to be ship navigation units, except for the most powerful one. I think that's the air traffic control set for Seychelles International."

"Are they detecting us?" Fuller asked.

89

"No the signal's too weak for any kind of a return," said the ESM operator. "They won't detect us for about ten minutes."

"Good, just enough time for us." Fuller reached for one of his overhead panels and switched his radio to a scrambled military channel. "This is Mako One to Olympus Control. We're approaching Apache Territory. So far, no hostile activity. This will be our last message. We're going to scrape some waves. Mako One, out. Pilot to crew, I'm sounding the dive alarm."

Fuller gave his men enough time to fasten their lap belts and lock their seats on the floor track most of them used, and then he dipped the Orion's port wing. The Lockheed patrol bomber swung away from the westerly course it had been flying for almost three hours and began a steep, spiralling descent. Uncharacteristic of its normal antisubmarine missions, it had been cruising at eight thousand feet, instead of less than a thousand.

As the P-3 wound down to the black waters below, its airspeed picked up, as did the G-forces. For just over a minute its ten-man crew felt like they were fighter pilots; the acceleration, the increase in gravity pushing them into their seats were unknown in their normal missions. All too quickly it ended as the four-engined turboprop levelled out, back on its original heading and doing nearly five hundred miles an hour.

"Altitude, three hundred and twenty feet," the copilot read off. "Airspeed, four hundred and thirty knots."

"God, after eleven years flying 'Charlies' I could count the number of times I did that on one hand," said Fuller, still feeling the exhilaration. "Pilot to crew, the Top Gun lesson is over. Tac-Co, switch radar to quiet mode and activate the FLIR pod. Let me know the minute the ESM detects any change or picks up new signals."

The momentum built up by the dive rapidly petered out, and soon the P-3 had returned to its original cruise speed. Slowly Fuller edged it closer to the waves, until its paddle-bladed propellers were whipping foam off some of the higher crests. For the rest of its run into the Seychelles, the patrol bomber would skim the ocean and remain as quiet as possible. Relying on its Electronic Surveillance Measures and Forward Looking Infra-Red (FLIR) system to avoid trouble.

"Time to go back under the bubble, Julie," said Reynolds, feeling the van reduce speed. "We must be there."

"I still have enough oxygen and power for four and a half-hours," Julie advised, checking the displays on her chestpack computer. "Let's hope we don't take that long."

Instead of attaching the helmet by herself, Reynolds lowered it over her head and helped her snap the locking rings in place. She slid her gloves on herself and connected their rings to the space suit's arms. By the time the van came to a halt, Julie had her suit pressurized, while the rest of the crew had their flight helmets on and their Personal Oxygen Systems connected.

"Ambassador, can you see anything?" Reynolds asked.

"Nothing," said Griffen, trying to peer through the steel slats covering the windows in the rear doors. "All I can see is light. You'd think we were in the center of Victoria on Market Street."

With little warning, the doors were pulled open, and the bright light flooded in. Griffen had barely enough time to push away from them before they were swung out. Since she and Goldman were closest to the doors, they were the first to be helped out. What they encountered gave the astronauts pause and only a few seconds to prepare.

"Visors up, you guys," Post warned. "They got a circus waiting for us."

Most of the illumination that stung their eyes came from the reactivated perimeter lights and vehicle headlights. But the truly painful glare was from the spots on video cameras and the strobe-like flashes on still cameras. In addition to the rescue crews, police and military personnel, the press had finally arrived.

"Well, spaceman. We meet again," said Lazare Sampras, stepping up to Reynolds as he was helped out of the van. "If I did not say so before, welcome to the Socialist People's Republic of the Seychelles."

"No, you didn't," said Reynolds, making Sampras wait an awkward moment before shaking the hand he held out. "Actually, I prefer your earlier, nine-millimeter welcome. It was so much more like you."

"Commander, please. Remember our situation," Griffen responded, a shocked look on her face.

"Yes, Mr. Reynolds," said Sampras. "Try to be diplomatic. Like your diplomats."

"I'm not here to be a diplomat," said Reynolds. "I'm an astronaut. And I'm here to finish shutting down my vehicle so it won't be a threat to your people."

"It would not threaten my people had you not made your illegal invasion in the first place."

"Invasion? Illegal? What we had was an emergency, and this was an emergency landing!"

"We're not here to discuss the incident," Sampras answered, smiling at the propaganda victory he had scored. "Merely to remove one of the threats it has created. As you said yourself, Mr. Reynolds, you are not a diplomat."

"Yes, I certainly walked into this one." Reynolds closed his helmet's visor as he spoke, causing his voice to become muffled. "Let's go."

Following his order, Post, Rebecca, and Glassner snapped down the tinted visors on their helmets while Julie activated the lights around hers. The security van that brought them to the runway's far end had parked in front of the shuttle, becoming part of a ring of vehicles starting a hundred feet out from it. The police, reporters, and soldiers kept outside the ring; anyone inside it wore the silvery asbestos suits of the rescue crews, except for Sampras. He escorted the astronauts up to the boarding stairs erected beside the *Phoenix.*

"Mr. Reynolds, these men will accompany you aboard your spacecraft," he said, pointing at two shimmering figures standing beside the stairs. "Major Alonso Parker and Corporal Ebo Dorson of the People's Security Forces."

"A pleasure to meet you, spaceman," said Parker, briefly removing his head gear to get a better look at Reynolds. "I hope we work well together, it'll make our future meetings much more pleasant."

"Just stay out of our way, and we'll do fine," Reynolds said slowly, and he did not respond by opening his helmet's visor. He was grateful for it; it kept Parker and Sampras from seeing the shock and anger on his face. All his plans for erasing programs and sabotaging equipment were dashed. "Let's . . . let's get to work."

Reynolds's only concession was to gesture up the

stairs, allowing Parker and Dorson to enter the shuttle first. Because its hatch door hung horizontally, the boarding stairs could not be pushed flush against the fuselage side. The last few steps onto the mid deck had to be done over the door's irregular surface. First to stumble on board was Parker, followed by his Corporal, then came Reynolds and Post.

"It doesn't look like much was touched in here, boss," Post noted, checking the galley and zero-gravity toilet on either side of the hatch.

"Your warnings we would cause an even greater accident were enough to keep us off," said Parker, speaking loudly so he could be heard through his asbestos hood. "Where, exactly, is this meteor damage you claimed?"

"Forward," said Reynolds. "The open locker to the left. That's where the meteor penetrated our pressure shell."

Squeezing around the seat still anchored to the floor, Parker and Dorson pulled out the drawer Reynolds had indicated and began examining the orange-stained photographic gear inside.

"What is this?" Parker asked, trying to rub an orange crust off the lens case he held.

"It's hydrazine residue," said Post. "If you were to touch it with your bare hands, your skin would blister immediately. The same thing would happen to your lungs if you were to inhale it. Until we wash down the deck that could happen to anyone."

"I see . . . and where is the meteor you claimed caused all this damage?"

"Ambassador Griffen has it," said Reynolds. "We felt you would have lost it in the nearest ocean."

"You mean you don't trust us, Mr. . . . Where are they going?"

Parker waved his hand at the bulky white space

suit trying to climb up the mid deck's ladder. Immediately behind Julie, Rebecca was trying to help guide her through the narrow roof hatch to the flight deck.

"They're heading topside to enter our shutdown programs into the GPC," Post quickly added.

"What? You've assigned your women to that task?" said Parker. "I don't believe you."

"They do similar duties while in orbit," said Reynolds. "Why shouldn't I assign it to them? Why do you think we bring them into space to begin with? Companionship?"

"Very well. Corporal, follow them to the cockpit."

The other silver-suited individual saluted Parker, then turned to the back of the deck. By the time he reached the ladder attached to the air lock, Rebecca had succeeded in pushing Julie through the roof hatch. For a few seconds, while she stood on the ladder's top rungs, they were able to talk privately.

"What will we do with him looking over our shoulders?" Rebecca asked, briefly raising her visor.

"Do what we talked about doing," said Julie, speaking just loudly enough to be heard through her bubble. "One of us will have to distract him while the other does the sabotaging. I'll ask him to help me remove the mission specialist seats while you fix the GPC."

"Control to Sonar, what do you have?" said Carver, using the periscope stand's hand mike.

"Actively pinging, Captain," was the response on the control center's speakers. "Our only surface contact is the *Simpson* and we have no sub-surface contacts, even at maximum range."

"Good, continue active pinging and finish retracting the BQR array. Clarence, get ready to take us to nine hundred feet. Greg, stand by on the Subscape panel."

"Captain, the BQR's been secured," said Clarence Jefferson, when a status light on his panel changed from green to red. "Diving planes, fifteen degrees down-angle. Flooding forward trim tanks."

The *Marshall's* senior helmsman pushed his control wheel forward until the angle-of-attack gage for the conning tower's maneuvering fins had dipped below the neutral mark. Despite their diminutive size, in relation to the massive submarine, almost at once they were pushing it for deeper waters. No longer towing a twenty-six hundred foot cable of hydrophones and multiplexers, the *Marshall* was free to dive and quickly reached its new level.

"Ballast Control is retrimming for neutral buoyancy," Jefferson advised. "Our heading is Two-Three-Zero degrees. Our speed is ten knots. Laser radar and thermal imagers are coming on line. Engine Room is answering, all speeds are available."

"Good. Control to Nucleonics, do you confirm reactor status?" said Carver, keying his hand microphone.

"Status confirmed," said another voice on the center's speakers. "The 'museum piece' is ticking perfectly."

"Stay on it, Don. Greg, what's your status?"

"Primary and secondary pumps are ready. All nozzle rings have been deployed," Gregory Burks replied. The *Marshall's* executive officer stood at the control center's safety station; on the panel that he had opened was a submarine's overhead silhouette. It was striped with bright green, glowing bars, indicating the Submarine Escape System had been activated. "The polymer tanks are full."

96

"Captain, laser and thermal systems show we're clear fore and aft," said Jefferson, motioning to the additional screens at his helm station.

"Captain to crew, stand by for Subscape run," said Carver, briefly holding down the intercom's Master Transmit button so he could be heard throughout his ship. "Sonar, keep pinging until you're at five percent efficiency. Mr. Burks, you may activate the system and give the call."

"Thanks, Terry," said Burks. "Tank valves, open. Primary pumps, on. Clarence . . . sorry. *Mr. Sulu, warp factor one.*"

As the Subscape system's pumps started up, the rings of tiny nozzles in the missile submarine's hull sprayed out a colorless, jelly-like substance. The water-soluble polymers quickly covered its four-hundred-and-ten-foot hull in an even coating, cutting its friction with the surrounding water to zero.

Moving at a sedate ten knots, Jefferson ordered the *John Marshall*'s engine room to give him flank speed. In minutes it was reaching twenty, just as the polymer film achieved peak coverage. The surge in speed was like kicking in afterburners on a jet fighter. In less than a minute the sub had reached thirty-five knots and continued to accelerate; all the while its engine noise grew quieter and its ride became glass-smooth.

"Glenn, how are your men doing?" Carver asked, turning when he heard the stamp of boots from the control center's back.

"Reading all the information we got on the Seychelles and its military," said Allard, stopping just short of the periscope stand at the stairs descending to the Tactical Attack, Situation Control (TASCO) Room. "Including the NASA info we got before departure."

"We should be doing the same thing, we got about twenty-one hours before we arrive at Reunion. Greg, you have the con. Glenn and I will be in the TASCO Room."

Just before they took the stairs to the tactical center, Sonar reported it was shutting down active pinging. As the *Marshall* approached forty-five knots even its passive sonar arrays were deactivated. Until it reached the vicinity of Reunion Island, it would have to rely on its short-range, infra-red imagers and three-dimensional laser radar. It would also have no communication with the outside world until it slowed enough to deploy an aerial.

"Colonel, I'm glad I got you before retiring," gasped an out-of-breath aide, when his commanding officer opened the door he'd been pounding. "We just got this from the Foreign Ministry."

The lieutenant handed Colonel Ahmad Nazih a densely packed teletype sheet nearly two feet long. He had not bothered to put it in an attaché case, or even a file folder. And at first it irritated Colonel Nazih.

"You violated all of Blood Revenge's security procedures," he said darkly, involuntarily touching the scars under his right eye. "By bringing this to me the way you did. If our experience last year taught us anything, it's we have enemies everywhere."

"I understand, Colonel," said the lieutenant. "But this report was marked urgent. And the initial incident happened more than three hours ago."

Nazih waved a hand at the aide to shut him up; the further he got into the report, the more intrigued he was by it. Near the end his dark mood had evaporated. He was smiling and, for the first time in many months, there was a light burning in his eyes.

"The one area where I thought the Americans were unassailable," he observed. "Now, we can strike at its heart."

"I recall you talking about the imperialism and hegemony of the space powers," said the lieutenant. "I thought you would be interested."

"In spite of your failure to follow procedures, you did well, Lieutenant. This will be better than dealing a blow to the Jews. It says here the American shuttle has one of their Keyhole spy satellites on board it."

"Should I alert our strike groups, Colonel?"

"No, this is not an operation suited to our 'terrorist' forces," said Nazih, not taking his eyes off the teletype sheet. "They train for specific targets, identified months ahead of time. What we have here is a target of opportunity, it requires forces that can be deployed rapidly. . . . Yes, they will do."

"What do you mean, Colonel?" asked the lieutenant.

"Colonel Qaddafi's Rapid Deployment Force. Our joint Air Force/Army command."

"But I thought it was created just for propaganda purposes. To counter the American and French forces of the same name. It isn't very large."

"Whether or not it was created for propaganda, it has the units and weapons we need for this situation. I know many of the officers assigned to it, their base is close by. Quick, we must go to Communications and . . ."

Nazih only had to take one step out his door, and into the already cool desert night, to realize he was dressed in just a T-shirt, briefs, and socks. He had been minutes away from going to bed when he was disturbed and had not bothered to put on a uniform.

"Damn. Lieutenant, you go to the center," he said. "I'll meet you there after I get clothes on. Get a secure phone line to Tripoli and another to our base at Kufrah. Hurry, we have much to prepare before this night grows any older."

"Pilot to Observers, what was that we passed by?" Fuller asked. "It damn well wasn't a fishing boat."

"Right waist to Pilot, I think it was a patrol boat. Not a big one, probably one of their *Simba*-class British Vospers."

"Big or small, it's probably reporting us to their headquarters," said the copilot. "Should we abort or continue?"

"What? With the island in sight and our target only three minutes away?" said Fuller. "We'll be there before that boat finishes sending its report. Look at the FLIR, you can see the shuttle plain as day."

Fuller motioned to the cockpit's Forward Looking Infra-Red screen, where the *Phoenix's* thermal image glowed brightly, standing out clearly from the airport lights and the vehicles circling it. The spaceplane was only a few hundred yards from Mahé's eastern shoreline, an easy target for the approaching patrol bomber.

"Jesus, four hours after its reentry and it's still hot," said the Orion's crew chief, strapped into the cockpit chair just behind the pilots' seats.

"This'll be easier than finding a virgin on the Rock," Fuller remarked. "Let's take her up a hundred feet and reduce airspeed. Pilot to crew, stand by for course change. Activate all cameras and recording systems. Tac-Co, keep a watch on your ESM. Sing out if anything changes."

After more than an hour of skimming across the Indian Ocean and avoiding the occasional fishing boat, the Lockheed giant pulled away from the waves, leaving behind four propeller-induced wakes. At its new altitude it dipped a wingtip and turned for a cluster of lights at the end of an island.

"Major, what's that noise?" asked the corporal, standing at the flight deck's floor hatch.

"It's an aircraft! Probably American!" Major Parker shouted. "Get down here immediately."

For a moment, the corporal leaned forward to glance out the cockpit windows. Then he was gone, climbing as best he could down the ladder. In seconds Julie and Rebecca were alone, just what they had wanted since they reboarded the *Phoenix*.

"Don't bother looking for it," said Julie, when she caught Rebecca trying to slide between the pilot and commander seats. "We got work to do. You wreck the payload bay doors, I'll erase the programs. Hurry girl."

With the mission specialist seat stowed, Julie and Rebecca had enough room to maneuver easily around the flight deck. Rebecca stepped lightly to the aft crew station while Julie remained forward, going to the overhead panels that held the master controls for the General Purpose Computer. Before she went to work, she glanced through the floor hatch and saw not only the Seychelle officials leaving the shuttle, but the rest of the crew as well.

"Right Waist to Pilot, I think I see the crew coming out of the *Phoenix*."

"Get it on film if you can," said Fuller. "The next pass we make will be from another direction."

Coming in over the tops of the coconut palms and Takamaka trees, which bordered the airport, the ghost-grey Orion finally materialized in the glare of its perimeter lights. It dipped its right wing slightly as it roared past the *Phoenix* and the surrounding ring of vehicles.

In moments the P-3 was gone, hurtling over the hangars and support buildings on the other side of the airport. It pulled into a steep climb, gaining several hundred feet before turning to the left and heading back out to sea.

"That's an Orion. An antisubmarine bomber," Post identified, as the roar of its turboprops receded from its deafening levels. "It's probably from Diego Garcia."

"It's a spy plane!" said Parker, charging down the steps behind Post and Reynolds. "And what it's doing is an illegal act of espionage."

"What the hell do you mean, illegal?" said Reynolds. "Arresting us and taking my ship is illegal. My country has the right to keep an eye on its people and property."

"My country also has the right to defend itself," Sampras responded, walking into the quarantine area without wearing any breathing equipment. "And it looks like your aircraft isn't finished violating our sovereignty. This is Sampras to Colonel Mooradian, you are authorized to open fire on the intruder."

Sampras spoke his order into the walkie-talkie he had been carrying and received a crisp, cryptic reply. Moments later the rumbling of heavy engines drifted across the runway from the perimeter tree line. Only then did Reynolds and Post realize they had not seen the armored cars which first surrounded the shuttle since their return to it.

"Activating Leigh light," said Fuller, tapping a switch on an overhead panel. "And since they already know we're here we might as well turn everything else on."

A last holdover from World War Two sub hunting, the powerful beacon under the Orion's right wingtip snapped on and burned through the night. After it, the anticollision strobes and formation light strips came to life, turning the patrol craft into a sparkling constellation.

Fuller swung the patrol bomber again to the left, holding it in the turn until it was lined up on the runway's eastern threshold. Levelling the aircraft, he dipped its nose, putting the Leigh light's strong beam on the threshold. In seconds it had moved far enough down the asphalt to illuminate the *Phoenix* and the vehicles surrounding it.

"Left Waist to Pilot, I think the astronauts are still out there."

"Good, get it all down," said Fuller. "Jesus, what the hell's that?"

"Right Waist to Pilot, tracers! They're shooting at us!"

"My God, I don't believe it," Julie uttered, catching sight of the intermittent flashes through the cockpit's port windows. "They're firing at our plane!"

"What should we do, Julie?" said Rebecca, looking up from the exposed service panels she had been working on.

"Keep working! Maybe they'll forget about us! It's taking longer than I thought to call up and dump all these programs."

"Take cover! They're strafing us!" Parker shouted, ripping his hood off and charging for the safety of an airport crash truck.

"Strafing? Hell, it's a *patrol* bomber!" said Post. "It doesn't have any guns! Guns . . ."

While most the personnel scattered at the Orion's approach, the military guards stood their ground and raised their weapons. The AK-47s started snapping out short bursts, even though the P-3 was not yet in range of small arms fire.

"Walt? Don't! Those guys can take care of themselves!" Reynolds warned, when he belatedly noticed his pilot was no longer at his side.

The few seconds' lead that Post had allowed him to sprint ahead of Reynolds and Glassner. Ahead of the few people still standing around the vehicles. He reached the ring's outer side before any of them fully responded to him, and threw himself at the nearest guard. Caught by surprise, the enlisted man tumbled to the ground, his Kalashnikov flying into the air. The rest of the guards immediately stopped firing, to train their weapons on Post and the other astronauts.

"Hold it! We're unarmed!" Reynolds managed to say, before the roar of turboprops drowned out everything else.

"Lights off, Chappie!" said Fuller. "Everything! Evasive maneuvers! Full throttles!"

While the crew chief behind them extinguished the bomber's exterior lights, Fuller and his copilot threw their control wheels about the cockpit in unison. For a moment the Lockheed giant drifted toward the tree

104

line and continued its shallow dive. Then, it abruptly levelled out and began to jinx to the left. The lines of tracers from the BRDM-2s at first came perilously close to the Orion, only to flash overhead and behind it as the maneuvers were initiated.

When the last of the P-3's external lights were killed, the armored car gunners lost their principal aiming points. All they had left was a black silhouette bobbing and slewing back and forth as it thundered down the runway. It was below the height of the airport's control tower, causing the gunners to briefly cease firing when their tracers arced dangerously close to it.

"We got a break, let's take her up!" Fuller ordered. "Their guns aren't radar-directed. They can't follow us once we climb out of this glare."

With no weapons and several thousand pounds of fuel already consumed, the lightly loaded patrol bomber leaped away from the airport. It traded some of its newly acquired speed for altitude as it rose above the glow from all the airport lights. After several seconds the tracer fire resumed, more erratic and less coordinated than before.

"No, no . . . the idiots!" said Sampras, raising the walkie-talkie to his mouth again. "Mooradian, control your men! Order them to stop!"

So they could keep firing on the Orion, several of the BRDMs had broken from the tree line and were driving across the airport's runway and taxiways. They chased after it, their firing much less accurate because of their bouncing across the landscape. By the time they were charging down the runway and firing steadily, the aircraft had climbed beyond the range of even their heavy-caliber machine guns.

"All right! Way to go, Navy!" Glassner shouted, waving his arms, in spite of the pain it caused.

"Shut up! Shut up!" Sampras responded, turning to the astronauts. "Major Parker, take them away!"

"You're going to have to shout louder," said Reynolds. "I think he dug a hole in the runway, and pulled the asphalt over him."

"Shut up, your insults will not help you! Added to your other crimes, your pilot will now be charged with assault."

"Well you shouldn't have had your goons fire at a Navy plane," said Post, being pulled off the asphalt by the guards. "I'm a Navy pilot myself. If you wanted to shoot at something, why didn't you wait for an Air Force plane?"

"Thanks, Walt. I'll remember that," said Glassner.

"I want that man taken to the hospital," Sampras ordered, ignoring what the astronauts were saying. "Ambassador Griffen, your government will be responsible for his medical expenses."

"Send us the bill, Mr. Sampras," said Griffen, stepping up to him. "We'll pay what is reasonable. What are your plans for the crew?"

"They're ours, Mrs. Ambassador. Major Parker, arrest them."

"I thought we already were under arrest?" Reynolds questioned.

"Shut up, Commander," said Sampras. "Collect them all, Major. Where did you leave the women?"

"Pilot to crew, I want a complete check for damage," said Fuller. "Especially any penetration of the cabin."

"I wish we were flying the Neptunes my father flew," the copilot observed. "They had guns."

106

"This is certainly going to make an interesting report when we get back to the Rock. In my fourteen years I've never had anything like it. Admiral Nicolson's going to have some real reading when we land."

At three thousand feet, with its airspeed down to two hundred miles an hour, the P-3C levelled out rather than risk a stall. It was already out over the water, on a direct line for Victoria, when it finally turned to the right, and continued turning until its new heading was due east. The patrol bomber picked up some of the speed it had lost during its escape, in approximately three hours it would be home.

"I've bypassed all the safety lockouts," said Rebecca, nodding her helmet at the control panels she cross-wired. "Get ready to rip those out when we're done. Here goes. PBD latches, engaged. Activating payload bay doors."

Normally, the systems that operated the shuttle's payload doors would not activate if the bulkhead and centerline latches were still in place. However, because of the jury-rigged overrides, the systems came on-line and began working. Almost at once their torque tubes and gear actuators started to bind. In seconds the tubes were warping and the gears bending their teeth. The wrecking of the systems was completed when their power drive motors shrieked mechanical death cries and burned out.

"Good heavens, they never told us at Rockwell they'd make noises like that!" said Rebecca, jumping away from the aft crew station. "Think they heard it outside?"

"If we heard it, everyone else sure did," Julie advised, pulling the jury-rig wires and closing the panels. "We only got a few minutes before they come for us, we better hide as much of our work as we can. The emergency power will die soon, and for a little while they won't get any secrets out of this Lady."

"Do you think they will head back to strafe the airport?" asked Yegorov, tracking the Orion from the *Navarin's* port bridge wing.

"No, it's an antisubmarine plane," said Raina, lowering his binoculars and handing them over to his watch officer. "They're not equipped with cannons."

"Thank you, Captain. We should probably be grateful it's not so armed. Our 'comrades' provocation was certainly enough to warrant an attack."

"And if they try it again, they may find the Americans prepared to respond. If they want a confrontation, this government is going about it the right way. We haven't done anything like this since the early sixties. I remember my uncle talking about those provocations. They frightened him then, they frighten me now. . . . We better let both Moscow and our Indian Ocean Fleet know what's happened. This is going to get very dangerous."

Using Raina's binoculars, Yegorov tracked the Orion until it was a black speck on the eastern horizon. By then the sky was at last growing light. With its first night almost at an end, the first day of the crisis was about to begin.

Four

Forces Deploy
New Friends

"When did you last see the crew?" asked Ray Fernandez, sitting in Griffen's office at the embassy.

"As they were being put inside the security van," she said, leaning back in her chair to get a little rest. "I wasn't allowed to return with them to the airport's detention center. If indeed that's where they were taken. Did your lookouts spot where the van went?"

"I'm sorry, no. They've only been watching activity around the orbiter. With so much else happening at the airport, a single van can get easily lost."

"We're in luck, people," announced Goldman, entering the office after being absent for nearly half an hour. "Finally got an answer from Diego Garcia. That Navy plane just landed, and it wasn't damaged."

Goldman went first to the ambassador's desk and gave her the tear sheet he had just taken from the embassy's communications center. He quickly took one of the office's few remaining seats; the rest of the personnel had to wait their turn to read the other sheets he brought with him.

"Hell, is everyone screaming for information?" said Fernandez, after scanning through his third sheet.

"Why shouldn't they be?" said Goldman. "We got a full-fledged crisis here. The White House, State Department, Pentagon and your agency all want to know."

"Not to mention the press and the tourists," added Chargé d'Affaires Donald Griffen, another embassy staffer. "While the Major and my wife were out visiting your astronauts, I was taking phone calls from the local press and a lot of frightened tourists. This whole island's waking up to discover it's in a crisis."

"God, it *is* morning," said Fernandez, checking his watch. "We must've been here for hours. What's it like outside?"

Fernandez hauled himself out of his uncomfortable seat, realizing how long he had been there by how stiff his legs had grown. He walked over to the office's picture windows which, like all the others, had heavy curtains drawn across them. Parting the curtains slightly to look out, he allowed in a glaring shaft of sunlight.

"Make sure you close them when you're done," Lynn Griffen warned. "They're made of sound deadening material. So no one can listen in, not even with one of those laser devices."

"It looks wonderful outside," said Fernandez. "Some rain clouds hanging over the mountains. And I don't see any anti-U.S. demonstrations either."

"Don't laugh about that," said Griffen's husband. "The government radio is claiming the shuttle landing is a pretext to invasion. They claim airport workers were killed by our astronauts. We're being painted as the aggressor, and it's going to damage us."

"So what should we do?" Fernandez carefully drew the curtains back together and returned to his chair. "Start filling sandbags?"

"Make evacuation plans, Ray," Goldman answered.

"In addition to supplying information to Washington, we better make plans to get our people and U.S. tourists out of here."

"Tourists? But the airport's still open, it's still receiving civilian flights."

"It's also swarming with military and security personnel, and their Libyan and Cuban advisors. They could shut it down in an hour. And since the Pentagon is already working on this, we should as well."

"What is the military doing?" Lynn asked, looking up from the tear sheets that made their way to her desk. "What else did you see at the center?"

"Diego Garcia's heating up," said Goldman. "And it's not just those Navy bombers. A Navy warship, the *Simpson,* has set sail to rendezvous with French and British warships. They'll be ready to help us should an evacuation be needed."

"Well, if they're going to cooperate with our Allies we should, too. Gentlemen, we've been at this long enough. I suggest we have some breakfast before we do anything more. I hope we can at least have that in peace."

"NASA Three-Nine-Nine, this is Edwards Tower. You are over the outer marker, there's no other traffic in your area. Once you're down you may taxi directly to the orbiter handling facilities. This is Edwards Tower, out."

"Roger, Edwards. I have three green, here I come," Cochran answered, watching his landing gear warning lights change color.

Four hours and one refueling stop after leaving Houston, the gleaming white T-38 appeared in the threshold lights of the primary runway at Edwards Air Force Base. High in the California desert northeast of

111

Los Angeles, the flight research and test center was relatively quiet after its day's activities. The NASA trainer was the only aircraft in its pattern, and no others were expected for the rest of the night.

Cochran finally slid his T-38 onto the runway at its halfway mark. Its enormous length still gave him the room for a safe rollout, and he didn't want to spend a lot of time taxiing over to the Dryden Flight Research Center. In spite of his shortcut, it still took him several minutes to reach the civilian side of Edwards.

Unlike the heavily illuminated military side, only the NASA main hangars still had their work lights on. None of the other government facilities, and the civilian contractor hangars, were active. Cochran rolled up to a line of demilitarized jet fighters and more NASA T-38s before shutting his engines down. The moment he opened his canopy he felt the cold night air flow in; he would have his flight jacket zipped up by the time he reached the ground.

"Ed, I thought they wouldn't let you fly anything but a desk," said one of the men who attached the ladder to the cockpit side.

"They can try but they know better than to stop me," Cochran answered, jumping off the last rung on the ladder. "Brenner, it's been too long."

Cochran grabbed Philip Brenner and hugged as best he could someone who stood five inches taller. In turn, he got squeezed and briefly lifted off the ground.

"God, I forgot how strong you are," he said, once he was able to get air back in his lungs.

"Piloting Nine-O-Five tends to put muscles on your arms," said Brenner. "And NASA says I'm too big to fly anything else."

"Well, we would need a shoehorn to fit you inside the shuttle's cockpit. How are the preparations going here?"

"We're making good time, have a look yourself."

Brenner motioned over his shoulder at the two aircraft which dominated the NASA flight line. Towering above the fighters and trainers, the silver and white Boeing 747 was the space agency's largest aircraft and its only shuttle carrier. Still wearing some of the markings from its days as a civilian airliner, it also sported the outrigger fins on its stabilizers and the roof attachment points for the role it had been flying for nearly twenty years.

Walking toward it, Cochran needed a few minutes to reach the behemoth and circle it. Around it were service vehicles, fuel trucks, and scaffolding. There was a work platform under each engine, all in various stages of being overhauled. Boarding stairs had been rolled up to the 747's port side entrance doors, and a steady stream of workers were carrying supplies into it.

Off the Boeing's starboard wingtip was the flight line's other giant, a Lockheed C-5B Galaxy. Squat and ugly in comparison to the airliner's rotund elegance, the military transport also had a distinctly evil look — courtesy of its grey-green camouflage scheme. The effect was enhanced by its raised nose section, a gaping mouth which appeared to devour the vehicles being driven into the aircraft.

"Our gift from the Air Force," said Brenner, stepping up to Cochran. "It can carry as much as two Starlifters and will accompany us all the way to the Seychelles."

"How soon will it and Nine-Zero-Five be ready?" Cochran requested.

"Working throughout the night, we'll be ready by around seven o'clock tomorrow morning. Then, all we have to do is wait for our commander to be assigned."

"You don't have to wait for that, I'm going to command this recovery force."

"What? You?" said Brenner, surprised. "But you're

113

the Director of Manned Flight Operations. You've got to stay here and help manage this crisis."

"Manage? Goddamn it, I want to command something," said Cochran. "I'm a pilot and an astronaut. I'll let Engleberg and the other bureaucrats do the 'managing.' My friends and my Lady are in trouble, and this is the best place for me. Where are the crews?"

"Either on board the planes or in the hangar ready room."

"Good, I want to meet them and your ground crew leader. We'll plan our trip as far as Diego Garcia, then rest. I have the feeling tonight will be the last best chance any of us will have for some real sleep."

"Squad, attention!" barked the unit's senior sergeant, the moment he got a nod from the highest-ranking officer on the tarmac.

The dozen members of the Libyan Army unit snapped stiffly erect and shouldered their weapons as a faint buzzing grew rapidly louder. The dark speck on the western horizon became a sand and green mottled Mi-8 helicopter. It circled the Al Kufrah Air Base once, then came in for a landing in front of the assembled officers and men. Once the helicopter settled firmly onto the tarmac, its side hatch rolled open and the boarding stairs were deployed. For all the ceremony involved, only a single Libyan Army intelligence officer emerged from the aircraft.

"Colonel Nazih, welcome to my airfield," said one of the other colonels waiting to greet him. "It's an honor to be visited by the commander of Blood Revenge."

"The pleasure is mine," said Nazih, returning the salute he was given. "I see you're preparing to take advantage of the opportunity this American blunder has given us."

114

"Yes, I would like to present to you Colonel Hazem Mashari of the Libyan People's Air Force. He's one of our most experienced officers, and he would be the best to command your Rapid Deployment Force Viper."

The base commander motioned to one of the younger, similarly ranked officers behind him. He stepped forward and shook hands with Nazih, who at first did not recognize him, until a gleam lit up in his eyes.

"Yes . . . yes, from our liberation of Chad," Nazih responded. "I remember you now. 'If you arrive first with your best you win,' did you not say that?"

"It appears as though I will become famous for that remark," said Mashari, smiling at the recognition. "It's something I believe in."

"Good, you'll have to if you're to succeed. What have you been preparing for the Seychelles?"

"The four Tupolevs and three Ilyushins you see here, they'll be refueled by one of our tankers in Somalia. One Ilyushin will carry a hundred and fifty paratroops, while another will carry the antiaircraft tank."

Mashari pointed down the flight line to the right of Nazih's reception group. First in line were the Tupolev Tu-22 bombers. Painted in the same sand and green scheme as the Mi-8 helicopter, their only external markings were the Arabic characters on their tails and the plain green discs on their fuselage sides and wings. Their smoothly tapered, needlelike noses belied the massive bulk of the rest of their airframes, which ended with the huge engine pods mounted on either side of their tails.

Farther down the flight line were the larger Il-76T transports. Painted a less militaristic-looking white and dark grey, they still wore the same Libyan Air Force markings, and their tail gun mounts stood prominently above their open clamshell doors. While the first Ilyushin had just begun receiving its squads of paratroopers, the other two were topping off their loads of supplies and munitions.

Among the last items to go aboard was a sand-colored ZSU-23 antiaircraft tank. Its broad, flat turret was the same width as its chassis, giving it a toad-like appearance. Even with its gun barrels depressed below the zero degree elevation mark and the Gun Dish radar lowered, the tank was still a tight fit for the I1-76T. It was slowly being inched up the tail ramp, stopping every few feet to check its alignment.

"When can your force deploy to the Seychelles?" Nazih asked. "You must arrive there before the Americans. They have an aircraft carrier and Marines in the Arabian Sea."

"The Seychelles government has already made a secret request for our aid. They will make their request public only after these planes are in the air. Then, our ambassador and their ambassador will go to the United Nations and charge the U.S. with aggression. We've been assured by the Chinese that they will veto any opposing resolutions in the Security Council."

"This revenge on the Americans must taste like sweet milk to you."

"It does," said Nazih, squinting when he faced the early morning sun. "We can cripple their space program, and pay them back for our humiliation in the North Sea. My only regret is we will have no opportunity here for revenge against Israel. That must wait for another day. Introduce me to the rest of your officers, Hazem. They will be the sword of our revenge."

"Radio Room to Bridge. We have a priority message for you, Lieutenant."

"Roger, I'll be down," answered the man sitting in the captain's chair. "Harry, you have the conn."

The *Simpson*'s executive officer, Lieutenant Robert

Stine, eased out of the seat he had been spending most of the last ten hours in. Even with his youth on his side, his legs had grown stiff, and he hobbled slightly until he reached the back of the bridge. There, he grabbed hold of the handrails and slid down the stairs to the ship's central passageway. From that point he only needed to walk a few dozen feet to reach the communications center.

"Lieutenant, are you ready for it?" asked the lone petty officer manning the cramped room.

"Fire away, Chris," said Stine, and in response the teletype beside him buzzed noisily. He pulled the sheet off its roller the moment it was finished and hurriedly read through the contents. "Diego Garcia confirms we're going to be rendezvousing with French *and* British warships. I think Stony would like to see this."

"Are you sure he should, Lieutenant? Does he have the security clearance to see that? I don't think Commander Correy would let him."

"Well I'm not 'Captain Homer,' and I don't think a security leak will be a problem out here. Constable? Hold on for a minute."

Stine quickly realized the shadow passing behind his shoulders was one of the two policemen on the *Simpson.* He turned and sprinted to catch up with him, stopping the officer just before he entered the Combat Information Center.

"Well now, Captain. What's this?" said Baxter, examining the tear sheet handed to him.

"We're going to have more company," said Stine. "Would you care to transfer your prisoner to the British ship when it arrives?"

"To the *Alacrity?* I don't think so. You're more likely to return to the bloody Rock than she is. Besides, your quarters are a little better than they would be on a smaller ship."

117

"I take it you're satisfied with the arrangements we've made?" Stine remarked.

"I wish you had a real brig on your ship," said Baxter, glancing into the CIC to check on his prisoner. "But I suppose that went out with HMS *Bounty*. I also wish Mr. Brody wasn't quite so valuable to you."

"I know, but a good tactical man is hard to find. Is this the end of his shift?"

"No, it's the end of Mallory's shift. I'll replace him and, in about five hours, I'll put Mr. Brody in his 'cell.' How is Commander Correy faring?"

"Our corpsmen are keeping him doped up and off his feet," said Stine. "So long as he can't walk, he won't be of much trouble to us. I'll be happy when we meet up with the other ships. I don't relish going in on our own. I've been a captain for about as long as you've been at sea."

"We're now six hours, twenty-three minutes from Re-union Island," Carver observed, seated at the main console in the Tactical Attack Situation Control Room. "Nice of you to finally join us, Glenn. I thought I'd have to do this briefing with your exec."

Carver glanced over his shoulder at the stairs leading down from the *Marshall*'s control center. Allard had only a few more steps to go before he reached the stairs' landing. From there he easily slid into the seat between his executive officer, Lieutenant-Commander Michael Jaskula, and Carver.

"We had a little munitions problem," said Allard. "We couldn't find all the Glaser rounds we're supposed to have in our armory. It took a little hunting, but we located them."

"You webfoots have more exotic bullets than James Bond ever thought of using," said Carver. "Now that we're all here, we can begin."

With a brief flurry of clacking from his keyboard, Carver brought up information on the TASCO Room's main and auxiliary display screens. In moments he had readouts on all the available military forces in the Indian Ocean.

"Here we go, United States, Great Britain, France, Russia, India and the Seychelles," he continued, pointing to each of the lists. "If you wish, I can bring up peripheral states like Australia and Madagascar?"

"No. In fact eliminate everything except Britain, France, and the Seychelles," said Allard. "And bring up something on their home islands."

With a few key strokes, Carver wiped his main screen clean and replaced the data blocks with a color map of a loose cluster of mountainous islands.

"This is the main group for the Seychelles," he said. "Mahé, Silhouette, Frégate, Praslin, La Digue, Cousin, Aride and Denis and Bird Islands. On auxiliary screen A you can see the atolls which also belong to the Seychelles. The Platte, Aldabra, Desroches and Amirante atolls. Total population is sixty-eight thousand, here are the population demographics."

"Good Lord, more than fifty thousand are on Mahé alone," Allard remarked, when another key stroke brought up the population figures beside each island. "There's less than five thousand on any of the other islands. We could use one of the sparsely populated ones for our insertion point."

"Insertion point? What are you thinking about?" said Carver.

"My officers and I have concluded that we need our own set of eyes and ears on Mahé.' We'd like to insert a recon squad, in much the same way we conducted exercises with the French on Tromelin Island."

"Oh yes, the operation we did four months ago. Are

119

you sure one of their Transalls has the range to reach the Seychelles?"

"With in-flight refueling it can," said Allard. "The problem is we need a nearly deserted island to drop our squad on. And I don't see one close enough to Mahé for us to use."

"How about an uninhabited one?" suggested Jaskula, speaking up for the first time. He nudged Allard in the arm and pointed at the main display screen. "That round one to the west of Mahé."

"You mean Silhouette?" said Carver, studying the screen and hitting more keys on his keyboard. "By God, he's right. It has no population, the readout says it's been set aside as a nature preserve and only gets daytime tour groups from the hotels on Mahé."

"How far is it from Mahé?" Allard asked.

"Fifteen miles. Well within the operating range of one of your zodiacs. There are two smaller islands much closer to Mahé, Conception and Therese."

Punching up a cursor for the main screen, Carver used his board's steering ball to position it on each of the two islands less than a mile off Mahé's southwestern coast. As the cursor touched each, they began to flash.

"They'd be perfect for observation points," said Allard. "But they're far too close, even with a night insertion. My men would be easily seen from the main island."

"How many men will you send?" said Carver. "And who have you selected?"

"I'll assign one sniper team, one communications team, and Gordo Hassler will command them. He did some of the jumps during the Tromelin exercises."

"Let's hope the French will cooperate to the extent that we need them to. Let's see their forces." Carver shifted his attention to another of the room's auxiliary screens and started to read off its list. "They have three

C.160 Transalls, and four helicopters. One frigate, the *Admiral Charner.* One destroyer, the *Aconit.* And my friend's command, the nuclear attack sub *Casablanca.*"

"When did you last see Captain Jacoubet?" Allard asked.

"Back in 1990," said Carver. "I know that's several years, but what we went through together makes for a strong respect and friendship. His being at Reunion is a good sign that we'll get the help we need."

"We better. Using a C.160 for the parachute drop would be a lot easier than a Starlifter or an Orion. Let's see what the Seychelles military has. I know they got a lot of new equipment from Libya in the past year. I hope they haven't any nasty surprises for us."

"I could order us out of Subscape and surface for the latest update. A lot must have happened in the world above. Unless you want to stop now, we won't find out for another six hours."

"Can you see anything up there?" said Reynolds.

"Not much, boss," Post answered, standing on a chair and trying to glance through one of the room's high windows. "I think I can see the runway, but no *Phoenix.*"

"Well at least this time they gave us a room with a view. Rebecca, Julie, have you found anything?"

"I found a critter," said Julie. "A common drawer beetle."

In addition to its five metal frame beds, the room also had three desks and a centrally located table. Since being placed in it, the astronauts had been examining it and its furnishings for any eavesdropping gear; which had proven fruitless until Julie held up a drawer from the second desk.

"Yes, you're right," Reynolds confirmed, glancing at

the microphone on the bottom of the drawer. "A pity we can't call in an exterminator. Allan, you find anything?"

"A couple of silverfish," said Glassner, standing in the bathroom door. "One of them's hiding there and another over here."

He turned and pointed to the toilet's water tank, then over to its shower stall. Rebecca and Reynolds joined him at the door, straining to see the bugs he had located. They had only been there a few seconds when a sudden banging on the room's main door startled them all.

"Do you like your new quarters, my friends?" asked Major Parker, entering the room at the head of a large contingent. This time, he wasn't wearing a silvery asbestos crash suit but a crisply pressed uniform that looked more police than military. "They were laid out specifically for you."

"Where are we?" said Post, climbing off his chair. "We're not back in the terminal. It looks like you got us in some building on the military side of the field."

"This is our detention and interrogation center. Jointly operated by the People's Defense Forces and People's Security Forces. I will be in charge of your care. I'm the commander of the Seychelles People's Security Force's interrogation unit."

"You're a fucking cop," said Reynolds, stepping up to the contingent. "And I thought you were military. Who the hell are these goons? Your rubber hose squad?"

"My assistants and advisors," Parker answered, smiling. "This is Gonzala Torres and Victor Esparza. They're from the *Direcciòn General de Inteligencia*. As my newest friends, I thought you would like to meet my oldest."

"They're DGI, Clay," warned Glassner. "Cuba's KGB."

"I see you know of us, Major," said Gonzala Torres, the senior of the two Cuban officials. "In Cuba, we know you well, too. For years we have lived with the terror of NASA rockets falling on our country. In incident after incident you've poisoned our land and damaged our property."

"Don't hand me this shit," said Reynolds. "The best Castro ever claimed was we killed a few cows with a booster."

"We're not going to hand it to you. The world's press is falling over itself to get here. We'll hand it to them."

"And with our expertise you'll help us," added one of the other men in Parker's contingent. "I'm Captain Mohammed Halim, Libyan People's Army. If I were you, I would be most cooperative with Colonel Torres. They call him *Escorpiòn* and he deserves his reputation."

"I think that means Scorpion," said Julie. "Maybe he can help us with our bug friends."

Julie threw the drawer she was still holding at Parker's feet, causing it to splinter and his group to jump as if they just heard a gunshot.

"And stealing U.S. property won't help your country either," Reynolds snapped back. "I want to know where my ship is, and when are we going to see Ambassador Griffen again?"

"Your spaceship has been towed to our military hangars for its protection. You will see your ambassador at *our* convenience. Before that, we have questions we want answers to. Starting with what your women did on the spaceship while we were driving off your Navy's bomber?"

Five

"Get enough sleep, Terry?" asked Burks, when he saw a hulking form appear in the control center's forward hatch.

"I think four hours is enough for now," said Carver, though he was still yawning. "What's our position?"

"Inertial navigation says we're about thirty miles north-northwest of Reunion Island."

The moment he got inside the center, Carver stopped at the helmsman's station to examine the readouts on the *Marshall*'s speed, heading, and the latitude and longitude of its position. It had been twenty-one hours since it left Diego Garcia, it was now twelve hundred miles southwest of the atoll and still running at nearly sixty miles an hour.

"End the Subscape run," Carver ordered, picking a hand mike off the periscope stand. "Clarence, start slowing us down. Control to Nucleonics, start reducing power on the reactor. Control to Sonar, stand by to resume pinging."

By the time Carver was finished giving his commands, Burks had reached the safety station and was

124

opening the panel to the Subscape system. Already the submarine was cutting its speed, and its glass-smooth ride was growing rough. Throughout its four-hundred-and-ten-foot hull, it had begun to vibrate softly and would continue to do so until the high speed ended.

"Primary and secondary pumps, off. Closing polymer tank valves," said Burks, hitting the switches on the panels. "The nozzle rings are retracting."

Without the Subscape system operating, the thin coat of water-soluble polymers was no longer being renewed, and friction with the surrounding water stripped it off the *Marshall*'s hull in a few minutes. As its speed reduced, its BQQ sonar once again became effective. Below twenty-five knots it resumed active pinging for surface ships and other submarines.

"Conn, this is Sonar. We have a submerged contact at fifteen hundred yards. Depth is six hundred feet and it's pinging actively as well."

"Roger, Sonar. Can you identify?" Carver asked.

"Yes, Captain. It's a *Rubis*-class boat," responded the same voice on the control center speakers. "At this speed I can't be any more definite, but I think it's your friend."

"In this part of the world it has to be. Keep watching it, Eddie. Conn, out. Clarence, take us to periscope depth. Speed, twelve knots."

"Aye, Captain. Periscope depth," said the senior helmsman, before turning to his subordinate. "Blow forward trim tanks, I want positive buoyancy. Diving planes, ten degrees up angle."

Now travelling at less than a quarter of its former velocity, the *Marshall* started to rise from its cruising depth of nine hundred feet. Though its ascent was gradual, it only needed a minute to reach sixty feet. Once there the sub again felt the effects of wave action, and Carver raised the search periscope.

125

"Conn, this is Sonar. The attack boat is also at periscope depth and is now running parallel to us."

"Roger, Sonar. I have him," said Carver, stopping his 'scope walk and adjusting the focus rings on the handles.

"Conn, this is the Radio Room. We have a short-range transmission from the Frenchies," another voice on the speakers reported. "They're identifying themselves as the *Casablanca* and want to know if we're going to be surfacing now."

"Tell Captain Jacoubet yes, and we'll see him topside. Down scope. Clarence, blow the tanks. Take us up."

A deep rumble shook through the *Marshall's* hull as its ballast tanks were emptied of enough water to make it highly buoyant. With its periscope retracted, the submarine's conning tower first broached the surface of a calmly rolling sea. Barely noticeable in the darkness, another sub rose out of the black waters on its starboard side. Just over half the length, and one-third the displacement of the *Marshall,* the *Casablanca* was not fully visible until its running lights came on.

"Activate all exterior lights," Carver said to the petty officer who accompanied him to the flying bridge. "Including the floods. Bridge to Radar, begin sweeping. I want to know who's in the neighborhood."

"Ahoy, *Marshall!*" A voice boomed across the water from the other collection of lights. "Ahoy, *Marshall!* You have a wonderful command, Terry! So much better than the *Delta* boat!"

"External speakers, on." Carver hit one of the buttons on the intercom panel before picking up its hand mike. "Yes, Alain! It's my alma mater! I'd rather have her than an *Ohio!*"

"I understand, my friend! As they often say about us, we lose our hearts to the first ship we serve on."

126

"Very true," Carver answered. "Can we proceed to Reunion and dock? There's much for us to discuss, Alain."

"Indeed there is, a lot has happened since you set sail!" was the echoing reply. "You will not be allowed to dock! A helicopter is en route to pick us both up! Have any crew you wish to take ready for transfer!"

"What, does this mean we're going to have to dangle at the end of a rescue hoist?" said Allard, just climbing through the bridge's floor hatch.

"I think it does," said Carver, hitting another button on the intercom panel. "Bridge to Radar, have you anything to report?"

"Aye, Captain. We have incoming traffic," responded a voice on the intercom's speaker. "It's either a helicopter or a slow-moving aircraft. We have no other traffic in the area, not even fishing boats."

"Roger, give me an ETA on the helo. Bridge, out. Glenn, you better go below and get all the data we need from the TASCO Room. I'll delay the helo if it gets here before you do."

"Good evening, Major. Did you have any trouble making it through the roadblocks?" asked Fernandez, walking up to the latest car to enter the tracking station's parking lot.

"Not when they saw I was driving an embassy vehicle," said Goldman, climbing out from the sedan's driver's seat. "When did the roadblocks go up on this road?"

"They weren't up as I drove into Victoria, but they certainly were there when I came back at four o'clock."

"That's about the same time the rest went up around the island . . ." Goldman's response trailed off as a deep rumble cut through the humid night air. He

127

turned in time to see a dark green BRDM-2 roll past the tracking station's main gate; behind it was a similarly painted Suzuki jeep filled with noisily drunken soldiers. "This government's taking on a siege mentality. No doubt encouraged by Major Yashin and the other Libyan advisors. Have you completed your evacuation plans?"

"Finished," said Fernandez. "In fact we have two sets of plans. One for our families and nonessential personnel, the other for the rest of us if things really get hairy."

"Good, we may have to put your first set into effect sooner than expected." Even though he and Fernandez were the only two people in the parking lot, Goldman lowered his voice and turned his back to the main gate. "Tomorrow morning there will be a government news conference. In light of their actions, and continued overflights by our P-3s, I believe the Seychelles government will ask the Libyans for military assistance."

"My God, what does Ambassador Griffen say about this?"

"She's still hoping for a diplomatic solution. I don't think there's going to be one," Goldman said darkly. "She hasn't even had a follow-up meeting with the astronauts. And we don't know where they're being held. We think they're in one of the buildings on the military side of the field."

"What are our forces doing? You have anything new?" asked Fernandez.

"Our frigate and the French destroyer will be rendezvousing in the next few hours. As of yet, the *Eisenhower*'s battle group hasn't left its station in the Arabian Sea. Let's move this discussion inside. I want to meet with your senior officers and review your evacuation plans. And let's do it in a room without any windows."

* * *

"Ahoy, *Aconit*. We are inbound," said Dean Marron. "Let's try it again. C'mon, Marge, do it for me."

For the third time the ghost-grey Seahawk lined up on a cluster of lights moving northeast across the Indian Ocean. The *Aconit* was the largest warship the French had based at Reunion Island. The prototype for the later *Tourville* and *Georges Leygues* classes of destroyers, it had once been the most modern ship in the French Navy. Now, twenty years after its commissioning, the *Aconit* was an orphan. Unable to operate with the newer destroyers, it was now the flagship of a token naval force in a far-flung colony.

The SH-60 again approached the *Aconit*'s stern, dropping closer to it and slowing until it was barely moving faster than the ship. The target was a landing pad between the ship's aft gun turret and its antisubmarine mortar. Smaller than the flight decks on modern destroyers and frigates, it had given Marron endless problems. With no air traffic control center to talk to, he and his copilot had to judge the approach by themselves. Finally, they had the right combination of speed and descent rate to plant their helicopter on the impossibly small pad.

"Good luck, Jack!" Marron shouted, as the side hatch rolled open. "See you again in the morning!"

In addition to the ensign Marron spoke to, two seamen jumped out of the helicopter with him. Once their gear was also dumped on the pad, the rotorwash increased until the SH-60 had lifted off and swung away from the destroyer.

"Ensign John Kilworth, welcome aboard the *Aconit*," said one of the officers waiting at the landing pad, once the roar of turbines and the slapping of rotor blades had died away. "I am *Capitaine de Frégate*

Yves De Mozay. I'm sorry my ship is not better equipped to receive helicopters, but your pilots appear to have overcome the problems."

"Yes, Dean and the rest of our chopper jockeys can fit their helos into pretty small places," said Kilworth, returning the salute the French officers gave him. "We haven't heard anything since our lift-off from the *Simpson*. What have you heard about the crisis?"

"Nothing new on your spacecraft. But our governments are considering a possible evacuation of dependents from Mahé. It all depends on what happens at their news conference in a few hours."

"We better start going over our coordination plans. Have you heard anything about the British ship?"

"The *Alacrity* is en route from the Persian Gulf and will rendezvous with us in another day or so," said De Mozay. "Yes, let's have your gear stowed and begin talks on our joint operations. Have you and your men eaten yet? If not, you will find our chefs most excellent."

At first Reynolds thought the pounding he heard was part of his dream. Not until he felt Post shake him did he rise out of his sleep, and start rising from his bed.

"Who? What the fuck's going on?" he grumbled, rubbing his eyes and shielding them from a painfully bright light.

"I think we're going to have visitors," said Post, standing over him. "These lights suddenly came on and somebody's banging on the door. Why don't you open it yourselves, you assholes! You got the keys!"

"Ow! Walt, please, my ears."

Post's barking caused a bigger jolt in Rebecca and Julie than the pounding did, which stopped immediately. Seconds later the main door flew open.

"All right, who said it?" Torres demanded, the first to enter the crew quarters. "Who called us assholes!"

"Sorry, Bug Man, negative on the asshole," said Post.

"We're in a negative asshole mode here," Reynolds quickly added.

"Enough arguing," said Parker, entering the room after his Cuban advisors. "You can do it later. Right now we have more pressing matters. Bring it in, Corporal."

"What's going on here?" said Reynolds. "Is it time for your favorite game show? 'Let's Make A Hostage Deal'?"

"Hardly, Mr. Reynolds. You and your crew are prisoners," said Parker. "Not hostages. We brought in the television for you to see our press conference. We're certain you'll find it interesting."

Adjusting the set's rabbit ears until he got the best picture, Corporal Dorson stepped away, and the other interrogators allowed the *Phoenix* crew to gather in front of it. Less than a minute after the television was fired up, the pastel green and red flag of the Seychelles appeared on its screen, dissolving to a shot of the reception hall in Revolution House.

"I am Foreign Minister Felix Boigny," said one of the men seated at the table; his title immediately appeared in simple dot matrix letters under him. "In the name of our great leader, Albert René, I address the people of the Seychelles in our hour of national crisis . . ."

"The smaller the country the more pompous the officials," Julie remarked.

"Shut up, woman!" said Torres. "This is important to you. Listen to it."

"Watch it, Julie. I think he likes you," said Glassner.

"In response to the invasion of our country by the imperialist space power, and the continued provoca-

131

tions by its racist armed forces, we have today made requests for aid from our socialist brothers in other countries," Boigny continued to drone on, his latest remarks passing almost unnoticed because of his bland voice. "We have asked the Soviet Union, Libya and Cuba to send us military forces to resist this aggression."

"Wait! What the hell did he say?" Reynolds asked, motioning for his crew to stop their small talk. They quieted down just as a flurry of questions from the assembled reporters momentarily interrupted the Foreign Minister.

"So far, the Libyan People's Republic has responded and will send forces," he answered. "The Russian embassy has said it would not be proper to send military forces at this time. The Cuban Foreign Ministry expresses its solidarity with us and is considering what it can send."

"Mr. Boigny, has the American ambassador been allowed to see the astronauts recently?" asked one of the reporters, her voice barely audible on the television.

"Are you crazy? Do you want a confrontation with us?" Reynolds said incredulously. "I'll remind you the last country to try that was Iraq."

"Yes, she will be allowed to visit the spaceship crew sometime today," said Boigny. "And we will choose the time."

"We have not invaded a neighboring country," Parker answered. "You have invaded us. Many in the Third World feared Saddam Hussein, but they all resent you and they'll be on our side."

"Mr. Foreign Minister, many tourists are fearful of the invasion and wish to cut short their vacations," said another reporter. "Will they be allowed to leave?"

"Yes. They will be allowed to leave," said Boigny.

"The airport is open, and we're making arrangements for extra flights."

"When will we be allowed to see Mrs. Griffen?" Post asked. "Now that your Foreign Minister said we could."

"As I told you yesterday. That will be done at *our* convenience," said Parker, this time he was smiling instead of responding angrily. "Enjoy the rest of the news conference. We'll be back soon."

Not quite as rapidly as they had burst into the room, Parker and his advisors filed out to leave the astronauts by themselves. In a few seconds they were the only ones left in a room with a loudly blaring television.

"Clay, do you think the Libyans are serious?" said Julie, once the door clicked shut.

"How could they be?" Glassner replied. "If they tried flying anything out here their planes would run out of fuel and crash off the coast of Africa."

"I wouldn't be so sure," said Reynolds, thinking a little longer. "Walt, didn't the Libyans have some Tu-22s when you hit them in eighty-six?"

"Yes. Two squadrons I believe," said Post. "And now some air tankers. They could get something here, but what about the carrier the major told us of?"

"That's probably still near the Persian Gulf, but it'll get here faster than anything a bunch of camel jockeys can whip together. Don't worry about it."

"Don't worry, they can't hear us through these doors, these walls," said Parker, standing in the hall outside the astronauts' quarters. "We'll have breakfast, then we'll return to interrogate them."

"When do we let the American ambassador see them?" asked Torres, starting to walk down the hall to the building's first-floor entrance.

"In the afternoon, at our leisure. First we'll have to move them to the civilian side of the airport. We can't let the Americans know where we're holding them."

"Yes, and after that meeting we should split the crew up. Move them to separate locations like I suggested."

"Are we going to start that again?" said Mohammed Halim, rolling his eyes. "Remember what their commander just told us? 'Let's Make A Hostage Deal'? If we split them up, the world press and the American government will treat this as a hostage situation. That will only complicate matters. My government and the Arab people know this well."

"It will also complicate any American attempt to rescue the hostages," Torres maintained, starting to grow angry once again. "In fact it will make rescue impossible."

"You can't turn them into hostages. Two of these people won Nobel peace prizes last year for rescuing Russian cosmonauts. You don't see us Libyans taking hostages. We have learned the hard way."

"What difference does it make if they won peace prizes?" said Victor Esparza. "It's only further proof of American hegemony and control over this new world order."

"The defense of your superior's position is admirable, Victor," said Halim. "But surely you see it's insanity?"

"Insane! Are you calling me mad?" Torres demanded, a cold fire glowing in his eyes and his voice becoming hard. He stopped short of the first-floor entrance and turned fully to face Halim. For a few tense seconds, they eyed each other silently.

"No one's calling anyone anything," said Parker, stepping between the two advisors. "Stop it, the both of you. I don't like it, Gonzala, any more than you do. However, there is truth in Mohammed's argument,

134

and we have to accept it for the time being. Come, let us have our breakfast in peace and save our arguments for the Americans."

"Sorry to have gotten you all up so early," Carver apologized, as he and Allard entered a briefing room overlooking the French air base at Reunion Island.

"Don't be sorry for it," said the French Army colonel who greeted the two American officers. "Your crisis has given us some excitement, and we're grateful you asked for our help. Please, take your seats."

Capitaine Jacoubet was already sitting at the room's table and motioned to the seats beside him. Carver took the nearest one while Allard momentarily detoured to the windows for another look at the base's flight line.

"The island's different and the planes aren't the same but this sure is familiar," he said, glancing down at the row of C.160 Transalls, Alouette II and Puma helicopters. The Puma that brought in the three naval officers still had a ground crew going over it on postflight checks.

"Glenn, time to join the party," Carver warned. "Colonel Béchereau's about to call us to order."

"Thank you, Captain," said Béchereau, taking his seat. "I know you're eager to move your operations so this will be brief. Gentlemen, all French forces in the Indian Ocean are now on alert in response to this 'space crisis.' The destroyer *Aconit* has rendezvoused with an American frigate, and they're now waiting for a British warship to join them. We will cooperate with our Allies but I must tell you, less than fifteen minutes ago I learned that the Seychelles government has asked Libya for military assistance and they will send forces."

"Then we better get underway as fast as possible," said Allard, shocked enough to drop into his seat instead of sliding into it. "Terry, you better tell him what we need."

"Colonel, with your permission we will need the following equipment," Carver began, pulling some sheets from his leather document pouch. "One of your C.160s to parachute a SEAL reconnaissance squad onto Silhouette Island in the Seychelles. Because of the distance involved, it will be necessary to modify another C.160 for in-flight refueling. In addition, I would like the presence of Captain Jacoubet's submarine to escort my boat and coordinate with it."

"Coordinate with it," Béchereau repeated. "I've been military commander here long enough to know that submarine captains usually give a 'wide interpretation' to their orders. This gives me some concern and, to be frank, were it not for your reputation from the *Ocean Valkyrie* rescue I'd be reluctant to give you help. From his previous association with you, I know *Capitaine* Jacoubet is eager to work with you again. It remains to be seen if Major Hebrard and Captain Turcat would wish to join."

"We have the kits available to modify our Transalls into flight refueling tankers," said Major Jean Hebrard, commander of the French Air Force detachment on Reunion. He examined the pages Carver had laid out, before passing them to the other Air Force officers. "It would take us perhaps four hours to convert one of our Transalls into a tanker. Commander, how long would it take to bring in your men and equipment?"

"Using one of your Pumas, I'd say about two hours," said Allard, after thinking over his answer for a moment. "A vertical transfer, even for seven men, can be an involved operation."

136

"My crews are up to it. Bernard, what do you say?"

"Do I get to fly the tanker sortie or the para-drop?" asked Captain Turcat, examining the same papers.

"Since you flew most of the parachute missions during the Tromelin exercises, you'll fly the para-drop."

"That's what I wanted to hear. I can have my aircraft and crew ready before the tanker conversion is finished."

"Good, but you'll have to wait until after the tanker has left before you can take off," said Hebrard, before he turned to the U.S. and French naval officers. "Commander, Captain, you better send an order to your submarine to prepare for a crew transfer. I'll send out one of my Pumas."

"Gentlemen, since this operation is largely a Navy and Air Force affair I'll leave it in your hands," said Béchereau, rising out of his seat, temporarily causing the other officers to do the same. "There are other duties I must now attend, so our activities today don't look too unusual. The warning I'll give you is this: whatever you plan must not bring French forces into direct conflict with either Seychelles or Libyan forces."

"Don't worry, Colonel. That's not what we want your men to do," Carver promised. "We'll let you know what our plans are before we leave your base."

"How does she feel, Ed?" Brenner asked, as he entered the 747's cockpit and found Cochran seated in its pilot seat.

"After flying that little white rocket for four hours this is quite a handful," said Cochran, glancing up at the mountain of a man trying to slide into the copilot's seat. "Thank God there are so many systems to help me fly her."

"That's one of the nice things about a Boeing. She

137

can practically fly herself, you only have to give her a 'suggestion' every once in a while."

"What's the rest of the crew been doing? I haven't seen anyone but you in so long I almost think we're the only ones on the plane."

"The others are either sleeping or listening to a report on the Seychelles," said Brenner, sitting uneasily in a seat he did not normally occupy. "There was supposed to be a news conference there. Diana, is there anything new?"

Diana Danforth, the 747's official copilot, slid through the cockpit's partially open door. Heavyset but tall, she was a good match for Brenner. When she came forward, she slipped an affectionate hand into one of his before turning to Cochran.

"Edward, you better put her on autopilot," she advised. "I just heard some bad news."

"Don't worry about me, Di," said Cochran. "I'm not going to let a plane fall out of the sky because someone told me something bad."

"All right, here goes. The Seychelles has just asked for military help from Libya to counter the threat of a U.S. invasion over the shuttle landing."

"Jesus Christ, they're turning this accident into an international incident." In spite of his attempt to hold the control wheel level, Cochran's angry reaction caused the three hundred and fifty ton aircraft to raise its nose and drop its port wing slightly. "Sorry, I got it. What the hell's going to happen to my Lady and our friends now? Are the Libyans going to send forces?"

"They said they would," Diana replied. "But there's no word yet on what they'll send."

"Well that's some good news," said Brenner, still holding onto her hand. "You have any more for us?"

"U.S. and French warships have rendezvoused off the Seychelles and the Navy's finally sending a carrier battle group to the area. The British are sending a ship and the Russians turned down a request for their aid."

"Sounds like we still have our friends in Glavkosmos. What do you think, Ed?"

"We're not going to do a layover in Hawaii," said Cochran, after thinking quietly for a moment. Then he glanced at the instrument panel's clock. "We're about one hour out of Oahu. We'll only need three hours to refuel and then we'll head on to Australia. Phil, you better contact the C-5 and let them know our change in plans?"

"You think we should?" asked Brenner, finally releasing Diana's hand so he could grab a headset. "How will the crews sleep?"

"The way we're doing it now, we'll use the tiny, cramped bunks on our planes. We can do a proper layover in Australia. From there we'll only be one day out of Diego Garcia. It's now more imperative than ever that we reach Garcia."

Some two miles off the 747's starboard wingtip there was another strobing collection of lights in the early evening sky. Ever since their departure from Edwards the C-5B Galaxy had been either paralleling or trailing behind the NASA transport. Now, as they approached the Hawaiian Islands, the two giant aircraft would draw closer together. Eventually the Galaxy would pull ahead to land first at Hickam Field.

Six

"This is Viper One to Oasis. I am ready to receive," Mashari advised, activating his flight refueling controls.

"Roger, Viper One. Continue for hookup."

Less than fifty yards in front of Mashari's cockpit floated a light grey Boeing 707. Once an airliner for Brazil's Varig airline, it had since been converted into a flight refueling tanker for the Libyan Air Force. Trailing back from its tail was a heavy black hose with a shuttlecock-shaped fueling drogue.

Holding his Tupolev Blinder steady, Mashari nudged his twin throttles forward slightly, pushing his nose-mounted probe into the drogue's cup. The moment the connection was made thousands of pounds of jet fuel flowed to the bomber's partly empty tanks. Almost at once the aircraft started to grow heavy, and he had to work his control wheel to keep it level.

"This is Viper One to Oasis," said Mashari. "I'm nearing my transfer limit. Ready to disengage."

Eyeing his row of fuel gages, he waited until they showed he was approaching his fifteen-ton transfer limit before calling for the flow to end. With a brief plume of white mist the connection was broken; for an instant the mist clouded over the Blinder's canopy. When it cleared, Mashari saw the drogue being retracted. Free to maneuver once again, he dipped his port wing and slid away from the tanker.

Behind him were three more sand and green mottled Tu-22s while farther in the distance was a trio of Il-76 transports. With Mashari's operation completed, another of the bombers climbed up to take his position under the 707. After swinging around the formation, Mashari brought his huge Tupolev up on the Boeing's left wing.

"Viper One to Oasis, are there any new reports on the crisis I should know about?" he said, loosening his shoulder straps so he could stretch a little, even in the cramped cockpit.

"There are some developments Nazih said you should be told of," the tanker's pilot responded. "The U.S. Navy is sending its carrier battle group from the Persian Gulf, and there may be enemy warships gathering to the east of the Seychelles. Over."

"If those ships give us any trouble we'll sink them." Mashari could not help but smile. When he heard a tapping behind him, he turned to find his systems engineer smiling, too, and giving him a thumbs-up. "And the American carrier cannot arrive before we will. We'll be there to greet them with our Otomats."

"Viper One, will you be waiting for all your aircraft to be refueled? Over."

"Only for the other Blinders. The Ilyushins have their own navigation systems, they can make it on their own and in fact have been holding us up. I'll let them know they will next see us at Seychelles International. This is Viper One, out."

It took another twenty minutes for the other three

Tupolevs to connect and have their tanks topped off. By then the loose formation had crossed the desolate Somali coastline and were heading out into the Indian Ocean. When the last dropped away from the 707 tanker, the four quickly reassembled and accelerated to a higher altitude. At their optimum cruise speed, they were more than thirty miles an hour faster than the Ilyushin's top speed. By the time the slower transports had completed their refueling, the Blinders were only visible on their radars.

"Mako Three to Olympus Control, the target is in sight. Do you read? Over."

"Affirmative. Good luck and stay high, Mako Three."

"Roger. Mako Three, out. Pilot to crew, look sharp. Mahé Island dead ahead."

Like the other four Orions to visit Mahé since their commander's encounter, Lieutenant Keith Moffet kept his aircraft at eight thousand feet, just above the limit of light antiaircraft fire. An uncharacteristically high altitude for an antisubmarine patrol bomber, it also meant the P-3 was detected by Mahé radar while still more than half an hour out.

"Increasing airspeed to three hundred knots," said Moffett, nudging his quartet of throttles up a notch. Then he turned to his copilot. "This should throw 'em off if they're trying to track us. Pilot to Observers, can you spot the *Phoenix?*"

"Left Waist to Pilot, I got it. They still have her sitting in front of their military hangars. It's kinda hard to hide something that big and that white."

"Pilot to Left Waist, is she still intact?"

"Roger, she is undamaged. But there are a few trucks around the shuttle."

142

"Tac-Co to Pilot, I got something on ESM. It sounds like air-to-ground transmissions on a military channel."

"Pilot to crew, you hear that?" Moffett asked, anxiety rising in his voice. "We got visitors. Sing out when you see them."

"Keith, there they are," said the copilot. "One o'clock."

Pointing out the canopy, he tracked a pair of small green and brown aircraft as they curved in front of the Orion. They crossed from right to left, climbing steeply on an apparent intercept course. It did not take long before Moffett and his cockpit crew were able to identify the planes by their straight wings, tip tanks, and shimmering propeller discs.

"They're trainers," said Moffett, almost laughing. "Some of those Italian SF.260s. Some interceptors, we can do more than twice their top speed."

"Then we better do it," said the copilot. "They may be slow, but those are either rocket or gun pods under their wings."

"Right. Pilot to Observers, take all the pictures you can. We're out of here."

Moffett pushed the throttles to their gate stops, getting a surge of power out of the bomber's four Allison turboprops. They emitted slightly thicker trails of black smoke, and the P-3C jumped from three hundred knots to four hundred, close to its maximum speed. The Seychelles Air Force trainers never got closer than half a mile to it and were not able to get a favorable firing position until the ghost-grey Orion was little more than a dark speck on the eastern horizon.

"So much for our Libyan-supplied air force," commented Lazare Sampras, watching the SF.260s break off their intercept from the airport tarmac. "Your pilots will not be returning victorious, Comrade N'tow."

"This won't be happening much longer," said Dhawon N'tow, Minister of Defense and Commander of the Seychelles People's Defense Forces. "Soon our Libyan allies will be here and no American planes will dare overfly us."

"If this crisis could only have happened a year from now," said Major Nayef Yashin, the Libyan embassy's chief military attaché. "You would've had your Mirage fighters, and the Americans couldn't intimidate you. Have you recalled all your planes from the outer islands?"

"The last G.222 will be here soon. The rest have already arrived." The black Defense Minister pointed to the flight line beside them, where a ragged collection of four SF.260 armed trainers, various Bell helicopters, and a single Aeritalia G.222 light transport stood. "What shall we do with them?"

"Arm all the trainers and the Aeritalias to attack ships and even submarines. Strip the rescue equipment from the helicopters, prepare to use them as troop transports. We may have to fight insurgent forces. Captain, what have you managed to learn about our prize?"

Yashin turned away from the Seychelles officials and walked over to a newly arrived jeep and greeted its passenger, almost before he had finished stepping to the ground.

"We're still questioning the crew," said Mohammed Halim, as the major's embrace ended. "We're not getting much from them. They know how to infuriate that idiot Cuban we're forced to work with. Right now it's a shouting match over the imperialism of the American space program. Useless."

"I know Mr. Torres can be 'trying' at times. However, because we must face the Americans together, it will be necessary to work with him. And don't worry about your lack of success with the astronauts. Soon, our experts will be here to go through this prize."

While he spoke, Yashin finished moving toward the shuttle and started walking around it. The *Phoenix* was parked lengthwise in front of the military hangars, which were not long enough or tall enough to accommodate it. The spaceship's nose pointed toward the airport's civilian end, where a line of airliners from British Airways, Air India and Air Seychelles stood taking on full loads of passengers.

"She will not keep her secrets from us for long," Yashin continued, getting close enough to touch the shuttle's wingtip but no closer.

"We could have many of those secrets if our former 'comrades' were still our comrades," said N'tow, bringing up the Seychelles officials to join the Libyans.

"Yes. The Russians," Sampras added, glancing out to sea at the *Navarin* riding at anchor. "They've been a bitter disappointment for us."

"It just proves the changing nature of the superpowers toward each other," said Yashin. "They're betraying us and their own revolution, and one day they shall pay for it. Halim, let's bring the astronauts out here. Let's make them explain what our crew found."

"Just hang your legs over the side and I'll tap you on the back when we're ready to lower you," said the French Air Force sergeant crouching behind Allard.

"Don't worry," he said. "I've done this before. All too often."

Unlike his departure from the *Marshall,* Allard was returning to it alone and in a much smaller helicopter. An Aèrospatiale Puma had been used to lift him,

145

Carver, and Jacoubet out, along with the SEAL reconnaissance team. Now it was down for needed maintenance and a diminutive Alouette II was taking him back to the submarine.

Both the *Marshall* and the *Casablanca* were still running on the surface, heading due north at twenty knots to avoid being spotted by the fishing boats putting out from Reunion. The Alouette descended toward the much larger U.S. submarine until it was matching its speed and remaining stationary over its conning tower.

With his legs already dangling out the helicopter's bubble, all Allard had to do was slide forward and grab hold of the rescue hoist's cable. Swaying slightly, he was lowered to the *Marshall*'s flying bridge where two seamen grabbed him and pulled him on board. The moment the rescue sling was unhooked, the Alouette was reeling it in and turning away, heading back to what appeared to be a low bank of dark clouds on the southern horizon.

"Secure the conning tower," Carver ordered, after Allard and the seamen came through the control center's roof hatch. "Get ready to take us down, Clarence. Control to Radio Room, send final message to *Casablanca* and wish them luck. Captain to crew, secure boat for diving. Sound the alarm."

A horn blared loudly in the control center and throughout the former missile sub; by the time it ended the last hatches had been slammed shut and the safety station reconfirmed the boat's status with a row of green lights.

"Dive, dive, dive. Opening main tanks," said Jefferson, tripping the valve switches on one of his panels, and watching their status lights change to red. "Diving planes, five degrees down-angle. Captain, what depth shall I set her for?"

"Two hundred feet," said Carver, standing behind his two helmsmen. "Make speed, twenty knots."

"Aye, Captain. We'll run her shallow."

Carver moved back to the periscope stand and raised the search 'scope to observe both his command and the *Casablanca* glide beneath the waves. Though the French attack sub lagged behind the *Marshall* in flooding its ballast tanks, its much smaller size allowed it to disappear faster. When his view was obscured by an onrush of sea foam, Carver secured the periscope.

"Greg, you have the conn. Keep us on this course and speed," he said. "Let me know if anything changes. Time to head below, Glenn."

Turning to the stairs behind the periscope stand, Carver and Allard descended into the TASCO Room. By the time they reached the tactical center, the *Marshall* was levelling out at two hundred feet, leaving most of the surface's wave action above it. At the stairs' landing the two Navy officers were greeted by a third dressed in a dark blue Marine *Nationale* uniform.

"This is Ship's Ensign First-Class Arlan Dupuis," Carver introduced, as the third officer snapped out a salute. "He's our exchange officer from the *Casablanca*. Ensign Dupuis, this is Commander Glenn Allard."

"Ensign, a pleasure to have you aboard," said Allard, returning the salute and shaking his hand. "Terry, who did you exchange for him?"

"Stackpole. He's done so much scut work here I thought I'd give him a reward."

"I hope I will serve your boat as well as I did my own," said Dupuis. "Commander, did your special team depart Reunion?"

"Lieutenant Hassler and my recon squad won't take

147

off until later this afternoon," Allard replied. "It will only take 'em four or five hours to reach the Seychelles, and I want them to make their para-drop at night. What news have you heard out here? The only report Reunion got is a Brit frigate will be meeting our ships soon."

"That's a couple of hours away," said Carver, taking a seat at the TASCO Room's console. "I'll show you what else we have."

Stroking a few control keys, he brought up a world map on the main screen. Across it, an orange line snaked from California to a position well to the west of Hawaii. To the north and east of the Seychelles, two target cursors floated in the Indian Ocean.

"NASA's 747 carrier and an Air Force C-5 are en route to Australia," said Carver, pointing to the line. "An update on their schedule says they'll be in Diego Garcia in another day or two. This is where the Allied evacuation force will meet. And the northern mark is the latest position of the *Eisenhower*'s battle group. They've been ordered to the Seychelles following their aid request to Libya."

"Have our ships in the Med spotted any activity with them?" Allard asked, standing behind Carver while Dupuis took the seat next to him.

"So far, there's no unusual activity among Libyan military forces. At our first Communications Stop we may get some satellite pictures of Libya to look over. Strangely, there's been activity with the Russian's Indian Ocean fleet. It cut short its visit to Goa, India and is now at sea."

"You think they will create problems for us?" said Dupuis.

"We've had our diplomatic ups and downs recently," said Carver. "But nothing would make them side with these nuts, and they publicly turned down their request for military aid. Still, the fleet will bear watching."

"Will you use your high-speed, Subscape system for your journey to Mahé'?"

"No, we'd easily outrun the *Casablanca* if we did. We need to stay with your sub and make frequent Com Stops. At twenty-five knots we'll reach Mahé in under forty-eight hours. Let's hope there's no more serious developments until we reach it."

"Pilot to Navigator, are you detecting the Amirantes?" Mashari asked, becoming more fully awake when he realized what time the clock was showing.

"I have them at long-range," said the plane's bombardier/navigator. "Northern part of the island group only."

"Don't worry, that's just what I was told to expect." After hours of having it on "Receive Only" mode, Mashari switched his primary radio to "Transmit/Receive" and held down the control wheel's microphone button. "This is Viper One to Guard Point. Viper One to Guard Point. Do you read? Over."

Releasing the button, Mashari listened to several seconds of static before repeating his broadcast. He was starting to grow impatient when, on his third repeat, he finally heard a weak but understandable response.

"Viper One, this is Guard Point. Welcome to the territory of the Seychelles People's Republic. What are your messages? Over."

"Inform Mahé we're still more than one hour out," said Mashari. "Our second flight will be contacting you in approximately two hours. Please be better prepared to answer them, out. Viper One to flight, follow me down. I want strict radio silence from here on in. Viper One, out."

While the other three bombers gave brief acknowledgements to his orders, Mashari quickly deactivated his autopilot. The Tupolev wobbled as he wrapped his stiff fingers around the control wheel. Stopping the erratic movements took almost as much work as maneuvering the needle-nosed giant. When he had it flying smoothly once again, he glanced out his cockpit side windows to check on the rest of his flight.

More than a mile had separated one Tu-22 from the other; now it was reducing to a few hundred feet as they slid up to each other's wingtips. When they were close enough for their pilots to see one another, Mashari gave them a hand signal to stop, then pointed down.

Instead of dropping one wing and rolling into their dives like fighters, the big Tupolevs merely lowered their noses below the horizon line. Even at their modest rate of descent, they were soon accelerating past seven hundred miles an hour. At this speed they rapidly fell from thirty-five thousand feet to within a few hundred feet of the Indian Ocean's surface. As it had been since they crossed the Somali coastline, no ships and no other planes could be seen; it would remain that way until the bombers neared Mahé.

"Bob, anything new from the sonobuoys?" asked Commander Fuller, stopping at his Orion's Tactical Coordinator's station.

"Apart from some biological noises, we're getting nothing," said the lieutenant, motioning to the CRT screens and glowing readouts around his seat. "Nothing that could even be mistaken for a submarine. Will we lay down some new buoys?"

"Not right away. With half our squadron doing surveillance runs over Mahé, we got a lot of ocean to cover."

"Commander, we're picking up something on the FLIR and ESM systems," said the petty officer a few feet down from the Tac-Co's station.

"What've you got?" Fuller requested, hurriedly finishing off the rest of his hamburger. He moved down to the Electronic Surveillance Measures station and glanced at the Forward Looking Infra-Red control panel.

"At extreme range, Commander. Infra-red emissions at bearing Zero-Three-Zero degrees. Appear to be heat plumes from marine gas turbine and steam power plants. We also have radar emissions from the same position. As of yet, they're too weak to identify."

"Well, we're going to be finding out real soon. Lou, change course to Zero-Three-Zero degrees!"

Fuller ran down the fuselage's main cabin to the cockpit, jarring the four-engined patrol bomber with each stride he took. Before he reached his pilot's seat, the P-3 had started to bank gently to the right, changing direction from northwest to northeast.

"Am I going to get a chance to take my lunch break?" DeMarino asked, a disingenuous whimpering in his voice.

"Sorry, the galley's just been closed," said Fuller, strapping into his seat. "And don't give me that hurt puppy routine. You can eat when this is over. Let's take her up, start number four engine. We got a potential fleet in the area, and it ain't ours."

From its standard patrol altitude of fifteen hundred feet, the Orion initiated a gentle climb while still making its turn. Its modest rate of ascent received a boost when the starboard outer engine was restarted. Shutdown to improve the bomber's range and endurance, its added power also increased airspeed to three hundred miles an hour.

"Tac-Co to Pilot, ESM has been able to identify radar types," said the Tactical Coordinator. "He says they're Top Sail, Head Net, and Top Steer Soviet radars. From a variety of sources."

"It's their Indian Ocean surface action group," De-Marino identified. "Should we drop back down and circle it?"

"No. Keep her climbing," said Fuller. "Pilot to Tac-Co, activate search radar. Nicolson doesn't even want the potential for a confrontation with the Russians. So we're going to be a nice, big target for them."

"Tac-Co to Pilot, we're getting multiple returns. We're cross-referencing with the radar and infra-red emissions. We have two large contacts, possibly a *Kiev*-class carrier and a *Slava*-class cruiser. So far we have five smaller contacts, two *Udaloy*-class destroyers and three *Krivak*-class frigates."

"Pilot to Tac-Co, can you confirm the carrier?"

"Not directly. But we are detecting Top Knot aircraft control radar and Palm Frond navigation sets."

"We're probably going to get a confirmation real soon," said Fuller. "If the carrier's Top Knot is operating, we may get intercepted."

Levelling off at ten thousand feet, the P-3C continued to increase speed until it was doing nearly four hundred miles an hour. At its new velocity, what had been on the extreme range of its sensors was in minutes far closer and being scanned in much sharper detail.

"Tac-Co to Pilot, we confirm earlier ship identities. We got the *Baku* and her escorts. We also confirm one *Kresta Two*-class cruiser trailing the carrier, two more destroyers and what looks like a fleet oiler."

"Roger, Tac-Co. Are you detecting any fire control radars?" Fuller requested.

"Negative, only air search and navigation sets. We've just picked up a high-speed target departing the *Baku*. We can't identify it, but it's closing on us."

"Pilot to crew, stay alert. We're going to have company. Communications, squirt a message to Olympus Control that we've spotted the Soviet fleet."

Ironically, in spite of his warnings, it was Fuller and DeMarino who spotted the approaching aircraft first. Before it had even grown large enough to be a speck on the horizon, sunlight glinted brightly off its canopy. Moments later, when it was finally identified, the rocket-like fighter with diminutive wings swung wide of the Lockheed giant and came up behind it.

"Left Waist to Pilot, I have him. It's a Forger all right. And guess what? He's not armed."

"What? Are you sure?" said Fuller, incredulous.

"See for yourself, Commander. He's slowing to match our speed."

Glancing over his left shoulder, Fuller watched the Soviet Vertical Takeoff & Landing (VTOL) fighter slide past his bomber's port wingtip until it was abreast of the cockpit. The pilot waved briefly, then rocked his wings to show they only held a pair of bulbous fuel tanks.

"He's right," said Fuller. "No missiles, not even rocket pods or gun pods."

"What the hell are they doing?" DeMarino asked, holding the Orion level on his own.

"Showing they don't want a confrontation either. Slow her down, Lou, we're coming up on the fleet. Pilot to crew, get the cameras ready. We're going to make our first pass."

What had either been symbols on radar screens or thin plumes of smoke on the horizon were now taking shape as widely spaced blue-grey slabs of steel on a calm sea. In the lead were the smallest, the antisubmarine frigates, followed by the destroyers. In the distance the far more massive aircraft carrier finally came into view.

* * *

"Admiral. Captain. The pilot reports the American is maintaining altitude and slowing his speed," said the lieutenant, stepping onto the bridge wing holding the ship's two highest-ranking officers.

"Did he say if the bomber was carrying any weapons?" Captain First Rank Nikolai Fedorov demanded. "Especially Tomahawks and Harpoons?"

"Nikolai Dmitrevich, they likely don't have any," Admiral Oleg Khomenko said calmly, waving a hand to quiet his friend. "And if they wanted to use such missiles, they could have fired either when they first spotted us. Right now, they could drop real harpoons on us and cause almost as much damage."

Khomenko glanced up to keep track of the ghost-grey turboprop bomber and its tiny, dart-shaped, companion as they glided over the Soviet aircraft carrier *Baku*. He watched them from bow to stern, then looked down at the carrier's flight deck where Kamov helicopters and more Yak-38 fighters were being prepared for flight.

"I still worry, Oleg Viktorvich," said Fedorov, continuing to watch the P-3 and its escort. "The Seychelles government tried to draw us into this crisis. Them, and their 'advisors.' I worry the Americans could be believing their rhetoric."

"The Americans can be naive and idealistic, but we needn't worry about them," said Khomenko. "Most are sophisticated enough to know empty rhetoric and hyperbole when they hear it. No, our real problems will be the people you just mentioned. Our one time 'comrades' on these islands, the Libyans and Cubans. Comrades . . . now there's a word few of us use or hear anymore. We must become familiar with it again if we're to be successful."

154

"Do you wish to maintain fleet speed at twenty knots? I fear for our smaller escorts and our replenishment ships falling behind us."

"Maintain speed. I want us to arrive at the Seychelles a full day before the American carrier. We need the time to work the miracle Moscow wants. Paying back the Americans by rescuing their astronauts and freeing a caged *Phoenix*."

Seven

"*Alacrity* Air Traffic Center, this is *Simpson* Helo Zero-One. We have you in sight. What's your situation? Over."

"*Simpson* Zero-One, this is *Alacrity.* We're running at twenty-five knots, sea conditions are calm, and we are in positive stability. Our deck lock system is ready, and our landing pad has been cleared for you. Please make a standard approach and descent. Over."

"Roger, *Alacrity.* Here we come," said Dean Marron. "*Simpson* Zero-One, out. Okay, Marge, this is going to be a lot easier."

Approaching the Royal Navy frigate from its starboard quarter, the ghost-grey Seahawk overflew it before swinging to the left and dropping from its cruise altitude of two thousand feet. Marron lined up on the warship's empty stern and slid his aircraft down a glide path until it was hovering some fifty feet above the pad.

An *Amazon*-class frigate, the *Alacrity* was of a more modern design than the French *Aconit.* It had both a landing pad and a hangar deck; its own Lynx helicopter peered out through the open door. While it had no gun

156

turret aft, there was one forward, along with box launchers for Exocet missiles. Amidships it had 20-mm cannons, torpedo tubes, and a Seawolf antiaircraft missile launcher on the hangar roof.

As the Seahawk hovered in front of its door, part of its crew came out to grab the cable the helicopter lowered and connected it to the deck lock system. When they signalled to Marron that the warship was ready to take him aboard, powerful winches started to haul the furiously buzzing machine onto the flight deck.

Unlike his troubles with landing on the *Aconit,* he was able to set his SH-60 down with relative ease on the British frigate. As soon as its landing gear stopped bouncing, wheel chocks were blocked around them. The scream from its turbines rapidly died away, and the gale-like rotorwash ended as its blades windmilled to a halt.

"Welcome aboard Her Majesty's Ship *Alacrity,*" said the officer who greeted the Seahawk's passengers. "I'm her captain, Commander Edwin Aldiss."

"A pleasure, Commander," Marron answered, stepping out of his aircraft with its passengers. "This is Ensign Locke, our ASW officer. He'll head the coordination team. I hope we don't have to do this with too many other ships. We're beginning to run out of officers."

"Not to worry, the larger forces are gathering far away from us. Ensign, I'm happy to have you and your detail aboard." Aldiss briefly turned to the next three men to come off the helicopter and greeted each with a salute before they were led into the open hangar. "Lieutenant, how far away is your ship and the *Aconit?*"

"They were around three hundred and twenty miles away when I took off. Between their speed and your speed, they're now about eighty miles closer."

"Good, we should meet in another five hours," said

157

Aldiss. "Of course, by then we'll have you refueled and back to your ship. Tell me, during your flight here were you approached by any Seychelles Defense Force aircraft?"

"No. But some of their fighter trainers tried to intercept our Orions when they overflew Mahé," said Marron, stripping off his helmet and opening his flight jacket to cool down. "Why? Have you had any trouble?"

"Some hours ago we did. Then, we were passing rather close to Denis Island. We were approached by one of their Aeritalia transports. They opened its tail ramp and made repeated passes at us like they were going to drop something. While we held our fire, we were tempted to shoot the bounders out of the sky."

"This sounds like the other crap they've been pulling. Who the hell do these people think they are? Arabs?"

"No doubt they've learned well these tactics of defiance and confrontation from their Libyan allies," Aldiss observed, motioning toward the hangar and for the Seahawk crew to follow him. "If my ship's incident fits the pattern of their behavior then we can expect more of it."

"Maybe you should talk to Bob Stine and the French Captain now," said Marron, gathering his copilot and crew chief. "Instead of waiting to meet them in five hours."

"Good idea, Lieutenant. We'll go to the wireless office after seeing to your passengers. Hopefully, this will just be another evacuation of our civilians, like last year in the Sudan. Somehow, though, I don't think it will be."

"I get the feeling they're driving us around in circles," said Julie, after standing in the center of the van's cabin for the last few minutes; and allowing her body to sway with the vehicle's movements. "And we've been on both paved and gravel roads."

"Very good," said Reynolds, extending a hand to hold her steady. "Looks like our astronaut training is proving useful for something other than space flight. Now if we could only figure out how far we've been driven."

"These guys are good," Glassner remarked. "Especially that Cuban. They don't want us telling our people where we think we're being kept with any accuracy."

"Bug Man is an asshole," said Post, still checking the van's painted-over windows for any cracks he could look through. "But a determined one. Boss, I think we're slowing down."

"We are," Julie confirmed. "And we're back on a paved surface."

The van glided so smoothly to a halt most of the astronauts were not aware it had stopped. The moment it did so its rear doors were pulled open, catching Post in his examination of their windows. Embarrassed, he and the rest of the crew stepped out to find they were on the People's Defense Force tarmac, standing in front of their shuttle.

"Walter. Clayton. How have they been treating you?" Lynn Griffen asked, as she and Major Goldman walked up to the crew.

"They're feeding us well and we've had some interesting conversations," said Reynolds, shaking her hand and Goldman's. "However, I can't tell you much about our 'accommodations.' "

"We understand," said Goldman, casting an eye at Sampras, Parker, and the other Security Force personnel. "Is there anything you'd like to know?"

"What have they done to my ship?"

"Externally, they haven't touched it. Just moved it

159

off the runway. But we know they've been inside it."

"Major, is this true?" Reynolds demanded, a sharp tone in his voice.

"For the safety of the Seychelles people we had to," said Parker, coming forward. "And what we found has raised many questions."

"We'll be happy to answer them. Walt . . ."

While Reynolds motioned for Julie, Rebecca, and Glassner to stay behind with the ambassador and her people, he and Post walked over to the *Phoenix*. Apart from a tow bar still attached to its nose gear, the space-plane looked exactly the way it had after it landed. The same set of boarding stairs was nestled up to its side hatch, and many of the same military and security vehicles stood around it. Before entering it, the astronauts and those who would escort them donned breathing systems.

"Looks like your people have been busy ransacking our ship," said Reynolds, instantly noticing the open lockers and galley station when he stepped onto the mid deck.

"Well isn't this just fine," Post added, coming in next. "They took all our fucking food. What the hell did you need that for? You got plenty of food on this island."

As he turned to face Parker and the other escorts, the air tank on his back hit and clanged loudly with the one on Reynolds's back. The heavy collision caused both to jump, and the security people to finish rushing on board.

"Be careful with our equipment!" said Parker, shouting to be heard through his mask. "We were careful with yours! We had to check everything to make sure they weren't dangerous. We found where you claimed the meteor came into your ship. But we didn't find the meteor. If there ever was one."

"Oh there is one, all right," said Reynolds, facing Parker. "As we told you before, we gave it to Ambassador Griffen for safekeeping."

"Major, ask them why we can't get any electrical power on their ship," ordered Sampras, his distinctive voice coming through clearly in spite of the face mask.

"We must've left the headlights on when we were here last," said Post, trying to act innocent.

"Maybe *you* left some of our systems on and drained the power?" Reynolds added.

"Neither of you are funny," said Parker. "Either you, or the other members of your crew, intentionally sabotaged your spacecraft. You created dangerous electronic booby traps."

"Booby traps catch boobs. And right now I'm looking at a prime pair."

"Your ambassador should be here to listen to you," Sampras said coldly, his remark seemingly frigid enough to lower the temperature of the oppressively hot cabin. "Your insults do not help your country, and only make your situation worse."

"Go ahead, bring her in! I like working before an audience!" Reynolds shouted, hoping it was loud enough to carry outside. "Don't try to threaten me, pal! NASA once locked me up because they didn't like what I said!"

"Major! Mr. Sampras! Come quickly! They've arrived!"

At first the warning could not be heard above the argument. Only when Reynolds paused did it become audible, along with the sound of jet engines. Though still distant, they did not have the high-pitched whine of civilian airliner turbofans. Instead they were a deeper, more ominous rumble which rapidly grew to earsplitting levels.

Air tanks again clanged loudly as the personnel, crowding the mid deck, rushed to the side hatch and charged down the boarding stairs. Stripping off their masks and wiping the sweat from their eyes, Post and Reynolds needed a few moments before they could see properly and locate the incoming aircraft.

They came out of the west, having evidently overflown Victoria before reaching the airport. At their low altitude they were not fully visible until they had roared past the airport's control tower. The needle-nosed giants flew wingtip to wingtip in a perfect four-ship flight. They were low enough for the Arabic characters on their tail fins to be seen, low enough for the sound of their engines to cause everyone on the ground to cover their ears until they were heading out to sea.

"Christ, those were Blinders!" said Reynolds. "I thought the Russians got rid of most of theirs?"

"They did," said Post, tracking the flight as it pulled up and swung to the west, its aircraft stringing into a line astern formation. "Those aren't from the Soviet Air Force. Did you see those green roundels on their wings? They're Libyan Air Force markings. Things just suddenly got worse."

"Clay, what the hell's going on?" asked Rebecca, joining Reynolds and Post while Julie and Glassner stayed with the embassy personnel. "I damn well know those aren't any of our planes."

"They're Libyan Air Force Tupolev Blinders," Reynolds said darkly. "These assholes have their reinforcements. You can tell Julie and Allan it's official; we can start worrying."

Though it had taken off more than a half-hour ahead of the second Transall to depart Reunion, the first C.160 was unable to maintain its lead. Heavily laden with both fuel bladders and a buddy-pack flight refueling kit, it was steadily overtaken by its more lightly loaded sistership.

They flew line abreast until they reached Tromlen Island, a remote speck of rock a third of the way between Reunion and the main island group of the Seychelles. There, the first Transall opened its tail ramp and deployed a refueling drogue while the second one swung in behind it.

"This is Renard Three to Renard One, cut the transfer flow," ordered Bernard Turcat, as the fuel gages on his instrument panel neared their full marks. "Prepare to disengage."

A plume of white mist spilled from the drogue cup when the spike-shaped probe on the second C.160 withdrew. For a moment its canopy was coated by the mist; after it cleared Turcat watched the tanker/transport pull slowly away from his aircraft and reel in its drogue line.

"Now, we are the heavier machine," he said before glancing over his shoulder. "Lieutenant, we're on our way. Next stop, Silhouette Island."

"How long before we reach it, Captain?" asked Gordon Hassler, commander of the reconnaissance team.

"Approximately three hours. That's if we encounter no trouble or have to avoid anyone. We're going to begin our descent soon, better let your men know."

As the tanker C.160 curved to the south and headed back for Reunion, Turcat eased his into a gentle descent. He circled Tromlen's uninhabited shoreline until he was holding his aircraft a few hundred feet above the waves rolling against it. The Transall broke away from the island when its heading returned to due north; some eight hundred miles over the darkening horizon lay the Seychelles main island group.

"Holding at periscope depth, Captain," said the relief helmsman. "Speed, eight knots."

"Keep her steady," Carver ordered, walking the search periscope a full three hundred and sixty degrees. "There's nothing in the air. Nothing on the surface, except for the *Casablanca's* 'scope. Take her to thirty feet, Patrick. Control to Radio Room, stand by to raise masts."

By chopping its current running depth in half, the *John Marshall* pushed the top of its conning tower above the waves. Its diving planes were still slicing through the water, giving its helmsmen better control than had it surfaced completely. As its periscope mast was lowered, the sub's HF and VHF antennas were raised. Like the *Casablanca* sailing half a mile off its port side, in moments it was receiving the latest information on the crisis.

"Jake, what do we have?" said Carver, appearing at the hatch to the *Marshall's* radio room.

"Patrol Forty-four has spotted the Russian's Indian Ocean fleet," said the black lieutenant standing in the tiny compartment, beside him the secure teletype was still clacking loudly. "In fact it was the squadron commander who spotted 'em. Says they'll arrive a day ahead of our fleet."

"I hope this doesn't complicate the situation." Carver accepted the first tear sheet and glanced through its contents while Jacob Hawkins waited with the others. "I know the Seychelles government asked them for help, but I thought they refused."

"Well, here's something that will. Latest report from our embassy in Victoria . . . and this was sent to Diego Garcia by the Brit ship rendezvousing with the *Simpson*."

"Good God, this *is* going to make it more dangerous," Carver responded as he started reading the embassy report. "Send these down to the TASCO Room. Glenn must be chomping at the bit for them. And raise the *Casablanca* for me. I need to talk with Alain."

Before Hawkins could turn around and work the communications panel, the seaman had a channel open and was talking to the radio room aboard the French attack sub. In moments Carver was handed a table mike, and the compartment loudspeakers were activated.

"Tie me in with Glenn. Since this concerns his men, he has to be in on the decision," he said before keying the microphone. "Alain, this is Terry. Have you received a report from your embassy on Mahé? Over."

"Affirmative, my friend. It appears as though the Libyans are intent on causing us trouble," said Jacoubet, his voice coming in strong and with no breakup. "My embassy says a flight of bombers and a flight of transports have landed. Do you confirm? Over."

"Roger, we have the same information. Do you think we should continue with the para-drop? Over."

"I think so. Though we should leave it to the discretion of the transport crew. Over."

"Agreed. Glenn, what do you think?" Carver asked.

"The Libyans flew in bombers, not fighters," said Allard, his voice booming over the same compartment speakers. "Whatever else they brought in will take time to set up. I think we can still sneak the mission in. It's about two hours from the drop point."

"All right, let's contact the Air Force. Jake. Kelly. Lock onto the secure frequency the *Casablanca* will use to reach the transport. And don't break in unless we get permission."

Apart from getting the channel and the scramble/descramble code to access it, the *Marshall*'s radio room remained silent as Jacoubet transmitted to and finally contacted the French Air Force C.160. Unlike the sharp, clear sub to sub talk the Transall was nearly six hundred miles to the north, and its communications were weak and crackled heavily with static.

"*Casablanca,* this is Renard Three. We can understand you," Turcat answered slowly, so the breakup would not distort his words. "What is the problem we have? Over."

"Libyan bombers and transports have landed on Mahé Island," said Jacoubet. "We don't believe anything they have is yet operational. However, you may abort your mission if you so desire. Over."

"Roger, *Casablanca.* Let me talk with the Americans. Renard Three, out."

"Terry, if they decide to abort have them rendezvous with us," said Allard, right after the transmissions were halted. "The recon team can parachute back to the sub, and we'll take them to Mahé."

"We can do a Subscape run," Carver suggested. "But that would mean leaving the attack boat behind. I don't like this, our carefully laid plan is coming apart."

"Carefully laid? Who are you trying to kid? We've been making this up as we go along."

"*Casablanca,* this is Renard Three," said Turcat, his transmission stopping all side conversations. "*Casablanca,* this is Renard Three. We have decided to continue. We feel this is our last opportunity to make the drop. Our American friends think it would be too dangerous to abort and try another day. Over."

"Understood, Renard Three. Good luck," said Jacoubet, the relief noticeable in his voice. "Advise Reunion of your decision. This is *Casablanca,* out."

"Roger, *Casablanca.* Lieutenant Hassler wants Commander Allard to know that the next transmission will be from him. This is Renard Three, out."

Minutes after the last broadcast from the distant aircraft had been received, the submarines were retracting their radio masts and extending their periscopes. As

166

their conning towers slid beneath the waves, they picked up speed. By the time the periscopes were lowered, they had increased to ten knots. And by the time they were back at their cruise depth, they had returned to their twenty-knot running speed.

"Colonel Mashari, I'd like you to meet the rest of our hosts," said Major Yashin, stepping up to the group of Libyan Army and Air Force officers standing under the nose of the lead Tu-22. "This is Dhawon N'tow, Minister of Defense. Lazare Sampras, Minister for People's Security. Felix Boigny, Foreign Minister. Army Commander Colonel Mooradian. Air Force Commander Colonel Lefevour. And airport manager Benoit Aubin."

As the head of Libya's military mission walked down the line of Seychelles officials, a very tired Hazem Mashari followed him, trying as best he could to eagerly shake their hands. When the introductions were finished, he turned back to his group to start his own.

"Comrades, thank you for your welcome," he said wearily. "We will stand with you together in this crisis, but I'm afraid I cannot stand much longer. I've spent most of today in a very small cockpit and I must have some rest. This is Major Osama el-Jabr. He is commander of all ground elements in Rapid Deployment Force Viper. He can answer your questions. Good evening, comrades."

Mashari smiled and saluted, then turned for the staff cars which had brought his latest visitors. When he did so, his gaze swept across the airport's opposite side: across the local and international airliners at the civilian terminal; the helicopters, trainers, and transports of the Seychelles Air Force; and finally to rest on the *Phoenix*.

"You'll be given a tour of our prize in the morning," Sampras promised, noticing the way he was staring at the shuttle. "Before you leave, could you tell me when you think your bombers can start flying reconnaissance missions? We do have an American carrier sailing for us and still more warships to the east."

"Before noon tomorrow," said Mashari. "The Ilyushins have our spare parts, weapons, and extra flight crews. While I will not fly that first mission, I can assure you someone will. Good evening."

"Looks like all the VIPs are on the other side of the field," said Post, glancing at the row of newly arrived aircraft and the vehicles surrounding them. "But you can bet they're talking about us."

With the airport's civilian and military flight lines already filled, the Libyan Tu-22s and Il-76 transports were forced to use its longest taxiway as their hardstand. Parked so each could have access to an exit ramp, the seven warplanes were widely spaced along the taxiway. Each had at least a few vehicles sitting around it, though by far the largest number were at the Ilyushins and the lead Tupolev. Work lamps had been erected around the transports, bathing the three huge aircraft in pools of light to facilitate their unloading.

"Shit, that's a tank they're driving off that one 'seventy-six," said Reynolds, when the rumble of a diesel engine drifted across the field. "First it was bus loads of troops, now this."

"It's a ZSU-23," Goldman identified, using a compact pair of binoculars from his attaché case. "It's an antiaircraft tank. They've brought in both offensive and defensive weapons. A good mix, and just enough of each to cause us problems if this crisis turns dangerous."

168

"It will turn more dangerous," said Griffen. "Look at the way the people around us have been acting? They're almost delirious with power. They think four bombers and a few hundred troops have made them invincible. And the Libyans have encouraged it."

Griffen motioned to the hangars, where the celebration by the Seychelles troops and their advisors had moved. Cheering, laughing, and an eerie mixture of Arabic, Spanish, and Creole patois rolled onto the tarmac from them. Occasionally the din would flare loud enough to drown out almost all other sounds, which caused the guards still watching the shuttle to be repeatedly distracted.

"If you guys want to join the party, go ahead," Reynolds taunted, eliciting angry stares from the soldiers. "We won't be going anywhere."

"Yes you are, Commander. We've allowed you to stay here far longer than planned," said Parker, walking out from one of the hangars. "You must all return to your quarters. Say goodbye to them, Ambassador."

"Unfortunately, we must go," said Griffen, turning to the astronauts, hugging Julie and Rebecca, then shaking hands with the men. "We have to finalize our evacuation plans for tourists and nonessential personnel. Don't worry. I promise we'll be in contact with you."

The farewells trailed off when the security van materialized out of the gathering night. Again the astronauts were piled in through its back doors. And as soon as they were slammed shut, it sped into the darkness, leaving Griffen and her staff to wait beside the *Phoenix* until their embassy car arrived.

Eight

"Running lights, Captain. At two o'clock," warned the Transall's copilot, stopping his repeated sweeps with his light-enhancement scope. "Possible fishing boats."

"Let's open some space between them and us," said Turcat, easing his control wheel to the left.

For the last hour, the C.160 had been skimming across the Indian Ocean at altitudes of less than five hundred feet. With no terrain-following or avoidance radar to help them, its pilots had to rely on a sniper scope borrowed from the SEALs in order to spot any approaching obstacles too small to be noticed by the plane's navigation radar.

Though the lights were too faint for Turcat to see, he dipped the Transall's port wing and banked it to the left. At more than three hundred miles an hour, it did not take long for the threat to even slide out of the scope's enhanced vision, while the glowing outline of Mahé Island crept nearer.

"Lieutenant, there's Silhouette Island," Turcat advised, nodding at a darkened hump rising above the ocean's surface. In the cockpit's nearly blacked-out conditions, it was almost as visible as Mahé. "We're about ten minutes from the drop point."

"I'll get my squad ready," said Hassler, standing between the pilots' seats. "Thank you for your delivery, Captain. I know it hasn't been a milk run for you."

"You've given us something to do, Lieutenant. After a month of training for such 'milk runs.' Would you wish for your Starlight scope returned."

"Don't worry, our sniper team always carries spares. You'll need it for your egress flight. Good luck, you guys. Hold her steady during the jump."

Gordon Hassler needed to step backwards in order to exit the transport's cockpit. He was now wearing both his parachute backpack and his chestpack. The moment he was on its cargo deck, he swung around and took stock of his squad. Five of the six men under his command already had their packs on and were now preparing their equipment canister for the drop. As for his sixth man, Hassler walked down to a curtained-off section near the tail ramp.

"C'mon, Belford. I know you're going to miss using a toilet, but we've got less than ten minutes," he said, banging his jump helmet on the curtain's support frame.

"All right, Gordo, all right. Can't a guy have a last minute of peace around here?" asked Petty Officer Thomas Belford, throwing back the curtain only after he finished buttoning up his pants and locking his belt.

"Not when we have so little time left. Ty. Nick. Help him get his packs on. Sergeant Bellonte, hit the low lights please."

The Transall's crew chief immediately changed the deck's lighting over to a soft red glow to prepare the commandos' night vision. While two of them helped Belford with his packs, the other three finished drag-

171

ging the matt green cylinder down to the tail ramp and hooked its parachute cord to the overhead static line.

As it approached Silhouette Island the aircraft bounced and swayed, then its nose tipped up and it started to climb. In half a minute, it reached the assigned jump altitude and levelled out. The sound of its turboprops changed as its airspeed was reduced; the moment the jump warning light flashed Bellonte hit the tail ramp controls.

Even at the reduced speed, a hurricane of wind and noise swept into the cargo deck. By then Hassler's squad was lined up and attaching their cords to the static line while the loadmasters anchored their safety tethers. Through the opening tail ramp the SEALs got their first, brief look at their insertion point, until the ramp finished extending and the jump warning light changed from red to green.

"Good luck, Lieutenant!" Bellonte shouted, leaning over to Hassler. "May you all have soft landings!"

Hassler could only manage a smile before his men pushed the canister out and charged down the ramp. He was the last to leave the C.160, the last to feel the slipstream pull him out and the last to feel his parachute explode open. The jarring deceleration swiftly ended with the parachute canopy's full deployment; at last allowing Hassler to see his men strung out in front of him, and the Transall diving away to his right.

Though they had been released at a thousand feet, the SEALs still only had a few seconds to prepare for their landing on Silhouette Island's western shoreline. Once they dropped below its central peaks they lost sight of Mahé Island, some fifteen miles to the southeast. Then, a field of glowing white sand seemed to rush up for them.

They had been released over the beach's widest section, not even the uncontrolled equipment canister landed in the water. The SEALs managed to steer themselves to landing points midway between the sea's edge and the line of startlingly tall Takamaka trees. The first two down left their parachutes where they dropped them and ran to get their weapons. Hassler and the other three worked under their cover, collecting everyone's chute before joining them.

"Ty, get your scope out and scan for any sign of locals," Hassler said softly. "Let me know if you see anything."

"Hey, this ain't so bad," said one of the other men. "It's just like our jumps on those French islands."

"Keep your voices down!" Hassler's angry whisper cut through the chuckling and effectively silenced it. "We're near enough to the water for them to carry. Let's do this fast. We have to inflate our raft, complete our loading, and be off this island within the hour. We'll need the rest of the night to reach Conception."

"Yarmouth Field to NASA Nine-Zero-Five, use Exit Ramp Bravo-Four once you are down. We have everything ready for you. Over."

"Roger, Yarmouth. We're on final," said Diana Danforth. "We have five green and we're passing the outer marker."

With all five sets of its landing gear extended, its flaps and leading edge slats drooping from its wings; the 747 was in the last minutes of a fourteen-hour flight from Hawaii. Over the runway approach lights it finally became something more than a collection of strobing anticollision beacons and running lights. The Boeing giant settled smoothly onto the ground, decelerated to a crawl by the time it reached its assigned exit ramp, and swung toward Yarmouth's flight line.

Already dominated by the newly arrived C-5B, the line held a meager scattering of Royal Australian Air

Force C-130 and BAe 748 transports. The 747 was guided into the slot beside the Galaxy, where NASA personnel from the nearby tracking station gathered around it as its engines spooled down.

"Director Cochran, I'm Stuart Schiano, NASA operations manager," said the official standing at the top of the boarding stairs. "Welcome to Australia. How long will your planes be staying here?"

"No more than a day," Cochran answered wearily. "All of us need a layover, I'm sure the Air Force crew is just as tired as we are. The Boeing is going to need some maintenance. You got someone outside of our crew to do it?"

"The Aussies have flown in a Quantas ground crew for us. They're just waiting to go to work on your plane."

Schiano motioned to the bottom of the boarding stairs, where Cochran finally noticed some of the people gathered around it were wearing uniforms from the Australian airline. Moments later, after Brenner and Diana joined him, Cochran was led down the stairs and introduced to the NASA and Australian personnel.

"How long do we have to work on your bird?" asked the leader of the Quantas detail.

"About a day," said Cochran. "Maybe a little longer. We want to get to Diego Garcia as soon as possible."

"Did you hear about Garcia, mate? Those bloody Marxists are saying you and the pommies should leave it. They say they brought in the Libyans because of your buildup there."

"Excuse me. Pommies?" said Brenner. "Who are the pommies?"

"The British," Schiano explained. "Around here, if you like the Brits you call 'em pommies. If you don't, you call them pommie bastards."

174

"Let's not get into this," said Cochran, rubbing his eyes, then glancing over at the hangars. "Who are those people? This is the middle of the night and the middle of the outback. There shouldn't be anyone here but air crews and ground crews."

"They're reporters and cameramen. They've been here for half a day waiting for you, ever since you did that fast refueling stop in Hawaii. Frankly, the press is mad at you. They think you did it to avoid them."

"Oh yeah? Well, frankly I'm pissed, too. My Lady's the cause of yet another international crisis, and it shouldn't be. Since I don't have my French speechwriter with me, keep the press away from my people, my planes, and me. I'm not about to play twenty questions with someone who's out to score a few ratings points."

"Bring up the map of Silhouette again," said Allard, standing behind the seat his executive officer was using. "And mark their insertion point."

Mike Jaskula tapped a few keys on the console keyboard, recalling the map of Silhouette Island and putting it on the TASCO Room's center screen. The map had contour lines showing the island's elevation and was color-coded to indicate its topography: mountains and tropical rain forest, boulder fields and stretches of open beach. On one of the beaches on its southwestern side, a bright yellow cursor floated the indicated jump point for the Reconnaissance Squad.

"If they haven't had any trouble on their insertion, they should be off the island by now," said Jaskula, glancing at the event clock above the main screen. Activated at the moment the parachute jump was to have started, it was only a few seconds away from the forty-five minute mark.

"They should be in their zodiac," Allard noted.

175

"Either finding a spot to sink the equipment canister loaded with their parachutes, or heading out across the channel to Mahé. How I hate this waiting and not knowing."

"We could always surface and try raising them," Burks suggested, his voice and the stamp of his shoes on the stairs catching both men by surprise. "I'm certain Terry would understand."

"So am I, but it wouldn't do any good. The squad won't set up their Satcom gear for hours. Not until they reach Conception Island. What's it like upstairs?"

"Still running at twenty knots, and the French boat is keeping pace with us. If you'll punch up the inertial navigation program, you'll see we're almost halfway there."

By the time the *Marshall*'s executive officer was standing beside Allard, one of the side screens had the sub's plotted course from Reunion to Mahé, and a flashing arrow indicated how far it and the *Casablanca* had sailed.

"We could surface and contact the Transall?" Jaskula intoned. "At least we'd know Gordo's squad jumped on time."

"That would be nice to know," said Allard. "But it wouldn't be worth the effort to slow down and surface. When will Terry wake up, Greg?"

"In about two hours," said Burks, checking his wristwatch. "I guess until then you'll have to fume and wait."

"Bring the munitions pallets out one at a time," ordered Major el-Jabr. "And load them immediately into the new pit."

Rumbling loudly, a forklift backed out of the Ilyusin, holding a semicircle-shaped container in its steel tines. The container was one of two filled with 23-mm shells for the ZSU-23 antiaircraft tank. Watched closely by the Libyan support crew, the forklift moved faster once it was on the taxiway. It finally swung to the side and started to roll forward after clearing the big transport's tail.

"Major, would you know if Colonel Mashari is still awake?" asked Sampras, stepping out of the sedan that brought him to the taxiway.

"No. He's asleep, and it would be advisable not to awaken him," said el-Jabr. "Why do you need to speak to him?"

"Since he is now the highest-ranking officer on the island, he's the senior military commander. And we have an unusual incident to investigate."

"If it's just an incident and not a threat then we don't need to awaken Mashari. What's happened?"

"Radar briefly detected a large aircraft moving at low altitude. It was heading south when we detected it and soon moved out of range. We have reports from fishermen who claim an aircraft flew by Silhouette Island."

"Silhouette? Not Mahé?" asked el-Jabr. "Do you think it was American?"

"What else could it be?" said Sampras. "Since the night that spaceship landed, our territory has been regularly violated by their P-3 bombers. However, this one didn't come from the west. It apparently came from the south, and it did not overfly Mahé. We don't understand what happened."

"Commandos. It's a reconnaissance flight for commandos. Is not Silhouette uninhabited?"

"Yes, it's a wildlife sanctuary. Why would they land there and not here on the main island?"

"Because their commandos could land, regroup, and watch us from there without worrying about a local population. Those are the reasons I would choose it.

And if I need to move, this island is only ten or fifteen miles away. What are you going to do about this sighting?"

"We've requested an Islander." Sampras turned and pointed to the far side of the airport. At the military flight line an Air Seychelles Islander was having its main hatch removed and a flare rack installed. In minutes it would be departing, with a military crew at its controls. "It will investigate the island. We were wondering if some of your troops could sweep it for invaders?"

"Not until the morning," said el-Jabr, irritated. "My men are almost as tired as the Tupolev crews, and I need some rest, too. Unless your plane finds something unusual, any sweeps or operations can wait until morning."

"All right, we're far enough into the channel," Hassler whispered. "Release the canister."

In place of the weapons, munitions, communication systems, and other gear once packed in it, the equipment canister now held the squad's parachutes. Not as heavy as it had been, it rode buoyantly alongside the squad's zodiac raft until Silhouette was miles behind them both. At Hassler's command, the squad members holding onto it pushed its nose below the surface. With a bubbling hiss, the canister filled with water and sank noisily. For several moments the raft slowed and circled the area where it went down until Hassler was certain it had disappeared from sight. Then, he ordered the raft to resume its course and increase speed.

"Gordo, I'm picking up a new radar source," warned the SEAL sitting in the middle of the zodiac, hunched over the backpack he had carried on board it. "And it isn't ship-based, it's airborne."

"Reduce speed," said Hassler. "And listen."

178

The outboard motor propelling the raft was heavily muffled and, even at full power, emitted no more than a soft rattle. However, when the power was cut, the sound fell to a quiet puttering, allowing other noises to be heard. Above the slapping of waves on the raft's sides, a weak drone was eventually heard and its location identified.

"Over there, Lieutenant," said the man in the raft's bow. "I think it's coming this way."

The seaman pointed almost directly ahead at the cluster of lights appearing over Mahé's spine of mountains and moving through the star-filled night sky. Once it was past the mountains, the cluster dove and appeared briefly in the glow from the hotels on the island's fabled Beau Vallon shoreline.

Its high wing and fixed landing gear immediately identified the Britten-Norman Islander. Even from a half-dozen miles away, the drone of its twin Lycoming engines could be heard reflecting off the water. And it rapidly grew louder as the light transport dropped closer and drew nearer to the raft.

"Arm submachine guns," Hassler ordered, drawing back the bolt on his weapon. "Be prepared to abandon the raft if we're hit. Nick, can you identify the type of radar you're detecting?"

"I think it's the plane's radar altimeter," said Nicholas Foreman, adjusting the controls on his ESM pack. "It's not I-band or J-band, and I'm not getting any Doppler shifting. So it's not interception or surface search radar."

"If they've got lights or flares, they can still see us. Snipers, don't break out your weapons. These aren't the conditions to make a few well-placed shots. We need volume of fire, and nobody opens fire until I do."

Instead of heading straight across the channel, the Islander turned south. For nearly a minute, it seemingly flew toward the gently bobbing zodiac. Those SEALs armed with MP5 submachine guns trained them on the aircraft. When Hassler flipped the safety off his weapon, the rest did likewise. Some were raising their weapons when the aircraft suddenly broke to the right and flew toward Silhouette from the southeast.

"What the hell's going on?" said the point man, lowering his weapon. "Another few seconds and they would've been on top of us."

"They're repeating the approach our plane made," said Hassler. "Quick, gun the engine. Let's get out of here."

The quiet puttering jumped back to a rattle, causing the raft to surge ahead. In seconds it was traveling at its top speed for the weight it was carrying. While most eyes scanned the light-studded bulk of Mahé, Hassler made sure a few kept watch on its dark neighbor.

"Gordo, it's dropping flares," Belford warned, raising his voice just high enough to be heard.

All eyes immediately swung back to find a string of sputtering fireballs hanging in the sky over Silhouette's western side. The Islander could again be seen, turning around and diving under the line of flares it had dropped. For a time it disappeared from sight, until it reemerged above the island's mountains and started ejecting another line of flares.

"They're on to us," Hassler said finally. "They must've detected our plane."

"You think they'll come after us?" asked Hall.

"Well, we're not going to wait here and find out. The best way to stay ahead of them is to keep moving. Tom, keep the engine at full throttle. It's at least another hour to Conception."

"We're clear, Terry. No surface or air contacts," said Burks, finishing his walk with the search periscope.

"Take us up," Carver ordered. "Once we've surfaced deploy the VHF mast. Don't deploy the radar mast, we'll get a data feed from the French. You have the con, Greg."

Carver stood at the back of the periscope stand, his hand on the guide rail to the TASCO Room's stairs. The moment his commands were acknowledged he disappeared into the control center, where Allard and Ensign Dupuis had already activated its systems.

"Glenn, I thought Mike was going to join us?" he said, moving up to the console.

"I got him on the phone," said Allard, holding a receiver in his hand. "He's in the aft briefing room with the rest of my officers and CPOs. They're sweating through this just like me."

"Just like all of us," Dupuis added. "Captain, I'm getting a transmission from the *Casablanca*. They must be on the surface."

The French officer flipped a toggle on the Joint Tactical Information Data System (JTIDS) panel, releasing the information to the center's computer. In an instant the main screen showed a digitalized version of what the DURA-33 surveillance radar on the attack sub was detecting: the increasing size of the *John Marshall* as it surfaced, but little else.

"This is the way we'll do it in the future," said Carver. "If we both come up together, only one of us will activate our radar. So if anyone's looking, they'll only detect one radar source. Glenn, you getting anything?"

"Radio mast up and operating," said Allard, listening to the soft static on the center's speakers, and adjusting the volume until all could hear it. "We're now at the designated time for the squad to contact us. Remember, it's going to take a little time for them to do so. First, their signal goes up to a satellite in geosynchro-

181

nous orbit, and then back down to Diego Garcia for rebroadcast to us."

"All of which takes about a quarter of a second. How long will you wait before you try raising them?"

"About five minutes. After that we'll broadcast a few times. If we get no answer, we should advice Garcia to listen for us and send out a message on the VLF when Gordo finally contacts them."

"I hope your squad is keeping to its schedule," Carver admitted. "I don't relish the idea of dragging a seventeen-hundred-foot wire behind me. Especially at —"

A loud burst of static and some heavy breathing on the speakers drowned out the rest of Carver's sentence. As their volume was quickly readjusted, Hassler began his transmission.

"Home Port, this is Spectacle. Home Port, this is Spectacle. Do you read? Over."

"Roger, Spectacle. We read you," said Allard, grabbing the microphone stand and pressing its button. "Have you conceived? Is everyone safe? Over."

"Affirmative. Everyone is safe and we confirm conception. Phase One, complete. Have you any news for us? Over."

"No changes to report. Will advise of any on next broadcast. Take care of yourselves. This is Home Port, out."

"Will do. This is Spectacle, out."

"Home Port? Spectacle? Is it necessary to use code names and such on secure channel transmissions?" Dupuis asked.

"It adds another layer of security," said Carver. "Just in case someone with sophisticated hardware is listening. Well, Glenn, what do your men have to say?"

"They're happy we got our eyes and ears in place," said Allard, cupping his hand over the receiver's mouthpiece. "And they want to know when we'll join them."

"The faster we submerge the faster we'll get there." Instead of using any of the center's microphones, Carver jumped back up the stairs. And before he had reached its top, his voice was filling both the TASCO Room and the control center with orders. "Greg, tell the Radio Room to let Jacoubet know we're resuming the run, then secure the mast. Clarence, open the tanks. Sound the diving alarm."

Nine

Finalizing Plans
Challenge

"Ray, how was your trip from the station?" Goldman asked, greeting Fernandez at the briefing room door and shaking his hand.

"Apart from all the security check points, it was easy," he said. "I've never seen island traffic so light."

"It's the crisis," said Donald Griffen. "With the arrival of those Libyan forces, I think everyone has realized this is a real crisis. We got a big upsurge in tourists requesting evacuation. And so have the British, French, and German embassies. We've all received our orders to evacuate civilians and nonessential staff. Lynn is still talking to the State Department and will join us soon."

The Chargé d'Affaires motioned to the seats at the room's table set aside for Goldman and Fernandez. Again they were all meeting in a room with heavy curtains drawn over its windows. Nothing of the early morning sun was able to peak through them. Only when the room's main doors were briefly opened did a soft yellow glow flood in.

"Mr. Fernandez, I believe you know our security officer, Henry Savage," Lynn Griffen announced, entering the room and quickly shutting the door behind her. "He's been reviewing your evacuation plans and will coordinate them with ours."

"When I haven't been worrying about embassy security," said the youngest man in the room, reaching over the table and shaking the station chief's hand. "Last night's protest got out of control, even for its government handlers."

"You think the same problem could happen today?" Fernandez responded.

"It could. When can your people be ready to leave?"

"In a matter of hours. Everyone who's leaving has already packed their bags, and all our vehicles have been checked. Do you want them to leave singly, or in a convoy?"

"A convoy would be more obtrusive but safer." Savage folded out a map on the table and pointed to the NASA station, then traced the route he had drawn onto it. "This is the fastest way to Victoria. Once in the city, this would be the easiest route to the waterfront. Of course, it's all dependent on the number of security checkpoints the government has set up."

"I take it we're going to be evacuated by sea?" said Fernandez, looking over the rest of the map.

"When you consider what's at the airport, it's the only way out. U.S., French, and British warships are en route to Mahé. They'll be here by mid-afternoon, and we have to be ready for them."

"Hank, could we have any trouble with the People's Security goons?" Lynn asked. "They've not only harassed us here, but also at our homes."

"Frankly, I'm also worried about the local population," said Savage. "I think the government's been successful at inflaming them against us. They've constantly been running your comments to Benoit Aubin and the remarks by the astronauts on both radio and TV."

"I didn't know I was being recorded at the time," Fernandez said defensively. "And you know they're quoting the astronauts out of context."

"You know it, and I know it," said Lynn. "But the local population doesn't know it. And more importantly, nor does the rest of the Third World. I've seen reports from embassies in the Middle East, Africa, and Asia. 'Space Imperialism' and 'Space Hegemony' have become the new catchwords. And then there are the groups inside the U.S."

"Yes, I know. The Proxmire Foundation, Concerned Americans For A Sane Defense, not to mention Phil Donahue. We're not diplomats in NASA, just space experts."

"Then leave diplomacy to the diplomats. And we'll leave space matters to you. Especially this piece of space matter . . ."

Lynn pushed across the table a clear plastic box with a marble-sized, angular piece of iron and nickel inside it. The meteor's irregular surface was spotted with deposits of orange powder, the dried remnants of the hydrazine fuel it released.

"We think someone in your group should take care of this," she added. "Not unless you believe a diplomatic pouch would be safer?"

"Our 'proof' that our space disaster was indeed a disaster," said Fernandez, picking up the container and surprised at its weight. "We'd know how to handle it. But it could get confiscated from us if the security goons were to search our convoy."

"We should give it to Joyce," Goldman suggested. "She'll be the ranking diplomat to be evacuated."

"Okay, we'll give it to her," said Lynn. "Ron, have you

heard anything more from the Pentagon or Diego Garcia?"

"The *Eisenhower*'s battle group is now about twenty-six hours away. The Russian carrier and its fleet will arrive in the next six hours. And so far, no more Libyan forces have arrived on the island."

"That fleet worries me," said Fernandez, handing the meteor back to the ambassador. "I thought the Russians turned down the Seychelles request for military aid. What has their embassy told you?"

"So far they've been very quiet about what their Navy will do," Lynn admitted. "Though I have heard Moscow is unhappy over the way their intelligence ship helped you. Donald, I'm going to leave you in charge of this meeting. I have another one that starts in one hour with the British and French ambassadors. If you have any questions you want me to ask them, better tell me now."

"It's been so long since we've done any antisub ops, we'll have to go back to ASW school at North Island when this is over," Marron commented, helping anchor a machine gun mount in the hatch of his Seahawk.

"Dean, after we've finished arming Lisa, do we leave the door on?" asked a black ensign, standing in the open door to the *Simpson*'s starboard hangar. Behind him, the frigate's second SH-60 helicopter could be easily seen.

"Yes, Kevin. It's too difficult to put back on, and it won't interfere with the gun's arc. Have you finished removing your ASW gear?"

"We're just taking out the sonobuoy rack. God, I never saw it look so empty in there."

"That's just the way we want it to look for the evacuees," said Marron, wiping the sweat off his brow. "Let me know when you're done."

In spite of the constant wind coming down from the ship's bows, the crew working on its flight deck was sweating heavily in the mid-morning sun. In addition to arming the helicopter with flare and chaff pods and a light machine gun, they were also pre-flighting it for the day's operations.

Before he returned to his work, Marron glanced over the stern at the two ships moving in formation with the *Simpson*. On its starboard side was HMS *Alacrity,* less boxy and angular than the American warship; it had hangar facilities for only one helicopter and mounted its main gun forward, instead of its missile launcher. On the port side was the destroyer *Aconit.* With no aircraft hangars, its superstructure's most dominant feature was the kettle-shaped dome for its DRBV air surveillance radars. All three ships were maintaining a cruise speed of twenty-five knots, which would have them arriving off Mahé by early afternoon.

"Brody, you've been a good lad so far," said Baxter, as he unlocked the handcuffs he had only moments before slipped over his prisoner's wrists. "Keep up this proper behavior, and it will likely go well for you."

"Yes, Stony . . . I mean, Constable Baxter," said Jerry Brody, correcting himself the second he noticed the hard look in the policeman's eye. "Are you going to be staying here?"

"Today? Of course. This may be the most exciting cruise I've been on since the *Queen Elizabeth* went to the Falklands."

"Brody, you better get over here," said the Anti-Air Warfare officer, Lieutenant Walter Stover. "We just picked up a high-speed bogie."

Rubbing the marks that were pressed on his wrists, Brody moved through the darkened Combat Information Center almost by memory. He dodged around the antisub, surface warfare and tactical coordination consoles to the anti-air warfare station. Before he had finished taking his seat, Stover was filling him in on the latest situation.

"It popped onto the screen about twenty seconds ago," he added. "It's at twenty thousand feet, and its heading indicates it is flying straight from Mahé."

"Okay, let's see what we have," said Brody, glancing at the scope and CRT screens at his station. "Lieutenant, are you going to be the Tactical Action Officer?"

"Of course, I'm TAO. No one else is qualified. Don't pull any of your Bart-shit, Jerry. We don't need it here."

"Just thought I'd try. We have a large target, its speed is six hundred knots, it's at one hundred and forty miles and closing. At current speed, it will be here in twelve minutes. ESM is detecting Short Horn weapons targeting radar . . . we got ourselves a Blinder."

"Energize weapons systems," said Stover, hitting the transmit switch to his communications headset. "Warm up the missiles in the ready magazine. Bridge, this is CIC. We have a Libyan bomber inbound. ETA, twelve minutes. I think you better sound General Quarters."

"Mr. Locke, it appears as though you're going to begin your duties early," said Commander Aldiss on entering *Alacrity*'s own CIC. "What is your ship reporting?"

"We have an inbound high-speed target," Locke answered, sitting at the center's tactical coordination console. "It looks like a Libyan Tupolev, and the *Simpson* is going to General Quarters."

"Lieutenant, sound Action Stations." Aldiss first turned to the CIC chief, then to the seamen at the weapons console. "Activate the Seawolf launcher and its Nine-Ten radar. Load the main gun's ready magazine with proximity fused shells and call out the Oerlikon crews."

"Dean, something's happening on the British ship," said Marron's copilot, stepping out of the Seahawk's main cabin and walking over to the landing pad's starboard side.

From their vantage point, the *Simpson*'s lead helicopter crew could see the *Alacrity*'s 20-mm gun mounts getting their tarpaulins stripped off and ammunition drums hauled out to them. Though several hundred yards away, the shrill blasts of its alert Klaxons could be faintly heard. Before anyone was able to comment on it, the General Quarters (GQ) alarm went off on the pad and echoed from inside the hangars.

"We're going to have visitors!" Marron shouted. "Howard! Carl, get your helmets! Secure the fuel line!"

"Dean, shouldn't we pull her into the hangar!" the copilot asked, motioning to the Seahawk as the crew scattered.

"If we're attacked, it won't make much difference if it's in a hangar or not! Get moving, Howard!"

Over the boxlike hangars, and through the ship's lattice masts, a dark speck appeared high on the western horizon. As it grew larger and sprouted wings, it began to descend toward the warships. By the time it screamed over them, the lone Tu-22 had dropped more than three miles to around two thousand feet.

"Bob, did you get a look at our friend?" said Stover, when he caught sight of another figure entering the CIC.

"For about three seconds," said Stine, stumbling through the dark until he reached the communications console.

"Well, now that you've seen him you can talk to him." Stover handed the executive officer a headset and plugged it into a buddy jack on the console. "Libyan aircraft, this is U.S. warship. You are now speaking to our captain."

"This is Lieutenant Robert Stine, Captain of the USS *Simpson*. To whom am I speaking? Over."

"Major Tariq al-Rayes, Libyan Air Force," answered the same voice that had first challenged the ship moments before. "What are the identities of the warships with you, and why are you violating Seychelles territorial waters? Over."

"The other ships are the French destroyer *Aconit* and the British frigate HMS *Alacrity*. We are on a peaceful mission to evacuate foreign nationals and diplomatic personnel. Over."

"Understood, Lieutenant. If you are indeed on a peaceful mission then why are your ships so heavily armed? If you want to continue with your mission, you must *disarm* them. Over."

"What? Are you crazy?" Stine blurted out, incredulous at the demands. "This operation has been agreed to by the Seychelles government."

"I know what the government agreed to, Lieutenant. They did not agree to the presence of such provocatively armed warships in their territory."

After its first pass the Tupolev almost disappeared over the eastern horizon before it had slowed and turned around. Even at several miles range it still looked like a large, black dart as it banked steeply, then almost disappeared when it levelled out after completing the turn.

"He's coming in again," said Marron, now wearing a Kevlar helmet. "Might as well stand and wave."

With the fuel line stowed, Marron's copilot and crew chief joined him at the stern to watch the bomber make its second pass. Even the crew from the second helicopter and the landing pad detail moved out of the hangars to get a better view of it.

Because it cut its speed in half, the Blinder needed several minutes to overtake the ships again. It had dropped even lower to a thousand feet, allowing the ships' crews to see its leading edge slats popped open for low-speed maneuvering. Its bomb bay doors pulled back, revealing a cluster of dark grey missiles attached to a rotary launcher.

The sight of the weapons transfixed Marron and the others as the Tupolev flew between the *Simpson* and the *Alacrity.* So much so that they didn't see either their ship's Phalanx cannon, or the *Alacrity's* Seawolf launcher, track the bomber until it broke away and started to circle the formation.

"We could've sawed its wing off if we had wanted to," said Stine, watching the gunner's mate at the Phalanx control station target the aircraft.

"Lieutenant, we got more problems," Brody warned. "In fact we got six more problems."

Both Stine and Stover responded to his call; in seconds they were standing over him while he pointed to the new blips on his scope.

"We got two bogies coming out of Mahé," he added, motioning first to the targets at the top of the scope. "And four more coming out of the northeast."

"Four? Can you tell what they are?" said Stine.

"These two are large aircraft travelling at high speed. ESM is detecting Short Horn emissions from them, they're probably more Blinders. These four are smaller, also at high speed, but we're detecting no radar from them."

"None? Could they be decoys? Or are they fighters that haven't turned their radars on?"

"American warship, American warship. This is Libyan aircraft," said al-Rayes, his voice coming over the CIC's speakers. "You have seen my weapons. My brothers and I can easily sink you. If you do not turn around or disarm your ships, action will be taken."

"Bob, the helo crews on the fantail report the bomber has a load of antishipping missiles in its bomb bay," Stover advised, cupping his hand over one of his earphones to hear better. "Type unknown."

"Libyan aircraft, this is American warship. Do not threaten us," said Stine, briefly pressing the transmit switch on his headset controls. "We are fully capable of defending ourselves, out. Walter, activate the SPG radar. If the Standards in the ready magazine are warmed up, run one onto the launcher. Seven planes could overwhelm our defenses, especially if three of them are carrying bellyfuls of antishipping missiles. Brody, what can you tell me about the new threats?"

"Blinders Two and Three are at five hundred knots and have descended to four thousand feet," said Brody. "The four unknowns have increased speed to five hundred and twenty knots. They're at one thousand feet, and will reach us about three minutes ahead of the Blinders. They're definitely fighters, not decoys. I think they may be Forgers."

"What! *Six* more?" Aldiss responded, surprised. "What are the other ships doing?"

"The *Simpson* has armed its Standard launcher," said the *Alacrity*'s Anti-Air Warfare officer. "And both

193

her and the *Aconit* are arming their ECM systems."

"Activate deception jammers and the Corvus launchers. Warn the gun crews. Mr. MacCowin, which of these groups will arrive first?"

"The four ship flight. The *Simpson* claims they're smaller; they could likely be fighters. The other two are more bombers."

"Whatever they are, if they try anything we'll shoot the bounders out of the sky," said Aldiss, studying the CIC's tactical board.

"Bounders?" asked Locke, confused. "I thought they were called Blinders?"

"Dean, he's changing direction," said Marron's copilot. "I think he's making another pass."

The black dart, which had been circling the warships for the last several minutes, nearly disappeared as it swung in toward them. Seconds later it had grown large enough to be clearly seen once more, though by then most eyes were not scanning the southern quadrant but looking to the northeast.

Appearing just above the *Alacrity's* aft superstructure, the approaching fighters held to a tight formation. Not until they were almost on top of the frigate could they be identified. Their diminutive wings, slender fuselages, and large air intakes immediately marked them as Yak-38 Forgers. They moved almost too fast for the red and yellow stars on their wings to be seen. What were more observable were the white and grey Aphid missiles on their outer wing pylons. In an instant they flashed over the Allied ships and closed on the Tupolev, causing it to break off its pass.

"Damn! Bastards!" snapped a familiar voice on the

CIC speakers, causing its crew to laugh. "Bastards, you are interfering with our mission!"

"*You* are interfering with a multinational evacuation," said a calm, heavily accented voice. "An operation approved by the Seychelles government."

"My planes have been ordered to defend this country, and these warships are a dangerous provocation."

"These ships are on a peaceful mission. And while they are, they will enjoy the protection of the Russian Navy."

"I don't believe this," said Stine, the surprise clearly audible in his words. "We're getting a Yak CAP! This may be the first time since World War Two that the Russians are giving us an escort. Walter, stand down the Phalanx and the Standard. Keep the RBOC armed, the Slick Seventeens and Thirty-twos active. Advise the French and Brits to do the same."

"Libyan aircraft, I have ordered my flight to arm our missiles," the Russian pilot continued. "You and the rest of your planes will not be allowed to threaten the multinational ships. You will stay away from them or risk being shot down, out."

"Captain, the other Blinders are closing to visual range," said Brody. "And I have still another target. It's also coming out of the northeast and is at five hundred feet. It's not closing on us, but will pass within visual range. The target is at low speed. I think it's a helicopter."

"There they are, Admiral," said the crew chief, pointing out the hatch window. "Climbing away from the ships."

"Yes, Sergeant. I see," Khomenko replied, watching three black darts rising away from the warships. Though he did not normally show emotion, he could not help but smile. "Colonel, your fighters are performing well."

"Admiral, surely you're not enjoying this incident?" said Colonel Vladislav Burdin, the *Baku's* air group commander. "The Libyans are our Allies."

"We have no 'Allies' in the Third World, Vladislav Petrovich. Only those who want to use us to counter the Americans. Even if the Libyans were truly our friends, the arrival of their forces has changed the equation of this crisis. It complicates matters and, as we've just seen and heard, makes them more dangerous."

"Admiral, do you think the Americans will attack them?" asked one of the other officers seated in the helicopter's main cabin.

"I hope we can convince them to show restraint," said Khomenko, moving away from the hatch. "Perhaps our little escort mission will help. Uncaging the *Phoenix* will be more difficult now. I know if it were our people who were in danger, I would certainly attack."

Since its coaxial main rotors spun in opposite directions, there was no need for the Ka-27 to have a tail rotor to counteract torque. It gave the rotund helicopter a squat, abbreviated look, and the coaxial rotors made it clatter like an angry, mechanical bumblebee. The Kamov flew within several miles of the Allied warships but no closer. It continued on toward Mahé, and, at a cruise speed of one hundred and forty miles an hour, would need just over an hour to reach the island.

"Don't put the antenna up too high," warned Hassler. "Even if it is camouflaged, I don't want us spotted because of it."

"Don't worry, Gordo. I'll just put it up high enough to get good reception," said Foreman.

The dark green telescope antenna continued to be

raised until the picture on the surveillance set's two-inch LCD screen lost its snow and came into sharp focus. Tuned to one of the two UHF stations on nearby Mahé, the picture showed a long tracking shot of the Libyan flight line at Seychelles International.

"Glenn'll be happy to know his family's latest high-tech gadget is working well," said Hassler, watching part of his squad work on the Allard Technologies AT-90 Full-Spectrum Electronic Surveillance Set. The size of a large attaché case, it appeared to have more antennas than any other feature. Yet it was capable of detecting and identifying electronic emissions across the spectrum of radio and microwave frequencies.

"I didn't think it would hold up to all the bouncing, but it has," Foreman added. "Do you want me to try the other station? I think it was playing a movie."

"No, what is this program reporting?"

"That three of the bombers are out looking for the evacuation ships." Foreman pressed one of his headphone cups down over his ear to listen to the broadcast better. "And one of the transports is taking off for Libya."

"I better let the snipers know," said Hassler. "Keep listening and keep watching. Glenn will want a full report on the airfield and any defenses."

Hassler crept away from one point on the jungle-covered ridge to another where the cover was not so dense and there was a clear view of Mahé's southwestern shore. Two members of the three-man sniper team were nestled among the granite outcroppings. In addition to their camouflaged fatigues, they wore the same two-tone green paint on their faces as Hassler did. They repeatedly scanned Mahé's shoreline and nearby Therese Island, with the Hensoldt scopes from their PSG1 rifles.

"Heads up," Hassler said quietly. "One of the Libyan

197

'Seventy-sixes will be taking off soon. Anything new to report?"

"McRibs are available, but for a limited time only," said the black petty officer, while he continued to scan the shore.

"I gotta pee," Belford remarked. "Can I be relieved to relieve myself?"

"Very funny, you two. Aren't you taking this seriously?"

"Shit, Lieutenant. It's kinda hard to take this crisis in paradise seriously," said Tyrone Hall, finally looking away from his scope. "Especially when there are so many hot babes on the beaches."

"Yeah, but there aren't as many now as there were earlier in the morning," said Belford, suddenly tilting his scope up. "There it is, Gordo. It's an Ilyushin all right."

Appearing above Mahé's central spine of jagged mountains, the white and grey Il-76T was still climbing moderately and heading due west. Approximately a minute later the low rumble of its jet engines reflected over the water to Conception Island.

"Okay, Tom. Go take your leak," Hassler ordered. "Give me your scope and your pad. If this kind of activity keeps up, we're going to have a lot to tell the *Marshall* when we contact her again."

Ten

Old Comrades
The Hunt Begins

Clattering through the approach pattern to Seychelles International, the angry bumblebee was a conspicuous sight, especially when the red stars on its fuselage sides became visible. Buzzing down the civilian flight line of local and overseas airliners, the Kamov helicopter slowed to a stop as it neared the airport's military side. It hovered next to a line of black limousines before settling furiously to the ground.

"Admiral Oleg Khomenko, on behalf of the People's Revolutionary Government, let me be first to welcome you and your staff to the Seychelles Islands!" said Benoit Aubin, beginning his announcement the moment the Kamov's side hatch rolled open. He had nearly finished it by the time the first Soviet officer stepped onto the tarmac.

"I am *Colonel* Burdin. This is Admiral Khomenko," said Burdin, pointing to the second officer to emerge.

"Admiral, on behalf of the People's—"

"Yes, yes. I heard you well enough the first time," Khomenko replied, cutting off Aubin, though he also shook his hand. "Thank you for your gracious welcome, Comrade. You have already met the commander of my carrier's air group. Colonel, why don't you introduce the rest of my staff to Mr. Aubin? I need to meet with Ambassador Samarefsky."

Releasing Aubin's hand, Khomenko immediately turned to the Soviet ambassador and the rest of the diplomatic staff. As they gathered around him, he quickly moved away from the local officials and toward the *Phoenix*.

"This Benoit Aubin is a buffoon," he said quietly. "You should've told me more about him, Yuri Ivanovich."

"Don't dismiss him so lightly," Samarefsky warned. "For the last two days, he's been something of a hero here. The first Seychellois to resist the American 'space invasion.' He maneuvered the NASA station chief into making several damning statements."

"I'll try to watch my words better." Khomenko stopped and looked over the shuttle from its port quarter. "Such a beautiful machine . . . with a company of Naval infantry I could easily take it from these 'comrades.' "

"That is the kind of violent ending I hope our intervention will avoid. So far, apart from their reconnaissance overflights, the Americans seem to be willing to operate in an international framework."

"There's an American phrase we should do well to remember, Yuri Ivanovich. It's 'keeping your options open.' I know if I were an American I would be thinking that way."

"I know you have requested to meet with the American commanders when their fleet arrives," said Samarefsky. "I hope when you do that you don't start giving them ideas. . . . Admiral, I think all your officers have finally deplaned. It's time for us to leave, our meeting at Revolution House begins within the hour."

Samarefsky motioned back to the limousines, and herded Khomenko and Colonel Burdin into the first one in line. As soon as they were all filled, the procession started to roll, turning off the flight line and threading their way through the maze of buildings beyond the hangars. At the airport's military entrance, they picked up an escort of People's Security Force motorcycles and accelerated down the coast road to Victoria.

"Captain, have the aircraft overfly the beach as we land on it," said Major el-Jabr, after scanning the southwestern shore of Silhouette Island with his binoculars. "If there's anyone on it, they will likely attack us then."

In broad daylight the island rose like a vibrantly green knoll of tropical forest from the sparkling blue waters surrounding it. An unbroken necklace of white sand beaches and its central peaks were Silhouette's most prominent features from the tiny bridge of a Vosper patrol boat. Not much larger than an airliner's cockpit, it had just enough room for the boat's captain, helmsman, el-Jabr, and the commander of the Seychelles forces' landing party.

"This is Assault Group Marlin to Kestrel One," said Captain Peter Matubis, squeezed against the bridge's communications panel. "Sweep the invasion area as we make our landing. Over. Major, should we have the ship's guns lay down suppressing fire when we go ashore?"

"Of course, and why not have the planes fire their rockets as well?" el-Jabr added sarcastically, though at first the sarcasm did not sink in.

"Really? Should I contact them again?"

"No! If anyone on this island doesn't know we're here, they will when they start firing. We'll maintain contact, but we'll only order support fire if we encounter hostile forces. Time to lead your 'assault group.' "

As the Vosper turned in toward the beach, both Matubis and el-Jabr left its bridge and worked their way forward. Clustered around the 40-mm gun in its bow were a half-dozen Libyans and three times that number of personnel from the People's Security Force and People's Defense Force. When they spotted their commander, the Libyans came immediately to attention. The Seychelles forces did not respond as rapidly.

"Stand up, now!" Matubis barked. "We're about to go ashore and face enemy American forces. If we find anyone we're to capture them if possible, kill them if we have to. If they resist, let their blood run into the sand of our islands."

"Not unless they're *friendly* American forces," said el-Jabr. "I'm sure the captain knows what to do with them. . . . If you come across any evidence that someone has been on the island, don't touch it until I arrive. Captain, order your men to re-safety their weapons until *after* we disembark."

Moments later the patrol boat tilted awkwardly as its keel dug into the sand. With a draft of less than six feet, the British-built Vosper was able to push its bow a fair distance up the beach without fear of getting stranded. The soldiers who climbed over its sides scarcely got more than their boots wet.

They hit the shore with a two-plane element from the People's Defense Force's sole combat squadron roaring overhead. The SIAI-Marchetti SF.260s emitted deafening howls from their Lycoming six cylinder engines; all out of proportion to the amount of power they produced. The fighter-trainers swept down the beach wingtip to wingtip, so low their machine gun pods and Matra rocket pods could be clearly seen. So low they passed below the crowns of the taller Takamaka trees

202

along the jungle's fringe. They continued down the beach and did not pull up until they were almost out of sight.

"Spread out and search carefully," el-Jabr ordered, once he could be heard again. "This whole island is an animal preserve; there isn't supposed to be anyone here. So any sign of humans is to be reported."

Mingled together, the Libyan paratroopers and Seychelles personnel spread out along an otherwise empty beach and worked their way up it, while their two commanders stayed behind them.

"Major, what should I tell the aircraft to do?" Matubis asked, as he watched the SF.260s return at a higher altitude.

"Tell them to search the island's interior," said el-Jabr. "If the enemy is here, perhaps their observers can spot them moving. We'll get enough fire support from your patrol boat, should we need it."

El-Jabr glanced out at the Vosper, which had since pulled off the beach and had taken up station about fifty yards from it. The fore and aft 40-mm guns on the hundred-foot-long boat were trained on the island and swept it continually. The major then looked down at his feet and realized he was standing on a broken string of debris running parallel to the shore.

"I take it this is the high tide mark?" he asked.

"Of course it is," said Matubis, now it was his turn to be sarcastic. "Have you never been on a beach before?"

"I live in the desert, not on an island. Only the sand and the heat are the same. Sergeant, have the men only search between this debris line and the trees. We'll move into the jungle later."

"What do you expect to find? A weapon someone dropped?"

"Nothing so obvious," said el-Jabr, moving along just below the debris line. "But perhaps we'll find their parachutes buried in the jungle. Since you cannot land an Orion bomber here, whoever the Americans dropped had to have parachuted in."

"Major! I have something! Down here!"

"Hold the line! Captain, tell your men to stop advancing!"

El-Jabr glanced up and broke into a run, quickly overtaking the column and zeroing in on the paratrooper who had raised his hand. When he reached his man, he knelt beside him and ordered the rest to step back.

"What do you have?" Matubis asked, arriving a few seconds later.

"A footprint," said el-Jabr, clearing the dried seaweed and decayed palm fronds. "More exact, a boot print. From its direction, the man who left it was moving down the beach to the waterline. From its tread design it's military, I think. And it's definitely recent."

"And it's definitely not from a superman. Look, this American must be much smaller than me."

The footprint el-Jabr had been carefully revealing was obliterated in an instant when Matubis planted his own boot on it. For a second the major was too shocked to respond, until he looked up at the grinning black face towering over him.

"You jabbering idiot!" he screamed, tackling the Seychelles officer and throwing him off-balance. "You've destroyed the only evidence we found!"

The second Matubis crashed to the ground el-Jabr was scrambling up him, trying to get his hands around his throat. But Matubis managed to kick him in his side and sent the Libyan officer sprawling down the beach toward the waterline. By the time they both stood up to take each other on again, their men were restraining them.

"Stop playing at detective and be a soldier!" Matubis said angrily, the cadence in his voice accentuating his anger. "If I had wanted a policeman, I would've asked for one of the Cubans!"

"Until we track down these Americans we must be detectives!" said el-Jabr. "Understand who we're facing. They could be Green Berets, Army Delta Force, Navy SEALs or Marine Reconnaissance. There are probably no more than a dozen of them. *Very* difficult to track down, even on an island. And I don't think they're on this island. They're probably on your main island."

"Major, it's fifteen miles from here to Mahé. Are you saying they brought a boat with them? Or did these American supermen swim?"

"Of course they brought a boat with them. The inflatable kind. A few gas cartridges and they can inflate it whenever they need it. You can release me now and return to your duties. Concentrate above the high tide line and move into the jungle. Look for any signs of recent digging. And as for you, Captain, stay away from me!"

"Take us down, Clarence. Two hundred feet," said Carver, moving away from the periscope stand. "Resume twenty knots running speed. Mr. Doran, you may have the conn until Greg wakes up. I'll be below with Glenn."

Once he was certain his weapons officer was safely commanding his submarine, Carver turned for the TASCO Room. By the time he reached the bottom of its stairs, he could feel the *Marshall* levelling out. When the creaking from the increased pressure ended, the vibrations from its power plant and propulsion system increased as it jumped back to its cruise speed.

"What's the news from Purgatory?" Carver asked the two men in the tactical room.

"Excuse please, Purgatory? I thought we contacted Diego Garcia?" said Arlan Dupuis, confused.

"We did," said Allard. "Purgatory is a name we sometimes use for Garcia. Especially those of us who want to get off it. We have an interesting report about the Russians. Yak-38 Forgers from the carrier *Baku* stopped the harassment of the evacuation ships. They intercepted the Libyan bombers that were making low passes against them. The ships also report a Russian helicopter flew into Mahé, and our embassy says Russian officials will be meeting soon with the Seychelles government."

"This could be trouble," Carver replied, looking through the tear sheets Allard handed him. "I said these guys could complicate the situation. They may yet do so."

"What do you mean?" Dupuis questioned. "So far, the Russians have been helpful. If not gallant."

"There's a billion dollar spy satellite in that shuttle's payload bay. It's far in advance of anything they have in space, or even on the drawing board. I know I'd sure love to have it. And there's a more basic way the Russians can cause trouble. They can detect submarines, whereas the Seychelles People's Defense Forces cannot."

"Another reason why we wanted your boat along," said Allard. "If we had to deal with hostile surface forces, two subs would confuse them."

"If necessary, Jacoubet could run interference for us," said Carver, whose mood suddenly grew darker. "I just thought of another way the Russians can create trouble. They know the disposition of all Allied forces in the Indian Ocean. They know about the *Marshall,* and could tell the Libyans and the rest about us. Perhaps even show them satellite photos of Diego Garcia, and that we're not at anchor."

"Terry, the Russians aren't the only ones who can spill the beans about us. Anyone who has copies of last year's *Proceedings* will know we were banished to Garcia. So far, we've been lucky."

"I suppose we should feel lucky that some reporter or network anchor isn't blowing our cover on nationwide TV half a world away. I guess the Soviets aren't the only ones who could ruin it for us . . . but they are the only ones who could hunt us down and destroy our secrecy. We need that to operate at all. Let me see the rest of Garcia's report, including the *Eisenhower*'s last position and when it expects to arrive off the islands."

"We helped build this," Samarefsky commented, as he and the Russian naval team were escorted into Revolution House by way of a side entrance. "Us and the East Germans. When there was an East Germany."

"Yes, I recognize socialist architecture when I see it," said Khomenko, slowing his stride just enough for a long glance at the building's exterior. "Bleak modernism thoughtlessly placed in the center of an historic old city. Completely out of style with the rest of its architecture. There can be no doubt we helped them put this here."

"Admiral, please. Your mood must be lighter if we're to succeed."

Once inside Revolution House, the Russian delegation was led to a meeting room on its second floor. To Samarefsky the destination was a familiar one, and he was actually ahead of the Foreign Ministry escorts when they walked through the room's double-door entrance.

"My old friends," he began, going first to Felix Boigny. Then he worked his way down the line of familiar faces at the room's table. "I'm glad you could all arrange to meet us. Admiral, this is Foreign Minister Boigny, Security Minister Sampras and Defense Minister N'tow. These are the Cuban and Libyan ambassadors. This is Major Yashin, senior Libyan military advisor. And Gonzala Torres, the ranking Cuban intelligence advisor. Gentlemen, this is Admiral Oleg Khomenko, Commander of the Russian Indian Ocean Fleet, and his staff."

"Comrades. I am pleased to meet you," said Khomenko, after going down the row of men and shaking their hands as they were introduced to him. "It's always a pleasure to meet with my revolutionary brothers."

"Indeed. Perhaps, Admiral, you would give us the pleasure of explaining why your intelligence ship helped the American shuttle land here and why your fighters are protecting the warships of the Western powers?" Boigny asked, with a diplomatically correct but cool tone to his voice.

"Yes, the *Navarin*." Khomenko turned and looked down the table to the Foreign Minister. He tried his best to keep the forced smile on his face. "Captain Raina may have overstepped his bounds, but he did so to help a crippled spacecraft make an emergency landing. International aviation accords require that every assistance be lent to an aircraft in distress."

"This was hardly an emergency landing, Admiral," said Sampras. "It was a calculated provocation to enforce the hegemony of imperialist space powers. Your ship's actions have nothing to do with international aviation law."

"Comrades, please. I don't see how you can make such a statement."

"International aviation accords only apply to *aircraft*, Boigny answered. "This shuttle does not have a certificate of airworthiness from the U.S. Federal Aviation Agency. It is, therefore, not an aircraft and cannot hide behind international law."

"My old friend, I warned you before this is a grey area you're dealing in," said Samarefsky. "A *very* grey area. It is not clear-cut."

"Then let's talk about a more clear-cut incident," said Yashin, not concealing his anger toward the Russians.

"Your fighters interfered with our bombers performing a legitimate mission in the defense of the Seychelles."

"Legitimate? You people agreed to the evacuation those ships are going to perform," Colonel Burdin snapped out. "I didn't like having my men used in such a matter. But clearly we had no alternative. You were violating an agreement this country made with the Western powers. You don't change an agreement after it goes in effect."

"Colonel . . . Colonel! I will handle the negotiations," said Khomenko, glaring sternly at the air group commander. "Please forgive my subordinate's lack of discipline, Comrades. But in his foolishness he makes a valid point. You agreed to this evacuation with the British, French, and American embassies. International law forbids one party from changing such an agreement after it's in effect."

"Perhaps we should say the commander of those aircraft overstepped his bounds," said Boigny, smiling. "A familiar, phrase, Admiral? Tell me, why are you here? And why is your fleet here before the American fleet?"

"To uphold international law," Samarefsky answered, jumping in ahead of Khomenko. "There is a United Nations Astronaut Return Treaty. All nations must return whatever spaceship and crew that lands within its territory to the launch nation. I've told you of it before, my old friend. The treaty is internationally recognized."

"This treaty can only be enforced on its signatory members. When it was originally signed into law, the Seychelles was not an independent state. We were a colony of the British empire. You cannot force upon us a treaty signed by our colonial masters. I've told you this before, Comrade Samarefsky. Our laws were violated, and our sovereignty must be respected. We will not be dictated to in our own country."

"The Soviet Union is not dictating to you. We merely

wish you recognize what all the other nations agreed to. You do it in so many other areas, why not here?"

"Because we recognize this crisis as a fight between the oppressed nations of the world and its space powers," Sampras responded, clearly enjoying the chance to put the Russians on the defensive. "Which side is the Soviet Union on? The side of space imperialism? Are you here because this spaceship rescued some of your cosmonauts? Do you wish to repay the favor? Do you still want the world to think you're a superpower?"

"We are here in an effort to be, what you could call, an honest broker," said Khomenko, trying to sound diplomatic while suppressing his anger. "Moscow wishes to have friendly relations with all countries. Not merely the other space powers."

"I doubt you would be here, Admiral, with your fleet if it were one of us who had this trouble. One of your 'revolutionary brothers.' You've betrayed the world's oppressed nations, for whom you were once their champion. You've betrayed socialism. You've betrayed your own revolution, just like the Americans did."

"I see you've been a good student of your Cuban teachers," Khomenko glanced down the table to Torres. He was surprised by the cold, fiery glare he got back; for a moment he was even intimidated by it.

"What are you here for, Admiral?" Torres asked, an icy bite to his question. "To prove what willing lackeys you are for the Americans?"

"To ensure there will be a peaceful resolution to this crisis. That is all we're after. You are holding an American spacecraft and an American crew, if you do not quickly agree to release them the Americans have the right to end it militarily. And don't think we can stop them."

"To help your revolutionary brothers? We never thought you would. If the Americans even attempt to

210

recapture their precious shuttle, we'll destroy it and kill the crew."

"You do that and the Americans will destroy this island," said Khomenko, showing his anger in spite of the intimidating stare. "And unlike Iraq, they won't need a hundred thousand sorties to do it in. They can accomplish it with as little as a hundred. And what do you care, Mr. Torres, this isn't *your* island."

"Admiral . . . Admiral, please," Samarefsky requested, laying a hand on Khomenko's arm. "You're doing what you admonished your officer about. My old friend, your country's action is jeopardizing normal space operations and space exploration. All complaints your country and other Third World countries have about space operations can be brought up at the U.N., after you have released the *Phoenix* and the astronauts."

"Mr. Ambassador, I have checked the U.N.'s record with regard to *all* space treaties," said Boigny. "Not just the one you keep mentioning. Those brought to the Security Council by so-called Third World countries have been rejected. Your country and the other space powers aren't interested in space exploration but space *exploitation*. Tell Moscow if they want the American astronauts and shuttle released, the matter of space exploitation must first be resolved. We will not be dictated to in our own country. And the oppressed nations of the earth will not be dictated to about the use of space by those who think they own it. Good day, Ambassador. Admiral . . ."

Samarefsky opened his mouth to try another defense, but when he saw the look on the Foreign Minister's face, and those of the other men seated at the table, he knew it would be in vain. He turned to Khomenko and his staff, then motioned to the doors at the room's opposite end.

"Come along, Admiral. We've done all we can," he said finally, before glancing at the table one last time.

211

"My old friend, I hope you understand well the path you're taking your nation on."

The Russians filed out of the meeting room without saying another word. They were escorted down the same stairwell and out the same side entrance as before. Fortunately, they did not have to encounter any of the reporters who gathered in Revolution House's main hall. In fact none of them spoke until they were back inside their limousines and returning to the airport.

"We should've expected to hear what we heard," Samarefsky dourly observed. "After all, we taught them that ideology."

"Out of date. Just like the architecture we gave them," said Khomenko, equally sullen. "We've failed. No, we did worse than fail. We've been pushed into the same corner as the Americans. For better or worse, our lot is with them."

"At least we are being recognized for the one area, apart from military strength, that makes us a superpower." For the first time in nearly twenty minutes, Samarefsky's mood lightened a little and he began to laugh. "If only it were not so negatively."

"Yes. . . . Space Hegemony. Space Imperialism. And now, Space Exploitation. They're the old words we and the Americans once accused each other of. Only now 'space' has been added to them, and it puts us together. We tried to uncage their *Phoenix*. Now the best we can hope for is to convince the Americans we have nothing to do with this crisis's outcome."

Eleven

Evacuation
Changing the Deal

"Sorry, Colonel. But we feel you must still wear this for breathing," said Parker. "We think there's still a residue of dangerous fuel inside the ship."

First he opened the flow valve to the air tank Mashari was wearing on his back, then helped him strap the diverlike mask over his face. When he had finished with Mashari, Parker moved down the row of Libyan officers, checking to make sure each had properly donned their breathing systems. When he was satisfied, he took his group up the boarding stairs to the *Phoenix*.

"It's much smaller than I thought," Mashari commented, stepping onto the mid deck, and nearly colliding with the galley cabinet beside the hatch. "And it's very cramped. This is a spaceship? It's not much better than our Tupolevs."

"I had the same question myself," said Parker, his smile broad enough to be seen through his face mask. "But the Americans say it's different when you are weightless."

"This level is used for equipment storage, sleeping and hygiene," said one of the other Libyan Air Force officers, glancing in at the zero-gravity toilet. "Where's the cockpit and how do we get to it?"

"The ladder beside you. Here, I'll go first."

Grabbing the sides of the access ladder, Parker hoisted himself up on its lower rungs. He climbed rapidly to the flight deck, only slowing when he got to the roof hatch and had to squeeze both himself and his air tank through it. Mashari followed him and, once on the flight deck, immediately slipped into the pilot's seat.

"Beautiful. Beautiful," Mashari repeated, running his hands over the panels of switches and controls surrounding the seat. "The Americans know how to build magnificent toys. By comparison the cockpit of my Tupolev looks primitive."

"It drips with the arrogance of American technology," said Parker, standing between the pilot and commander's seats. "But, it is ours. And soon we'll learn its secrets."

"Wait, what's going on here?" Mashari finally clicked some switches he felt comfortable in operating, and was puzzled when nothing responded. Not even the cockpit lights came on. "Why will nothing activate?"

"Because the Americans did something to drain the power. We can't operate anything. We can't even open the cargo bay roof doors."

"We can handle this," said Mashari, turning carefully and sliding out of his seat. "Captain Walid. Captain Halim. Bring one of our ground crews here and an auxiliary power cart. The astronauts may have drained the internal power, but we can hook up an external power source. There are two auxiliary power umbilical panels at the tail of this spaceship."

"But, Colonel. What about the evacuation?" asked one of the Libyan officers standing at the aft crew station. "Shouldn't we prepare for it?"

"We already made our stand on that, and failed. At this stage Major Parker's government can handle it better than us. It's not our concern now. Learning the se-

214

crets of our prize and the satellite in it are. After we've finished touring it we'll go to work."

"Joel, are signs attached to all the vehicles?" Fernandez requested, turning when he heard someone coming up behind him.

"Yes, and most also have U.S. flags," said Lomberg. "I don't see why we had to mark them. They already had NASA written on their sides."

"In nice, discreet, little letters. Not identifiable at any range. This way, there will be no doubt."

Fernandez looked past Lomberg to his station's parking lot. Crowded to one side of it was a motley collection of private cars owned by his staff. On the other was a neat line of blue and white vans and four-wheel-drive trucks. Squares of cardboard with "NASA" crudely painted on them either adorned their sides or were taped to their windows. For a few vehicles the available American flags had been attached to their radio antennas.

"We've all had enough problems with the People's Security Force roadblocks in the last few days," said Fernandez, turning again to face the crowd milling before him. "If our evacuation is going to go smooth we can't have any more. People, can I have your attention! We'll be moving out soon to our evac point. All assigned drivers know our route to the Victoria Docks, just in case we get separated. Those of you who are staying will have to live here at the station. Surveillance and confrontations with the PSF and PDF have made your homes and apartments too unsafe for you to use them. You'll be safer here, and our families will be safe once we get them out there."

Fernandez pointed beyond the tracking station's satellite dishes, transmission towers, and the western wing

215

of its administration building to the three grey slabs of steel waiting outside of Victoria harbor. Though they had been in view for less than an hour, all three warships were already lowering their service boats into the water. And on the sterns of two of them could be seen helicopters being prepared for flight. Circling above them was a flight of Yak-38s, occasionally passing close enough to Mahé to be heard.

"There they are again. Those are fighters, damn it," said Post, responding to the sudden, sharp roar of jet engines which quickly fell to a dull rumble. "I'd know that sound anywhere."

Abandoning his lunch, Post ran to one of the room's tiny windows and twisted his head to see what he could of the sky. His silverware was still clattering after the engine noise had died to a level that indicated the aircraft had long since passed out of view.

"We all know that sound," Reynolds answered, looking up from his plate of fried bananas and fish. "The last thing I may have flown for the Air Force were B-1s, but I know what a jet fighter sounds like. Even four of them."

"I have a twelve-year-old nephew who acts that way whenever a plane flies over his house," Julie added. "It's irritating when he does it. When are you going to grow up?"

"Yeah, Walt. I was twenty when I stopped it," said Glassner, swallowing his mouthful of food. "When are you going to stop?"

"When I find out what those jets are," said Post. "Something's going on, boss. And it probably has to do with us."

He was still returning to the table when a sharp banging stopped Post in his tracks and everyone else from eating. He had just turned to the room's one entrance

216

when the door flew open and a familiar figure stepped inside.

"Well, if it isn't Bug Man," said Reynolds, pushing away his lunch. "The one guy who can kill an appetite. What's on for today? More history according to Fidel?"

"Today, you can *watch* history being made," Torres informed him, stepping far enough into the room to allow the guards behind him the space to wheel in the television set from the previous morning. "Your fleet and your lackeys will be humiliated in front of the world."

"What the hell's going on?" said Post. "What are you doing to *my* Navy and our shuttle?"

"Your shuttle? That spacecraft is now the property of the world's oppressed people. The sooner you accept that reality, the better it will be for you. As for your Navy, Mr. Post, have a look."

Torres motioned to the set, which had its rabbit ears up and a burst of static rattled its speaker. Moments later its picture tube brightened and its image fluttered until stabilizing. The view was a telephoto shot of the three warships outside of Victoria Bay. While the astronauts had difficulty identifying the two end ships, Post labelled the one in the center as an *Oliver Hazard Perry*-class frigate.

"*Alacrity*. Ahoy, *Alacrity*. This is *Simpson*," said Stine, moving around the Combat Information Center of his ship. "We're ready to launch our helos. What is your status? Over."

"*Simpson,* this is *Alacrity*. Our Lynx is armed and is being launched," replied a voice with a heavy Scottish accent. "Once airborne she will rendezvous with your machines. Are you lowering your boats? Over."

"Roger, our boats are away. They'll be joining up with yours and the *Aconit's*. *Simpson,* out. CIC to Air

Traffic Control, launch Marge."

"Roger, Control. We're ready," said Marron, placing his feet on his rudder pedals, and taking hold of his collective stick. "Unlocking RAST hook."

Marron glanced at the phone booth-shaped Air Traffic Control station between the frigate's two hangars. When he got his final waveoff from the director inside it, he increased power to lift his Seahawk from the landing pad. It floated away from the *Simpson* on a cushion of rotorwash that roiled the surface of the calm waters outside Victoria Bay. Before it had started to gain altitude, the frigate's second SH-60 was being hauled out of its hangar by the Recovery, Assistance, Securing, and Traversing (RAST) system and positioned on the pad's center spot.

Forming up in front of the warship was a miniature flotilla of their service boats and captain's skiffs. Each had at least one seaman operating it, with a Royal Navy lieutenant in command of the formation. From the *Alacrity* a dark grey Lynx helicopter clattered into the air and climbed to join the lighter grey Seahawk.

"We're getting our first wingman," said Marron, watching the British machine climb onto his starboard side. "Carl, open the hatch and deploy the gun."

The Seahawk's black crew chief, the only other personnel on board beyond the pilots, unstrapped himself from the last remaining seat in the main cabin and went to the starboard hatch. What had been a muted thumping became a deafening roar the moment the hatch was pushed forward. It forced the crew to switch over to their intercom system to continue talking.

"Machine gun deployed, Lieutenant," Carl reported, unlocking the M60 from its stowed position, and swinging it until its barrel pointed out the side. "Do I

218

arm it?"

"Not until we run into trouble," said Marron. "And so far these clowns seem to be keeping their distance."

Visible from the SH-60's cockpit were a pair of Seychelles Air Force SF.260 trainers, orbiting over the mountains behind Victoria. Closer to the warships, the flight of Yak-38s orbited, now banking steeply as they passed the airport, where the Kamov helicopter was just lifting off.

Crammed with people and luggage, the NASA four-wheel drives and vans made their way down the winding La Misére Road from the tracking station. Once they descended from the mountains, they would connect with the coast road that ran from Seychelles International to Victoria. The route had the fewest stops and the shortest distance to the evacuation point at the docks.

"What the hell? This wasn't here when I drove up," said Fernandez, the instant a roadblock appeared in front of them. "Hit the brakes. And start contacting the embassy evac team when I hop out."

Tires screeched softly on the convoy's lead truck as it slowed to a stop. The vehicles behind it did likewise, and were still screeching and groaning when Fernandez opened the passenger door to disembark. Less than twenty feet separated his truck from the roadblock's sawhorse barricades. He was met at the halfway point by an Asian-looking man wearing the uniform of a People's Security Force captain.

"This road is closed," he announced. "You'll have to go back to your tracking station."

"Why isn't this a surprise to me?" said Fernandez, mostly to himself. Then he met the captain's gaze. "Look, we told your government the route we would

219

take to the evacuation point and they approved it."

"Independence House has issued us new orders. This section of the road is closed to all but military traffic."

"Independence House? I thought that was the tourist trap and Revolution House was the real power."

"It should make no difference to you . . . Mr. Station Director," said the captain, an angry glare in his eyes. "Either you turn around or you'll face arrest."

To emphasize his point the captain motioned forward, and the BRDM armored cars flanking the road swung their gun turrets on Fernandez and his convoy. Above the rumble of their engines, Fernandez thought he heard the click of bolts being pulled back on their machine guns.

"All right. We'll deal with this in another way," he said nervously. "Tell Revolution House you haven't stopped us. Only delayed us. George, let's turn 'em around! It's back to the fort!"

"Bob, it's the embassy evac team," said Lieutenant Stover at the CIC's communications console. "They have a problem."

"I suppose the tourists don't like the room service on our boats," Stine responded absently, before switching his headset to the channel being used by the embassy. "Evac Team, this is the Captain. What's your status? Over."

"We just got word from the NASA convoy. They've been turned back at a roadblock. Can your helicopters evacuate them from the tracking station? Over."

"It will take time, but they can do it. Our second helo is ready to launch, and we'll ask the Brits if we can borrow theirs. Have our boats arrived? Over."

"Roger, *Simpson*. They are dock side. The station will contact you when the convoy returns. Over."

"We'll be waiting for them. *Simpson,* out," said Stine, then he switched his headset back to the ship's intercom. "CIC to Air Traffic Control, get Lisa in the air now. Communications, activate the satellite antennas. Diego Garcia's going to know about this. And so is Washington."

"Yes, Joel. They'll be back in a couple of minutes," Savage advised, holding a CB radio handset to his ear. "The Navy will help you with the convoy. Contact 'em on something more secure. Evac Team, out."

"Hank! Hank, we got trouble," said another embassy staffer, weaving through the groups of tourists lining the dock. "You better come with me."

"It never rains but it pours . . . what now?"

"At our impromptu press conference, Joyce decided to show off that meteor. Then Lazare Sampras appeared. And the rest, you better see for yourself."

In place of the souvenir vendors and tour guides who normally worked the dock, a crowd of American, Australian, and other foreign tourists now filled it. Divided into squad-sized units of a dozen, two could fit in the open service boats pulling alongside the dock, while one could go aboard most of the captain's skiffs. Savage weaved among the groups, following the staffer to the base of the dock, where he could see a sizeable knot of local and foreign correspondents being broken up by Lazare Sampras and his men.

"This conference is over, people!" Sampras instructed, waving his hands and raising his voice to be heard above the crowd. "No more questions here! The Minister of Information is holding a news conference. Over at the Tourism Office!"

"Well, Lazare. I thought you were meeting with the Russians," said Savage, finally getting close enough to

221

see him. "Or as you call them, 'our new lackeys.' "

"How did you know I was meeting them?" Sampras spun around and confronted the security officer, flashing him a smile as he recognized an old adversary. "Who told you? Which informant?"

"You did. I said I *thought* you were with them. You just confirmed it for me."

"Clever, Mr. Savage. But your wit will be of no use to you now."

"Hank! Hank, he took the meteor from me," said a woman in her thirties, clearly distraught and pointing an accusing finger at Sampras. "His men bumped me when I showed it to the press. And then he picked it up."

"You stumbled, Mrs. Richmond," Sampras corrected. "You must be more careful on these wharves, the footing can be unstable."

"Damn right more careful," said Savage. "What the hell possessed you to take it out of the pouch?"

"The Cuban reporters said we staged the emergency landing," Joyce answered. "They said there was no proof of the meteor strike. I thought showing the meteor remains would prove our case. That's when they bumped me."

"You let them sucker you, Joyce. You should've been smarter. Whatever the reason, the meteor is United States property. Hand it back, Lazare."

"Mr. Savage, you should know well the laws concerning diplomatic pouches. Anything removed from one loses its diplomatic protection," said Sampras, taking out of his pant's pocket a clear plastic box with a marble-sized chunk of metal in it. "This is now property of the Seychelles People."

"And what do 'the people' plan on doing with it?" Savage asked.

Sampras held it up high enough for the diplomatic personnel to see it, and shook the box to make what was inside it rattle. Then he stepped back from the personnel and turned, giving him enough room to launch it on a high, arcing flight into Victoria Bay. It landed with scarcely a splash some fifty yards from the shore.

"That is the will of the People," said Sampras, smiling triumphantly. "Prove your meteor story now, Mr. Savage. Enjoy the rest of your evacuation."

"Admiral, the flight leader wants to know if he's to accompany us back to the carrier," said Burdin, stepping down from the Kamov's flight deck.

"No. They're to remain over the international force," Khomenko responded, his expression brightening a little at the question. "It's the least we can do for our 'Space Power' allies. Tell the fighters they will be replaced in an hour, after we land on the *Baku*. Have you heard from her yet?"

"Yes, they're holding at two hundred kilometers northeast of the islands. They also report the *Eisenhower*'s battle fleet is still a thousand kilometers to the north. Though once they get within five hundred they could launch their aircraft."

"Add yet another dangerous element to this crisis," commented another officer in the helicopter's main cabin.

"If any nation's warships have the right to be off these islands it's the Americans," said Khomenko. "I fear our old 'comrades' will play their same old tricks and provoke the Americans. We'll lose still one more chance to be peacemaker."

"What will you do next, Admiral?" said a third.

"I'll confer with Moscow, then tomorrow I'll go to the American carrier and talk with my opposite number. Colonel, have a helicopter prepared for long-range flight."

After clearing the airport's traffic pattern, the Ka-27

set a northeast course and climbed to five thousand feet. Behind its twin tail fins was Victoria Bay, with the three warships suspended in water so clear their shadows could be seen on the seabed. High above them the Forgers continued to circle while the Allied helicopters appeared to fly inland.

"All right, here they come," said Lomberg. "Open them up."

The chain link gates swung away from the main entrance within seconds of the convoy's return to the tracking station. They were still folding back when the first vehicles drove into the parking lot. Moments after the lead truck stopped, Fernandez was climbing out of its cab.

"Ray, I got the Navy on a secure channel," Lomberg added. "The Evac Team's been talking to them about flying our people out by chopper. What do you think?"

"Clear these cars off the parking lot," said Fernandez, after taking a moment to scan the area. "Convoy vehicles, too. Park them around the satellite dishes, anywhere else there's room. We have to give the Navy the largest unobstructed landing pad we can."

"Shouldn't we wait and discuss it with the rest of our people?"

"Joel, this isn't the time for a management meeting. It's time for orders. Now clear the lot. I'll go to the Ops Center and talk with the Navy."

"All right, we'll do it," said Lomberg. "And when you talk to the Navy, the ship's captain is Bob Stine."

"Marge, this is Lisa. We are airborne," advised the second SH-60's pilot. Swinging his aircraft away from the *Simpson*'s fantail.

"Roger, Lisa. We're heading inland," said Marron.

"Join us over the NASA station. The Brit helo is heading over Victoria on a decoy mission. Over."

"We have you in sight, we'll be with you in a few minutes. Marge, my ESM is detecting Gun Dish triple-A radar emissions."

"Roger, Lisa. We have it as well. It's the ZSU antiaircraft tank at the airport. So long as we stay clear of that area he won't bother us. Over."

After clearing the *Simpson,* the Seahawk rose over the *Aconit* as it turned to the southeast. It headed away from Victoria, which the Lynx was already circling, and flew into the mountains overlooking Seychelles International, toward a prominent cluster of buildings, radio towers, and satellite dishes.

"Christ, they're talking like it's some sort of damned invasion," Foreman said quietly. "Lieutenant, I think there's going to be trouble."

He gave Hassler one pair of the surveillance set's headphones and plugged it in. On the set's TV screen was a live shot from a vehicle in a People's Defense Force convoy. Ahead of it was a BRDM-2 armored car and a flatbed truck crowded with troops. Farther down the road that the convoy was travelling upon could be seen the rim of a satellite dish poking above the foliage.

"They're talking the way the North Koreans did in the 'fifties," Hassler observed, after listening to the broadcast for nearly a minute. "Or the Cubans in the 'sixties. Or the North Koreans in the 'seventies . . ."

"We get the point, Gordo," said Hall, relaxing a little from his watch on the ridge's clearing. "What are we going to do about it?"

"Hope our ships are watching Seychelles TV. Apart from that we can't do anything. Just watch, record what we see, and report it when contacted."

"They've cleared the parking lot for us," said Marron, glancing down through his cockpit side window. "And they're lining up the people to be evacuated."

"We also got an Army convoy moving along the road," the copilot warned, looking out the port side windows. "We better start our taxi service before they arrive."

"Right. Lisa, this is Marge. Begin your descent immediately. The station's cleared the parking lot for us. Take no more than ten people with their luggage. We'll ride shotgun for you. Over."

Looking forward, Marron caught sight of his ship's other Seahawk. As it slowed and began to descend, he swung his machine around it and took up a position on its starboard side, allowing his crew chief to watch the convoy with the door gun. For a time both helicopters descended, until Marron saw his rotorwash swaying the higher treetops. Then he stopped, hovering his aircraft, while letting the second SH-60 continue.

The omnipresent buzzing of the first helicopter initially masked the arrival of the second. Until the people gathering for evacuation looked behind them and noticed two of the ghost-grey dragonflies dropping toward the station. One pulled into a hover just as it was disappearing behind a satellite dish. The other sank from view completely. Only to reappear seconds later, its irritating buzz growing to an angry roar, its rotor blades slapping the air and churning up a sheet of dust and sand that preceded it across the parking lot. The squat, sleekly contoured machine gingerly bumped its main wheels on the lot's asphalt surface before touching down.

"Start moving! Avoid the tail rotor!" Fernandez shouted. "Keep to the right! Do what they tell you!"

Moving alongside a single-file column of women and children, Fernandez walked out to the helicopter, keeping his head down until he was next to its cockpit. While the evacuees were hurried inside the main cabin, he managed a brief conversation with the pilot.

"There's a convoy driving up to your gate! Just thought you should know!" the lieutenant shouted, then he turned his head and leaned an ear into Fernandez.

"We do!" he answered. "Think they'll interfere?"

"They better not! How many people do you have?"

"About a hundred!"

"That may take us a dozen trips! But we got enough fuel and helos!" said the lieutenant, before he was tapped on his shoulder by the crew chief. "Stand away! We got our first load!"

Fernandez waved at the column to stop and ushered them back to the grass field beside the parking lot. The Seahawk was moving before its side hatch had rolled shut. It waddled forward, then lifted its tail as it rose off the ground. The SH-60 quickly assumed the typical, nose-down attitude of a departing helicopter. As its roar diminished to a buzz, Fernandez noticed he could hear bursts of a strange, mechanical chattering. They seemed out of place, until he caught sight of the tracers arcing over his head.

"They're shooting at him!" Marron blurted out. "Carl, return fire! Howard, call the ship. We got us a shooting war! Lisa, you're being fired on!"

The departing Seahawk reacted immediately, breaking to the left and diving down the mountain's slope once it cleared the treetops. All the fire it received came from the BRDM-2 at the head of the convoy. Its saucer-shaped turret fired both heavy and light machine guns

227

at the helicopter, only stopping when hits sparkled all over its angular body.

"That's it, Carl! Keep it up!" Marron added, banging the cyclic control stick to one side as he increased power on his collective stick. "Keep it up! Hose down any other vehicle that fires at us!"

Breaking out of its hover and increasing its forward speed, the lead Seahawk banked sharply to the right. Unlike the armored car's gunner, whose aim was spoiled by the foliage overgrowing the road, all Carl had to do was aim his M60 out the hatch and squeeze the trigger.

He fired long bursts at the BRDM, concentrating on it even though he could see troops jumping out of the trucks behind it. He continued to fire as the SH-60 swept down the convoy, only stopping when he saw his tracers curving erratically. His bursts had been too long; they had partially melted and deformed the machine gun's barrel.

"You people are fucking crazy!" said Reynolds, turning away from the TV while his crew was transfixed by what they saw. "You're firing on a helicopter loaded with civilians."

"Commander, I see an American warplane that made an illegal landing in this country and is now escaping," Torres replied, a cold fire showing in his eyes. "Did you see civilians climbing on board it? I didn't."

"No, the trees hid it. But that's —"

"Commander, please." Torres cut off Reynolds with laughter as cold as the look in his eyes. "Whatever you claim is there doesn't matter, for it is illegal to land. The oppressed nations, the Third World, will see it as an invasion. And that's exactly what we'll tell them."

"If you and your buddies keep this up, the U.S. will

228

respond militarily," said Reynolds. "I'll let Post tell you, our ships have enough firepower to blow that convoy off the road."

"Don't bother, Mr. Reynolds," said Torres, still laughing. "We know how long it takes for your country to respond militarily. And we're not going to wait here for months."

"Bob, it's Diego Garcia. Admiral Nicolson himself," Stover warned. "He's on the secure channel."

"I hope he's got good news," said Stine, working the controls for his headset. "Yes, Admiral. What do you have for us? Over."

"I just got the word from CEN COM," said Nicolson, his voice sounding strangely altered by the electronic scrambling and descrambling. "If Seychelles Forces threaten your aircraft again, you may open fire on the convoy with warning shots first. If the threat doesn't end, you have permission to destroy it. What have you heard from the other ships? Over."

"*Alacrity* already has Admiralty permission to lend fire support. *Aconit* is still trying to get Paris's permission. We're just getting our first boat loads of evacuees. Over."

"Go with what you have, Lieutenant. Keep me informed. Garcia, out."

"Roger, Admiral. *Simpson,* out," Stine replied, then he changed his headset back to the ship's intercom. "Weapons Control, activate three-inch gun. Load with laser-guided GP shells. Walt, contact Marge. Tell them to break out their designator. Hey, where did Stony go?"

"Stony? Oh yes, the Brit. He left when he heard Air Traffic Control ask for more help with the evacuees."

"Air Traffic Control, this is Lisa. We're on final. We're lowering our haul down line."

When the Seahawk was within a thousand feet of the frigate's stern, it dropped a steel cable from its underside. Part of the RAST rapid haul down system, it allowed for a faster landing, secured the helicopter to the pad and would even help move it into a hangar.

This time all it had to do was land; once it was over the pad, the deck crew quickly attached the cable to the system. When the pilots signalled they were ready, the powerful winches started pulling the SH-60 down. The speed it was recovered at was controlled by the RAST's computers, which measured the ship's movements and compensated for them. Today, with calm seas and the ship itself virtually hovering, it only took minutes for the first load of evacuees to be delivered.

"Sorry, Lieutenant. I think I overheated the barrel," said Carl, finishing his examination of the M60. "This never happened to Rambo."

"I know, he has a Hollywood machine gun," said Marron. "It never jams or runs out of ammo. Forget it, we have another job. Unpack the designator. We're going to do a little artillery spotting."

Abandoning the hatch position, the crew chief moved forward and opened a case under the pilot's seat. Inside it was a laser range marking and target designator. The size and shape of a large, stylized target pistol, it had a sniper's scope for sighting and a power umbilical ran from an end plate where its hammer would have been located.

Hooking the umbilical to a power distribution panel in the main cabin, Carl tested the designator before returning to the hatch. He reattached his safety line and watched as Marron realigned the Seahawk until he was looking down at the convoy, which had since reached the tracking station's main gates.

"Goddamn it, if they want a war let's give 'em one," said Belford, raising his voice above a whisper for the first time in half a day. "Let's find something and shoot it up!"

"There's another patrol boat out there," said Hassler, pointing to the open ocean on Conception's southern shore. "Why don't you fire at it? Or better yet, just keep shouting and they'll hear us."

"Yeah, man. Hold it down," Hall whispered. "We're supposed to see and listen. Not be seen and get captured."

"But they shot at one of our helos," said Belford, lowering his voice. "They're trying to kill Americans."

"If they were trying to kill the President we couldn't do anything but sit and watch," said Hassler. "Those are our orders. I'd like to do something, too. But we'll all get our chance later to kill. Ty, go up and relieve Patterson. Nick, you got anything new?"

"That convoy's now at the station's main gate," Foreman answered, temporarily pulling the headphones out of his ears. "I think there's going to be trouble."

"I am Major James le Blanc!" announced the light-skinned black, standing in the open hatch ahead of the BRDM's turret. "Seychelles People's Defense Forces! I order you to stop your illegal operations and allow us in!"

"Illegal operations?" said Fernandez, puzzled and growing angry. "I think the pot has just called the kettle black. Joel, have you found the megaphone?"

231

"Are you sure you should do this?" Lomberg replied, rooting through the glove compartment of a NASA van.

"The worse they can do is shoot me. I doubt they'll want to do that on live TV."

Finally, a compact speaker/amplifier handset popped out of an overstuffed glove compartment and fell into Lomberg's hands. The moment he turned it over, Fernandez was heading across the cleared parking lot to his station's main gates, where only a length of heavy chain and a padlock were effectively stopping the BRDM-2 and the trucks behind it from entering the grounds.

"I am Major James le Blanc," said le Blanc, pressing the switch on his hand mike again. "Open your gates and let my patrol inside!"

"All right, we heard you the first time," Fernandez answered, hitting the trigger switch on the megaphone. "Your roadblock prevented us from reaching the evacuation point. We had no choice but to call in the choppers."

"If any more of your helicopters attempt illegal landings, we will shoot them down."

"I'll let the Navy know that. Our evacuation is peaceful. But if you threaten it, we will respond with force."

"We've already survived one of your attacks," said le Blanc. "If another happens, we'll have no choice but to invade your station!"

"Dean, Lisa's inbound," the copilot warned when he caught sight of a grey silhouette climbing over the mountains.

"Good. Let's see if the Brits are still with us," said Marron, glancing at the rearview mirror attached to the canopy frame. In it he saw the *Alacrity*'s dark grey

Lynx still hovering behind him. "CIC, this is Marge. Lisa's getting in position to make her second landing. The Brits are still with us. What are your orders? Over."

"Marge, this is the TAO. Has the convoy changed its position?" Stover asked.

"No, the BRDM is still facing the main gate and the rest of the convoy is backed down the road behind it. Over."

"Good, we want you to straddle the armored car. Aim your designator for its right side, then its left. Make sure you give the car at least a fifty-foot berth. Over."

"Roger, CIC, will do. Marge, out," said Marron. "Carl, did you hear that?"

"I got it, but I don't like it," he replied. "Even at this distance I could lase a shell down one of her hatches."

"I know, but for now we have to be nice guys. Get ready, Carl. Here comes Lisa."

Several hundred feet below the first Seahawk, the second initiated a gentle descent toward the station's parking lot. In minutes it would be touching down; while hovering out of small arms' range, its sistership and the Lynx were designating targets for their frigate's guns.

"Lieutenant, the Mark Ninety-two is in gun-laying mode," reported the seaman at the weapons control panel. "The ready magazine is loaded with laser-guided GP shells and the computer has plotted the trajectories. We're ready to shoot."

"Fire number one shell," said Stover, after getting a nod from Stine. "Now, now, now."

Located atop the frigate's superstructure, and behind its latticework masts, the compact gun turret raised its barrel and swung it to the left. The instant it finished moving, a three-inch shell was loaded into its breech. An instant later a spurt of flame and smoke erupted from the muzzle, and the entire ship briefly shook as the shell began its flight.

"She's opened fire!" shouted the copilot, watching a faint smoke ring rippling away from the *Simpson*'s port side.

"Well, it better get here in a hurry," said Marron. "I see muzzle flashes below."

"Everybody get down!" Fernandez ordered, when he noticed several heads poking above the overturned tables and around the vehicle sides. "You'll see it later on TV!"

The high-pitched whistle they all heard dropped several octaves as the first shell fell toward the earth. It impacted less than forty feet away from the BRDM idling at the front gates. The fountain of dirt covered it, and the shrapnel, unleashed by the shell, ricocheted off its armor plate. The dust had yet to settle when a second explosion went off on the other side of the armored car. Raining shrapnel not only on it but on the convoy vehicles strung down the road behind it.

On top of the second shell, a third one came whistling in. Its tone was much deeper; when it exploded on the opposite side of the road, its blast uprooted a Takamaka tree. The tall palm crashed across the road, creating its own obstacle. The *Alacrity* had joined the bombardment.

"Major, if you continue firing on our helicopters our ships will destroy your convoy!" said Fernandez, standing up and using the megaphone. "Can we continue our evacuation or not?"

"This imperialist aggression only serves us and deepens the crisis!" le Blanc answered, though he did not bother to show himself as he had before. "We will not be dictated to in our own country! However, in order to prevent the loss of life, we will allow your escape from revolutionary justice to continue!"

The rhythmic slapping of rotor blades drowned out whatever else was blared out on the armored car's speakers. The second Seahawk repeated its earlier descent and landed on the parking lot. Moments after its touchdown, it was approached by a line of evacuees with Fernandez at their head.

"Is that it?" said Belford, watching the tiny screen on the AT-90 Surveillance Set. "A couple of shells and it's over? Our ships could plaster that convoy."

"If that was their mission, yes," said Hassler. "But they came to evacuate civilians, not start a war. If it comes to it, that's what we're for. I hope I don't hear any more suntan and girl jokes from you. Our little crisis in paradise is *real*."

"You think this will make it more difficult to slip into Mahé?" asked Bruce Patterson, the third member of the sniper team.

"It probably will. We've seen how many patrol boats so far? Five? I hope they don't keep up that kind of schedule tonight. Nick, your people better start checking out the SAT COM gear. We're scheduled to contact the *Marshall* before we leave."

Twelve

New Tactics
Arrival

"NASA Nine-Zero-Five, this is Garcia Control. The runway is clear for your arrival. Winds remain light, out of the west and blowing at three knots. Visibility is unlimited. Over."

"Roger, Garcia Control. We have five green and here we come," said Cochran, occupying the copilot's seat. "We're turning for the final."

After circling the island for nearly half an hour, mostly waiting for the C-5B to land and taxi off the runway, the Boeing giant was finally able to swing in toward the footprint-shaped atoll. Crossing its southern rim, the 747 flew over Eclipse Bay, tracking straight for the three-mile ribbon of concrete extending into it. Riding at anchor in its waters were more than a dozen U.S. Navy ships. Uniquely, among the transports and supply ships no warships or submarines could be seen.

NASA's shuttle carrier touched down within the first one thousand feet of the runway's southeastern end. It completed its rollout a mile and a half later, and used the nearest taxiway to follow the Galaxy to the airfield's flight line. An incongruity among all the military aircraft, the 747 was the first civilian-registered plane to visit the island in months. And its passengers and crew were among the few civilians to be allowed on the remote base.

"Mr. Cochran, welcome to Diego Garcia," said Nicolson, extending his hand. "I'm Admiral Adam Nicolson. How was your flight in?"

"Restful after what went on at Yarmouth," Cochran answered, shaking hands. "I'm happy to be out here in the middle of nowhere. At least I'm not going to be chased around by reporters who want to play twenty questions."

"Were you able to talk with your Russian friends?" Nicolson pulled Cochran from the line of arriving NASA personnel and, leaving his subordinates to greet the rest, walked down the flight line with him. "I heard you have a lot of contacts in their space agency."

"Yes, my Glavkosmos friends were very informative. They said their efforts were only to help free the *Phoenix* and her crew. They're not after my Lady or the satellite she's carrying."

"That's pretty much what their spokesmen in Moscow have said. But a lot of us think the Russians wouldn't be above taking advantage of an opportunity. Especially if it's presented to them by an old friend, like Libya."

"I understand," said Cochran. "And some of my friends hinted at that. I was told not every Russian official was unhappy that they failed to change minds. Some would like to see the old ideology triumph. Or have us rush in and brutally destroy this little country to rescue our shuttle, and make us an even greater villain to the Third World."

"And after today's events we may have to,"

237

Nicolson said, soberly. "The Eighty-Second Airborne's alert battalion is leaving Fort Bragg. They'll be here in about thirty-six hours. By tomorrow morning the *Eisenhower*'s battle group will be off the Seychelles. And in eight hours the commando submarine *John Marshall* will arrive there with its SEALs."

"Commando sub? Wait a minute, I heard of the *Marshall*. Didn't it sink a Libyan sub in the North Sea last year? I'd completely forgotten about it."

"Apparently so has the rest of the world. And for the sake of their success, I hope everyone will continue forgetting about them."

"Terry, are we on our way again?" Allard requested, when he heard the stamp of shoes on the stairs behind him.

"Yes. We'll be off Mahé in another eight hours at our cruise speed," said Carver, stepping up to the TASCO Room's main console and finding all its seats occupied. "Well, how did the evacuation go after the three-shell bombardment?"

"There were no further incidents or delays after it. And the ships have since withdrawn to rendezvous with the USS *Comfort*."

"However, the bombardment will make the crisis worse," Arlan Dupuis warned, scrolling through the latest transmission's written text on one of the side screens. "It will be used against the West. It'll make us look like villains and gain sympathy for the Seychelles government."

"Are you kidding?" said Jaskula. "It was only three shells."

"I'm inclined to agree with our exchange officer," said Carver, glancing over Dupuis's shoulder at the screen. "And so does the thinking ashore. I see the

Eisenhower's group will be arriving not long after we do. I hope they can draw enough attention for us and the *Casablanca* to operate effectively."

"The Recon Squad reports they've seen the Tu-22s flying more sorties," Allard informed. "And the local forces have increased their air and naval patrols."

"Will that interfere with them landing on Mahé?"

"Gordo's delaying the squad's departure from Conception until after eleven. He feels he can't push it back any later or they'll be tramping around Mahé's forest in daylight. Apart from that, I sure hope not. Mike and I will go over the situation here, then take our findings back to the rest of the team."

"Good," said Carver. "Are you keeping them busy?"

"They're breaking out the anti-air and anti-armor weapons from storage. And Artie's checking through his explosives, I may have a little diversion for him."

"That wouldn't have anything to do with those messages you sent to the *Casablanca,* would it?" When Allard turned around, he caught the look in Carver's eyes. And the wide, knowing grin on his face. "You can't keep much from me, Glenn. Not on my Lady. Tell me about it later, after I'm back from dinner."

"*Simpson,* this is *Aconit.* Do you have an update on our rendezvous operation? Over," asked De Mozay, his voice coming over the bridge speakers beside the captain's chair.

"Affirmative," said Stine, shuffling through the tear sheets he had stuffed into the chair's side pocket. "We will link up with the *Belleau Wood* at zero-seven hundred hours tomorrow morning. We'll then use our helos and the Marine Hueys on the *Wood* to transfer our passengers to the hospital ship *Comfort*. How are your charges doing, Captain? Over."

As he asked his question, Stine involuntarily glanced out the bridge's starboard windows to catch sight of the French destroyer. In the post-sunset glow the warship was a dark silhouette, identified by the kettle-shaped radardome and its unique array of running lights. From the *Simpson*'s bridge, he could just barely discern the red glow on the *Aconit*'s.

"They are enjoying our food," said De Mozay. "Though they do complain of the crowding. It'll be a difficult night. Over."

"I quite agree," added Commander Aldiss. "We have so many guests we'll need to keep our Lynx secured to its pad. And they'll certainly draw down our food stores. Over."

"I know, we'll all get resupplied at Diego Garcia," said Stine, briefly glancing out his bridge's port windows at HMS *Alacrity*. "Sorry, Captain, I don't think you'll get any champagne."

"Not to worry. I understand," said De Mozay. "Will your helicopters try picking the guests off my ship tomorrow? Over."

"If it was difficult to get a Seahawk on your pad then I don't think we should try a Marine Huey. We'll have to transfer your passengers to either us or the *Alacrity* by breeches buoy. We'll have to do the same thing with the stragglers the *Navarin* picked up. Commander, are the Russians still with you? Over."

"Still tucked up on my port side," Aldiss replied. "And so long as we don't exceed twenty knots she'll stay there."

Unlike the three warships, which sailed only with their running lights on, the *Navarin* was ablaze with light. Except for the telltale satellite dishes, the intelligence gatherer looked like a brightly illuminated cruise ship chasing after a trio of ghosts. Their presence was better marked by the phosphorescent glow in their wakes than by the few lights they burned.

"God, will you look at that glow," said Belford, pointing out to sea. "What's causing it?"

"The patrol boat that went by twenty minutes ago," Hassler answered, not looking up from his work. "You've seen it before, Tom. A ship moves through the water and causes the bio-luminescent critters in it to light up."

"Yeah, but I never saw it last so long before. Think it could cause us trouble?"

"Our draft is measured in inches, not feet. Don't worry about it. You better worry about getting that rifle case in here. The rest of us are set to go."

Reinflated, and reequipped with its outboard motor, the zodiac was once again filled with the squad's equipment. While one manned its tiller, the other six members of the squad grabbed the raft sides and hauled it off the tiny beach on Conception's southern shoreline.

The moment it started to float the two SEALs at its back released the rope and cleaned up the beach as best they could. They swept away the footprints and the marks the raft left in the sand above the high tide debris line. When they got back in the water they tossed away the palm fronds they had used and were the last to climb inside the zodiac, whose motor was already puttering quietly.

"Dale, increase speed," said Hassler, turning to the SEAL manning the tiller. "Nick, get your surveillance set working. The rest of you, keep quiet unless you see something."

Puttering a little louder, the engine pushed the zodiac away from Conception's desolate, rock strewn shore. Several hundred yards out, it changed course from south to due east. Ahead of it lay Conception's sister island of Therese and Mahé's southeastern shore. Unlike its western shore and the beach north of Victoria, few lights burned along this side of the island. There were few beaches for tourists, and still fewer hotels and restaurants. Making it the perfect location for a commando landing.

"Pilot to crew, we're at cruise altitude," advised Tariq al-Rayes, watching his altimeter needle stop at the twelve-thousand-meter mark. "Lieutenant, what is our position?"

"We are just south of Bird and Denis Islands," said Lieutenant Riad Kalmendi, seated in the Tupolev's radar navigator/bombardier station. He was located in front of the cockpit and below it, where his only view of the outside was through tiny windows in the lower nose. He got a much better perspective from the radar scopes and navigation systems around him. "I'm no longer detecting the enemy warships or the Soviet fleet."

"Sergeant, can you still detect them on our electronic surveillance systems?"

"Yes, Major. I still have them," said Sergeant Badran, seated directly behind al-Rayes in the fuselage's dorsal spine. "I used them to calibrate our radar and infra-red systems."

"Good. Now start scanning for the American fleet," al-Rayes ordered. "You'll probably detect them before Riad does. They know where we are; now we have to find the Americans so they can't surprise us."

In place of the antishipping missiles it carried earlier in the day, the Tu-22's bomb bay now held extra fuel tanks to extend its range. Instead of challenging warships, it now had to search for them. And from its forty thousand foot altitude the needle-nosed giant would be able to sweep hundreds of square miles at a time for the approaching fleet.

Again the pounding felt like it was part of a dream. Reynolds turned over in his bunk to escape the noise, then awoke with a start. Stumbling to his feet, he moved toward the door a few strides ahead of Post and Rebecca. When he opened it, a familiar set of faces greeted him.

"What, you again?" said Reynolds, annoyed. "I thought we already had our confrontation for the day?"

"Clay, maybe they're bringing the TV back," Post added. "Do you guys get Arsenio?"

"We're changing our procedures," said Torres, ignoring the responses to his team's appearance. He led them into the room while the remaining astronauts were still waking up. "From now on there will be no more group interrogations. Instead I will conduct them individually. Victor, her . . ."

Julie froze in mid-yawn when she realized Torres was pointing at her. Esparza was at her bed in an instant and jerking her to her feet. For the moment the other astronauts were too stunned to act, until Julie tried to break the lock Esparza had on her wrist.

"Now wait just a damn minute," Reynolds protested, moving toward the beds. "She's my crew."

"Tell your stooge to let her go," said Post, laying a firm hand on Torres's shoulder. "If you want a fight on your hands you got one."

Before Post could start another sentence, Torres pried his hand off his shoulder and had spun around.

He felt a small iron hand sink its fingernails into his neck. The cold fire he had seen earlier was now burning only a few inches away from him. Moving too fast to be stopped, Torres had Post slammed against the wall while the rest of his team were drawing their weapons.

"I'm not called *Escorpiòn* for nothing, spaceman!" Torres shouted, breaking away from Post and pulling his Skoda automatic on him. "Commander, if your crew resists, their deaths will be on your hands!"

"Okay, okay! Let's chill it, guys," said Reynolds, for the moment his eyes were transfixed on the revolver levelled at him. "Chill it! We'll have our chance later."

"Later indeed . . . Victor, take her to the privacy room." Torres brandished his weapon longer than the others, he waved it at the door before finally putting it away. "None of you need worry about her. She won't be taken from this building."

"Boy, that's reassuring," said Post, his fear ebbing enough for him to speak "What are you going to do with Julie?"

"She can tell you on her return. Good night, my friends."

Torres left the detention room in charge of the Seychelles security staff who entered with him. In the hallway outside, he trailed Esparza and Julie into a room marked "Maintenance." Inside was far larger than a storage closet, furnished with a table and a handful of chairs. One of which was set in a circle of light stands.

"Have a seat, Mrs. Harrison," said Torres, trying to be courteous as he motioned to the interrogation chair.

"No thanks," said Julie, glancing darkly between Torres and what he offered. "I'll stand."

"As you wish . . . Victor, I think you can leave us alone. She's of no threat to me." Torres nodded to the door and fell silent until Esparza had closed it behind him. "I'm so glad we can now meet this way. I've wanted to for some time."

"Why? You think without the men around you can rape me? You just try it. If you win, I'll guarantee you'll be raping a corpse."

"There's no need to be defensive, Julie. There's no need for us to be antagonists," said Torres, softening his tone until he was almost purring his response. "You are black, my mother was black. We're both from the same race, the most oppressed race in America. Yet you work for its government, the same government that kills black leaders like Malcolm X and Martin Luther King."

"Don't hand me this 'we're of the same race' shit," Julie answered, circling Torres warily. Always moving out of range as he stepped forward. "King tried to teach us not to look at the color of their skin but at the content of their character. And the more I see of yours, the less I like."

"Your attitude will not help you, Julie. Or your friends. In the oppressed nations of the world there is little sympathy for you. There isn't much sympathy or understanding for you in your own country. Even your own family . . . are you aware your own mother appeared on the Phil Donahue show yesterday? She cried and wanted to know why NASA forced you to fly again."

"My mother has never understood why I wanted to be an astronaut. I had to fight her and a lot of others to get my dream. And no one forced me to fly again. I wanted to be on the first mission *Phoenix* did after the rescue, and I had to pull a lot of strings to get it."

"Who is pulling whose strings?" Torres said, smiling. Something Julie immediately felt uneasy about. "Don't you see how your racist government is using you? Open your eyes, Julie. They say, 'Racism? What racism? We have a black woman who's an astronaut and a Nobel prize winner.' But if you work with me, that can change."

"I'd no sooner work with a scorpion than kiss one," said Julie, briefly making eye contact with Torres and giving him a hateful glare. "And for your information there are *two* black women astronauts who've won Nobel prizes. The only people who want to use me are you and your friends. What will you offer me for my cooperation? A trip to Disney World?"

"The status of your crew mates," said Torres, shedding some of his newfound charm. "There could even be freedom for some of them. Especially if you cooperate with our joint investigation of the satellite your spaceship is carrying. We already know Major Glassner is the satellite's expert from your own media."

"You want me to sell out my country and my friends? To you and the Libyans?"

"It would serve the cause of world peace." The tone in Torres's voice grew icy and the fire was igniting again in his eyes. "You should understand that. You won a peace prize."

"Not by betraying my country!" Julie shouted. "You can call it what you like. And maybe some of it is true. But it's still my country, and I'm not a traitor!"

"Sit down," Torres ordered, pointing at the chair surrounded by the circle of light stands. "Now! Or my people will come and tie you in it! I now see I must first educate you on your country's racist past before I can expect you to cooperate."

"Gordo, I have a new radar source," said Foreman, the moment another light on his AT-90 set started flashing. "It's a surface search and navigation set."

"Patrol boat?" Hassler asked, glancing over his right shoulder at the figure huddled behind him.

"You got it. Frequency identical to the standard systems the Brits put on those Vospers."

"Range and bearing?"

"Range, five miles. Bearing . . ." Foreman let his words trail out as he readjusted the surveillance set's controls for a better reading on the new target's direction. "I'd say zero-seven-zero degrees. Right off our port bow."

"Christ, five miles? How the hell did they sneak up on you?" said another SEAL, his voice too low to be identified.

"They might've come out from one of the bays along this shore," said Hassler. "There's certainly enough of 'em. Tyrone, you see anything?"

"Just lights on a big, black outline," said Hall, sitting in the zodiac's bow. Instead of using the scope on his rifle, he used Hassler's binoculars to sweep both Mahé and the smaller islands off its southern coastline. "Wait, wait. A couple of these lights are moving."

"Switch to the Starlight scope. Patterson, Riker, arm your weapons. Barton, start taking us south."

After heading east for more than an hour, the zodiac was now abreast of Therese Island. Still puttering quietly, it tried to weave around the higher swells in an effort to remain inconspicuous. Even as it changed direction, the helmsman still attempted to hide it; even though the farther into the Indian Ocean the raft sailed, the rougher the seas became.

"It's a patrol boat all right," Hall advised, raising

the light-enhancement scope to his eye and training it farther off to port. "Just like all the others. *Simba*-class, thirty-one meters long. Forty-millimeter guns fore and aft. . . . And it just activated its search-lights."

"Shit, they're on to us," said Belford. "They waited until we were stuck out here before springing their trap. Now we'll either get shot or drown."

"Knock it off," Hassler ordered. "They're still look-ing for us on Silhouette. Riker, get the Armbrust case. If it gets too close we'll treat it to an antitank round. Ty, what's going on?"

"I really can't tell, sir. I'm constantly losing it in the swells," said Hall, half-crouching and half-standing in order to see over the wave tops. "But I don't think it's changed course."

"Nick, what do you have?"

"Range, four miles and closing," said Foreman. "I can't give you a good bearing because we keep chang-ing ours."

"Gordo, if this sea state gets any worse we're going to start shipping water over the sides," Barton warned, gunning the engine and throwing the tiller to one side. Even so, he did not completely avoid the swell rearing up on the zodiac's starboard bow. When it hit, water spilled briefly over the side soaking some of the men.

"Great," Belford sputtered, trying to wipe the sting-ing seawater out of his eyes. "We're either going to have to shoot or bail."

"Sir, it's disappearing!" said Hall, briefly raising his voice. As another swell pushed the raft up, he got a momentarily clear view of the distant patrol boat. "It's heading into the channel between Therese Island and Mahé."

"All right, let's not go crazy," said Hassler, quelling

the cheer that was starting among his men. "Sound can still carry, even in these conditions. I don't know about you guys, but I still wouldn't want a firefight. Dale, take us back in."

The moment Barton reversed the zodiac's course the ride smoothed out. Now moving in the same general direction as the waves, he was able to take advantage of them, maneuvering the raft so it would sail down their slopes and pick up their speed. While Hall kept an eye on the retreating patrol boat, those who had produced their weapons safetied them; everyone felt their hearts beat a little slower when the boat completed its disappearance between Therese and Mahé.

"Finished, Colonel," said Captain Jassem Walid, climbing off the shuttle's port wing. "All the ground crew has to do is throw a switch and the spacecraft will have power."

Behind the captain, near the base of the shuttle's tail, a jury-rigged set of lines had been connected to its launch umbilical panel. With a nod from Mashari, the sergeant commanding the Libyan Air Force ground crew pulled a switch on an auxiliary power cart. As he did so, several people moved away from the *Phoenix,* but all that happened was the activation of the lights on its mid deck and flight deck.

"You can stop cowering," Mashari observed, glancing at the personnel around him. "It isn't going to explode, and it's time for us to go aboard."

Before he did so, he finished slipping on his breathing system's face mask, as did the other members in his team. They climbed the stairs and entered the *Phoenix* through its side hatch, stopping only briefly on the mid deck while they mounted the ladder to its cockpit.

"Now we can start learning her secrets," said Walid, standing beside Mashari at the aft crew station. "I think these control the lighting."

Walid ran his hand down a row of switches on the station's main panel, activating the flight deck lights aft of the cockpit. The next row turned on the floods inside the payload bay, illuminating the KH-12 reconnaissance satellite. The billion dollar vehicle still sat in its customized cradle, its solar cell panels still tightly folded against its sides.

"Ahh, I never thought it would be so large," Mashari gasped, the shock and delight clear in his voice. "The best of American technology, and it's ours. Find some way to open the cargo doors, I want to see all of it."

"These control the latches," said Walid, locating another row of buttons on a side panel behind Mashari. "And these, the motors that open the doors."

With no other systems on the shuttle operating, they both could hear the soft clicking as the dozens of bulkhead and centerline latches unlocked. When all their status lights had changed to green, Walid tripped the switches to the payload bay door motors and Mashari waited at the observation windows for them to open.

"Jassem, what's wrong?" said Mashari. "Why aren't they opening?"

"I . . . I don't know," said Walid, hitting the buttons repeatedly. Until he noticed the service doors below the panel were slightly open. He swung them open, and in moments realized what had been done. "Someone's tampered with these. There's been sabotage."

"It was the astronauts! Other than security-cleared personnel, they were the only ones who've been here.

They *are* the only ones who know how to damage this ship! Said, what's wrong?"

"I can bring nothing up on the computer!" shouted Viper's weapons control officer, Captain Said el-Reedy. He banged his fist on the center pedestal between the pilots' seats, until he broke some of the toggle switch stems. "They erased everything in its memory! All the programs that could reveal their secrets! Gone! We should destroy this plane and send them the wreckage."

"No. We'll leave the Americans a bare airframe," said Mashari. "In the morning our resupply jet will arrive. It'll have the equipment we need to pull this spaceship apart."

"But, Colonel, if we destroy the shuttle, won't the Americans attack us?" asked Walid.

"You forget, Jassem. We have their astronauts. If Saddam Hussein taught us anything, it's the value of human shields. By the time the Americans realize what we're doing, it will be too late. Captain, I'll leave you to discover the rest of their treachery. I can't breathe with this equipment anymore."

"Major, electronic surveillance has just detected weak radar signals," said Badran, speaking for the first time in nearly half an hour. "They are northwest of us. Intermittent. Not strong enough to get an accurate fix."

"Can you tell if they are surface or airborne radars?" asked al-Rayes. "We must know if the Americans have launched any interceptors."

"Difficult to tell. At least one signal is the same frequency as used by American Navy Hawkeye planes."

"Then we have them." In spite of the exhaustion several hours of high-altitude flying had put on him,

251

al-Rayes felt his adrenaline surge and he quickly grew restive. "Lieutenant, do you have anything on radar or infra-red tracking?"

"Nothing yet, Major," said Kalmendi. "But if you turn us in the direction of the signals, I should have a return echo of the fleet in minutes."

"Agreed, Lieutenant. Changing course," said al-Rayes, switching off his aircraft's autopilot system. In seconds the bomber would be under his control again. "Sergeant, what bearing do you have on those signals?"

"I have. . . . Strong radar sources, aft!" Badran shouted, his voice jumping from calm to terror in seconds. "Two sources, airborne intercept radar! Closing fast. Activating tail gun!"

"Andy, I've detected Bee Hind radar," said the Naval flight officer in the F-14's second seat. "And I'm jamming it."

"Good work, Larry. I guess they know we're here," said Commander Andrew Kearns, glancing at his own threat-warning panel. "Green Hornet One to Green Hornet Two, split up and reduce speed to match the Blinder. Over."

The two Grumman F-14As had spent almost an hour stalking the Tu-22. Tracking it, first by its own radar emissions, then by its infra-red signature. Maneuvering at low altitude to avoid being detected by its radar, it later climbed behind it and remained far enough back not to trigger its tail-warning radar. Now, with the Tupolev finally approaching the *Eisenhower*'s battle group, they had hit their afterburners and activated their AWG-9 fire-control radars.

Kearns, the commanding officer to one of the carrier's two Tomcat squadrons, broke to the left while his wingman banked right. They cut their afterburners and popped their fuselage-mounted speed brakes, shedding velocity until they had drawn alongside the bulky, needle-nosed giant. In the clear night at forty thousand feet even its camouflage paint could be seen. The cockpit lights virtually glowed, making the pilot readily visible.

"Bastards! You may have us but we'll find where your ships are," said al-Rayes, shaking his fist at the fighter on his port wing. "You'll lead us to them."

"Major, should I try jamming their intercept radar?" asked Badran.

"No, let's save our tricks for later. Right now we need an accurate fix on their fleet, so we can radio it back to Victoria. Switch off the tail gun radar. We'll let them take us right to their carrier."

"Think that guy was giving us the finger?" the flight officer requested.

"If he did, that's all he can do to us," said Kearns, before he switched his radio to a secure channel. "Green Hornet One to Turntable. I have our night visitor; will maintain visual contact with him. Might as well advise the fleet to end their M-Com conditions. He's going to find them sooner or later."

"Gordo, the beach is secure," Belford whispered, rejoining the team crouching around the zodiac. "There's no one here for miles."

"A few hundred yards will do us just fine," said Hassler, glancing over Belford's shoulder when he caught sight of some movement in the beach's tree line. "It looks like Bruce found us a place to hide the raft. Tom, get behind me. Squad ready, lift."

In unison the six men shouldered their weapons and raised the zodiac out of the water. Apart from the creaking and shifting of some equipment, they made no more noise than the sound of the waves lapping against the isolated beach and then receding. For the fifty feet of open ground they crossed, they were covered by Patterson. Even after they reached him he continued to sweep the area with his submachine gun.

"Nick, deflate the raft. The rest of you, remove the ground cover and start digging," Hassler ordered, removing a spade from his backpack and clearing the forest debris from a section of ground. "Barton, detach the engine and fuel tank."

With a loud, squeaking hiss, the zodiac's escape valves were opened and the air inside it rushed out. As the noise continued, spades dug into the sandy soil; with four men working on it, there would soon be a hole deep enough to bury the zodiac and its gear.

"Gordo, she's all folded up," said Foreman, pointing to the neatly squared-off pile of rubber and Kevlar. "What next?"

"Get on the short-range radio and listen for the *Marshall*," said Hassler. "By now our home should be here."

"Slow to ten knots," Carver instructed, standing behind the helmsmen's seats. "Sonar, what do you have?"

"Coral reef, one and a quarter miles ahead," said Seidel, the *Marshall*'s sonar officer. "We have one high-speed surface craft, rounding Mahé's western side. Possibly a patrol boat. We have three more sur-

254

face contacts at long-range, they all appear to be fishing boats."

"Continue active pinging, let me know if anything changes. Bring us up to two hundred feet and alter course to Zero-Nine-Zero degrees. Radio Room, stand by to release com buoy."

Rising from its nine-hundred-foot cruise depth, the submarine gently curved into a starboard turn. By the time both maneuvers were finished, it was sailing due east at two hundred feet, roughly paralleling the reef now on its port side. Several miles behind it, the *Casablanca* was just coming to the same course and depth.

"Radio Room, release the buoy," Carver added, keying his hand mike again. "Glenn, you can start hailing your squad as soon as it surfaces. Clarence, reduce speed to ten knots."

Directly aft of the *Marshall*'s conning tower, a small hatch was opened and a six-inch-diameter capsule ejected. Attached to the sub by a fiber-optic cable, it rose swiftly. When it broke the surface, the buoy raised an antenna shaped like an umbrella's skeletal framework.

"Gordo, I got her," said Foreman. "Glenn's on the line."

"Okay, I'll take it," said Hassler, jumping out of the pit and accepting the radio. "Tom, finish burying the gear. Then replace the cover. Home Port, this is Spectacle. We read you five by five, over."

Hassler released the transmit bar on the handset-sized radio and pressed its top end closer to his ear. Partly to hear the response better, it also cut down on any of the conversation leaking out.

"Roger, Spectacle. Glad to hear from you," said Allard. "What's your situation? Over."

255

"We have reached Phase Two. Repeat, Phase Two. We will proceed soon to Phase Three. So far, conditions are nominal. We'll have a full report when we reach Phase Three, over."

"Roger, Spectacle. We have no changes to report, you may proceed. We'll wait for your transmission at the scheduled time. This is Home Port, out."

"Roger, Home Port. This is Spectacle, out," said Hassler, releasing the transmit bar and hitting the power switch. "All right, let's get ready to move. Tyrone, clear our trail off the beach. From the waterline to the tree line. Bruce, cover him. The rest of you, get your gear together. We have two and a half hours before daybreak. By then I want our observation post established."

"Gordo, is this going to be the easy part?" asked Belford, still breathing heavily from his burial work.

"Hell, the easy part is what we just went through. From now on it's all uphill."

Thirteen

Conspiracy
Illusion of Progress

"We have installed long-range tanks in the Kamov's ventral bay," Colonel Burdin advised, walking across the *Baku*'s angled flight deck. "That should give us the range to make the U.S. fleet and return without refueling."

"I still wonder if you should go, Admiral," said Captain Fedorov. "Would it not be easier to merely contact the American commander by radio, and confer that way?"

"It would, Nikolai Dmitrevich," said Khomenko, holding his wheel cap so the twenty-knot wind would not blow it off. "If we wanted everyone to listen in on our conversation. The ways we scramble transmissions are not compatible, and, besides, I would prefer to have a more personal meeting with the Americans. I doubt they'll be as confrontational as what we had to put up with yesterday. Goodbye, my friend, and don't worry. The Americans know we're coming."

Their shoes clacking loudly as they walked across the flight deck's heat resistant tiles, Khomenko and his entourage reached the one Ka-27 helicopter the *Baku* was preparing for flight. High above, a quartet of Yak-38s were gathering into a formation, readying to fly the morning's first patrol.

Before boarding the Ka-27, Khomenko turned and shook hands with the carrier's captain. By the time they parted company, the turbines had started to whine. By the time Fedorov had returned to his ship's bridge, the Kamov was lifting off. After it circled to gain altitude, it would eventually head to the north-west, to an expected rendezvous with the USS *Eisenhower.*

"Thank God our headache is over," commented Griffen, standing in her embassy office. She briefly pulled the heavy curtain back from its window, letting the morning sunlight flood in. "But we still have our nightmare. I see the 'spontaneous' protest is being trucked in on time. Ron, when will the evacuation fleet reach the hospital ship?"

"The choppers from the *Belleau Wood* are already flying the evacuees to the *Comfort,*" said Goldman, checking his wristwatch. "From there they'll sail to Oman where they'll be flown home."

"Oman? Why there and not Diego Garcia?" said Fernandez, seated in front of Griffen's desk.

"The Pentagon is building up forces on the island. The Eighty-second Airborne will be arriving there soon. They'll bolster the Marine and Navy units we already have."

"How close will the fleet come to us?" asked Griffen, returning to her desk.

"If you think the Navy's going to sail a ninety-thousand-ton aircraft carrier off Victoria, guess again," said Goldman. "The islands of Cerf and Saint Anne make the channel far too narrow. However, we can expect a visit from her planes."

"Nothing closer? Seeing those warships yesterday did unsettle some people at Revolution House."

"Well we do happen to have something closer. There's a squad of Navy SEALs on Mahé right now."

"What? Here? What are they doing and where are they?" said Fernandez, just beating out everyone else in the office.

"They're here for reconnaissance," Goldman responded. "The commando submarine *John Marshall* is lying off Mahé with her entire SEAL team. Where they all are I don't know and we don't need to know. If we have to free the astronauts and the shuttle, they'll be the ones to do it."

"I hope they'll be able to remain hidden," said Henry Savage, speaking up for the first time. "People's Security Force and military patrols have increased here and on the surrounding islands. There are more roadblocks; traffic into the airport is restricted; and more Air Seychelles airplanes are being modified for military use. This place is resembling Cuba during the 'sixty-two missile crisis."

"And unlike then I don't think there will be a diplomatic solution to our problem," Griffen added darkly. "Not even the Russians were able to break through the 'oppressed nations' rhetoric yesterday. And all our resolutions are being vetoed in the Security Council by China and Libya. It looks like the U.N. won't be able to help us this time. Unless there's some movement in the negotiations soon, the major's military options may have to be used."

"I wish the Russians would sell us some of those," said Torres, nodding at the trio of sand and green painted giants on the airport's opposite side. "They have plenty of more modern bombers in their Air Force."

"They'll never give you anything like those Tupolevs," said Mashari, smiling. "You're only ninety miles from America, and the Soviets learned thirty years ago about the folly of putting strategic weapons in your country. However, they have given you other long-range aircraft. You have Ilyushin 'Seventy-sixes, why don't we see some of your troops here?"

"Because as you just said, my country is only ninety miles from America. They can watch us very closely, and there are fears in Havana that they could attack us from Guantanamo Bay. There is talk of creating a nonaligned nations' task force of ships to resupply us. Until then we must rely on your men and weapons. When do you expect your transport to return?"

"By noon today." Mashari turned to the runway at the sudden burst of engine sound. Lifting off from it was a pair of SF.260 fighter-trainers, their underwing pylons laden with rocket pods and external fuel tanks for an extended patrol of the outer islands. "The Ilyushin will bring another ZSU tank and a special lifting frame. We used it to change engines on our Tupolevs, but I believe we'll find it capable of removing the satellite from the shuttle. When it's done, my people think a diversion should be made to distract the Americans. Is anything planned?"

"Foreign Minister Boigny has suggested we give back the women astronauts," Sampras offered, speaking for the first time since the officials gathered on the hangar apron. "He made it at our meeting last night, saying it would be a useful publicity ploy. Following the bombardment of our island by the warships, it would show us being flexible and humanitarian to the brutal Americans."

"In my country we're always surprised at the value the West places on women," said Mashari. "It's a mystery to us, but we know it's there and how to use it. That would make an excellent diversion. And it would give the illusion of progress in your negotiations. What do you think, Mr. Torres?"

"I would prefer we keep the women," said Torres, irritated at the idea. "Given time, I think I could break them."

"Well you obviously didn't succeed last night with Mrs. Harrison," Mohammed Halim remarked sarcastically. "From what I heard, the woman got the better of you—"

"Don't get me started, Captain. In time I can break them and you know it."

"Yes, Captain, let's not argue with our ally. I've irritated him enough for one day," said Mashari, at first treating the situation lightly, until he saw the cold fire igniting in the Cuban's eyes. "I've heard about the problems you two have had, let's not continue them. If not the women, who would you suggest we release?"

"Their commander," said Torres. "I doubt I can break Mr. Reynolds. His personality is—"

A distant, growing rumble caused Torres to end his answer early. All eyes turned skyward as the noise became deeper and omnipresent. The officials were unable to sense a direction from it; not until the first dots were spotted on the western horizon and approached the airport in perfect formations.

"My God. It's them," said Sampras, an edge of fear in his voice. "But how? Their fleet is still hundreds of miles away."

The first aircraft to roar over Seychelles International was a five-ship flight of Grumman A-6s. The center one had a longer fuselage than the others, and a streamlined pod on its tail which identified it as an EA-6B Prowler. Flanking them were two four-ship flights of F-14A Tomcats, their wings swept forward for their low speed pass. Several hundred yards back, was a four-ship flight of Lockheed S-3B Vikings. And swarming around the boxy, tall-finned, antisubmarine bombers were a dozen F-18 Hornets divided into similar-sized flights.

Having first overflown Victoria, the stream of warplanes now roared past the airport, over the Tu-22s and Il-76s sitting on its principal taxiway, over the few remaining international airliners that were still flying out tourists, finally, over the *Phoenix* and the People's Defense Force aircraft at the flight line's eastern end. It took the nearly thirty warplanes more than a minute to complete their flyby. As the last of them turned out to sea, their ear-numbing decibel level fell back to the original rumble.

"An arrogant display of power," said Torres. "Something the Americans are good at."

"And frankly, intimidating," Sampras added. "I never knew a sound like that could be made. Then again, I never saw so many jet fighters in the air before."

"It was also an empty display," said Mashari, almost laughing at the fear he saw in the Seychelles officials. "Didn't you see? The bombers only carried fuel tanks. The fighters carried fuel tanks and defensive missiles. None of their vaunted smart bombs. It was just a show designed to frighten us. And from appearances, they've succeeded."

"Then we should not release the women," said Torres. "We shouldn't let the Americans think their act of intimidation has won them anything."

"And I say release those two astronauts precisely for that reason. Let the Americans think they won something through an empty demonstration of power. If they think they can win through bluster, they'll be less likely to resort to military action. It will contribute to what I mentioned before our 'interruption,' the illusion of progress. Of course, Mr. Sampras, it is not for us to decide—only to advise. It's for your government to do so. Which will it be?"

"Soviet One. Soviet One, this is *Eisenhower* Traffic Control. You are on proper final approach, you need not acknowledge any further transmissions. The deck crew is ready for you, please follow their instructions. This is *Eisenhower* Traffic Control, out."

In order to minimize radio contacts which could be monitored in the Seychelles, the Kamov had been escorted for the last hour by a Sikorsky SH-3H helicopter. Now, after watching the Sea King land on the carrier, it repeated the procedure and clattered over the four-and-a-half-acre flight deck. For several minutes it hovered abreast of the block-like island until finally settling onto the spot indicated by the yellow-suited deck crew.

"Welcome aboard the *Eisenhower,* Admiral," said the one man not wearing a brightly colored jacket. "I'm Captain David McQuay. If you and your staff could follow me, Admiral Bryant is waiting for us."

Deplaning with most of the same officers he had taken earlier to Victoria, Khomenko followed the *Eisenhower*'s captain into the island and up a series of stairs until they were several stories above the flight deck and deep inside the structure. There, in a richly furnished room insulated against the screech and roar of regular carrier operations, he met his opposite number.

"Admiral Khomenko, this is Vice Admiral Richard Bryant," McQuay introduced, as the two senior officers exchanged salutes and handshakes.

"A pleasure, Oleg Victorovich," said Bryant, releasing the Russian's hand, and motioning to the room's arrangement of chairs and tables. "Please, take your choice. On behalf of my government, I would like to thank you for assistance in yesterday's evacuation and initiative in resolving the crisis."

"You are most kind," Khomenko responded, selecting a chair close to the one Bryant dropped his much taller frame into. "In the cause of peace it was the least we could do. I do hope that yesterday's unfortunate incident where you fired on Seychelles forces will not lead to further military action."

"That depends on what the Seychelles government and those Libyan forces do. The State Department reports you weren't able to make much headway with them. What happened?"

"The local government still believes in the old revolutionary rhetoric, they're very much under the control of their Cuban and Libyan 'comrades.' " Khomenko started rubbing his hands together and looked down, a hint of despair edged into his voice. "What they said to us is what we said to you twenty years, thirty years ago. Exactly, with one change. Instead of exploitation of the masses, it's the exploitation of *space*. It's no longer superpowers but *space* powers, and *space* imperialism. We no longer have influence with them, we're no better than you."

"From what's happening at the U.N.," said Bryant. "It appears as though China holds more sway with the Third World. We know you were at both Revolution House and the airport yesterday. At any time, did you see or were you told where the astronauts are being kept? So far, we've only seen them at the shuttle."

"We only saw your spacecraft," Burdin answered, all heads turning toward him. "Our 'revolutionary brothers' didn't take us into their confidence. They never mentioned where your crew is being held. I suspect they're somewhere inside the airport's military compound. With the right forces, it should be easy to find them."

"Yes. Colonel Burdin and I decided we could retake your *Phoenix* with a company of Naval infantry," said Khomenko. "While such forces are available in my fleet, I know you have similar. Your commando submarine *John Marshall*, for instance."

"How do you know about the *Marshall?*" said Bryant, trying to maintain an impassive face as his heart skipped a beat. "And what do you know?"

"We've been interested in her since the *Ocean Valkyrie* incident of last year. Because of a personality clash, we know she was banished to Diego Garcia since then. And since this crisis began we've not been able to locate her."

"Have you told anyone else about the *Marshall?*" asked McQuay, his face draining of the color Bryant was able to maintain.

"If you mean our 'revolutionary brothers' in the Seychelles, they didn't cooperate with us; we didn't with them," said Khomenko. "Even if we did, we don't know where your sub is."

"And for operational security, I hope you understand why we can't reveal where the *Marshall* is," said Bryant, uttering a barely noticeable sigh of relief.

"I understand. However, if I had such—"

"Captain, this is CIC. That Libyan Blinder snooping around us is changing tactics," warned a voice on the office speakers, ending the conversation.

"This is McQuay, what's he doing?" McQuay replied, using a hand mike from the wall-mounted intercom panel.

"Heading for us and descending. The fighters want to know what to do."

"Tell Sunburst Three to follow our new orders and escort the bomber in. Tell the Flying Bridge to expect me there. Sorry, Admiral, you're going to have to continue on your own."

"Under the circumstances, Admiral Bryant, could we not adjourn this meeting to the flying bridge?" said Khomenko. "The aircraft's behavior is unusual."

"I see no problem with that," said Bryant, rising out of his chair. "Captain, lead the way."

Ascending another level in the island, the Russian officers were shepherded to the mostly glass operations center extending out over the flight deck. Though they crowded the Air Boss's staff, they had a commanding view of the *Eisenhower* and the sea around it. Within minutes of their arrival, a formation of dark specks appeared behind the carrier.

Growing rapidly from mere dots to aircraft-shaped silhouettes, and finally to identifiable warplanes, they were still descending and overtook the giant ship. The lead plane's swept wings, needle nose, and tail-mounted engines quickly identified it as a Tupolev Blinder. The F-14s flanking it had to sweep their wings forward to maintain their positions as it visibly slowed down.

"I think the Libyans are trying to shake your interceptors," said Burdin, after he realized what was happening.

"Why do so now?" McQuay inquired. "In the past, these maneuvers were tried when the planes were still far away from the battle group, not right over it."

"I don't know, Captain. But if there is a reason for it, I fear it will be provocative."

Despite its attempt to shake the Tomcats, the bomber still had them sitting on its wingtips as it roared over the carrier at less than a thousand feet. Just before crossing the ship's fantail, the doors on its mid-fuselage undersides snapped open. Inside its bomb bay, in place of the expected missiles or fuel tanks, was a pallet with reconnaissance cameras.

"It's nearly the same stunt they pulled on the evacuation ships," said Bryant, tracking the planes through the bridge's overhead windows. "If it wouldn't be revealing too many of your secrets, could you tell us what missiles they're using?"

"In fact it would betray none of our secrets," said Burdin, briefly shielding his eyes against the sun's strong glare. "Their missiles are Italian-built Melara Otomats, very similar to your Harpoons."

"But the Otomat is a ship-launched missile only," said McQuay. "There is no air-launched version for sale."

"It would not take much to modify the Otomat for air-launching. All you need do is remove its boosters and change its ignition circuits. The launcher they're mounted on was built for Libya by the Brazilians, just like their flight refueling systems and tanker planes."

"They bypassed us very effectively," Khomenko added. "As have several of our former clients. It's a problem with many disturbing aspects."

"Would you care to take our meeting back to my office?" said Bryant, wiping the sweat off his brow with a handkerchief.

"Not quite yet, my friend. Let's see if the Libyans have any more stunts for us. However, I would like to complete what I was saying then. Though it's my government's hope there will be a peaceful ending, I know if I had such a submarine as the *Marshall* I'd be planning to use it."

"C'mon, you guys. Time to wake up," Hassler said quietly, tapping the figures sleeping in the camouflaged tarpaulins. "It's noon. You've had your six hours."

Grumbling slightly, Belford and Hall turned and unzipped their bags. Sliding out of them, they quickly folded the bags, collected their gun cases, and followed Hassler up to the ridge of their observation post. The reconnaissance squad had selected a bowl-like depression near the summit of a mountain in Mahé's central spine. They were on its eastern side, which allowed them to overlook both the NASA tracking station and the international airport. Weaving around the prehistoric ferns, teak, and other hardwood trees, Hassler and his two snipers crept up to the lookouts he had posted earlier.

"Dale, anything new?" he asked, settling down beside the man using his binoculars.

"Nope. Just those four Yaks buzzing around Victoria Bay and the airport," said Barton.

"Let's see what I can see," Hall added, opening the snap locks on his rifle case.

This time, unlike the previous day they spent on Conception Island, both Hall and Belford pulled out of their cases their PSG-1 rifles. The matt black weapons had a sleek, functional look to them. Their only parts that were not black and made of metal or composite materials were the wooden pistol grips; each customized to the hand of its user. In seconds both snipers were attaching their Hensoldt scopes to the guns; the only sounds they made were the rasp of the mounting screws being turned.

"Gordo, should we load clips?" said Belford.

"Not now," said Hassler. "We haven't seen or heard another human being since we crossed that last road."

"I can see a few," Hall remarked, already shouldering his rifle and pointing it at the airport. "They're walking around the shuttle. If we were a couple of miles closer, I could pick 'em off."

"Any of them look like the astronauts?"

"Can't really tell. But none of 'em are wearing those blue NASA flightsuits."

"Keep looking," said Hassler. "One of the things we have to do is discover where they're being held. So far, the people at the station haven't been able to spot them. Dale, what do you have?"

"Three new bogies," Barton advised, sweeping the binoculars as far west as he could. "Coming out of the northwest. Looks like something big being escorted by a pair of fighters."

The snipers quickly trained their weapons, and their scopes, in the direction Barton was pointing the binoculars. As the Yak-38s departed the area, a large, high-winged aircraft came into full view. The noon sun glinted off its high-gloss finish and the glass panels in its nose when it turned to enter the airport's traffic pattern. Its white and grey paint scheme identified it as an Ilyushin Il-76T, the same one which had departed just over a day before.

Its two escorts wore a lighter grey camouflage, Navy ghost-grey, and were identified as F-18 Hornets. While they broke off and climbed, the Libyan transport gradually descended to Seychelles International. It touched down on the runway. Instead of turning off to take its old spot on the field's main taxiway, it rolled across to the hangar apron.

"It's not going to the civilian terminal," said Belford, his rifle tracking the aircraft's movement. "I think it's heading to the military side."

"It must be," said Hall. "There's a group of people on the apron that I didn't see a minute ago."

"Where are they?" Hassler asked.

"Near the *Phoenix*. Say, you don't think they're going to try dismantling it? Or ripping off the satellite inside it?"

"Anything's possible. We'll just have to wait and see what the cargo jet has brought."

"Gordo, we got visitors in the neighborhood," Barton said quietly, now pointing the binoculars down the mountainside. "A convoy's just stopped on the road below. I think its troops are going to do a sweep."

"Let me have those," said Hassler, taking back the binoculars and scanning the same area. "Yes, they are doing a sweep. Just what we saw earlier around the tracking station . . . I hope this doesn't mean what it could mean."

"What's that, Lieutenant?" Hall asked.

"That we could find ourselves in a firefight before the rest of our team lands. Before Washington even decides to use force to rescue the shuttle."

Fourteen

Reinforcements
Freedom

Towering even above the airliner-sized spacecraft, the Ilyushin transport dominated the military flight line the moment it swung onto the hangar apron. It was forced to maneuver carefully so its drooping wingtips would not hit helicopter rotor blades, and its jet blast wouldn't knock over the SF.260 trainers. When the scream from its Soloviev turbofans died, it was replaced by the lower-pitched whine of its Auxiliary Power Unit. By the time the crowd awaiting its arrival had gathered around the grey and white giant, its tail ramp had finished opening.

"Excellent. Just what we need," said Mashari, smiling as he surveyed a compacted set of yellow I-beams and the sand-colored antiaircraft tank behind it. "This is the lifting frame. Once we assemble it around the shuttle, we'll be able to force open its payload doors and take its satellite."

"What will you do with it then?" asked Sampras, stepping up to the deployed ramp to get a better look at the equipment.

"Send it to Libya in this same aircraft. We'll have to

271

work fast; I want it to coincide as close as possible with your release of the women astronauts. We need to take as much advantage of the illusion of progress as we can. Yes, Major, what is it?"

"I just received a report from Captain Mashat," said al-Rayes, jumping out of the Suzuki jeep which had driven up to the Ilyushin. "Colonel, he says he has photographs of a Russian helicopter sitting on the American carrier."

"Excuse me, the *American* carrier?' said Sampras.

"Yes. Why should it surprise you?" Mashari replied, his smile breaking even wider. "When you met with the Russians, you accused them of Spacepower Hegemony. Now we have proof of it. Major, how did Mashat discover the Russian?"

"His electronic warfare officer recorded several scrambled radio messages," said al-Rayes. "Then, his radar navigator tracked the inbound flight."

"This is a stroke of good fortune for us. His entire crew is to be commended. I'll order him to return early and be replaced with the next aircraft."

"You, Colonel? Aren't you going to finish welcoming the new personnel?"

"I have another appointment to keep," said Mashari, glancing at his wristwatch. "I can stop at our operations control while on the way to the Security Headquarters."

"What will you do there?" asked al-Rayes.

"As they say in the American police shows, I will play 'Good Cop.' Mr. Torres is currently interrogating the other woman astronaut. I'll be happy when they're gone, we can interrogate the men about the sabotage they committed here. Time to go, Mr. Sampras. We'll both be playing 'Good Cops.' "

"Conn, this is Sonar. The active pinging is growing

272

weaker," advised the voice on the control center speakers. "The patrol boat is moving off. Should we resume pinging?"

"Not yet," said Carver, keying the hand mike he held. "Not while Glenn's still squirting messages to the *Casablanca*. You'd interfere with him. Concentrate on your passive arrays. I'll let you know when you can go active. Conn, out."

"Captain, you want us to continue this maneuver?" said Jefferson. "Or should I cancel it?"

"No, keep us on Auto Program. We haven't had any problems with it so far. If Mr. Doran sees any trouble, disengage the moment he says so. Jim, you have the conn. I'll be checking on Glenn's progress."

Even though the *Marshall* had been performing the same maneuver for the last two hours, Carver still felt the slight drop to starboard in the control center's floor. Both the former missile sub and the *Casablanca* were engaged in a slow right turn, circumscribing a ten-mile-diameter circle. Some nine hundred feet down, they maneuvered just off the barrier reefs along Mahé's southern coast. They dared not rise any higher, not for fear of being detected on hostile sonar, but because the water's clarity allowed visible sunlight to penetrate nearly five hundred feet.

"That last one got pretty close, Captain," Jaskula said nervously, turning when he heard footsteps on the TASCO Room's stairs. "Are we gonna go to deeper water?"

"If we did, we'd have to leave Jacoubet's boat behind us," Carver answered. "We're already near its maximum diving limits. Unless the Russians start sub hunting for these people we needn't worry. There isn't a ship in the Seychelles Navy that's big enough to carry a Variable Depth Sonar rig. Glenn, what have your people been doing?"

"We got your friend to agree to help us," said Allard, a mischievous gleam in his eyes. "Our little diversion is on."

"Did he contact Paris to get their permission?"

"After the way they delayed granting permission to the *Aconit* to open fire, he doesn't want to get them involved."

"Let me see those," said Carver, accepting a handful of tear sheets from Jaskula. "Did Alain notify Reunion of what he plans on doing?"

"Since Colonel Bechereau already acknowledged that sub skippers give a 'wide interpretation' to their orders," Allard recalled, "Alain decided it's not necessary to tell him. But he sure wanted to know every detail of what we're planning."

"I see he did, and I fully understand why. We're asking him to put his career on the line for a decoy operation. If anything goes wrong with it, they'll take his boat and his gold anchors away. I know I sure wouldn't like it."

"As you've often said yourself, they'd have to haul your black ass off this boat in chains. For all his questions about our plans, he made remarkably few changes in them."

"He wants us to surface much farther away from the island than we decided," said Carver, giving a careful read to the *Casablanca*'s transmissions. "Twenty miles instead of twelve. And he wants to use the channel between Mahé and Silhouette? Not circle around them?"

"About a year ago one of their *Agosta*-class subs surveyed all the islands here," said Allard. "Some political crisis on Mahé caused the French to send in the *La Praya,* and she spent three weeks prowling these waters. Now the French Navy has the best, most up-to-date charts on the whole archipelago."

"I'm glad we can take advantage of someone else's handiwork. Have you webfoots decided how big a team you're going to put ashore? The Pentagon may have okayed the general idea, but they still want the specifics."

"Chen will go ashore with one demolition and one anti-air/anti-armor team. They'll create enough hell to look like an insurrection, and that's all I can afford. I'll need to reserve as much manpower as I can to make whatever rescue attempt Washington calls for."

"Artie always gets to do the fun jobs around here," Jaskula complained, trying to stretch in the confined room. "When am I gonna get to do something?"

"If this situation gets any worse, you will," Allard said more seriously. "Since the ELF antenna is still deployed, we better start transmitting the data now. Terry, do we have permission to begin?"

In addition to trailing the twenty-six-hundred-foot cable for the BQR-23 passive sonar system, the *John Marshall* also ran a thousand-foot wire antenna from the back of its conning tower. Designed to transmit and receive messages in the Extreme Low Frequency (ELF) radio bands, it nonetheless needed fifteen minutes to send a three-letter group. Even in a compressed, coded form, Allard would need more than an hour to transmit all the details of his decoy operation.

"At colleges across your country there are demonstrations against your imperialist space policies," said Torres, circling the ring of lights in the interrogation room. "When will you understand your people don't support you?"

"When you tell me *my* mother cried on 'Phil Dona-

275

hue,' " Rebecca answered, trying to follow the movement and sound of footsteps beyond the light stands. However, the glare was too strong, and there were too many people walking for her to keep track of Torres.

"Do not act smart with me, Mrs. Wheeler!" At the last moment Torres stepped though the ring and came up behind Rebecca. Because of his soft-soled shoes, she never heard him until he was shouting in her ear. "Your *intelligentsia* knows your mission was to push your imperialism into space! The oppressed nations of the Earth know it! When will you admit it? Stop crying and answer! Who sabotaged the computers on your shuttle? What orders did your commander give you?"

"Enough, Torres," a distant voice advised, coming from outside the ring of light stands. "I said enough! This session is over. Mr. Esparza, turn off these lights. I said turn them off!"

One by one, the powerful floods encircling the chair were extinguished, killing both the strong glare and the heat they produced. Until her eyes adjusted to the sudden drop in illumination, all Rebecca could see were blurred figures entering the room.

"What's the meaning of this?" Torres said finally, confronting the visitors to his interrogation room. "I'm about to break her and gain valuable information for our case against American hegemony."

"The decision has been made at Revolution House, Mr. Torres," said Sampras. "Untie her and take her back to the crew."

Rebecca heard the handcuffs, that bound her arms behind her, unlock and felt the links slide off her wrists. The first thing she did was rub them, then she wiped the tears from her eyes. By the time she could see clearly, Sampras was kneeling in front of her.

"Mrs. Wheeler, yours and Mrs. Harrison's ordeal

will soon be over," he continued. "Tomorrow, you will be freed. When you go back you can tell her that."

"What . . . what about the others?" Rebecca said, regaining her composure.

"Ah, yes, their freedom is more difficult. It's dependent upon your government's actions. Take her out."

Her legs stiff from sitting in the chair for more than an hour, Rebecca had to be helped to her feet by Alonso Parker and Dorson. At the door to the interrogation room, their way was momentarily blocked by a short, stocky man wearing a green flightsuit.

"Your freedom is an act of goodwill," said Mashari, smiling coolly. "My country was able to impress on another people's government the need for one, in spite of your country's aggression. I hope you and Mrs. Harrison will take that message with you when you go."

"You're late," Torres remarked, after the door was finally shut behind Parker. "What delayed you? I was beginning to enjoy myself."

"We knew you would. We decided to have a lunch first, and allow you a little more time with the woman. Did she tell you anything new?"

"No. But I did have her close to breaking when you came in. I still think this is unwise. Have you told the press about your 'act of goodwill'?"

"Not until much later," said Sampras. "We want to give the Americans the night to think it over and guess what our motives are."

"And the euphoria we create tomorrow will give us the time we need to steal their most prized technology," Mashari added, still smiling. "The next transport I send home will have a billion dollars worth of their secrets on board it."

"Clay, someone's at the door," Glassner warned, his ear pressed against it until he heard its lock start clicking.

"Okay, back off from it," said Reynolds. "And stay cool. Let's not have a repeat of last night."

Post, Reynolds, and Julie abandoned their lunches to join Glassner at the room's entrance. Before they could reach him, the door was swung open by Parker and Dorson. Rebecca was pushed inside. It was all done without a word or even a smile from the security force personnel; it was over in seconds.

"Girl, what did you do to get out so soon?" said Julie, embracing her. "Torres kept me an hour longer than this."

"Nothing," said Rebecca, still wiping tears from her eyes. "We're being freed! That Lazare Sampras stopped my questioning and told me you and I are going to be released tomorrow morning!"

"Us? Free? Thank God!" Julie squeezed Rebecca again and laughed, a momentary elation. Until her expression grew somber and she glanced at the other members of the crew. "What about the others, Rebecca? What about the guys?"

"They're not being freed . . . our release is a good-will gesture. Theirs will be dependent on what Washington does."

"It's a publicity stunt," said Glassner. "We should've expected something like this."

"A distinctly Arab publicity stunt," Post added. "Like our embassy hostages in 'seventy-nine. The TWA airliner in 'eighty-five, and Iraq a few years ago."

"Well, I'm not going to be part of any stunt," said Julie. "Especially for these bastards."

"You're leaving tomorrow and that's an order,"

278

Reynolds commanded, trying to be stern all the time a smile crept onto his face. "The bastards can use you for a publicity stunt all they want. The important thing is you'll be free and you'll be able to tell NASA and the military everything you know. And anything you tell them will help whatever rescue forces are out there."

"I'd rather stay here. I took my share of the risks the last time I went into space, I'll do so now. I didn't become an astronaut to get preferential treatment. If I wanted that, I'd have stayed in college."

"If she's not going then I'm not going," Rebecca declared nervously. "I don't want to be the one who looks like she's a coward."

"Neither of you are cowards," said Reynolds. "And only the assholes will accuse you of being one."

"Like an asshole with a TV show?" Julie responded. "Phil Donahue had my mother on his show."

"Who cares about Phil-fucking-Donahue? I don't, and neither should you. I just want you guys safe. And telling our people everything you know. If these assholes want to use you for a publicity stunt, fine. We'll use their stunt for our own ends."

"Gordo, something big and yellow is coming out of that Ilyushin," said Hall, still watching airport activity through his rifle's scope. So long, in fact, that he had since attached the PSG-1's kit tripod to its stock.

"What the hell is that thing?" Hassler asked, sweeping his binoculars out to the airport and refocusing them.

"It looks like some sort of giant erector set." Hall pivoted his rifle a fraction of an inch in order to follow the lifting frame as it was towed off the Il-76.

"They're taking it straight into the hangar. I guess they don't want anyone to know what it is or what it's for."

"We'll take note of it, and report it to Glenn later. Wait, we got another arrival."

A squat, sand-camouflaged vehicle slowly inched down the ramp under the Ilyushin's tail. In spite of the distance between the airport and the reconnaissance team's observation post, the vehicle's wide, flat turret and quad gun barrels made it readily identifiable.

"It's another ZSU," said Hall. "That makes two. I suppose they'll try hiding it like the other. What's happening, Lieutenant? Where's that noise coming from?"

"One of the Blinders," Hassler replied, moving his binoculars around. "Strange. It's taking off earlier than the others. It's not following the schedule we've seen. Something's happening. I better get down its takeoff time."

Even in the distant mountains, the sound of the bomber's Koliesov turbojets could be heard. At the observation post, it was a long, muted rumble; much closer it grew to an earsplitting roar as the needle-nosed giant used most of the runway's length to get airborne. It hurtled away from Point Cascade, tracking straight for Victoria's harbor. By the time it reached the city, the Tu-22 had started to turn north; its twin engines leaving a single, dense trail of black smoke curving behind it.

After an entire morning of constant shuttling, the last Marine Corps UH-1N clattered away from the *Simpson*'s landing pad. Like all the other transfer flights, the sand and brown helicopter swung to the

280

east and climbed slowly because of its full passenger load. Below it, the *Alacrity* and the *Aconit* were already steaming in the same direction — not for the *Comfort,* but for Diego Gracia. Both would be refueled and reprovisioned there.

"Mr. Locke. Mr. Kilworth. Welcome back," said Stine, returning the salutes of the two officers who joined him on the starboard bridge wing. "I hope you enjoyed your duties on the other ships."

"I'll miss the food," said Kilworth. "The *Aconit* may not have been the most modern ship I've been on, but she was the best provisioned."

"How come we're not going to the Rock with them?" Locke requested, glancing at the two grey slabs of steel heading east.

"We already have enough fuel and supplies," said Stine. "And the Navy needs us elsewhere. Dean's refitting the helos for ASW work. We're being assigned to escort the *Belleau Wood.*"

"Captain, this just came on the evac channel," advised the seaman, handing over a tear sheet he had carried up from the Combat Information Center.

"Who's it from?" said Locke.

"Captain Raina on the *Navarin,*" Stine answered. "He says it was a pleasure to work with us, and hopes to do so again. He just got his orders to depart and join the Russian fleet. Barry, hold on. I want you to take a message back to CIC."

"It's from the *Simpson*'s captain," said Raina, glancing through the sheet the radio room technician handed him. "He thanks us on behalf of the U.S. Navy and NASA for our help. And wishes us luck in our next assignment."

"I think I see him, Anatoli Pavlovich," said Major

281

Yegorov, training his binoculars out the bridge's port side. "He and some of his officers are waving at us."

"Yes, I see them." Raina swung his binoculars onto the warship riding beyond the *Navarin*'s port bow and focused them. "I still think they assigned too young an officer to command that ship."

"After we rendezvous with our fleet, where do we go next?"

"Sri Lanka. After our navy refuels us, we'll make port at Colombo. I wonder how difficult it'll be to watch American space activities from there? Helm, steer course zero-four-zero degrees. Make ten knots."

Changing slightly from a due north to northwest heading, the *Navarin* slowly broke away from the *Simpson*. The last exchange the two ships had was the lowering of their flags as they departed. Minutes later the distance between the two had opened up to several miles. Inside of half an hour, they were only dark specks on the horizon to each other; *Alacrity* and *Aconit* were out of sight, too.

"Ladies and gentlemen, I'm sorry I'm late," Nicolson apologized, when he entered the briefing room overlooking Diego Garcia's flight line. "I was waiting for some last-minute information. Please, be seated."

Once he appeared, the assembled officers and civilians came to attention around the table. When he reached the empty chair at its head, they retook theirs. The moment the squeaking and rattling stopped he began the meeting.

"The hospital ship *Comfort* now has all the evacuees on board it from the multinational fleet," he said, opening his folder. "It will now head for Oman where civilian airliners will fly the evacuees to their home countries. The French and British ships are due in here tomorrow for reprovisioning. The *Simpson* is joining our fleet and the *Navarin* is joining Russia's. Earlier today Vice Admiral Richard Bryant, commander of the Persian Gulf Task Force, met with Admiral Oleg Khomenko. As Mr. Cochran's Glavkosmos friends suggested, the Russians want to cooperate, but they admitted they have precious little influence with the Seychelles government."

"If only this could've happened ten or even five years ago," Brenner commented, sitting with the rest of the NASA personnel. "Then the Russians could've wielded some real influence."

"Wishing the situation were different won't make it so. Those with real influence in the Seychelles have been active there. These satellite photos are only a few hours old."

Nicolson pulled from his folder a stack of black and white pictures and distributed them around the table in sets of three. The first one showed the nearly circular island of Silhouette to the west of Mahé, while the other two were detail shots of the international airport.

"What's going on in this one?" Cochran asked, examining the first picture.

"This is Silhouette Island," said Nicolson. "Where our SEAL recon squad was parachuted in. If you'll notice the boats in the lower left corner? That's the area where the team landed, and Seychelles forces are conducting a sweep in it."

"So, they know we got someone there," said Raymond Fuller. "Is the recon squad still on Silhouette?"

"No, they're on Mahé and are watching the airport. The other two photos show a Libyan Air Force Il-76 shortly after its arrival. They parked it next to your shuttle and under its tail appears to be part of its cargo. Can you identify it, Ed?"

"It's difficult to say," said Cochran, concentrating on the third shot and borrowing Diana Danforth's glasses to magnify it. "It looks like something we're carrying. Phil, let's have our ground crew look at this. Admiral, what else is happening? What about those subs you told us about?"

"Both the *Marshall* and the *Casablanca* have reached Mahé," Nicolson answered. "And they'll be active tonight. Washington's given Terry Carver the go-ahead to land another SEAL squad."

"I hope this kind of activity doesn't jeopardize our negotiations."

"Terry's an experienced sub skipper, I doubt it will. And I may have some good news about the negotiations." Nicolson reached into his folder again and produced a single tear sheet which he handed to Cochran. "That's a cable from our embassy in Victoria. There's going to be a press release later today and a major news conference tomorrow morning in Revolution House. From the way that sounds, it could be hopeful."

"In fact the press release should be ready any minute now," said Cochran, checking his watch after reading the sheet. "Can you contact the embassy directly? If it is good news, I'd like to hear about it as soon as possible."

Fifteen

Night Operations
Discovery

"We're clear," said Carver, finishing his periscope walk. "Patrick, take us up. Radar, this is the Conn. Raise your masts and start sweeping. Mike, tell Glenn to get his team ready to disembark. Lookouts, to the tower."

All the *Marshall*'s helmsmen had to do was tilt the diving planes up a few degrees and in seconds her conning tower was breaking the ocean's calm surface. The moment it did so both the radar and Electronic Surveillance Measures masts were extending into the air. At the top of the first mast, a crescent-shaped antenna rotated continually, scanning an almost empty sea for any planes or surface ships.

Standing at the control center's back, Jaskula flipped a toggle on a bitch box and quietly relayed Carver's orders to Allard. By the time the submarine had finished surfacing, a hatch was opening on its aft section at the point where its missile casing sloped down to blend into the hull. Apart from the lookouts who manned the tower's flying bridge, the team that climbed through the hatch were the only people to appear on the sub.

"Good luck, Artie. And no fireworks till we give you the word," said Allard, helping push the raft from the escape trunk below the hatch.

"Don't worry, Glenn. We'll be good boys," Lieutenant Arthur Chen promised. "All right, let's get this thing inflated! We'll do it just like the exercises! Glenn, tell 'em to raise the guardrails!"

As he pushed the heavy pack onto the missile casing, Chen grabbed its lanyard. When his men took hold of the raft, he pulled the cord, firing the gas cartridges inside it. In moments, the bundle of rubber and Kevlar was taking form, growing rigid enough for the SEALs to load their equipment in it. By the time its inflation had finished, the engine and fuel tank were being installed.

"Paul, get the engine started!" said Chen. "The rest of you, grab the rails!"

Chen raised his hand and lowered it in a chopping motion. Even in the early evening darkness, it was visible; Allard repeated the signal, then closed the hatch. An explosive hiss erupted from the submarine's hull, and the air filled with geysers of seawater. Its ballast tanks had been opened, and the air inside them was being purged.

The squad received a final wave from the lookouts in the conning tower before they disappeared below and waves started lapping over the missile casing. At a speed of five knots, the *Marshall* was settling into the water instead of diving. Even so, the SEALs strained to hold onto the guardrails until the zodiac was floating off the hull.

It drifted backwards until it cleared the rails, then the idling motor was gunned and the raft turned sharply to the left. With a last slap of waves against its tower, the *Marshall* disappeared except for its periscope. For a moment Chen's squad was alone on an empty sea, until another periscope flashed a signal light and the *Casablanca* started to rise.

More than a hundred and seventy feet shorter than the missile boat, the French attack sub also had a smaller silhouette. The detail that appeared on its forward hull was its most visible part. They threw a line to the raft and helped it pull alongside. The squad's equipment packs were hurriedly transferred to the submarine; the last to get passed through the hatch were the zodiac's engine and fuel tank.

"This is going to sound like one almighty fart," Chen warned, grabbing hold of two valves on the raft's interior. "Here goes!"

The moment the escape valves were opened they emitted a loud, flatulating hiss. The chorus was amplified when the valves on the opposite side were also unlocked. As opposed to its rapid inflation, the raft needed much longer to deflate. It was a wet, rumpled mess when it was manhandled down the forward hatch.

"It's nice to see an American face again," said the U.S. Navy officer standing at the bottom of the ladder. "Welcome aboard the *Casablanca*, Lieutenant."

"Very funny, Stackpole," said Chen, one of the last men to come off it. "Where's the captain? I thought he'd be here to greet us?"

"He's probably still talking to Carver. He thought it would be the best protocol if I were to welcome you. Come along, I'll take you to the attack center."

"Not before we deal with this." Chen pointed to the pile of rubber and Kevlar everyone was walking on. "Albért, let's take it to your torpedo room. We'll be able to refold it there."

Less than a minute after its forward hatch was

shut, the *Casablanca* opened all its ballast tanks. Unlike the *Marshall*, it crash-dived; within minutes of levelling off at five hundred feet, it was changing course to the northwest. Heading for the channel between Mahé and Silhouette as arranged.

"Viper One to Viper Three, we have reached the patrol area," al-Rayes advised. "Have you anything to report? Over."

"The Americans have their Tomcats and a radar plane airborne," said the pilot of the outbound Tu-22. "They approached us at the start of our patrol, but not after. Over."

"Roger, our ESM system has already detected them. They are expected. This is Viper One, out."

Though they were both at forty thousand feet, al-Rayes caught only a fleeting glimpse of the Tupolev heading back to Mahé. Its formation and anticollision lights streaked by his left wingtip. Apart from the moon and the stars they were the only lights he had seen since departing the Seychelles.

"Major, I have strong radar emissions. Both surface and airborne," warned Sergeant Badran, seated behind al-Rayes.

"Which are the closest and how far are they?" said al-Rayes.

"The airborne sources are nearest. They're a hundred and twenty kilometers away."

"Good. The game is about to begin. Arm ECM systems."

Al-Rayes pushed his control wheel forward, initiating a steep dive. Heavy with fuel for an extended patrol, the Blinder dropped out of the sky. In less than a minute it had fallen more than a mile and broken the sound barrier. From the back of its landing gear nacelles, tiny clouds of aluminum foil strips were ejected into its slipstream.

"Jeff, how come we have to fly the red-eye patrol?" complained the Naval flight officer in the lead F-14A. "I thought you were Andy's good friend?"

"What can I say?" said Lieutenant-Commander Jeff Easton. "He wants us all to have some night flying experience. Don't worry, your *Playboys* will still be in your cabin when we get back to the *Ike*."

"Green Hornet Three, this is Turntable. The relief Blinder has just started to dive and is releasing chaff. Prepare for intercept. Over."

"Roger, sounds like he's going for a low-altitude run. Better get the Quick Reaction Alert pair up. Over. Bud, you got this guy?"

"I have him. And he is dumping chaff," said Lieutenant Spader, watching his scope momentarily cloud up with multiple returns. "I'll fix this. Switching from track-while-scan to single target tracking."

"Good, don't let him weasel out," said Easton. "Green Hornet Three to Green Hornet Four, let's tag this camel driver before he gets over the fleet. Changing to one-seven-zero degrees."

Flying more than a mile apart since the start of their patrol, the two F-14s closed ranks before breaking out of their orbit and changing course to intercept the bomber. They left behind the fleet's guardian, an E-2C Hawkeye cruising about a mile below their altitude. Apart from the helicopters, it was now the only aircraft over the ships.

"Sergeant, stop firing the chaff systems," al-Rayes ordered, cutting back his throttles. "Pilot to Naviga-

289

tor, prepare to open bomb bay doors. Prepare to deactivate radars."

The reduction in power caused the Blinder's velocity to fall below the sound barrier. When al-Rayes pulled on his control wheel it quickly ended its dive; though it had less than a thousand feet of altitude left by the time it bottomed out.

"Open bomb bay doors," al-Rayes continued. "Release package. Deactivate all radars, including radar altimeter."

A lozenge-shaped canister fell out of the bomb bay, tumbling end over end until it hit the water. When it resurfaced the canister's transmitter deployed its aerials and began operating. By then the Tu-22 was miles away, heading due east and skimming the ocean at less than five hundred feet. All its radar and radio systems had been shut down, even its external lights were switched off. For all intents and purposes, it had disappeared.

"Green Hornet One, you are clear for launch."

"Roger, Sky Cap. Opening throttles," said Andrew Kearns, pushing his throttle levers forward.

The Tomcat strained against its catapult strop as its turbofans increased to full thrust. Behind it a blast deflector plate rose out of the *Eisenhower's* flight deck, while in front most of the plane crew jumped to their safety stations. Only a yellow-jacketed director remained, giving the last signal to Kearns before he felt his nose gear compress.

From a standing start, the Tomcat accelerated to a hundred and fifty miles an hour in three seconds. At the end of the catapult track, its nose gear strop disengaged from the lug and it hurled into the night sky; its afterburners emitted twin plumes of blue-white fire. In seconds the fighter's landing gear, leading edge slats, and flaps were retracted, and its wings sweeping back to increase speed. As it left the *Eisenhower* behind, a second F-14 was roaring down the carrier's number one catapult.

"Turntable, this is Green Hornet One. I'm airborne with Green Hornet Two," said Kearns, glancing over his shoulder to make sure his wingman was climbing after him.

"Roger, Hornet One," said the Hawkeye's senior controller. "Be advised that we've lost track of the Blinder, and we've picked up an ELT beacon. We think it may have crashed. Over."

"Understood, Turntable. What are your orders? Over."

"We are commencing search and rescue operations in the crash area. You and Hornet Two are to remain over the fleet until we decide what to do with you. Over."

"Will do, Turntable," Kearns answered. "Hornet One, out. Hornet Two, looks like the intercept's ended before it began. Let's get in a little night flying."

"Changing radar to surface search mode," said Spader, working the hand controller to the Tomcat's AWG-9 set. "If there's still something down there I'll find it."

"I hope we don't get accused of shooting this guy down," said Easton. "That's just what the Libyans would try pulling."

"If they want to fuck with eagles they better learn to fly first," remarked Ken Pickens, Easton's wingman.

"Eagles? You ain't flying no Eagle," said the back-

291

seater in Green Hornet Four. "You're flying a Tomcat. I always knew you were an Air Force man."

"Okay, you guys. Cool it," Easton ordered. "Keep your radar in velocity search mode. We'll do the surface search. Have you spotted the helos yet? Over."

"We got two inbound," said Pickens. "A Sea King and a Seahawk. They'll be here in the next ten minutes. I hope they find something quick. Over."

Now down to ten thousand feet, the F-14s had again separated and swept their wings forward for low-speed flight. They orbited in the area of the last radar contact with the Tu-22; waiting for the helicopters pulled off ASW operations to arrive and begin a more detailed search.

"Quiet. There's someone out there," warned Patterson, immediately causing the hushed conversation to fall silent. "Tom, is that you?"

"You're getting good, Bruce," said Belford, a dark figure materializing out of the night and dense undergrowth.

"What gives? I thought you were to be on watch for another two hours?"

"I know, but Gordo's relieved me so I can relieve myself. C'mon, I need an escort."

"What, you need someone to hold your hand while you pee?" asked Hall, still eating the brownie from his Meal, Ready to Eat (MRE) pack.

"No, I need an escort because that's what the lieutenant says we have to do," said Belford, irritated.

"I'll go," said Patterson. "But don't think I'm going to hold your hand."

Moving out from the reconnaissance squad's base camp, Belford and Patterson first had to climb over the depression's ridge before they could make their way down the side of the mountain to the slit trench that had been dug for latrine use. While Belford kneeled at its edge and unbuttoned his fly, Patterson stood watch a few feet lower on the slope.

"Before you left, what was going on?" he asked.

"The airport's pretty busy," said Belford. "Those Italian transports are getting racks loaded in them for sonobuoys. And some sort of frame is going up around the *Phoenix*."

"Tom, you okay? You're not getting sick, are you?"

"No, I'm taking a leak. Why?"

"Because I hear somebody barfing," said Patterson, his voice dropping to a whisper. "Get over here."

"What? Now?" protested Belford. "I'm taking a leak."

"Then tie a knot in it. C'mon, we got company."

Not bothering to do up his pants, Belford moved away from the trench and crept down to Patterson. The closer he got to his position the more audible the sounds of vomiting became.

"He's no more than a dozen feet away," Patterson said softly, pointing in the direction that the sounds came from.

"Christ, he's closer than that," Belford managed to say, before the snapping of twigs betrayed the intruder's true position.

Half-staggering, half-falling, a People's Defense Force soldier virtually blundered on top of the two SEALs. He bounced against the tree beside them and raised the bottle of rum he still managed to carry above his head. All that did was spill the rest of its contents over his already soiled uniform.

A flash of burnished metal in his hand was the only indication Patterson had drawn his commando knife. In a single motion he rose and lunged at the soldier, driving the knife's double-edged blade into his throat.

No scream or cry of pain came out of his lips, only a gargling noise and a few trickles of blood. In seconds the man was dead, his lifeless body slumping against the tree.

"Get Gordo down here now," Patterson whispered, pulling his knife from his victim. "And be quiet about it. This guy ain't the only company we have."

"Major, the Americans have fallen for our trick," said Badran, laughing. "In their radio traffic they're talking about a rescue operation. They're no longer hunting us."

"Good. Just as we hoped for," said al-Rayes. "Keep watching your equipment, Sergeant. Let me know the instant any radar signal changes or a new one is detected. Pilot to Navigator, what is our position?"

"Two hundred kilometers northeast of the fleet," answered Lieutenant Kalmendi, checking the panel to the Blinder's inertial navigation system. "And we're maintaining our course."

"Stand by for change. We're going to probe them."

Al-Rayes slowed his aircraft before swinging it to the west in a gentle port turn. When he levelled its wings, the Tu-22 was heading back to the fleet, still at five hundred feet and travelling at less than six hundred miles an hour. After skirting the battle group's radar coverage for the last few minutes, it would again be penetrating it.

"Jeff, I'm not getting much," said Spader, watching the returns from the AWG-9's surface scans. "If there was any debris down there I'd be getting it. What do the helos say?"

"They're not seeing any floating wreckage either,"

294

said Easton. "Or any oil slicks. They're still looking but I don't think they'll find anything. I got the feeling this jet either broke up completely or didn't crash at all. Something here just doesn't add up."

"Bruce, who else do you think is here?" asked Hassler, creeping up to the location of the dead soldier.

"There's a vehicle down there on the road," Patterson replied quietly, pointing at a set of head- and taillights barely visible through the dense forest of hardwoods and palm trees. "And there's someone in it. I've heard them laughing, and I think one of them is a woman."

"What the hell was this guy doing?" Hassler glanced over at the dead Seychelles soldier, a crumpled figure lying at the base of the tree where he had been killed. "Why was he climbing up this mountain?"

"I didn't think to ask him. Hell, he was drunk and so are the people down there. What are we going to do about them?"

Above Patterson's whispers, the echoing call from one of the soldier's companions could be heard. It was a singsong repetition of a man's name, friendly but incessant.

"We have to kill them," said Hassler, unpacking his Colt .45 and fixing a silencer to its muzzle. "I want it done quickly. I think there's only two or three of them. If there is, we'll use knives. If there's more, we'll have to use sidearms."

"Gordo, does that include the woman?" Belford asked, crouching beside Hassler.

"Of course it does. And remember, yesterday you wanted to kill somebody so now's your chance. Arm your weapons and move. Let's kill these people before they escape."

"Looks like all we're going to get here is some night flying experience," sighed Kearns, glancing out his canopy to recheck his wingman. The glowing strips of formation lights in the second F-14's nose, tail fins, and wingtips made it easy to locate. "How are those helicopters doing?"

"On our last sweep in that quadrant they were real busy," said the backseater. "Hold on, hold on . . . I got something at long-range, and I don't think it's one of ours."

"What's it look like?"

"Big and slow-moving, around five hundred knots. It's also at low altitude. I'm picking up no IFF from it, and the ALQ isn't detecting any radar signals."

"Someone's trying to be invisible," said Kearns, before he hit his transmit switch. "Turntable, this is Hornet One. We got a bogey, northeast quadrant."

"Major, airborne radar signals are growing stronger," said Badran, the moment his ESM panel lights changed. "The Americans may be detecting us."

"Stand by on your ECM," said al-Rayes. "We're retreating."

Pushing the throttles to their gatestops, al-Rayes used the surge of power from his engines to help swing the Tupolev around and lift it away from the ocean. At a thousand feet he cut in the afterburners; the jets of flame the Koliesov engines produced could be seen for miles, though the only people who could have seen them were beyond the horizon.

The bomber reversed its course and accelerated out of the area; breaking the sound barrier within minutes of the afterburners kicking in. From its main landing gear nacelles, more clouds of aluminum foil strips were ejected and scattered by the slipstream.

"David, what do you have?" asked Admiral Bryant, as he entered the *Eisenhower's* Combat Information Center and went directly to its captain.

"One of the Libyan bombers is playing games with us," said David McQuay. "At first we thought it crashed. Now it appears to be probing our northeast sector. I've ordered the planes aloft to use secure channels and the joint data system. We're scrambling a tanker and readying more fighters."

McQuay pointed to the CIC's main tactical screen, indicating the two pairs of F-14s already airborne, the E-2C Hawkeye, and the helicopters still conducting search operations. Beside the symbol for each, a block of data was displayed; the Joint Tactical Information Data System had been activated and was not only linking them to the carrier, but the rest of the ships in the fleet.

"Nail this bastard," said Bryant, starting to smile. "Relay that to the Hawkeye. Let them handle the intercept, they can do anything short of shooting it down."

"Charlie, Charlie, Charlie! C'mon man, it's getting late."

Much closer to the road, the call did not echo. The soldier making it stood on the road's tiny gravel shoulder; when he stepped one foot beyond it he was standing in the jungle. And he was almost on top of Hassler and Patterson.

"Not yet," Hassler whispered, almost subliminally. He laid a hand on Patterson's shoulder, then looked past him to the white Suzuki jeep the woman was sitting in. When he saw a shadow creep out of the jungle behind it, he tapped Patterson's shoulder.

The burnished metal of the knife's blade flashed a little brighter in the jeep's headlight beams. As he rose, Patterson drove his knife into the soldier's stomach and up; until it hit the breastbone. The soldier let out a loud moan and doubled up, wrapping his hands so tightly around the knife's handle that Patterson had difficulty letting go of it.

The woman in the jeep stood up and started to cry out a name, then shrieked when Belford's knife entered her back. It slid under her left shoulder blade and punctured her heart. She stiffened briefly, before sinking down into the passenger seat. The open bottle of rum she held in her hand fell to the floor and tumbled over when it landed, spilling what remained of its contents.

Belford allowed the body to settle into the seat before trying to remove his knife. When a pair of headlights curved into view on the road, he barely had enough time to arrange the body in a natural-looking pose before having to hide in the jungle. When the truck finally rumbled by the position, all its driver saw was a woman apparently sleeping in the front seat of a jeep.

"I'm turning to port," said al-Rayes. "Tell me if there's any change in the enemy radars."

At Mach One even a gentle turn produced G-forces; they pushed al-Rayes deeper into his seat and caused his arms to grow heavy. The effects ended when the maneuver did, by which time the Tupolev was streaking due west at just under eight hundred miles an hour.

"The airborne radars are still behind us but growing weaker," Badran remarked. "And I'm no longer detecting as many surface radars."

"Standard American response to a threatened air attack," said al-Rayes. "Perhaps we can use this . . . I'm slowing us down. Lieutenant Kalmendi, activate radar altimeter and main radar in surface mapping mode only. Be ready to switch them off when I tell you."

With some of its radar systems on, the Tu-22 got an accurate reading on its altitude and detailed scans of what was under it. Once its afterburners were turned off the bomber decelerated to subsonic speed. It did not porpoise when it dropped back to the heavier air at low altitude; when it turned due south, it did not get the same increase in G-forces.

"Lieutenant, deactivate radars," al-Rayes ordered. "Let's not give them any warning of where we are until we're ready to."

"Green Hornet Three, this is Turntable. Return to fleet patrol," said the Hawkeye's senior controller, his voice now slightly distorted by the secure channel's scrambling and descrambling. "Change your radar to track-while-scan. Over."

"Roger, Turntable. Will do," sighed Easton. "Bud, you got that?"

"Sure do. Switching modes to track-while-scan," said Spader. "This is better, I got Andy and his wingman."

"So do I. Shit, all the opportunity and none of the luck."

By lowering his cockpit lighting to minimum levels, Easton could discern the distant glow of jet exhaust from the other pair of F-14s as they headed to the northeast. Directly over the fleet a new set of formation lights had appeared: a KA-6D tanker just launched by the *Eisenhower*.

"I wish we could join the C.O.," said Spader, watching the two Tomcats on his radar screen. "But I suppose someone has to stay and protect the fleet from missiles."

"At least it's us and not the Sundowners," said Easton, mentioning the name of the carrier's other F-14 squadron. "I hope we can nail this bastard before the captain calls them in."

"What took you guys so long?" Hassler demanded, when the rest of his squad finally arrived at the location of the first body.

"Sorry, Lieutenant. But we had to secure our base camp before we left it," said Foreman, standing beside the tree. Until he realized someone else was leaning beside it. "Good God, who's he?"

"A future traffic accident. Ty, Dale, grab him and carry him down to the road. Riker, I hope you got some of those C-Four charges."

In spite of two men carrying him, the dead soldier proved a heavy, difficult load to bring down the mountain. By the time Hall and Barton appeared with him, the other two bodies were already strapped into the jeep's front seats, and Riker was lying under its chassis.

"Where's Nick and Bruce?" Barton asked, straining under his half of the soldier's weight.

"I posted them as lookouts," said Hassler. "So we won't get surprised. Dump him in the back."

300

Stepping over Riker's legs, Hall and Barton lowered the body into the well behind the front seats.

"Lord, she's beautiful," said Hall, circling around to the jeep's passenger side. "I'm sorry you had to kill her."

"I'm sorry, too," Belford added, pushing the tussled hair out of the woman's face. With the knife removed from her back, she rested normally in the seat, and the tightly fastened harness made sure she sat upright. "I don't think she's much older than a teenager. She had no part in this mess. She was only out to have a good time. Why did it have to be her that I killed?"

"Because I ordered it," said Hassler. "It was necessary. Don't go guilt-tripping yourself, it's my responsibility. Now open some of these bottles and raise the jeep's roof. I've got the perfect way to make this look like an accident."

"Coming up on our time," warned Lieutenant Stover, watching the Combat Information Center's LED clock display. "Mark . . . Fire up the SPS."

"SPS radar activated," said Brody, tapping one of the larger buttons on the Anti-Air Warfare console. "And it's on-line."

Since joining the battle group, the *Simpson* had been stationed at its back, where it was now trailing the helicopter assault carrier *Belleau Wood*. Like the other escort ships, it was tied into the Joint Tactical Information Data System, which allowed it to see what their radars and sonars were detecting, along with the airborne helicopters and aircraft.

Because of the threat posed by the Libyan bomber, the entire group was operating under potential air attack conditions. Only a few ships at a time would switch on their radars to hunt for the intruder. For the next few moments it would be the *Simpson*'s turn.

"Walter, I got something," said Brody, before the SPS-48 radar had finished its first rotation. "Single target track. Travelling at low altitude, and it's big."

"Where is it and what is it?" asked Stover.

"About thirty miles northwest of us. Bearing, Three-Four-One degrees. Slick Thirty-Twos aren't picking up any hostile radar emissions. But I say this is the Blinder."

"Good work, Jerry. Deactivate the SPS. They probably already know we're here. Keep this up, and you may just erase your 'Bart of the Month' award."

"Major, I have a new radar source!" said Badran, startled by the lights flashing on one of his panels. "Surface radar, very close. Possibly a warship."

"What's its location?" al-Rayes demanded.

"Ahead of us, on our port side. There was nothing in the area before and . . . the radar has just been turned off. We're no longer being scanned."

"That doesn't mean we won't be intercepted. Are the airborne radars changing?"

"There's one more," said Badran. "But the emissions haven't changed strength or frequency."

"Don't worry. They will," said al-Rayes, dropping his hand onto his throttle levers. "Stand by on your jamming systems. Use them the moment we're tracked again. Lieutenant, prepare to switch on main radar."

Al-Rayes nudged his throttles forward a crack, increasing the Blinder's already high airspeed. To compensate for it, he raised the aircraft another few hundred feet; in spite of his increased vantage point, he still could not see any ships in the fleet ahead of him.

"We got him," said Kearns, watching the latest data system update appear on his CRT screen. "Jim, switch to single target tracking."

"I'm way ahead of you," advised the backseater. "I'm already tracking, and I got a fix. Come to Three-Four-One degrees. He's ninety-six miles out, at seven hundred feet."

"Hornet Two, stay behind me. I need some maneuvering room."

Kearns watched the airspeed, heading, and altitude numbers change on his Head Up Display as he swung to the northwest and pushed his aircraft's nose below the horizon line. Sitting just off his left shoulder was his wingman, Kearns could see the glow and flash of formation and anti-collision lights. As each F-14 dove and increased speed, their wings were swept back and their glove vanes extended to keep them stable.

"We're being tracked," Badran announced. "Activating chaff dispensers."

"I'm taking us up," said al-Rayes. "Lieutenant, activate radar. Surface search mode only. Find me the carrier."

Rising to one thousand feet, the Tupolev dumped raw fuel into its afterburner chambers again and was soon breaking Mach One. Its Short Horn radar came on, and began sweeping the ocean in front of it for the fleet that was still invisible.

"Sorry, Gordo. I couldn't make the charge stick to

the gas tank," said Riker. "So I did the next best thing."

Riker pointed to the jerry can attached to the jeep's tailgate. Its cap was hanging loose, when Hassler lifted it he found a wire antenna rising from the can's interior. When he pushed it, he heard the plastic explosive charge and detonator splash around in the gasoline.

"It won't get knocked off in here," Riker continued. "And the antenna is sure to get the radio signal."

"Five gallons of gas will make one hell of a bang," said Hassler. "All right, let's get this accident rolling. Tyrone, are you ready?"

"Lord, yes," Hall gagged, reeling away from the driver's side of the now roofed-over jeep. "It smells like my uncle's den in here. Shouldn't we open all the bottles?"

"Hell, they're all made of plastic. What doesn't catch fire in the crash will melt and explode later. Put the rock on the clutch pedal and shift it into third gear. Gordo to lookouts, what's your status?"

Idling since it had been pulled over, the Suzuki jeep had all its passengers inside and its canvas roof deployed. The bodies were liberally soaked with the liquors which had been brought along for partying. Now, they would add to the incineration.

"Gordo, this is Bruce. We're clear to the east," said Patterson, his voice heard by everyone working on the jeep.

"Gordo, this is Nick. We're clear to the west," said Foreman.

"All right. Here we come," Hassler answered, pressing the transmit bar on his walkie-talkie. "Let me know the minute anything changes. Out. Ty, you walked the course so you steer. Release the brakes. John, get your detonator ready. Everyone else, push."

304

With its wheels turned hard left and three men straining against its back, the jeep moved off the road's one shoulder and picked up speed when it hit the downhill grade. Only the road's right side had a shoulder, the left side was a steep slope guarded by a wall of hand-carved volcanic rock. The wall was not in the best repair, in several places it had weakened and gaps had opened. Hall steered the jeep for one of the openings, until he could no longer run fast enough to keep up with it.

"Let go! Let go!" Hassler shouted as the four men either stopped or jumped away from the vehicle. "John, get ready."

Even with no one pushing it, the jeep's speed continued to increase. It hit the wall doing almost thirty miles an hour and easily broke through. Just as it disappeared from view, Riker triggered the detonator. The jerry can erupted with a jarring thunderclap; it had engulfed the jeep in a fireball before it finished crashing to the bottom of the slope. Hassler and the others only took a few moments to observe their handiwork, then retreated. By the time the unopened liquor bottles and the internal fuel tank were exploding, they and the rest of the squad were hiking up to their base camp.

"Shit! Andy, he passed right under us. How can something that big do Mach One so low?"

"You'd be surprised, Jim, at what brute force and ignorance can do," said Kearns. "And there's plenty of both in a Tupolev. Turntable, this is Hornet One. I don't think we'll catch him before he reaches the *Ike*. But if he's too busy watching us, Hornet Three could surprise him. Over."

"Roger, Hornet One. We understand," said the

Hawkeye's senior controller. "Keep the Blinder occupied, we'll take care of the rest."

"Will do, Turntable. This is Hornet One, out."

As they approached the ocean's surface, the two F-14s cut their afterburners to reduce speed. They broke hard left, for a time almost standing on their port wings, and levelled out. They were now at roughly the same altitude as the bomber and directly behind it. They increased speed again, though they would not be able to overtake it until it reached the *Eisenhower*.

"If I switch to single target tracking I can burn through the chaff he's dropping with velocity search," said Spader, watching the trail of electronic snow on his scope.

"No, don't change your modes," Easton ordered. "The E-2 thinks that will give us away. Just activate the ALE and set it on manual."

The original pair of F-14s dropped their noses and swept back their wings. They went to afterburners to increase their velocity, and soon were plunging through the broken cloud layers at Mach Two. Some sixty miles ahead and thirty thousand feet below them was the approaching Tu-22. At current closure rate they would meet in two minutes.

"Tail gun, on," said Badran. "And I'm tracking the fighters behind us. What about the jets in front of us, Major? They appear to be diving."

"Ignore them," al-Rayes replied. "They're not after us if they haven't changed their radars to intercept modes. I'm more worried about the chaff clouds the ships are firing. Lieutenant, can you find the carrier?"

"I believe so," said Kalmendi. "It's too big for the chaff to hide completely. In another two minutes we'll be buzzing it."

"Bee Hind radar on and tracking us," said Kearn's backseater. "Shall I break its track?"

"Break it," said Kearns. "Give 'em something else to worry about. Thirty miles and closing. Twenty-eight. Twenty-six . . ."

The closure rate between the other pair of F-14s and the Blinder was unreeling so fast it could not be read as single numbers. Kearns watched the changing figure on his CRT screen, then glanced up to his HUD to get the distance between his jet and the bomber. The moment he slid into range of its 23-mm tail gun, he saw the closure rate for Easton's ships fall below twenty miles.

"We're out of here," Kearns warned. "Hold on to something."

Breaking sharply to the right, the pursuing Tomcats ended their part of the engagement. Still travelling at supersonic speeds, in seconds they had climbed to ten thousand feet and were miles away from the Tupolev.

"Levelling out," said Easton, groaning under the strain the building G-forces imposed. "Bud, what's the distance?"

"Fifteen miles," said Spader. "Now twelve!"

"Fire the flares, full spread! Hornet Four, you copy?"

The ALE-39 dispensers on each Grumman fighter began firing patterns of flares from their ejector chutes. Designed to decoy infra-red guided missiles,

307

the flares burned bright and hot. They trailed out behind the two fighters, which had ended their dives less than five hundred feet above the Tu-22. For ten seconds they released flares; then Easton broke to the left, and his wingman to the right.

"Major, the Americans are leaving!" Badran said triumphantly. Until he felt the aircraft unexpectedly pitch up. "What? What's happening?"

"Bastards! Bastards!" shouted al-Rayes, pulling sharply on his control wheel the moment he realized the lines of sputtering stars were rushing toward him.

Because of its supersonic speed, the moment it tipped its nose up the Blinder was climbing swiftly. Its run had ended a half-dozen miles short of the *Eisenhower*. In minutes both F-14 elements had reformed and were drawing alongside its wingtips. For the rest of its patrol over the battle group, the bomber would be closely escorted by the fighters.

"If you want to fly with eagles," said Easton, giving the Libyan aircraft the finger. "Andy, my fuel gauges are getting low. Can you watch him for us?"

"No problem," said Kearns. "Go ahead, the tanker's ready for you. Only leave a little for your C.O. This intercept's eaten into our fuel supply, too. Hornet One, out."

"Gordo, listen. Can you hear?"

Foreman's question stopped not only Hassler, but the rest of the squad. The clinking and rustling sounds they made collecting their equipment fell silent and, above the forest's own noises, a lonely wail filled the night air.

"It's a police siren," Hassler finally answered. "Sounds like someone finally spotted the fire."

"Probably those trainers that flew by here twenty minutes ago," said Hall. "We're getting out of here none too soon. Where do we go now?"

"Glenn already planned a fall back position for us, it's the next mountain over. We'll see the airport, but probably not the tracking station. Is everyone ready?"

"For a little midnight hiking? You bet," said Patterson, grunting as he lifted his backpack onto his shoulders. The rest of the squad nodded or motioned they were set.

"Good. Tom, that shit trench of ours covered?"

"I buried it so deep, the next time somebody finds our shit it'll be fossilized," Belford promised.

"Then let's move out," said Hassler, lifting his own pack onto his shoulders. "We only have the rest of tonight to climb down this mountain and up the next one."

"Good luck, you guys," said Stackpole, undoing the line that held the zodiac to the *Casablanca*. "Don't do anything crazier than I would."

"Don't worry," said Chen. "We're not going to sink the island. Just shake it up a little. Thanks, Mike. Cast us off."

When the line slipped out of the cleat, the raft's quietly puttering engine was gunned, and it swung away from the French nuclear attack sub. The men on the *Casablanca*'s upper hull quickly secured their detail and dropped through the forward hatch. Stackpole was the last to climb down it, approximately a minute after he did so the ballast tanks were being flooded.

309

Before the raft had gone a mile, the submarine had vanished, except for its search periscope and ESM mast. They remained raised until Chen's squad arrived at a secluded beach on Mahé's North Point peninsula. Then, they, too, disappeared, and the attack sub headed for deeper waters and an eventual rendezvous with the *Marshall*.

Sixteen

Revelation
Go Code

"We'll bring the women in through that entrance," said Sampras, pointing to one of the reception hall's many side doors. "And because of where we'll place the TV cameras, they'll see them while still in the passageway."

"You will place the reporters in the front rows?" Mashari requested, glancing at the seats being arranged before the hall's raised platform.

"Only the TV crews and photographers. Print reporters will sit farther back. Also, we'll allow the American ambassador and her staff to sit in the front rows."

"You're stage-managing this very well. Congratulations."

"Certainly better than you managed last night's encounter with the American fleet," said Foreign Minister Boigny, in spite of his bland voice he was still able to sound irritated. "What you ordered was dangerous, reckless. You could've damaged 'the illusion of progress' you spoke so much about."

"I know," said Mashari, smiling malevolently. "It

311

will keep the Americans guessing about us. Tonight, they'll look for another incident to happen around their fleet. Hopefully, what I'm planning will be so great a diversion that they'll never see the Ilyushin transport leaving here."

"Provided the Americans have no commandos on the island," Major el-Jabr added. "I still feel there may be some."

"For the last several days you and Captain Matubis searched everywhere for them," said Boigny, who started raising fingers as he mentioned island names. "Silhouette, Conception, Therese, Cerf, Saint Anne. Are you not satisfied with your efforts?"

"No, sir. They could be here . . . on Mahé itself. And frankly, the search would go much better if I could work with someone other than Peter Matubis."

"Major, please. Let's be cooperative with our hosts," said Mashari. "Will you be concentrating your efforts here?"

"Yes. There was an accident in the mountains last night," el-Jabr answered. "I will investigate it when I leave Revolution House."

"I recall hearing about it. It happened near the airport. . . . As soon as the conference ends I'll join you there. Good luck, Major. I hope what you find will be easily explained."

The knocking at the door was gentle, not the pounding the astronauts had grown accustomed to. Even though they were all awake and had finished breakfast, they did not respond immediately; their level of conversation was drowning out all other noises.

"Commander Reynolds, we've come for Mrs. Harrison and Mrs. Wheeler," said Corporal Dorson,

312

who spoke in a kindly voice and did not enter the room when Reynolds opened the door.

"What, no Bug Man? No Parker?" he asked. "Just you guys?"

"Yes, Commander, just us. Mr. Torres and Major Parker are waiting below at the van. Are the women ready?"

"Ready," said Julie, zipping shut her crew bag and lifting it off what had been her bed. "I guess this is goodbye, fellas. Good luck, Allan."

"Let's just go with a handshake," Glassner replied, holding up his hands when he realized Julie was going to wrap her arms around him. "My skin's still a little sensitive."

Following her more polite farewell with Glassner, Julie embraced both Post and Reynolds. Rebecca repeated the procedure, shaking Glassner's hand; then hugging the others. And for each, Reynolds had the same message, whispered lightly.

"Don't forget anything you saw or heard," he said. "And tell it all when the time comes."

"Don't worry," said Rebecca. "What I won't remember, Julie will. I hope we'll see you soon."

"Sorry, ladies. I have orders to do this," said Dorson, producing a set of blindfolds. "If you'll please?"

Without protest, Julie and Rebecca accepted the elasticized bands of heavy fabric and slid them over their eyes. Dorson's contingent of guards led them from the room and out to the same blacked-out van that had been used to take them on their meetings with the ambassador. Only when they were locked safely inside it were they allowed to remove the blindfolds. They would not see the outside world until they disembarked at Revolution House.

"Radio Room, secure the com buoy. All messages

received and decoded," Carver said darkly. Then he punched another button on his control panel. "Conn, this is the TASCO Room. As soon as the buoy is secure take us back to the *Casablanca*. We got a lot to talk about."

"Roger, Terry. Will do," Burks responded. "Do you want us to redeploy the ELF aerial?"

"Only when we're at our original depth. I don't want to be dragging that wire around while maneuvering."

"God, I can't believe this," said Allard, glancing through the primary message the *Marshall* had received. A few moments later he began reading it aloud. "Concerned Americans For A Sane Defense spokesman Cecil Atwater revealed the basing of your submarine in the Indian Ocean and commented extensively on its possible use. These comments are being carried today by both the *New York Times* and NBC News. It is expected that this revelation will adversely affect negotiations, and may hasten a military solution to the crisis."

Partway through Allard's reading, he and Carver felt the room pitch down and the turbines increase speed. After cruising at five hundred feet for only twenty minutes, the *Marshall* was returning to its original depth. As it approached nine hundred feet, its dive angle gracefully diminished until the eight-thousand-ton attack sub was riding level. Approximately a mile off its starboard side was the *Casablanca;* by then Carver had raised it and was talking to its captain.

"What will your Navy's plans be, Terry?" Jacoubet inquired. "Over."

"The *Eisenhower* will launch two strikes," said Carver. "One will be a decoy. The other will bomb the Libyan planes at the airport, and attempt to destroy the ZSU antiaircraft tanks. Glenn's team will land before that, and strike when the bombing begins. He'll rescue the astronauts first, then the *Phoenix*. He will be reinforced by Marines from the *Belleau Wood*. And they'll be reinforced by a unit from the Eighty-second Airborne. If we get the word, it could all happen tonight. Over."

"An excellent plan. Still, I hope it doesn't have to be used. Has Glenn heard from the squads he has on Mahé? Over."

"Let me answer that," said Allard, accepting the microphone stand Carver pushed toward him. "Alain, I heard from both. Chen's squad is scouting out targets for diversionary attacks. And Hassler's men are at a new observation site. They report some sort of frame is being erected around the *Phoenix*. You can bet your last dollar the Libyans are planning something. Over."

"Actually. I would prefer to bet my last franc," Jacoubet corrected. "Beyond landing your team, what should we plan for tonight? Over."

"Well. Since you asked," said Carver, grabbing the microphone away from Allard, "and since your operation with Glenn went so smoothly . . . I think we should plan a diversion for your boat for tonight. Are you game?"

"Lieutenant, there's a panel van leaving the military compound," said Hall, starting to track it with his rifle. "I think it may be carrying the women astronauts."

"Did you see where it started from?" Hassler requested, raising his binoculars and focusing on the distant vehicle weaving its way out of Seychelles International.

"Sorry, I didn't. But from what Nick's been monitoring, it has to be them."

"Shit. If we could've seen where it started, we'd know where the other astronauts are. Make a note of it. The same vehicles are usually used for the same duties, and there's always a chance our ambassador will meet them again. How far can you track it?"

"Only about a mile down the coast road," said Hall, lifting his head from the scope's eyepiece and rubbing the mark it left around his right eye. "And I can't see much of the NASA station either. You were right about this place."

"Second best always has more problems than your first choice," said Hassler, getting off his stomach, but rising no farther than a crouch. "Tom will relieve you soon. I'm going to check on our other post."

Higher up on the slope than their previous observation post, Hassler's squad now had a commanding view of southern and eastern Mahé. However, their view north was limited, and to the west it was completely blocked by the other mountains in the island's central spine.

Nearly two thousand feet above sea level, the air was cooler though heavier with humidity; only half as much rain fell in the lowlands as on the mountains. The forest at the higher altitudes was largely hardwoods, which gave a denser cover and allowed the squad members to move around a little easier.

Staying well away from the forest line and sprinting quickly from tree to tree, Hassler circled the new mountain to its southwestern side. Though little could be seen of the island from their second observation post, it did give the squad an excellent view of the crash site.

"Dale, what's happening?" said Hassler, crawling up to the saplings at the forest edge.

316

"The ambulances finally took the bodies away," said Barton, lowering the binoculars he was using.

"How did they look?"

"Pretty crisp to me. I doubt they'll get much off them. Right now it looks like there's mostly Army and security people down there. What's happening at the airport?"

"They're finishing their antisub conversions on those Italian transports," said Hassler, glancing suddenly to his right. "They now have depth charge racks. . . . Get down!"

It was their movement more than their engine noise that first attracted Hassler's attention. The two SF.260s skirted so close to the mountain that he and Barton could almost reach out and touch them. As their engines' flat howl filled the air, Hassler could read the stenciling on their fuselage sides, and see their rocket and gun pods under their wings. In seconds they were gone, turning west and following the southern shoreline.

"Any lower and we could've seen inside their cockpits," Barton commented. "This shit's getting heavier, Gordo."

"I know," said Hassler. "We may have seen the women astronauts being driven to Victoria. This activity will probably continue until after they're handed over. So stay concealed. No sun bathing, no cookouts."

"That lead vehicle was a BRDM," said Chen, finally feeling safe enough to whisper. "Think an Armbrust can penetrate it?"

"Like a hot knife through soft butter," answered Petty Officer Ken DeBrandt, leader of the anti-armor team. "Did you see the uniforms on some of those guys? They're Libyan paratroopers."

317

"I know. We've got a real Third World fruit salad to contend with. Paul, you got the time the patrol passed here?"

"Sure do, Lieutenant," said Petty Officer Webber, breaking cover to slide over to Chen's position. "You want me to record that helicopter as well?"

"Everything," said Chen. "From the sound of the *Marshall*'s last message, we may be going into action tonight. Pass the word along to relax. We'll move across the road in ten minutes and scope out the power plant."

"Mr. Sampras, Mr. Boigny. The astronauts have arrived," announced a guard who approached a collection of Seychelles, Libyan, and Cuban officials.

"Good. Bring them to the passageway and hold them there," said Sampras, smiling. Then he turned to the other officials. "Gentlemen, it's time to begin."

With Boigny leading them, the officials moved out of the ante room as a group and entered Revolution House's reception hall. A few hours before it had been empty except for workers and security personnel. Now, the cavernous chamber was filled with reporters, camera crews, diplomatic staff from various embassies, more security personnel, and government and communist party functionaries. The moment the group appeared, the hall's clamor of voices quieted down and the flash units started firing.

"In the name of our great leader, the beneficent Albert René," said Boigny, after stepping up to the speaker's podium on the raised platform. Even with a sound system, his bland voice barely rose above the hall's background rumble. "I address you again in this hour of national crisis. In these past days the Seychelles people have been subjected to the bullying

318

and intimidation of the world's superpower. Our fraternal allies have been harassed for coming to our aid, and most of the world's space powers have attempted to use the United Nations to dictate to us what our response should be to this illegal invasion . . ."

"What now?" Mashari asked coldly, when one of his officers tapped him on his shoulder. "Can't you see what we're doing?"

"Yes, Colonel. I know," said Captain el-Reedy. "But something grave has happened. You're needed. And so is Mr. Sampras."

The Security Minister gave the captain the same icy glare as Mashari had, then followed him off the raised platform and back into the ante room. There, he and Mashari found Colonel Mooradian and the Libyan and Cuban military attachés waiting for them. The looks on their faces betrayed the seriousness of the news they possessed.

"These messages were forwarded from our U.N. embassies in New York City," said Major Yashin, nodding to his Cuban opposite number. He handed copies of teletype tear sheets to both Mashari and Sampras. "The American press reports there is a secret 'commando' submarine operating from Diego Garcia. It could be operating with the American fleet. They say it has an entire U.S. Navy SEAL Team on board it."

"The submarine is called the USS *John Marshall,*" Mashari added, reading through the report. *"Marshall* . . . it was assigned to Diego Garcia following its involvement in the controversial *Ocean Valkyrie* incident. Now I know where I heard of this submarine. Colonel Nazih told me about it."

"I recall when it arrived at Garcia," said Sampras, his face draining of color. "We filed our usual protest about it."

"What? You knew it was there, and you didn't tell us?"

"Colonel, please. That happened almost a year ago," said Mooradian. "We forgot about it. We thought it had departed. The Americans rarely assign a warship to Garcia for so long."

"Then perhaps Major el-Jabr wasn't wrong in his suspicions," said Mashari, slowly and quietly. Until his eyes grew wide with fear. "Lazare, we have to stop the release of the women. Now!"

"What do you mean?" Sampras responded. "Yesterday you urged us to release them. Why stop it?"

"Because they can give their government all the information it needs to rescue the other astronauts. This has to be stopped."

"I'll handle Boigny. You two, stop the women. Send them back to the airport."

Whereas only a few cameras had followed their departure from the reception hall, many more tracked the men when they returned and split up. Sampras mounted the platform and went straight for the podium; where he interrupted the Foreign Minister's droning by cupping his hand around the microphone. Mashari and Mooradian walked around the platform, heading for the open door beside it; they picked up speed when they realized the women were already in the passageway.

"Take them back," Mashari barked, walking through the doorway. "Return them to the van, now!"

"What the hell are you doing?" Fernandez demanded, jumping out of his front-row seat. "You promised they'd be released."

"The situation has changed, Mr. Station Manager," said Mooradian, turning and attempting to block the entrance. "Your country does not wish to negotiate.

You have a new terror weapon you wish to use against the Seychelles people. Guards, seize him!"

Fernandez had only taken a few steps toward the doorway, toward the two figures in blue flightsuits he clearly saw inside it; but it was enough for Mooradian. His order brought the security personnel around the platform rushing to Fernandez; physically restraining him as the hall filled with a barrage of flashes and a chorus of reporters' questions.

"Mr. Boigny, I must protest the way Mr. Fernandez and the women astronauts are being handled!" said Lynn Griffen, trying to be heard above the din.

"They do not have diplomatic immunity!" Boigny answered, for once his voice rising to a shout. "Unlike you, Mrs. Ambassador! If Mr. Fernandez continues to resist, he will be arrested! You have lied to us! You wish to destroy our people's revolution, with a terror weapon that circles these peaceful islands like a great white shark."

"I have no idea what you're talking about."

"A nuclear submarine, filled with your trained assassins and saboteurs. Operating such a vessel in our territorial waters is in violation of our declaration as a nuclear-free zone. Your treachery has been revealed to the oppressed nations of the Earth. Your astronauts will be held for trial, all of them! Especially Commander Post, who participated in the criminal bombing of Libya in 1986. That's all, no more questions! Mr. Sampras, clear the hall!"

"I said back!" Mashari continued to bark, his voice filling the passageway; even drowning out the clamor rising behind him. "Guards, if they keep resisting drag them to the van!"

"But you promised we would be released," said Rebecca, angry and crying. She continued to wrestle with the guards, even when more joined in. "You promised! Julie!"

"Hold on, girl," she said, as calmly as she could with two guards holding her arms in viselike grips. "It's up to the military to get us out now. At least this way we'll be together."

"I don't believe this," Foreman uttered. "I'm watching it, and I don't believe it. C'mon, you guys. Stop crowding me in."

Except for those assigned as lookouts, the entire reconnaissance squad was gathered around the Allard Technology surveillance set. On its two-inch Liquid Crystal Display (LCD) screen, the chaos in the reception hall continued to be broadcast, until the Seychelles flag faded in and the country's national anthem started blaring.

"At least they're calling us *trained* killers," said Hassler. "I wouldn't like it much if they called us untrained killers."

"You know what this means, Lieutenant?" said Hall. "They'll be taking those two astronauts back to the others. Maybe we'll find out where they're all being held."

"That's right. You better go join Patterson now. This may be our one chance to discover their location."

"Gordo, what should we do?" Foreman requested.

"Find a place to set up the Sat Com dishes," said Hassler, pointing to one of the backpacks leaning against a tree. "Barton will be coming off duty soon, he'll help you. We'll notify Diego Garcia of this. They'll call the Pentagon, and the Pentagon will send an ELF signal to the *Marshall*. We should be talking to Glenn in the next half hour."

"We should've expected this," Fernandez said bitterly, walking out the main entrance to Revolution House. "It's not the first time they double-crossed us."

"Quiet, Ray," Major Goldman advised. "You're on prime time, live."

Cleared out of the reception hall, the TV crews, photographers, and journalists had collected on Revolution House's front steps. The moment Ambassador Griffen's group appeared, they swarmed over them, shouting so many questions they could hardly be differentiated. Except for brief comments, none of them said anything substantial until they were all inside the embassy staff car.

"We'll have to tell Washington," Griffen commented, stating the obvious. "White House, State Department. Everyone."

"They all watch CNN," said Goldman. "It's likely they know already. But I suppose we do have to notify them officially."

"How the hell did they find out about our submarine?" Fernandez asked. "Do they know we already have forces here?"

"Washington is leak city. Somewhere someone told, or someone found an old story about the *Marshall*. I doubt they know we have people on the island, they can only guess. I don't know where the SEALs are, and none of us here need to know."

"You think they'll be used, Major?"

"We'll know for certain when we get back to the embassy," said Goldman, glancing out the windows to see how far the limousine had managed to drive from Revolution House. "However, my guess is the Pentagon will get the green light to act. Perhaps as soon as tonight. If it's needed, would your staff be willing to carry out a diversionary operation?"

"The way my people feel, you give us some guns, and we'll take the orbiter back ourselves," said Fernandez. "I hope you don't do that. We'd probably end up shooting ourselves in the foot."

"It was observant of you to remember our nuclear free zone declaration," Sampras remarked, as the officials gathered in the Foreign Minister's office. "It gives us one more crime to charge the Americans with."

"Do you want to proceed with a trial for the astronauts?" asked Boigny, settling into the seat behind his desk.

"We must substitute the progress in one area with progress in another," said Mashari. "I must also congratulate you for recalling our discussion about Commander Post. It lends credence to our claim that their crimes are against all the oppressed nations of the Earth."

"Do you still plan on flying the spy satellite out tonight?" said Mooradian.

"In spite of what happened, this would still be the best time to do so. Only now I'll have to plan a more involved operation to deceive the American fleet."

"We'll have to increase our patrols here," said Sampras. "And, now that our G.222s have completed their conversion, we can begin antisubmarine missions."

"What will you do about the astronauts themselves?" asked Oscar Rojas, the Cuban ambassador, standing near the back of the office. "Mr. Torres has suggested we split them up to complicate any rescue attempt. Since it now seems more likely the Americans are planning one, shouldn't we do so?"

"I heard about the arguing that went on from Major Parker and Captain Halim. Though the plan Torres advanced does have several advantages, it has severe political consequences if put into effect. Splitting them up would make them look like hostages, the Americans could charge us with being terrorists if we did so. Up to now we've managed to avoid that accusation. If we're going to put the astronauts on trial, we must continue to treat them as prisoners."

"I agree with Minister Sampras," said Mooradian. "And our security is better at the airport than here at the civil jail. One question we should resolve is which to guard more, the astronauts or the *Phoenix?*"

"That answer is easy," said Mashari, almost laughing. "In spite of what they've been saying publicly, the Americans will value a three-billion-dollar spaceship and a one-billion-dollar satellite more than the lives of three men and two women."

"Can you be certain of that, Colonel? The increased patrols will put an extra burden on our resources," Sampras advised. "Even with my forces joining Mooradian's, I don't think we'll have enough to adequately guard both the shuttle and its crew."

"Westerners may value women, but technology is their God. The Americans will try for the shuttle first, or it and the crew together. Those are the two attacks we must prepare for. If you wish to start now, I suggest we move to the meeting room next door and bring in your staffs."

"It's stopping again, Lieutenant," said Hall. "And this time it's not at a gate or checkpoint."

Ever since the panel van had reappeared, Hall had been tracking it with his sniper rifle. He followed it down the coast road to the airport, through the main gate at the field's military side, and into the complex of barracks, administrative buildings, and hangars. The van disappeared, then reemerged as it weaved around the one- and two-story structures in a seemingly erratic pattern. When it finally came to a stop, Hall could almost see inside it when its rear doors were pulled open.

"I'm getting too much distortion from the heat," Hassler complained, lowering his binoculars and glancing up at a hot, midday sun. "What can you see?"

"A bunch of people getting out the back," said Hall, giving his scope's focus knob the slightest touch. "And two of them are women. One white, one black, and they're both wearing blue flightsuits."

"We've got them." Hassler set aside his binoculars and pulled out his notepad. "Now, tell me everything about the building they were taken in to. Its size, exterior color and markings, location, antennas, power sources, security, and any auxiliary structures."

"Christ, Lieutenant. You want a lot."

"As Artie will tell you, ancient Chinese proverb say, 'One picture worth thousand words.' We can't send a real picture to the *Marshall,* so we'll have to send a verbal one."

"Think we'll go into action?" Hall asked, briefly looking away from the scope on his PSG-1.

"We'll have to hear what Glenn says," Hassler said. "But I think we probably will. After we talk to Glenn, we'll have to raise Artie's squad. They probably still don't know what's happened. Okay, start giving me the info."

"Good afternoon, Ed. What did your station manager have to say?" Nicolson greeted, when he noticed civilians getting out of the Hummer that had driven up behind him.

"Pretty much the same thing we heard from the ambassador," said Cochran, walking up to the group of officers standing on Diego Garcia's flight line. "Except the station's no longer being watched by Seychelles forces. It's been *surrounded* by them. And, they report traffic into Seychelles International has almost completely stopped."

"No doubt it would," said Commander Fuller. "With no more airliners flying to the airport, there's no reason for anyone but the military to go there. Admiral, there they are."

The assembled officers and civilians turned to the northwest and saw the expected formation of heavy transports appear on schedule. Their flight had begun at Fort Bragg, North Carolina, where they picked up the alert battalion from the Eighty-Second Airborne Division. The four grey-green Starlifters were trailed out in a line astern formation several miles long. As the first turned in toward the runway, the soft rumble of its turbofan engines could be heard.

"Where are you going to park them?" Phil Brenner asked, looking away from the transports and down a flight line already filled with P-3 Orions, the NASA 747, and the C-5 Galaxy.

"Trust a pilot to ask," said Nicolson. "It'll be a tight fit, but we'll have the room if we keep a few more of Raymond's patrol bombers in the air. Besides, I doubt they'll be here long enough to cause that much of a problem."

"You think you'll be given the green light to start the rescue operation?" Cochran responded soberly.

"In light of the way the Libyans have been acting, what the Seychelles government did this morning and threatens to do with your friends, I'd say it was a virtual certainty. And everyone concerned will tell you, the sooner the better. Even them!"

Nicolson was forced to raise his voice as the lead C-141 screamed in for a landing. Though the base's flight line was more than a quarter of a mile from the runway, the decibel level still rose to earsplitting intensity until the transport had finished its rollout and reduced power. Even then the group knew the relative quiet wouldn't last for long; they could already see the next Starlifter line up for its final approach.

"This whole operation hinges on your friend and his submarine," said Cochran, while the background noise was still a rumble. "You think they can do it?"

"Terry and his Lady are the best team you could have on your side," said Nicolson. "With everyone else's help, yes, they'll do it. From the way you've talked these last two days, I'd say you and Terry Carver were a lot alike. Once this crisis is over, we should get the two of you together."

"I can't think that far ahead. Right here and now all I want is for my people and my Lady to be safe. And to do that, I'll have to trust another man's Lady to rescue them."

"Is this all that's left?" Mashari remarked when he finally reached the slope's base and fully saw what he could only partially view from the road above it.

"Except for the bodies, this is it," said el-Jabr.

The major waved his hand at the incinerated remains of the Suzuki jeep. One could scarcely tell the vehicle had once been white. None of its vinyl upholstery, canvas roof, or windshield glass remained. Its body and tires were charred and melted; its most intact pieces were its axles and engine block.

"What you don't see either went up in flames or ran down the mountain," he continued.

328

"It's a mess," said Mashari.

"No, Colonel. It's too neat. This accident was arranged."

"Are you still playing policeman?" Captain Matubis asked condescendingly. "Is it to impress your superior officer?"

"Captain, please. I'd like to hear what my officer has to say," said Mashari, trying to keep the irritation out of his voice. "Continue, Major. Why do you say arranged?"

"Because the destruction is so complcte," said el-Jabr, trying to ignore the Defense Force captain's taunting chuckles. He circled around the wreck, pointing occasionally to what he wanted Mashari to notice. "Very little evidence remains. The bodies were burnt beyond recognition. The soldiers were only identified by their service tags. We'll have to identify the woman with them through her dental records. The fire was very intense, it destroyed everything in the passenger compartment."

"It was intense because of this," Matubis stated, holding up the broken remnant of a rum bottle. "You know we found some of these in the debris trail running down the slope."

"That explains the fire's intensity. But what explains the *bodies* remaining in the jeep as it crashed through the wall and down the mountain?"

"You know that, too, Major. The ambulance crew told us the bodies in front were wearing their seat belts."

"Exactly, Captain. Have you asked yourself *why* a drunken soldier and his girlfriend would wear their seat belts?" said el-Jabr, a vindictive smile on his face as he sprang his trap. "Have you thought of that, you jabbering idiot?"

"All right, Major. Enough," Mashari gently admonished. "However, you do have a point. Something is unusual about this crash. I want you two to put aside your squabbling and cooperate. Sweep this mountain, and pay particular attention to the NASA tracking station. It isn't very far from here."

"Colonel, we already have the station surrounded," said Matubis, trying to sound at least friendly to Mashari.

"Then increase the blockade. If the Americans have commandos on Mahé, the station would be their one refuge. And, since it overlooks the airport, it would be an excellent base for their operations. Keep that in mind when you conduct your sweep."

"Gordo, that officer who just showed up is leaving," said Riker, when he noticed Hassler had trained his binoculars in another direction.

"What? Oh, yes," Hassler stammered, turning and quickly refocusing on the crash site below them. "Stocky little shit. He must be some high-ranking officer, he's still giving orders."

"You better make a note of him for Glenn, when he contacts us again. When will that be?"

"Just after sunset. We'll probably know by then when and if the rescue will take place." Hassler took out his notepad and started writing a brief description of what Mashari looked like from half a mile away. "With all the vehicles and men they have below, I'd say they were getting ready to do a sweep. Let's hope these guys don't have any mountain troops."

"That's it, Captain. ELF transmission completed," said Lieutenant Hawkins, when the teletype in his tiny compartment clacked just three times. "Whiskey-Tango-Echo. Is this what we've been waiting for?"

330

"Sure is, Jake. The thinking ashore finally agrees with what the rest of us have been saying," Carver replied, ripping a sheet of paper from the teletype far larger than the three-letter message it contained. "This is our Go Code. We're going to rescue a spaceship."

"Do you want to use the intercom? I can arrange it for the entire boat to hear you."

"No, I want Glenn and his team to hear first. And I'd like to do it in person. Don't go putting this in the grapevine until after I'm done. If you want to keep busy, raise the *Casablanca*. Ask them if they've heard anything on their ELF."

Backing out of the *Marshall*'s radio room, Carver turned and walked down the passageway to the hatch at its far end, past the engineering and nucleonics center, past the submarine's primary air-conditioning plant and one of its dry stores room. When he reached the hatch, he pulled it open to enter what had once been the missile compartment.

Now, only a few of the Polaris launch tubes remained, used to house some of the *Marshall*'s defensive systems. The rest of the compartment was used to house the SEAL team's living quarters, armory, briefing room, and swim-out chambers. It was a section of his command Carver did not visit often. Still, he quickly found Allard and gave him the news everyone on the submarine had been expecting.

Seventeen

The Prize
Positioning Forces

"Stony, when's this going to end?" Brody complained, while he was being led down broadway to the *Simpson*'s Combat Information Center.

"When we put back in Garcia," said Baxter. "Mallory and I would like it to end. We'd like to put you in a proper nick. But first, we'll have to rescue your astronauts."

Within a few feet of the central passageway's end, Brody and Baxter turned right and entered the CIC. The moment they did so, they realized the atmosphere was charged and tense. All the consoles were manned, even Antisubmarine Warfare, and Stover was commanding the center.

"Good, you're finally here," he said, when he noticed Brody and Baxter. "Get over to the Anti-Air station. We need our best people tonight."

"What gives, Lieutenant?" said Brody. "I thought you were going to be off duty?"

"So did I, until about twenty minutes ago. That's when Stine got the word. We're going in for the astronauts and the shuttle. We'll be one of the escorts for

332

the *Belleau Wood*. We'll detach soon so get to your station, Jerry. Stony, you're going to have a ringside seat."

Before Brody finished relieving the seaman at the Anti-Air Warfare console, he and Baxter could feel the missile frigate pick up speed. A few minutes later it altered course to the southeast, as did the assault carrier *Belleau Wood* and the other escort ship, the frigate *Ainsworth*. Moving at twenty-four knots, they would be over the horizon from the rest of the *Eisenhower*'s battle group by the time the late afternoon sun had finished setting.

"Damn, that noise is terrible," said Mashari, holding his hands over his ears. "What's causing it?"

"The door operating mechanisms," Halim answered, pointing to the shuttle. "Our experts were able to remove the burned out drive motors. However, the mechanical systems were too complex and too badly jammed for them to do anything with."

The *Phoenix* was now surrounded by a framework of yellow I-beams that extended several dozen yards in front of its nose. The frame's roof was fifteen feet above its fuselage and contained the heavily reinforced track the power winches moved along. They were causing the metallic screeching and tearing which filled the hangar apron; they were being used to pry open the shuttle's payload bay doors. After several minutes of noisy operation, the sixty-foot-long doors were warped, torn by the hooks used to move them, and hanging loosely along the fuselage sides. The thirty-foot radiator panels under them had also pivoted out and, though they received far less damage, were leaking freon gas through pinhole tears and punctures.

333

"Still another environmental crime we can accuse the Americans of," Sampras laughed, gesturing at the tiny plumes of mist erupting along the radiator panel surfaces. "Can we go aboard to view our prize?"

"Of course," said Mashari. "And we don't need to wear those breathing systems either. Our experts have washed the rocket fuel off the mid deck and everything else it contaminated."

For the first time since it landed, people were able to go inside the *Phoenix* without having to use the cumbersome air tanks and face masks. With Mashari leading them, the officials climbed through its side hatch and up to its flight deck. At the aft crew station they found the port skylight window hanging open; the exit steps under it deployed.

One by one they squeezed into the emergency opening and were helped onto the top of the shuttle. From there, they could all look down into the payload bay. The forty-foot-long KH-12 satellite was still sitting snugly inside it; its polished metal surfaces gleamed brightly in the work lights.

"How much does this thing weigh?" asked Sampras.

"We estimate fifteen or sixteen tons," said Mashari, smiling triumphantly as he studied the satellite. "Far heavier than any engine, but our lifting frame is heavily built and can tolerate the load. Our only problem in erecting it was we had to build it backwards, and we had to remove the spaceship's elevons and flaps."

"How long will it take for you to remove it? I'm worried about the satellites America already has in space seeing it."

"Only a few hours. And don't worry about the satellites up there, most of them don't work well at night." Involuntarily, Mashari looked up at the darkening sky and its gold and red tinted clouds. Then he

334

glanced across the airport to the row of Il-76s and Tu-22s. "I wish I could stay here, but I'm needed elsewhere. I must check on the preflighting of the Ilyushin we're going to use tonight, and on the Tupolevs. They're tough beasts, but I'm going to ask a lot of them and their crews."

"Room, attention!" said the *Eisenhower*'s Carrier Air Group commander, when both Bryant and McQuay entered the main flight crew briefing room. Immediately, the more than one hundred and twenty officers and petty officers rose from their seats. They were the majority of the carrier's air crews, and all would be flying tonight.

"You can be seated," said Bryant, stepping up to the room's podium. "I know it's unusual for either myself or Captain McQuay to address a mission briefing, but this is an extraordinary event. As of five minutes ago the *Belleau Wood* is still moving to a position where the Russian fleet can shadow it, and it can launch its assault force.

"While only three planes will have an actual combat assignment tonight, I want the rest of you to know that it is likely at least some of you will be involved as well. Even after Gary's Intruders destroy the Blinders and the ZSUs, the SEALs, the Marines and the paratroopers will still need close air support. Which is why the Hornets and Intruders going on the decoy strike will carry air-to-ground weapons. Even the Vikings will be equipped with free-fall bombs.

"As for you Tomcat jocks, unless one of the Blinders escapes destruction in the strike, you won't have much opportunity for a kill. This doesn't mean it can't happen, just don't be trigger-happy. Gary, I see you've taken the opportunity to assign yourself to the strike. Will you be flying the HARM ship or the Blinder bust?"

"I'll fly the bomb run," said Lieutenant-Commander Gary Hatch, seated in the front row with the rest of the squadron C.O.s. "I'm an old-fashioned guy. Gerry Hartmann is the best in the squadron when it comes to smart weapons. He'll fly the HARM ship."

"Happy hunting, Commander," said Bryant, before he turned to the one black officer in the front row. "Alton, I take it you're following Gary's lead?"

"Us black boys know voodoo best, Admiral," Commander Alton Sumner answered, smiling broadly. "Whether the electronic or mumbo jumbo kind."

"Snow them in, Alton. Gentlemen, I'll let McQuay and Mr. Tompkins conduct the rest of the briefing. As of now we're still on schedule. Fleet M-Com and dispersal will begin as soon as the bomber shadowing us departs. All your aircraft are being prepared. The strike force and support tanker will be launched first. The rest of you will go about an hour later. I cannot stress how important what we're doing is. There are five brave Americans who'd love to see a sky full of Navy planes. Let's not disappoint them. Good luck."

"That's enough," Chen said quietly, when one of his SEALs molded another brick of C-4 onto the bridge frame they were hiding under. "Let's test the detonator."

While the SEAL pulled a small metal box from his backpack, Chen produced a flashlight-shaped transmitter. They briefly activated them, tested to see if one would pick up a signal from the other; then planted the detonator in the plastic explosive charge.

Snapping his fingers, Chen pointed into the jungle and led his demolition team up the embankment; to where the anti-armor team had been covering them.

"Are we gonna plant any more charges?" asked De-Brandt, once the squad's two teams were reunited. "It's almost nightfall, Artie."

"Just one more," said Chen. "Time for us to hike back to the power plant we scouted."

"Good, you wore us out climbing up to that TV tower," said another SEAL. "What'll we do at the plant?"

"Wait for our orders. And start our mischief once we get them. Move out. Ben, take the point. The rest of you, single-file it."

"God, how did you manage to get through the roadblocks?" Fernandez questioned, astonished when he met Goldman at the administrative building's front entrance.

"You can still get a lot done with a good, loud voice," said Goldman, shaking his hand. Then he motioned that he wanted to go deeper inside the building. "Though I probably won't be returning to Victoria. At least for tonight."

"Why? Are you and Griffen on the outs?"

"That would make a good cover story, but no. It's official, Ray, the rescue's on for tonight."

The news stopped Fernandez in mid-stride. His eyes widened nervously, and his mouth fell open. For a moment he didn't know if he would start cheering . . . or faint.

"Don't go crazy on me just yet," Goldman added, grabbing hold of the station manager. "I want you to get Joel and the rest of your top people into your office immediately. We have to stage a diversion. At one

337

o'clock this morning, we're to start all the vehicles we can and drive them around the station perimeter."

"Think that'll be enough to get attention?" said Fernandez.

"As you would say, 'you better believe it.' I just hope it won't make the People's Security goons out here trigger-happy."

"What else will happen? When will the rescue begin?"

"Sorry, I can't tell you," Goldman replied. "Mostly because the Pentagon and Diego Garcia didn't tell me. We just have to know what we have to do. Let's go to your office and get the rest of your staff in."

"What time did the *Casablanca* depart?" said Allard, working the main screen controls until the map of the Seychelles slid east and enlarged on Frégate Island.

"Just after four o'clock," said Carver, glancing at the TASCO Room's time display. Then he leaned forward. "About five hours ago . . . yes, Alain should be at the decoy point by now. Thanks, Glenn. It's time to contact him. TASCO Room to Radio Room, lower the So-Far Transceiver."

Unlike all the other communication aerials the *Marshall* carried, the So-Far Transmitter/Receiver unspooled from a hatch on its keel instead of its conning tower or upper hull. It dropped more than a thousand feet to a deep ocean region called the So-Far Channel, where the water pressure created a layer that allowed acoustic signals to travel hundreds, even thousands of miles. Once used only by whales, now submarines fitted with a special transceiver could make limited use of it.

"Terry, this is Alain. We have arrived at Frégate Is-

338

land," Jacoubet answered, speaking slowly so the distortions and fading would not garble what he said. "There are several boats in the area. Do you wish to begin? Over."

"Commence operations at the arranged time," said Carver, in the same measured cadence. "We are departing for our launch point and can no longer maintain contact. Good luck, Alain. This is Terry, out."

"Roger. Do not take any chances, Terry. This is Alain, out."

"Radio Room, raise the So-Far Transceiver," Carver ordered. "Be prepared to deploy the Com Buoy. Glenn, what are you doing?"

"Contacting Mike," said Allard, picking the hand microphone off the wall-mounted intercom panel. "He and the rest of my officers are in the briefing room. I'll tell them to start suiting up, then join them after we signal Artie and Gordo."

"We'll be doing that in about twenty minutes. Conn, this is the TASCO Room. Take us up, Greg, to one hundred feet. Change course to Zero-Three-Zero degrees. Increase speed to twenty knots until we raise the Com Buoy."

"Roger, Terry," said Burks. "You don't mind if Clarence shows off? Do you?"

Rising from nine hundred feet, the *Marshall* quadrupled its speed, which allowed it to bank and maneuver gracefully in the black waters until it was heading north-northeast. It skirted the coral reefs to the south and east of Mahé. If it could remain undetected by local air and naval patrols, the submarine would eventually come to a stop less than a mile off the eastern side of Point Cascade—the closest it could approach the island's airport without running aground.

* * *

"*Capitaine,* we are at fifteen meters," said the *Casablanca*'s senior helmsman. "Diving planes, level. Speed, ten kilometers."

"What's that in knots?" Stackpole asked.

"Just over five knots," said Jacoubet. "Keep her steady, Accart. Raising attack 'scope."

Smaller and more slender than the search periscope, the attack periscope had a much narrower field of view but also left less of a "feather," the telltale wake it created when slicing through the water. After deploying it Jacoubet quickly walked the 'scope, stopping briefly at three points during the walk and calling out bearings.

"Those are the positions of the fishing boats in our area," he continued. "The one on our starboard quarter appears to be the closest. That's the one we'll surprise."

"You want me in the tower?" said Stackpole.

"Yes, you better do so now. Man the bridge as soon as we surface and repeat what your captain told you. Robert, check on our escape routes with navigation. Marcel, activate the weapons station."

While Jacoubet gave orders to his executive and weapons officers, Stackpole cranked open the attack center's roof hatch and climbed through it. The cover plate was quickly shut after him, leaving him isolated in the tower's access tunnel. He entered the compartment just below the flying bridge, a cramped room cold and dripping with condensed moisture. A far cry from the warm, dry, and well-illuminated attack center he had left.

However, he could see the outside world through the room's observation windows. Even at some fifty feet below the ocean's surface, moonlight penetrated: a weak, ethereal glow that revealed the *Casablanca*'s smoothly rounded hull and the streamlined fairing for its DUUX sonar array. It was now scanning the immediate area for surface targets beyond the fishing boats already detected.

"There he goes," said Easton, watching a distant set of anticollision and navigation lights off his port wingtip partially disappear as the aircraft they had covered turned onto a southerly heading. "Green Hornet Three to Turntable, our visitor is departing. Over."

"Roger, Hornet Three. You better split as well. We got a pair of Sundowners already on the way to relieve you. We're advising the *Ike* of the Blinder's departure. Turntable, out."

As the Tu-22 departed for Mahé, the two F-14s which had been shadowing it turned to the northwest. They changed their AWG-9 radars to surface search mode, even though the orbiting Hawkeye was currently in radio contact with the *Eisenhower*. In minutes the carrier would be shutting down electronically, and the fighters would have to find their way to it on their own.

"The relief Tomcats are on their way, Admiral," said McQuay, watching two sets of afterburner plumes climb away from his ship. "CIC reports the inbound pair are tracking us with their radar and can land even under M-Com conditions. Do we begin?"

"Signal the fleet to disperse according to plan," Bryant ordered, joining McQuay at the bridge windows. "Go to Alpha-Two M-Com conditions. After those F-14s are recovered, go to Alpha-One. Accelerate to flank speed and change course for the southwest. Now it begins, David. I hope in the morning we have five astronauts and a spaceship in our hands. And not five dead heroes and a burned wreck."

With a nod from McQuay, the *Eisenhower's* bridge crew carried out all of Bryant's commands simultaneously. Several voices spoke at once, relaying information to the ship's Combat Information Center, Radio Room, and Nucleonics Center. In minutes the giant SPS-43 radar on the tower aft of its island had ceased operating; as had all the other SPS-series air, surface search, and navigation radars on the island itself. Outgoing radio traffic fell to a mere trickle on the scrambled and secure voice channels.

All around the carrier, the destroyers, cruisers, and frigates dispersed in a seemingly random pattern. They scattered to every point on the compass, except north. Inside their randomness a plan was unfolding; as the ships spread out, maneuvered, and fell back, all their radars and sonars were operating and transmitting information through the JTIDS data system. All except for the *Eisenhower,* which would only receive so it could remain hidden.

The ninety-thousand-ton giant vibrated and rumbled slightly as both of its nuclear reactors, and all four of its steam turbines, were put on-line. More than a half-million horsepower accelerated it to its flank speed of fifty knots. The only ship in the fleet moving faster than it was the nuclear cruiser USS *Texas,* which was just barely creeping ahead of it at fifty-five knots.

On the carrier's flight deck were just two A-6E Intruders, a KA-6D tanker, and an EA-6B Prowler. They were the Strike Team assigned to destroy the Libyan aircraft and ZSU tanks based at Seychelles International. Once the incoming Tomcats landed, and before the relief Blinder appeared, they would be launched.

* * *

"Gordo, we got another liftoff," said Belford, suddenly swinging his PSG-1 rifle after having held it steady for several minutes. "It's that G.222 transport."

Even miles away, the howl of turboprops and course-pitched propellers hauling an aircraft off the ground could be heard. Briefly, Hassler turned to watch the collection of flashing lights climb into the night sky. Below it, Seychelles International glowed brilliantly with its array of runway lights, fluorescent and sodium vapor lamps. It scarcely looked like a military base preparing for an attack.

"It must be going out for another antisub patrol," said Hassler. "If these clowns can tell the difference between a sub and a whale. Yes, Nick. Is it him?"

"It's Glenn all right," Foreman answered, handing over the walkie-talkie. "And he wants you."

"Glenn never wants to speak to me anymore," said Hall. "And I even changed my mouthwash."

"Quiet, Ty. Home Port, this is Spectacle," Hassler informed, pressing the handset's transmit bar. "What are your orders? Over."

"Commence Phase Four operations," said Allard. "Twenty-four, thirty hours Zulu. Good luck, Spectacle. Home Port, out."

"Roger, Home Port. Spectacle, out." Once he released the transmit bar, Hassler switched off the handset and retracted its antenna. Then, he looked up at the men clustered around him. "That's it, no more sitting back and looking. Thirty minutes past midnight you guys will finally get to shoot something. Arm your weapons. Break out the Armbrust and check its missiles. Bruce, go tell Riker. We'll probably attack the forces sweeping our old location."

343

Because of their proximity to it, the reconnaissance squad could not cheer their orders. Instead, they let out a nervous sigh of relief and started to unpack their munitions. For the first time since they unpacked their PSG-1, rifles, Hall and Belford loaded full clips into them and clicked on their safeties. The other squad members similarly armed their MP5 submachine guns and assembled their Armbrust antitank launcher.

"Okay, boys and girls. It's fifteen minutes to lights out," Reynolds announced, checking his wristwatch. "Christ, I didn't think I'd still be saying that."

"What? That they're going to turn our lights out at ten?" said Post.

"No, the boys and girls part . . . I'd give anything for you two not to still be here . . ."

Reynolds's words trailed off a second time when he heard the room's main door unlock. Characteristically, it burst open and Torres stormed in with a contingent of guards. Again, the lack of warning caused some of the astronauts to jump. Especially Rebecca and Julie, who eyed Torres nervously as he circled the room.

"If you don't mind, Bug Man, it's time for our beauty sleep," said Reynolds, motioning for Post and Glassner to join him in front of the women. "So just tell us what you came here for and leave."

"I'm certain you'll understand how sorry I am that we're disturbing you," Torres replied, putting his hand over his heart to emphasize his answer. "But today's events ruined our interrogation schedule. So we have to make up for lost time. Seize him."

At first, Reynolds thought Torres meant him and raised his fists to defend himself, but the guards

344

Torres ordered swept by him and grabbed Post by the arms. All Reynolds had to do was take one step toward the struggling men in order to hear slides being pulled back on automatics.

"Like all Americans you are so predictable, Commander," said Torres, levelling his Skoda pistol at Reynolds. The appearance of it and other weapons brought all attempts at resistance to an end. "Some day you must try something that will surprise us. Don't wait up for your friend. My Libyan comrades want to have a very long talk with him."

Using his free hand, Torres snapped his fingers and pointed at the door. Neither Post, nor the guards, nor anyone else made a sound until after the contingent had left the room, and the door locked behind them.

"I should've guessed they would take Walt," Julie said finally. "After what I heard them say at the conference this morning. They're going to question him about his part in the 'eighty-six Libyan raid."

"All he can tell them is how to ripple fire HARM missiles at multiple radar emitters," said Glassner. "What can they do with that?"

"Plenty. They'll cook the evidence to serve their needs," Reynolds concluded. "We're in for it now. Crimes against Libya. Crimes against the Seychelles. Crimes against the Third World. Sorry, against the Oppressed Nations of the World. Can you spell 'Show Trial'? Whatever tricks the Navy has they better use 'em before this circus sets up its tent."

Eighteen

Deceptions
Launch Point

"Turn on de lights, Cap'n!" shouted the man standing in the bow. "The tuna they be's a schoolin'!"

The fishing boat's diesel chugged a little slower as it reduced speed in preparation to casting its lines. From its bow to its stern, rows of powerful lights snapped on, making the fifty-foot boat more luminous than the darkened island on its port side. The lights were used to attract the fish the tuna fed on and the tuna themselves. Though an illegal practice, it was a highly efficient one; it also made the boat a much more visible target.

"The tuna, they be's a bitin' soon," said another crew mate, baiting a series of large hooks. Until he dropped his bucket of fish parts. "Adam, what be that?"

"It must be a whale," said the captain, stepping from the wheelhouse. "Unusual, so far north this time of year."

The crewman continued motioning to a patch of foaming, turbulent water off the fishing boat's starboard side. Less than a hundred feet away, it was well within the glow of the running lights. Out of the foam and chop a glistening black slab rose. At its front edge it had what looked like a set of airplane wings, and on its roof were gleaming steel poles; one of which mounted a radar antenna. Before the water had finished sheeting off it, a figure appeared among the poles and called out to the boat.

"Ahoy, Rabbit. This is the *Marshall!*" boomed an amplified voice. "Are you ready for transfer? Over."

"It's the Americans!" shouted the crew mate, picking up his bait bucket and heaving it at the conning tower. "It's their submarine! Cap'n, do something!"

Reaching inside the wheelhouse, the captain retrieved a double-barreled shotgun and levelled it at the tower. As he pulled each trigger, the weapon exploded; an instant later, the sound of pellets bouncing off the tower's steel skin could be heard. Before the captain finished reloading, a much louder hissing filled the air.

"Crash-dive! Crash-dive!" Stackpole urged. "These guys are shooting at us!"

The moment he secured the intercom mike and shut it down, Stackpole was jumping through the bridge's floor hatch. He remained just long enough in the compartment below it to lock the hatch plate and glance out the observation windows. He could see plumes of spray erupt from the forward ballast tank vents as they were opened, and felt the rumble of seawater replacing the air inside them. Then, he descended the access tunnel and returned to the comfortable, well-illuminated world of the *Casablanca's* attack center.

"Take us down, fast. One hundred meters," said Jacoubet. "Lieutenant, what kind of weapons were they using?"

"Shotguns, I think," said Stackpole, jumping off the ladder's final rung. "I don't know who scared who more, them or me? Are we going to get company soon?"

"Radar detected no aircraft in our area, only the three fishing boats. Before we retracted the ESM mast, we did pick up a radio message from the people we surprised. If we don't have company now, we will have soon."

"Diving planes, twenty degrees down-angle," Accart informed, lifting his helmsman's wheel and dipping it to the right. "Rudders, thirty degrees. Hold on."

Creaking because of its maneuver and the increasing pressure, the *Casablanca* entered a diving right turn, flying through the water like an aircraft. It swung away from the coral reefs surrounding Frégate Island and headed into the deeper, open waters south of it. The attack sub's decoy operation was almost complete; all it had to do now was remain in the area long enough to be detected by military forces before making its final escape.

"The deck crews are finding it difficult to work in a fifty-plus-knot wind," said McQuay, hanging up one of the bridge's growler phones. "That was the Air Boss. He says the strike team jets are ready for launch."

"We'll have to slow down when we marshal for the decoy strike," said Bryant. "Forty planes will be more of a headache than four. Has anyone spotted the relief Blinder yet?"

"No one. Not the Hawkeye or any of the ships. Not even the *Belleau Wood*'s escorts, and they're the closest to Mahé."

"It must be late taking off, like it was this morning." Bryant glanced at his watch, and rechecked by looking at the digital time display above the bridge windows. "And we can't be. Tell the Air Boss to launch the team."

At its fifty-knot cruise speed, the *Eisenhower* had no need to turn into the wind in order to launch its first group of planes. Once the command was received, the flight deck's Sky Cap control warned each of the Grummans sitting on the carrier's four catapults that they were going to be launched.

The first to roar into the night were the KA-6D and EA-6B. Though they carried no weapons, they were the heaviest aircraft and were fired from the two bow catapults. The two A-6Es were sited on the amidships catapults. Its wing racks loaded with two dozen stubby, white cluster bombs; Hatch's Intruder hurled off the carrier's port side angle deck. The last to go was the A-6 armed with four High-Speed Anti-Radar Missiles (HARM).

They circled the *Eisenhower* at low altitude until they assembled into a four-ship flight. Accelerating to over five hundred miles an hour, they departed on a southwesterly heading. Soon they would turn due south, then east. Skirting the Seychelles main island group until they received the signal to attack.

"Colonel, won't the Americans be suspicious when a replacement Tupolev doesn't appear?" asked one of the bomber pilots in the briefing room.

"We've been late in replacing our surveillance patrols before," said Mashari. "They would probably call this a delay. By the time their suspicions are fully aroused all four of you will be appearing on their radar screens. They'll be so busy preparing for what they think is an air strike they'll never see our one Ilyushin taking off."

"Colonel, what will be my flight plan and when will I leave?" asked Lafit Kawar, standing up when Mashari pointed to his crew.

"This will be your departure route." Mashari turned

to the map behind him and indicated the blue line heading east from the airport, then changing south and finally due west. "You will leave after the Tupolevs trigger a response from the American fleet. You will even take off west to east so you don't have to fly over Victoria and alert the American embassy to your departure. Yes, Lieutenant. What is it now?"

The tone of Mashari's voice sharpened when a People's Security Force officer entered the briefing room yet again and walked toward the platform. The harsh response to his reappearance caused him to break his stride and to begin explaining his return while still in the aisle.

"Excuse me, Colonel," he said nervously. "But we have a more serious incident. Naval Command just got a report from a fishing boat near Frégate Island. Apparently an American nuclear submarine surfaced near it and asked if it was ready for a transfer."

"A transfer? How could these fishermen be sure it was an American submarine?" said Mashari, his tone softening and a smile breaking over his face.

"They said the man in its conning tower spoke to them with an American accent. His exact words were "Ahoy, Rabbit. This is the *Marshall*. Are you ready for the transfer? Over." Their answer to the Americans was to fire a shotgun at the submarine until it submerged."

"The Americans have showed their hand and have made a mistake. The submarine was obviously going to transfer its commandos to a local fishing boat, but it selected the wrong one. Captain, how far away is Frégate Island?"

"About thirty-five miles," said Captain Sori Azziz, the senior instructor pilot of the Libyan Military Mission. "The Aeritalia can make it there in seven minutes. The Marchettis will need twelve."

"Send them in," Mashari ordered. "Perhaps they can

350

still catch the *Marshall* on the surface. If they do, they're to attack with rockets until it's crippled or sunk. Lieutenant, send your patrol boats to the island, have them search all the fishing boats around it. The Cubans may be right about an underground operating here after all."

"But, Colonel, I'll need Minister Sampras's permission to issue such orders," said the lieutenant, suddenly nervous.

"Then get it!" Mashari's smile evaporated and his harsh tone returned. "And don't return here until your boats and planes are heading for the island. If we're to unravel this mystery, we must do it now."

"Did you check that launcher out?" asked Hassler, joining his sniper team at their base camp.

"I've done everything but test fire a missile," said Patterson, cradling in his arms what looked like a submachine gun with two pistol grips, no barrel or rear stock. "Though with only four rounds I decided I shouldn't."

"Good idea, I'd have your balls if you did. Are you two ready?"

"Ready," Hall answered, speaking for both himself and Belford. They finished fitting lens covers to their rifles' scopes and plastic caps to their muzzles before standing up. "We've reloaded with Glaser rounds. So what we hit we'll kill."

"Will you use silencers?"

"At the ranges we'll be operating," said Belford, "no. They'd not only be useless, they would be detrimental. They throw the weapon's balance off and slow the bullet's velocity."

"Then let's start hiking," said Hassler, shouldering his own MP5. On his back were two of the containerized missiles for the Armbrust launcher. "Nick, you'll

351

be in charge until I return. Keep watching the airport, and don't use your weapons unless you're spotted. Don't expect us back until after one."

Hassler exchanged salutes with Foreman before he led the sniper team out of the base camp and down the mountain. Even though he tried to follow them, Foreman lost sight of the men within seconds; soon after that he could no longer hear them. It was as if the night and the forest had swallowed them up.

"Slow us down," said Captain Malcom Neveu, of the Seychelles People's Defense Forces. "Descend to two hundred meters. Pilot to lookouts, we've reached the search area."

The Aeritalia G.222 had the same general configuration as the C-130 Hercules, but it was one-third smaller and only had two turboprop engines. This still made it the largest aircraft in the People's Defense Forces Air Wing and, ironically, the fastest. On its departure from Mahé, the light transport had accelerated to over three hundred miles an hour. Now, as it circled the waters south of Frégate Island, it cut its speed in half and dove to within six hundred feet of the surface.

"There are the fishing boats," said the copilot, pointing to the clusters of light passing under the transport's nose. "Should we start dropping the sonar buoys?"

"They're called *sonobuoys,*" Neveu corrected. "And before we drop any, we should find out if there are surface targets. This is Sailfish to Kestrel Three, what is your radar detecting?"

"We have all three fishing boats," said a voice on the cockpit speakers. "No other ships are in the area."

"We know *that*. Are you detecting a submarine periscope or conning tower? Over."

"When you arrive, I want you and your wingman to

352

split up and sweep independently," said Neveu. "We'll begin dropping our sonobuoys."

Turning away from the boats and heading south, the Aeritalia transport waited until it had flown several miles before starting to eject a line of sonobuoys from the rack sitting on its open tail ramp. The canisters were still floating under their parachutes when the two SF.260 trainers arrived and split up to conduct their radar sweeps of the area.

"Rockets loaded, Artie," DeBrandt whispered, creeping over to where Chen was hidden. "Did you only plant charges on one tower?"

"That's all we need," said Chen, arming the remote detonator he was holding. "Remember your targets. Go back and wait for my signal."

"What about my Stinger?"

"Not now, that takes too long to set up. Just wait for the fireworks and join in."

A few feet in front of where Chen's squad had collected, the jungle came to an abrupt end. In the clearing beyond sat the island's main power generating station. The muted hum of its turbines and the soft crackle of static electricity from its transformers filled the air and drowned out the sounds of insects and other creatures.

Chen waited for the perimeter guards to reach the station's opposite side before raising the detonator and pointing it at the line of high-tension towers. In spite of the electrical interference created by the facility, the activation and triggering signals reached the line's fourth tower. The flash momentarily illuminated the jungle on the opposite side, and the explosion was a muffled bark. The tower immediately swayed in one direction, then slowly collapsed.

It was still falling as the anti-armor team's Armbrust

launchers were fired. Instead of emitting a telltale jet of flame and a roar, they banged loudly and ejected clouds of small plastic flakes. The missiles easily tore through the station's chain link fence and continued their flights until one exploded a transformer; the other punched a hole in the administration building.

The blast inside blew out every window in the building, it even jarred the doors open. In the parking lot the two vehicles marked "People's Security Forces" erupted into fireballs when hit by shotgun-fired sabot rounds. At the lot's entrance, the lone guard fell back inside his shack, a line of bullet holes stitched across his chest.

"Retreat! And move it!" Chen commanded, still firing his M16 in the parking lot's direction. "Don't bother to reload. Just empty your weapons and run. We've got a schedule to keep."

"Excellent. He's even early," Mashari commented, as the returning Blinder ended its landing flare and its main wheels hit the runway. "Once he taxis over here, we'll refuel the aircraft and arm it. Major, is it all ready?"

"Fuel truck and decoys are ready," said al-Rayes. "Colonel, we're using virtually all our Tupolev crews on this operation. Who will be our relief pilot should we need one?"

"I will. Why do you think I'm wearing—"

Mashari had started to motion to the flightsuit he was wearing when nearly all the lights at Seychelles International flickered out. Only the rotating airport beacon atop the control tower, vehicle lights, and the Tupolev's landing lamps remained on. Mashari completed his motion by pulling his Makarov automatic from its holster. As he cocked it, the rest of the officials around him similarly armed their weapons.

354

"What the hell is this?" he added, training his weapon wherever he turned. "An attack? You hear any sirens?"

"No. It must be a local power failure," said Sampras, before turning to the other Seychelles officials on the hangar apron. "Aubin, I want the emergency lights on. Now!"

"Yes, Minister. Of course," Benoit Aubin said nervously. "But I don't think it's merely a local failure. Look."

The airport manager pointed to the west, where the expected glow from Mahé's capital city could not be seen.

"This is no failure," Mooradian concluded, scanning what he could see in other directions. "All of Mahé appears blacked out. Lieutenant, contact the power station. Find out if it's been attacked."

"It probably has," said Mashari. "Your fears of an underground movement are being justified. Alert all your forces, Colonel. This and the submarine sighting are obviously part of an American attempt to recapture their shuttle."

"Just the shuttle? Not the astronauts?"

"They'll try for their spaceship first. They know where it is, they don't know where the astronauts are held."

"Should we continue with our operation, Colonel?" asked al-Rayes. "Given what the Americans are doing."

"Of course," said Mashari. "There's already been one mistake in their plan. Once our operation is launched they'll be thrown completely off-balance. Colonel, ready all available helicopters and strike trainers. They may be needed. Increase security around the shuttle, and make sure those forces aren't drawn off to fight local saboteurs. Major, put some lights on the fuel truck so the bomber crew can see it."

"Still no sign of a replacement Blinder, Richard," said McQuay. "CIC reports neither the Hawkeye, the *Texas* or the *Bunker Hill* have spotted anything but those fighter-trainers and that transport are going after the *Casablanca*."

"I have to wonder if the Libyans aren't planning an operation themselves?" Bryant pondered for a moment, as he stared at the planes being marshaled below him.

"You want to launch an RF-18? Or send in the Hawkeye?"

"No, if we go snooping around Mahé they'll get even more suspicious of us. Tell the Air Boss to launch the decoy strike. Let's get 'em airborne."

Now travelling at its normal, more sedate, flank speed of thirty-five knots, the *Eisenhower* had to turn into the wind in order to launch its second strike. Where there had been four aircraft less than an hour earlier, forty were now crowded on its flight deck. So many that only the bow catapults could be used.

Because they had the best endurance, the first in line were two flights of F-14As. Behind them was a similar number of S-3B Vikings, the carrier's remaining A-6E Intruders, an entire squadron of F-18s, two EA-6B Prowlers, and two KA-6D tankers. Of the aircraft that could be armed, only the F-14s carried air-to-air weapons. The rest were hung with low-drag bombs, cluster bombs, Maverick, and HARM missiles. The Prowlers carried jamming pods; the KA-6Ds, extra fuel tanks.

Once the command from Bryant was relayed through the Air Boss to the Sky Cap control center, the deflector plates were raised behind the F-14s already sitting on the bow catapults. As each ignited its afterburners, they were shot into the night sky. Before they had finished their climbouts, the deflector plates were lowered and the next pair of Tomcats were taxiing forward. If the deck crews encountered no problems with the rest of the planes, the entire strike force would be airborne in less than twenty minutes.

"Glenn, someone's coming," said Chief Petty Officer Landham. "From the sound I think it's Carver."

The warning caused an immediate halt to the clanks, rattling and squeaking that filled the *Marshall*'s briefing room and medical facilities. It allowed those near the briefing room's front hatch to hear the footsteps advance down the swim-out chamber compartment until a familiar figure appeared.

"Gentlemen, sorry to catch you while you're still suiting up," Carver apologized. "But we're at our launch position. We're riding at eighty feet and the shoreline's about a half mile to port."

"Any patrol boats?" said Allard, as he finished strapping on his air tank.

"One of their *Simbas* moved through this area just ahead of us. Based on the frequency of their rounds, it shouldn't be back for another seventy-five to eighty minutes. That should give you just enough time to deploy and make your landing."

"Just barely enough. Sure you couldn't get us another few hundred yards closer in?"

"We're scraping the outer edge of the reef as it is," said Carver. "This is as close as I can get you. Not quite as good as our last operation, but at least the water's warmer. Good luck, Glenn."

"Thanks, Terry. And stay out of trouble," Allard replied, shaking hands with Carver. "This time you won't have any Libyan submarines shooting at you."

"Got any famous last words for us?" said Jaskula,

standing in the hatch between the medical facility and the briefing room.

"Yes. Thanks to Gordo's squad, we know which building the astronauts are in, and we have our plans to take it. We just don't know which room or rooms they're in, so be careful when we search it. Don't shoot unless you know what your target is. I want us to rescue live heroes, not dead ones. Landham, your team will deploy with me. Mike, you'll be the last one out. To the rest of you, don't do anything that will ring the bell. I don't like writing letters to parents and widows."

Before he left the briefing room, Allard attached a chestpack to his air tank straps. Inside it were his weapons, ammunition clips, and other gear. Though heavy, it effectively counterbalanced the scuba tank on his back. Carrying his face mask and fins, he led the first group of SEALs to the next compartment forward.

The twin swim-out chambers stood side-by-side. A detail of seamen from the *Marshall*'s crew opened their curved hatches and allowed four divers apiece to enter them. When the hatches clanked shut, the cramped, claustrophobic feeling inside them increased. There was barely enough room for the divers to move their arms.

"Get your masks ready," said Allard, watching the signal lights on the hatch rim change from yellow to red. "They're opening the vents."

The work lights at the chamber's roof also changed to a soft red as seawater began swirling into the chamber. The nozzles were at its base and in moments the level reached the divers' knees. Allard and the other SEALs had just enough time to spit into their masks and clean them out before the water rose above their heads.

When it got to the roof, the signal lights started flashing, indicating it was time for the divers to leave. Allard pushed off the floor and grabbed the wheel lock to the chamber's exit hatch. After he rotated it several times, the hatch popped out of its frame and was pushed the rest of the way open.

Though the *Marshall* was riding some eighty feet below the surface, moonlight still penetrated far enough for Allard to see its hull and the outline of its conning tower. There was no need to use the submarine's exterior lights. The moonlight and the twin red glows from the open chambers provided the SEALs with enough illumination to emerge and collect at their designated spots.

"Capitaine, how are the SEALs doing?" asked Arlan Dupuis, when he heard the stamp of shoes on the stairs behind him.

"If it keeps going this well, they'll be ashore in an hour," said Carver. "Here, you can see for yourself."

As he entered the TASCO Room, Carver stepped up to its console and tapped several buttons on its surveillance control panel. One of the room's auxiliary screens came to life with a view from the low-light level camera mounted on the back of the conning tower. By now there were two dozen men clustering on either side of the submarine's aft hull. Carver gave the scene a cursory look, then turned his attention to the main screen.

"It looks like everything is moving into place," he said, keying in commands which showed him the estimated positions for each of the strike, decoy, and rescue forces moving around the Seychelles. "Did you get a confirmation that the carrier did launch their strike and decoy missions?"

"Yes. They both arrived just before we retracted the VLF aerial," said Dupuis. "Do you think the Russians will continue to shield your Marine carrier from detection?"

"They should. They've got a lot to gain for doing next to nothing. We won't know what's actively happening until we surface, and we won't surface until we hear that Glenn's taken both the astronauts and the shuttle."

Jaskula was indeed the last man to emerge from the *Marshall*'s swim-out chambers. When he closed the exit hatch behind him, the red glow ended, forcing the collected teams of divers to rely solely on the moonlight filtering down from the surface. Jaskula joined a team hovering near the conning tower and exchanged hand signals with Allard, who then swam up to the tower's aft-facing camera and waved.

Seconds later the aircraft wing-sized diving planes on the tower visibly pitched down, causing the huge submarine to slowly drop away from the SEALs. It did not move fast enough to suck any of them with it; they were easily able to turn and head for the wall-like coral reef.

Across its surface were the constant flashes of bioluminescent light from creatures out hunting. They avoided the coalescing groups of divers that rose until they were within a few dozen feet of the surface and headed for the deepest channel which cut into the reef. When they glanced back for a last look at their home, the SEALs found the *Marshall* had already been swallowed up by the dark waters.

"Has anything changed?" Khomenko asked on his return to the *Baku*'s Combat Information Center. On his uniform were a few crumbs of black bread and stains from the soup he had hurriedly eaten.

"The American carrier, the *Belleau Wood,* has moved even closer to our fleet," said Captain Fedorov. "I think it's preparing to launch its helicopters."

"And what of the *Eisenhower?*"

"It's out of range, even for our primary air search and surveillance radars, Admiral. But the rest of the fleet is dispersing the way the Americans said it would."

"So we have no way of telling whether they launched their strike aircraft or not." Khomenko walked over to the scopes for the Top Sail and Top Steer radars; then he looked back at the main screen. "And we can't tell where their submarines are."

"We'll spot the planes as they approach Mahé," said Fedorov. "And we're monitoring Seychelles and Libyan radio traffic. They're now hunting the submarine they spotted earlier, and there's just been a guerrilla attack on their main power station. I fear the American operation may be falling apart before it even starts."

"No doubt that's the way the Libyans and the Cubans are thinking," said Khomenko. "After all, we trained them to think that way."

"Should we prepare to help the Americans more actively? Colonel Burdin is readying his fighters."

"No. Moscow says we should only help passively and watch. One day we may have a similar problem, and we must learn from the Americans how to handle it. We must learn to be like them."

"Is that one of ours or theirs?" asked the Marine Corps officers, standing at the open stern elevator and watching a much smaller warship swing in behind the carrier.

"It's the *Simpson,* Colonel. One of ours," said the Naval officer beside him. "All the Russian ships are to port. The rest of your men have arrived and are waiting for you."

"Then let's get on with it. These guys still have a lot of work to do."

Colonel Wilson Harris turned away from the hangar deck's open stern and walked over to the microphone stands set up for him. As commander of the battalion landing team embarked on the *Belleau Wood,* he was one of the two highest-ranked Marine Corps officers on board. The other was waiting for him at the microphones: Colonel John Norwood, commander of the carrier's helicopter wing.

In front of them and the other officers stood nearly half of their battalion. Mostly infantrymen, they had been assembled on the hangar deck to finish gearing up and to receive their munitions. Only the helicopters that were down for maintenance were still in the hangar. The rest, some two dozen, were sitting on the flight deck, getting armed and fueled for the operation.

"Men, I know a lot of you are grumbling that we're only going to do the mopping up for the SEALs," Harris began, once his Marines had come to attention. "That once the space shuttle and the astronauts are rescued all the hard work will be done and all the glory will be theirs. I'm here to tell you what your sergeants and lieutenants have been telling you. The hard work begins *after* the *Phoenix* is rescued. The Seychelles Defense Forces and Security Forces have a combined total of over four thousand men. With their Libyan and Cuban 'advisors,' the total is closer to five thousand. And they have armored cars, patrol boats, helicopters and armed aircraft that are even now after a French submarine they think is the *Marshall.* It will be up to us, the *Eisenhower*'s air wing and the Eighty-Second's paratroopers to make sure they don't try to take the shuttle back."

The last unit Harris mentioned brought a scattering of jeers and catcalls from the Marines. They echoed briefly in the cavernous hangar until Harris quieted them.

"All right, there'll be plenty of work for all of us. Those of you who are part of the first assault wave will board the Sea Knights in the next hour. We'll lift off when we get word the A-6s are hitting their targets. The Sea Cobras will escort us, and the *Ike* will give us all the air support we need. We'll be reinforced by the Eighty-Second, and later by the tanks, artillery, and APCs our landing craft will bring ashore.

"Even then we may still be outnumbered, not unless we take a lot of prisoners or do a lot of killing. Whichever it is, I expect you to behave like Marines. Don't get sloppy, and don't get careless. Those are the two main reasons I lost men in the Gulf War. Remember them and we may all come out of this alive. As an Army general once said, 'I will be proud to lead you wonderful guys into battle. Anywhere, any time.' Well this is where it starts, and the time is approaching. See you ashore."

The Marines remained at attention until Harris and Norwood had disappeared through a starboard hatch and were climbing to the carrier's island. By squads they broke ranks and either started to climb for the flight deck, or descend to the aft docking well where the air cushion landing craft were already being loaded with tanks and other armored vehicles.

Night fell rapidly in the jungle. Less than half an hour after their attack on the power plant, the demolition squad found they had to use their starlight scopes to penetrate the darkness. The only place where moonlight reached the ground was the plant's service road,

363

which they followed until they reached the bridge.

"Finally," DeBrandt whispered, when a column of headlights appeared on the road. "Sure took their time getting here. Ready launchers."

"Hold off until I start the fireworks," said Chen, hitting the activation and arming buttons on his transmitter. "Those of you with shotguns, make sure you have sabot rounds in them."

The convoy's lead and tail vehicles were Defense Force BRDM-2s. Their turrets rotated constantly, sweeping the jungle to protect the rest of the vehicles, a haphazard collection of white Security Force and camouflaged military trucks and cars. As the convoy approached the bridge, it did not stop to let out an inspection team or even slow down. When the lead armored car was less than a dozen yards from it, Chen hit the detonation button.

A white flash ripped apart the bridge's far end, collapsing the rest of it into the streambed. The BRDM screeched to a halt, its driver slewing it sideways as its gunner fired wildly at the jungle. It had barely stopped when an Armbrust missile struck its left side.

The vehicle's thin armor offered no resistance to the warhead. It struck behind the turret, in the engine compartment, where it detonated the fuel tank. The BRDM nearly disappeared in the resulting fireball. It dwarfed the explosion created by the second missile, which destroyed a truck farther down the convoy line.

"Mad minute! Mad minute!" Chen shouted, setting a timer on what looked like a canister of firecrackers.

For the next sixty seconds the squad's M16s, MP5, and shotguns riddled the convoy's remaining vehicles. Initially, they drew little return fire from the soldiers diving for cover, but their muzzle flashes betrayed their position. By the time Chen's noisemakers started going off, the surviving convoy personnel were staging a counterattack.

Under the twin covers of darkness and confusion, the squad retreated deeper into the jungle. It would take nearly twenty minutes for the convoy to discover they were fighting decoys; by then they would have reported another guerrilla ambush and Chen's squad would be approaching its next target.

Once inside the channel, the open ocean's choppiness became a rhythmic surge and ebb. Rather than fight it, Allard and his SEALs used it, swimming ahead rapidly during the surge periods, trying to hover in place when the water swept back out.

In spurts they advanced through the reef, and on its other side they found the conditions much calmer. In addition to moonlight, they now had the more powerful illumination of the runway's eastern approach lights. Allard could almost use it to read his watch by when he checked the time. Though he was unable to accurately judge distance, he estimated his group would reach the shoreline in another fifteen minutes.

"Backshot One, this is Premium. I'm reeling her in. Good luck, you guys. Out."

"Roger, Premium. Backshot One, out."

Hatch's windshield briefly misted up from the plume of spilled fuel as the drogue cup disengaged from his probe and withdrew to the KA-6D's underbelly. The tanker pulled up to the right and broke away from the Strike Team. It was the first aircraft in the formation to rise above five hundred feet since being launched.

"They'll probably turn him around and send him out as soon as he lands," said Hatch's navigator, watching the tanker depart. "How long do we stay out here?"

"Until either the SEALs call us in or we reach Bingo fuel," said Hatch, pressing the transmit button on his right throttle. "Backshot Seven. Voodoo One. Let's close it up."

Now down to three aircraft, the formation regrouped into a tight vee with the A-6s flanking the EA-6B. Nearly a hundred miles southeast of Mahé, they orbited slowly, waiting for the commands to either return to the carrier or begin their attack.

"They needed what?" Sampras asked incredulously. "Water?"

"The guns on a ZSU are water-cooled," said Mashari, watching the sand-colored, antiaircraft tank rattle back out to its defensive position at the runway's eastern end. "Captain Walid's crew forgot to properly close the valve to its holding tank. Don't worry, it's no longer a problem."

"Minister Sampras. Colonel Mashari. The convoy heading to the power station has been attacked," said the Security Force's lieutenant, rushing up to the officials who were now standing around the fourth Tu-22. "We believe by counterrevolutionary forces."

"No doubt that's true," Mashari responded. "They've probably not heard of the American Navy's failure to deliver its commandos to their boat. This rescue operation is coming apart, just like Desert One in Iran."

"Has martial law been declared yet?" said Sampras.

"It will be soon," the lieutenant promised. "The Foreign Minister and Albert René will shortly arrive at the TV studios. They will make the broadcast jointly."

"Let us know when it begins. All of us want to see it!" Sampras was forced to raise his voice by the lift-off

366

of still another pair of SF.260 trainers. Now, almost all the airplanes in the Seychelles Defense Force air wing were airborne. At the airport's opposite end, only a few helicopters, the remaining trainers, and one of the Aeritalia transports were still keeping company with the *Phoenix*.

"Flippers, off," said Allard, as he removed the swim fins from his own feet. "And follow me."

They had been crouching in about two feet of water for the last few minutes, scanning the shoreline for any signs of activity while the rest of the team waited in deeper water. At Allard's command, Landham and the other two members of his team rose up and charged onto the deserted beach.

They moved in a single file and scarcely made any noise louder than the waves lapping against the shore. Allard led them to the point where the tree line came closest to the water's edge. Once inside it, they unclipped their chestpacks and slipped off their scuba tanks, freeing themselves of the seventy pounds of deadweight each was carrying.

"Form a watch," Allard whispered, pushing a clip into his silenced MP5 submachine gun. "Signal me if you see anybody. I'm bringing the rest ashore."

"Are we on time, sir?" said Landham, fixing a starlight scope to his own MP5.

"It's just after midnight. So far we're still on schedule. I hope Willis gets his Communications Team ashore fast. I need to contact Gordo and Artie, and then those A-6s waiting on us."

Returning to the edge of the tree line, Allard switched on his flashlight and briefly waved it in a circular motion. He got no immediate response from the quiet waters spreading before him. Then, the dark ob-

367

jects that appeared to merely drift on the surface accelerated their movements and coalesced into three- and four-man groups.

Like their commander, they came ashore in single file and gathered around him. While some armed their weapons and joined the perimeter line Landham had established, others collected the scuba gear all were shedding. In minutes the entire unit was ashore and breaking out their equipment for the coming assault.

Nineteen

The Last Interrogation
The Assault Begins

"*Capitaine?* This is Sonar, we have more splashes to port. It's another line of sonobuoys."

"Sonar, this is the *Capitaine*. Are they any closer?" said Jacoubet, in response to the voice on the attack center speakers.

"Much closer. Less than a kilometer away."

"They got lucky," Stackpole remarked.

"They undoubtedly did. And we should reward them for their luck," Jacoubet declared, stepping up to the helmsman's station and waiting for the symbols representing the sonobuoys to appear on its screen. "Pierre, increase speed to thirty kilometers. Steer course Zero-Four-Five degrees and take us up to thirty meters. Robert, advise reactor control we'll soon need one hundred percent power. Marcel, activate the decoy. Flood tube number four. It's time for us to be discovered."

The *Casablanca* had been running on a southeasterly heading ever since it detected the first sonobuoys entering the water and the noise of a turboprop aircraft overflying the area. Now, with the second line in the water and pinging actively, it turned and climbed for them. In minutes the attack sub had risen to less than one hundred feet from the surface and the sonar pulses could be heard through its hull.

"This is Sonar. They've detected us, *Capitaine*. The turboprop is growing louder. It's doubling back."

"Robert, what does reactor control say?" Jacoubet asked.

"One hundred percent available at your command," said the *Casablanca*'s executive officer.

"Tell them to go to one hundred percent power. Pierre, flank speed. Steer course One-Eight-Zero degrees and hold us at this depth."

"*Capitaine*, we have full power," said Accart, watching the readouts at his station for the sub's speed and reactor output change. "Altering course now."

Banking steeply to the right, the attack sub swung more than a hundred and thirty degrees, until it had changed course from northeast to due south. For a few moments it sailed closer to the newest line of sonobuoys. Their pinging echoed a little louder inside its hull, then grew quieter as speed increased to twenty-five knots.

"*Capitaine*, the decoy is programmed and ready for launch," advised Marcel le Brix, the *Casablanca*'s weapons officer.

"Fire tube four," said Jacoubet. "Pierre, steer course Two-Zero-Five degrees. Take us down, two hundred meters."

Briefly, the outer door to the fourth torpedo tube was retracted and a decoy simulator ejected. Smaller than the F17 torpedoes the submarine normally carried, the simulator also did not unspool guidance wires as it left the tube. Its own computer already had its instructions. It maintained heading and depth and

370

matched the *Casablanca*'s speed, while the attack sub turned to the southwest and dove.

"*Capitaine,* this is Sonar. We're picking up heavier splashes near the decoy," reported the sonar officer, his voice more urgent than before. "I think they're depth charges."

"Alain, should we start evasive maneuvers?" said Robert Dormé.

"The decoy will do all the maneuvers for us," said Jacoubet, watching the depth readout end at the level he ordered. "Unless our enemies get lucky again, our part in rescuing the *Phoenix* is over."

"Captain, look! Success!" shouted the copilot, pointing out the cockpit's starboard side.

"Excellent," said Captain Neveu, leaning far enough over to watch twin geysers of foam erupt out of the ocean's dark waters. "We have our first victory over the Americans. Pilot to Sensor Officer, do you confirm attack?"

"We confirm attack," answered a voice on the cockpit speakers. "But we're still tracking the *Marshall*. It is changing course."

"Then we will continue our attack. Prepare another bomb run. I'll tell our escorts they're no longer needed."

While the Aeritalia transport continued to circle the area where its depth charges had exploded, the SF.260s regrouped and climbed away. They turned due west for Mahé Island, leaving the G.222 to hunt the submarine contact by itself — until, however, the Defense Force patrol boats finally arrived off Frégate Island.

* * *

"Artie, it's Gordo's squad," said the seaman walking directly behind Chen. "They want to talk, now."

The seaman handed over the walkie-talkie he had been listening to on an earphone, monitoring the channel set aside for communications between the SEAL units. After he took it, Chen signaled for the rest of his squad to stop their march and rest for a moment. Even though the jungle canopy was thick, they could at least see the flashing lights on Mahé's sole TV transmission tower.

"Thanks, Spectacle. This is Alleycat, out," Chen responded, concluding the brief exchange. He returned the radio handset to its operator and pulled out a transmitter of his own.

"What's going on?" said DeBrandt, moving close enough for his whisper to be heard above the noises of insects.

"Gordo's Com Team says they're watching an emergency TV broadcast by the Prime Minister. It's time to pull his plug."

Chen raised the detonator in the tower's direction and repeated the same firing sequence he had used before. There was a brief, though seemingly eternal, wait for the flash of light from the exploding charges. The column of twinkling red lights slowly leaned to the right, indicating the tower was crashing down the side of the mountain it stood on. Seconds later a dull boom echoed through the jungle, followed by the snap and grind of tearing metal.

"Shall we go take a look at our handiwork?" asked one of the demolition team members.

"No. We'll move out to that clearing," said Chen, motioning to a pool of moonlight a few dozen yards away. "You hear what I hear, Kenny? I think it's time to break out your Stinger."

Above the sound of the tower's collapse, the drone

of propeller-driven aircraft could be heard. In response to the attacks on the power plant and its relief convoy, the fighter-trainers just launched from Seychelles International were now circling low over Mahé's northern peninsula. They were hunting for any sign of the counterrevolutionaries they had been told were there and awaiting orders to attack.

"Are all the teams ready?" Allard said quietly, when Jaskula reappeared at his side.

"All the scuba gear's been buried," said Jaskula. "All the weapons have been armed and checked. All the other equipment's been unpacked. They're ready, Glenn."

"Good. I've contacted Artie and Gordo. They'll be creating more havoc in about ten minutes. The Strike Team is orbiting at their holding station, they can begin their attack whenever we want them. Everyone's in place but us. It's time for our part to begin."

Allard stood and snapped his fingers, getting the perimeter guards' attention and causing them to fall back briefly. The other teams in his unit moved forward until all were close enough to hear him, even though he scarcely spoke above a whisper.

"If we encounter no obstacles or delays, we'll be in position to rescue the astronauts in twenty minutes," he advised. "All our deceptions appear to be working. Our enemies appear to be confused, but confident they're only dealing with an insurgent group. They think our rescue operation is falling apart, let's hope they keep thinking that way. Are there any questions?"

"What do we do if we run into any civilians?" asked a voice in the darkness.

"Knock 'em out if you can. Kill them if you're ordered to. Kill any military or security personnel you encounter, no questions asked. And remember, Demolition and Assault Teams only are to enter the astronauts' prison. I don't want anyone firing an M16 or an M249 inside it. I won't give you any more pep talks; it's time to do our jobs. Move out. Landham, I want your team in the lead."

"I thought I left orders we were not to be disturbed?" said Torres, incensed at the appearance of Major Parker at the interrogation room's entrance.

"I know you did," Parker said hesitantly. "But there have been some developments you and Captain Halim should know about."

The Security Force major nodded to the senior Libyan interrogator as well as Torres. When they left, the only one to remain with Post was Victor Esparza, who activated all the lights ringing him and continued with the questions. In the hall outside, Parker waited until the door had closed before speaking.

"The Aeritalia has confirmed a submarine contact and is attacking it," he reported. "So far as we know, the *Marshall* was unable to drop off its SEALs, and the attacks we're experiencing are being committed by subversive forces. They're operating north of Victoria, and have just succeeded in destroying our television transmission tower."

"There's been no activity from the American fleet?" Torres wondered.

"Nothing has appeared on radar, and radio traffic has actually decreased."

"Then the American operation is failing." The cold fire in Torres's eyes gleamed brightly, and a malevolent smile broke across his face. "Just like at the Bay of Pigs in my country. Only this time the imperialists aren't just abandoning their mercenaries, they also have to abandon their spaceship and crew."

"This time, I agree with Mr. Torres," Halim added. "It appears as though their attempt to rescue the shuttle is foundering. I'm still worried about their fleet, however. They could still launch punitive air attacks."

"Without the United Nations backing them, they're a helpless giant," said Torres, waving his hand to dismiss Halim's fears. "And we've heard even the American public is divided against their government. Your news will be very useful to us, Major. It may help us break Commander Post and the others. If you have nothing further to add, we should return to our interrogation. Captain, if you wish, you can tell Post that his own Navy is failing him."

"Lieutenant, I think I got their officers spotted," Hall whispered, moving his rifle almost imperceptibly to follow his newest target.

"Fire at your discretion," said Hassler, glancing at his wristwatch. "It's time to start. Everyone, we're cleared to fire."

A thousand feet farther down the mountain, the palm trees started appearing again. Bracing themselves against a fallen one, Belford and Hall waited until the soldiers they were tracking had reappeared before squeezing their triggers.

Though they had no silencers, the long barrels on the PSG-1 rifles were still able to muffle effectively the barks of the first shots and suppress their flashes. Their reports scarcely carried to the next mountain; by which time a sergeant and a lieutenant in the Seychelles People's Defense Forces were tumbling down its side.

"Here goes, Gordo," said Patterson, squeezing the trigger on the Armbrust's front pistol grip.

The launcher thundered briefly as the unguided rocket shot out its transport tube. While nothing could be done to hide or suppress the noise, the back blast was obscured by the cloud of plastic flakes ejected out of the tube's opposite end. Once they realized the rocket was in flight, Patterson and Hassler were pulling the empty tube off the Armbrust and replacing it with another.

"Captain! Captain! Lieutenant Adams is dead!" shouted the corporal, breaking through the forest undergrowth and stumbling onto the road. "And the third squad has lost its sergeant! We're being attacked!"

"Calm yourself! At once!" Matubis roared, charging up the road to where the corporal had appeared. "Regroup your men here! I will lead them!"

A sputtering hiss drowned out the orders Matubis barked next. The Armbrust rocket shot over his head with less than a foot to spare; an instant later it flew into the back of the convoy's last truck and exploded. The cab was ripped apart; the fuel tank beneath it consumed the rest in a fireball. The shock wave the blast created knocked everyone around the truck to the ground, including Matubis.

"Where did that missile come from?" he asked, as the corporal helped him to his feet. "Find out! We must counter . . ."

Matubis had barely straightened up when he stumbled himself and grabbed his chest. He glanced down to see a patch of blood forming above his right jacket pocket. Had it been a normal rifle bullet he may have survived, but the Glaser round's plastic cap ruptured the moment it entered his chest. Its load of Number Twelve shotgun pellets spread out from the entrance

376

wound and punctured both of his lungs, his aorta, and his heart. Matubis lived long enough to turn around, mumble something to the soldiers collecting beside him. Then, his tall frame sank back to the ground.

Almost at once, two of the men near his body screamed and doubled over. With Matubis's death, the sole remaining officer was a lieutenant, who started shouting for the entire convoy to retreat. The fiercely burning wreckage of its tail-end truck illuminated the remaining vehicles and personnel. Several more died or were run down as they scattered. A second Armbrust missile added to the panic as it hit the ground short of its target, skidded under the truck, and exploded against the road's barrier wall. A second hole near to where the jeep plowed through was created.

"Well, one out of two ain't bad," said Hassler, watching the search units abandon his former observation post. "Hall. Belford. Cease firing, let's get the hell out of here."

"Where to, Gordo?" Belford asked, clicking on his rifle's safety and snapping the lens covers over his scope.

"Back up the mountain. I'm not missing the rest of tonight's fireworks. We got the best seat in the house."

"What time do you have?" said Fernandez, even though he had just checked his own watch.

"One A.M. on the nose," Goldman answered. "If it's all on schedule, the SEALs should be entering the airport grounds. Let's hope this works."

Goldman turned the key in his car's ignition; the moment the engine fired up, he switched on its headlights. Within seconds the rest of the cars, vans, and four-wheel-drive trucks in the parking lot were also starting their engines. As their lights came on, they rolled out; although none of them drove for the lot's entrance.

Instead, they fanned out across the tracking station's grounds. Singly or in small groups, the vehicles circled the buildings, the satellite dishes, and antennas. A much larger group prowled along the station's perimeter fence. In minutes their activity had gained the attention of the surrounding defense and security forces.

"Sergeant, more lights are coming on in Victoria," said the private walking the airport's outer fence with his watch commander.

"They finally got the emergency generators working," the sergeant answered, stopping to look over his shoulder. "So much for the rebel victory in attacking our power plant. Private, did you hear that?"

The only responses he got from his subordinate was a moan and the crash of his body against the chain link fence. Above its clinking, he heard the soft popping that first attracted his attention. He swung his flashlight in its direction, only to have it blown from his hand when two bullets struck his right arm. Three more walked across his chest and spun him into the fence. Before he finished sliding down it, he was dead.

"You're nicked," said Landham, crouching next to the bodies and checking for pulses. "Well and truly. Commander, they're gone."

"Open the fence," said Allard, bringing the rest of

378

his SEALs up to it. Several moved forward and started clipping out links until they had two rectangular holes cut in it. "Willis, I need your radio. John, go scout the area. And Mike, start taking them in."

The head of the second Communications Team crept up to Allard and gave him the handset off his backpack radio. Landham's team was the first to use the holes, and spread out for the lighted buildings in the distance. Next to go through the holes were Jaskula and the fire-support teams armed with M16s and light machine guns. All the while Allard keyed in the channel the A-6s were using and started raising them.

"Backshot One, this is Leopard. Do you read? Over," he repeated, then he released the handset's transmit bar.

"Leopard, this is Backshot One. What are your orders? Over."

"Begin your attack twelve minutes from now. Mark, mark, mark. Your targets are still the same. Leopard, out."

"Roger, Leopard. Our Time To Target is twelve minutes. Backshot One, out."

"Shouldn't you contact Gordo's squad again?" Willis suggested, accepting the handset and locking it on its cradle.

"We will," said Allard. "Just before our first assault. Move, I'll cover you."

Allard pointed his submachine gun at the holes, then waited for the Communications Team to slip through them before doing so himself. The last team to enter the airport grounds was the unit's second sniper team. Their PSG-1 rifles already unpacked, they scanned repeatedly for signs of activity beyond the other SEALs. In less than a minute they had moved far enough away from the fence for darkness to envelop them. All that could be heard from the entire group was the rustle of sawgrass under their boots, the occasional clinking of a weapon, and the squeak of a wet suit.

"Backshot to Voodoo One, take the lead. We're going in. Our Time To Target is twelve minutes. Over."

"Roger, Backshot One. Change heading to Three-Four-Zero degrees," said Commander Sumner, watching his navigator update the flight's attack route to Mahé. Behind him, he could hear the Electronic Warfare Officers (EWO) running through their checks on the Prowler's ALQ-99 system. "Increasing speed to five hundred knots."

The EA-6B surged ahead of the two heavily loaded Intruders and swung to the northwest. The moment its wings levelled out, its nose dropped below the horizon line, initiating a shallow dive. From a thousand feet it dropped to one hundred, easily gaining the speed Sumner called for. The A-6Es briefly increased to more than six hundred miles an hour. They caught up to the Prowler before cutting their throttles back to maintain formation with it.

"Changing APQ to track-while-scan," Sumner's navigator informed, running his hand over the control panel to the jet's main radar system. "And the EWOs are arming their chaff dispensers and changing their jammers to penetration mode."

"Tell them not to activate anything yet," said Sumner. "Not until I say so. We are ten minutes to target."

"All right, what do you have that I so urgently need to see?" said Mashari, entering the control tower's radar room and walking up to its watch officer.

"Our search radar is detecting a large number of aircraft to the west," the officer replied, pointing to the scope on the center console. "We spotted the first ones three minutes ago. We now count more than thirty."

"Are we going to be attacked?" Benoit Aubin asked nervously, entering the room last. "Minister Sampras? Colonel Mashari?"

"I don't . . , I don't yet know," said Mashari, at first as nervous as the airport manager. He and Sampras bent over the scope to study it, watching the blips change position with each sweep of the beam. "There's forty in all. . . . It looks like a strike, this is almost half the carrier's air group."

"Have you noticed? They appear to be circling," said Sampras. "Is it what you would call a holding pattern?"

"Yes. Yes, you're right. This is a holding pattern." The color returned to Mashari's face, and the smile that had been absent since he was first told of the problem slowly returned. "They're confused. The routing of their commando submarine has upset the plans of all their forces. They must be waiting for an order from the SEALs to attack. An order that will never come."

"They could still attack us," warned Aubin, moving close enough to see what was on the scope. "Such a force could devastate our island. All of your planes are on the ground, they could be destroyed in minutes."

"They will not attack," said Mashari, growing angry. "You are not a military officer, I am. The Americans always follow a plan, and this plan is falling apart. However, I will push forward with our operation. Sooner or later their planes must land. And when they do, my aircraft will create havoc with them."

* * *

"Whiskey Grey One, you are cleared for takeoff. Orbit the carrier until your flight has formed. Over."

"Roger, Sky Cap. Whiskey One, out."

Sitting on the narrow forward neck of the *Belleau Wood*'s flight deck, the lead AH-1W Super Cobra had only to increase rotor speed to lift off. The moment it started moving forward, it was over the carrier's bow and gaining altitude. It rose out of the red glow suffusing the deck and became a set of flashing anticollision lights.

Behind the lead Super Cobra were three more of the slim-bodied helicopters and the first half dozen of the carrier's CH-46 Sea Knights. The gunships had their pylons filled with rocket pods, Tube-launched, Optically-tracked, Wire-guided Antitank (TOW) missile racks and fuel tanks; the transport helicopters were filled with squads of Marines. All had their rotor blades turning; in fifteen minutes they would all be circling the *Belleau Wood* before setting out for Mahé.

"Artie, the missile's ready for firing," DeBrandt announced, when another light came on in his sights. "And I got a target."

"All right, let's give Kenny some firing room," said Chen. "Move it! All the way to the tree line."

In moments DeBrandt was standing alone in a tiny clearing on the side of a mountain. On his right shoulder, he balanced a fifty-pound Stinger missile and launcher combination. The weapon's status lights indicated the missile was flight-ready and its seeker head was tracking the same target as he: an SF.260 just pulling out from a low pass over the fallen TV tower.

DeBrandt exhaled slowly as he squeezed the trigger on the Stinger's pistol grip. He closed his eyes the instant the launcher rose off his shoulder; even so, the missile's tail fire blinded him temporarily as it scorched into the night sky. A plume of hot, choking gases surrounded him, forcing him to stagger out of the clearing in the direction of Chen's voice. Not until the final seconds of the missile's flight was he able to see his handiwork.

More than two miles away, the fighter-trainer's crew saw the flash of light in the clearing. They had just enough time to radio in its location before a fireball obliterated the darkness. The missile exploded just below the Marchetti's right wing, detonating the rockets and ammunition in the pods under it and ripping most of it away.

The SF.260 tumbled out of control and impacted close by the tower. Its fuel and its remaining weapons were consumed in a blast that lit up the surrounding landscape. By the time its leader arrived in the area, Chen's squad was fleeing its location, moving as rapidly as it could to its next target.

"Captain Matubis and most of his officers were killed," Sampras continued, reading from a handwritten report. "At least one vehicle was destroyed. Most of the convoy retreated under fire from unknown counterrevolutionary forces."

"No, no! We just lost one of your aircraft," said Mashari, pointing to the radar scope. "I've seen planes go down before, and this one was either shot down or crashed."

"You think the Americans have supplied Stingers to the counterrevolutionaries?"

"We're facing a U.S.-backed uprising," Aubin

added, still nervous. "A subversion of our legitimate government. What does Libya plan on doing to help us, Colonel?"

"Continue our support of a legitimate people's democracy," said Mashari, irritated. "Minister, take all your forces not assigned to airfield defense or city patrols, and divide them into two groups. Send one to the north peninsula, the other to the area of the latest ambush. Send your airborne helicopter to this new site as well. If possible, I want the subversives and their weapons captured."

Deeper inside the airport compound, the shadows became fewer and fewer. After their ease in penetrating the perimeter fence, it grew increasingly difficult for the SEALs to surround the building where the astronauts were held. Even so, the sniper, anti-armor, and fire support teams were able to take up their positions while the assault and demolition teams split into two groups: Allard commanded one; Jaskula, the second.

"Commander, when do we kill them?" Landham asked, pointing to the guards and other security personnel around the building.

"Four minutes," Allard whispered. "When the Intruders start their bomb run. The demo team will blow the power and phone lines as we go in. Break out your night goggles and check them."

From their web belts, Allard and all the members of the teams around him pulled what looked like face masks with pairs of small telescopes attached to them. The SEALs took a moment to test them, then slipped the infra-red vision goggles over their heads. In the last few minutes before the attack, their eyes would have just enough time to adjust to the goggles.

"Nick, what do you have?" said Hassler, rejoining his communications team.

"After your turkey shoot, there's a lot of activity on the roads," said Foreman, getting up from his prone position. "And it looks like we got a helicopter inbound."

Foreman pointed to a set of lights floating in the night sky. They were almost at the same level as the mountainside observation post, and moving in from the east. As the SEALs talked about it, the popping of its rotor blades was faintly heard.

"The ground forces are too far away for us to do much about," Hassler remarked. "But we can do something about that chopper. Tom. Tyrone. Get up here."

Belford and Hall stepped back up to their old position, but did not lie down or even crouch. Instead, they braced themselves against some trees at the forest edge and popped the lens caps off their scopes.

"Have no fear, the T-Team is here," said Hall, training his PSG-1 on the helicopter and sighting it in.

"The T-Team?" Foreman questioned.

"It's what these two are calling themselves since they routed the convoy," said Hassler. "Can you hit it, Ty?"

"Sure thing, Lieutenant. Once it closes to six hundred yards."

"We better switch from Glaser to tungsten carbide rounds," said Belford. "Or else we'll just shatter its windows."

"Then switch," Hassler ordered. "Now's the time to make a few well-placed shots."

"Three minutes to target," said Hatch, glancing at

the event timer on his instrument panel. "Changing HUD to weapons delivery. Arm weapons. Activate TRAM."

With the press of a button, the Head Up Display on Hatch's side of the cockpit began showing air-to-ground targeting data as well as normal flight information. On the cockpit's right side, his navigator had his face pressed against the FLIR viewing scope and was working the controls for the Target-Recognition Attack Multisensor (TRAM) turret just ahead of the A-6E's nose gear.

"Infra-red is up and functioning," he said. "CBUs are armed. Ejector rack safeties are off. We're ready for weapons release."

"Hartmann reports his missiles have warmed up, and he's detecting Gun Dish radars," said Hatch. "And it looks like Alton's dispensing a little of his voodoo."

Off the port side of the Intruder's huge nose, the EA-6B could be seen releasing barely discernible clouds of chaff. The thin aluminum strips were immediately scattered by the violent slipstream and spread out in a wide trail behind all three aircraft.

"Colonel, something's happening!" shouted Aubin, at last allowed an unobstructed view of the scope. "The radar is clouding over!"

"What? Clouding over?" scoffed Mashari. At first not believing the airport manager, he turned and pushed him aside, just in time to see the electronic snow finish covering the scope. "It's being jammed. But I don't understand . . . the strike force is more than a hundred miles away. Not unless this is some kind of deception."

"What do we do, Colonel? As you said, you're the

386

military man."

"Sound the air raid sirens." Mashari glared angrily at Aubin, but kept it out of his voice. "Alert Captain Walid's ZSUs. And switch off all airport lights, just in case."

"What's that?" Rebecca asked, standing closest to the detention room's windows. "Clay, do you hear it?"

"Quiet. Quiet," said Reynolds, waving his hands until Julie and Glassner stopped moving and talking. In the stillness he heard a deep wail grow outside until it drowned out all other external noises. "That's an air raid siren."

"It's happening!" said Glassner, charging out of the bathroom. "Here comes the cavalry!"

Even though he ran from across the room, Glassner still made it to the windows the same time as Rebecca. However, try as they did, they only had a limited view of the base lights going out.

"Get down from there," Reynolds demanded, taking Glassner by the arm while Julie pulled Rebecca away. "Christ, and you complained about Walt doing the same damn thing."

"But this is different," said Glassner. "We're being rescued!"

"This field is also being attacked, and if you act like a fool you can get killed. We only got a few minutes before the shit starts happening. Pile all the beds in that corner, we'll use the pillows and sheets to cover us. Grab the med kit and put it there as well. Pile the desks in front of the door, just in case the bastards come after us."

"Clay, what about Walt?" said Julie, as she overturned a bed and started dragging it to the corner

Reynolds indicated. "He's still being interrogated."

"I'm afraid he'll have to take care of himself," Reynolds admitted. "And I hope whoever's leading this rescue will get it over quickly."

"Go and discover if this is a drill," said Torres, turning and motioning to his assistant to leave the interrogation room. Esparza saluted obediently and slipped quietly out the door. For the few moments it was open, the distant wail sounded louder, more ominous.

"You better hope this is a drill, Bug Man," Post laughed, glancing at all three figures still in the room: Torres, Halim, and Parker. "If it isn't, my Navy's going to fry your asses off the face of the Earth."

Seconds after Esparza left the room, all its lights went out, including the ring of lamps around Post. Since it had no windows, the room was plunged into total darkness; not even a single shaft of light crept under the door from the hall outside. Post was grateful that the heat and blinding glare finally ended. When he heard Torres shout after colliding with one of the lamps, he realized the others were no better off than he.

"I didn't know Cubans were afraid of the dark," he said, his laughter growing. "I always knew you were a spineless weasel, Bug Man."

"Enough!" Torres shouted, still tripping over the light stand he had toppled. "You'll die for that, spaceman!"

In spite of his soft-soled shoes, Post could hear Torres charging for him. After being handcuffed to the same rickety chair for three hours, he knew its weaknesses; all he had to do was roll to one side and it fractured as he crashed to the floor. The support rungs between its legs splintered, releasing the hand-cuff manacles that had forced Post to sit with his arms at his sides.

An instant later there was a heavy impact on the floor beside him, about where his chair had been. Torres let out an explosive grunt when he landed; then he was rolling off his stomach and reaching out to locate Post. Walt, in turn, was trying to get off his back and find a weapon, anything that could be used to defend himself.

"This is it," Allard whispered to Landham, with the base lights going out and the siren filling the air. "The Intruders must be jamming the radar. We go as scheduled in ninety-five seconds."

Darkness covered the airport, expanding the area of shadows Allard and his SEALs could hide in. For a moment he saw inside the detention building, when the guards and the other personnel outside retreated to its imagined safety. He saw a hallway extending straight to its opposite side; before the outer door slammed shut and he slapped his infra-red goggles over his eyes.

In the final ninety seconds, they adjusted to the monochromatic world the device presented. Allard could see the detention building almost as clearly as when the lights were on around it. He raised his head high enough so he could look to the east, where he hoped to catch sight of the approaching bombers.

Twenty

Phoenix *Uncaged*

"Alton, we're jamming everything but the Gun Dish radars," said the Prowler's navigator. "You want the EWOs to jam them as well?"

"No. Backshot Seven has a lock on both," said Sumner. "Let's give him a clear field of fire. Voodoo One to Backshot One, we're out of here."

Pulling his control stick back and to the right, Sumner caused the EA-6B to leap away from the Intruders, then break into a starboard turn. It arced high over the ocean east of Point Cascade, giving the ZSU tanks at either end of Seychelles International's runway their first real target.

Within seconds, 23-mm cannon fire was rising from both vehicles. They fired in the normal, twenty- to thirty-round burst patterns. The packets of green tracers reached out for the Prowler; however, it was already climbing above their range. Slightly closer a second target appeared, but the tank crews were too fixated on the first to notice it initially.

At five hundred feet Backshot Seven halted its climb long enough to fire two of its High-speed Anti-Radar Missiles. After they burned off their launch rails, the first AGM-88 HARM dove for the runway's eastern end while the second tracked straight for its western threshold.

"There's goes Hartmann," said Hatch, glancing quickly at the A-6E over his left wing as it broke to port and resumed its climb. "We're it."

"Gary, I only have three Blinders and two Ilyushins sitting on the taxiway," warned his navigator, working the TRAM turret's controls to sweep the entire airport. "I think the others are by the control tower."

"You're right. I'm afraid we're going to have to leave them for someone else. We're forty seconds to target. Line us up on the taxiway."

"New target, Captain. New target to the right," said the Libyan sergeant, seated at the console behind the commander's seat. "And it's in range."

"Switch automatic tracking to new target," Walid ordered. "Driver, relay the . . ."

Riding in on the emissions of the ZSU's fire control radar, the HARM's warhead did not detonate until its proximity fuse indicated it was only a few feet away from the transmitting aerial. The explosion occurred directly over the tank's squat turret. It twisted the barrels of the four 23-mm cannons, blew off the radar dish, and easily penetrated the turret's half-inch thick armor.

Walid and all three members of his crew were killed immediately by the missile blast. Their bodies, and what remained of their vehicle, were consumed by the detonations of its fuel and seventeen hundred cannon shells. Most were still going off when, half a minute later, a similar explosion illuminated the two-mile-long runway's opposite end. The second HARM had found its target; with the destruction of both ZSU-

23s the airport had lost its most advanced antiaircraft defenses. Now, it could only rely on vehicle-mounted machine guns and small arms fire.

The missile strikes were still lighting up the night sky when the first SEALs moved out of the shadows and up to the detention building. They attached charges to its front and rear doors: precut bricks of plastic explosives just powerful enough to destroy locks and hinges. Wiring them to detonators took thirty seconds; by then the strikes were over, tracers no longer crossed the sky, and an eerie quiet settled over the airport. Only the air raid sirens punctured it.

"I have you now, American!" Torres shouted, the instant his hand touched one of Post's arms. Immediately his fingers wrapped around it in a viselike grip; he threw himself on top of the much larger astronaut. "I'll kill you myself!"

"Torres, no!" said Halim, stumbling through the light stands. "We must put him on trial with the others!"

Halim virtually collided with the struggling figures, which momentarily disrupted Torres and gave Post the chance to throw him off. He rolled into Halim's legs, causing him to fall and entangling the two, but not for long.

"You've interfered with me for the last time," said Torres. "They don't call me *Escorpiòn* for just one reason!"

From his left boot, Torres pulled a small dagger with a four-inch blade. There was no flash of metal to warn Halim, not even enough light to see the cold fire in his killer's eyes, but it was there. Torres plunged the knife into his stomach, just above his belt buckle. The first time Halim screamed, the second and third times he moaned and slumped to the floor.

"American," Torres purred malevolently. "You're next."

"Coming up on release point," said the navigator. "Just hold her steady for ten seconds."

"You got it," said Hatch, as he finished slamming the throttles to the firewall. "Toggle them all. We're not coming back."

The last increase in power accelerated the A-6E to six hundred miles an hour, one last trick to break the track of radar-directed guns. The Grumman was tracking straight down the airport's main taxiway, less than a hundred feet above it and at current speed would reach its opposite end in ten seconds.

One by one the stubby white cluster bombs dropped from the ejector racks. They had barely stabilized their falls when compressed air charges split them open and scattered the dozens of bomblets each contained. Some were powerful enough to blow the treads off a tank, others just large enough to kill a man. They spread over the taxiway, the Tupolev Blinders, the I1-76s, the fuel trucks, munitions dumps, security and service vehicles on and around it.

The bomblet explosions sounded like a ripple of distant thunder. Roaring out of it were the heavier, earthshaking detonations of jet fuel, bombs, and missile warheads. Fireballs blossomed and rose into the night sky; they melted away the darkness and seemed to chase after the Intruder. For ten seconds the ghost-grey bomber was illuminated by them; until it banked steeply to the right and headed out to sea.

* * *

The rest of Allard's SEALs charged from the shadows the moment the thunder rolled in on them. They deployed as he had instructed; the fire support, anti-armor and sniper teams moved to covering positions while the assault teams ran for the building entrances. The demolition teams set off the charges they had placed on the doors; their explosions completely drowned out by the destruction of the Libyan aircraft.

"Pull it away! Pull it away!" Allard shouted when he saw the door was still blocking the entrance.

Two members of the demolition team grabbed the door and threw it to the ground. Inside, the people who had taken refuge in the hallway were still trying to get to their feet when Allard and Landham's team appeared at the entrance.

"You're nicked," said Landham in a voice loud enough to be heard over the bombing.

Landham, the members of his team, and Allard levelled their MP5s and opened fire. In a closed space the silenced weapons popped a little louder and their spent shells clinked when they hit the floor. But these noises blended in with the screams of the personnel, who had been surprised, and the detonation of bombs at the airfield.

"Search the rooms!" Allard ordered, when he saw Jaskula and his teams enter the hallway at its opposite end. "And do it fast! If they're not here, we'll have to search the second floor!"

"I'm . . . I'm going to get some guards," said Parker, when he realized Halim's cries were those of a dying man. "Torres, I'm going for help. Don't . . . don't let the American leave the room."

394

Parker reached out cautiously, until his hand touched one of the room's walls. He then moved swiftly along it, searching for the door. When he found it, he nearly tore the doorknob off as he opened it to escape.

"Go find help," said Torres. "If there's anyone left."

Finally, some light entered the interrogation room from the hallway. The muffled noises also became sharper but Torres ignored them. He concentrated instead on the dim outline he saw in the weak light and leaped at it, hitting Post in the chest.

The two collapsed to the floor again. Post was amazed at the strength Torres possessed. It was all he could do to prevent the much smaller man from ramming the knife into his throat. He could feel Torres's holster and the Skoda automatic in it, pressing against his side. He could easily reach it, yet dared not free a hand to do so.

The moment he stumbled into the hallway a body fell at Parker's feet. It was one of his guards. In the last seconds of his life, he realized the much-feared commando attack was underway. Then three Glaser rounds struck him in the chest and stomach. The pain made him want to scream, but the first two bullets knocked the wind out of his lungs and filled them with shotgun pellets. He was thrown against the door he had just opened and slumped to the floor where he died.

"Get in there!" Jaskula said to the men around him. "I don't care if it says Maintenance. What the hell was an intelligence officer doing in it?"

"The knife is more painful, American," said Torres,

395

so close Post could feel his breath. "And a gun is too quick. I know, I've used both."

"Thanks for the tip," said a voice neither Torres or Post recognized. It caused both to stop struggling momentarily, and Torres looked up.

The SEAL standing in the entrance moved the safety lever on his MP5 to semiauto before lowering its sights on the two figures. Even with the limitations of the infra-red goggles, he could clearly see the man on top was holding the knife and fired on him.

A single Glaser round struck Torres in the head, just above his left eye. Its load of pellets spread through his brain, killing him instantly. His body stiffened and spasmed before it sagged onto Post. His grip on the knife loosened, and it fell softly on Post's chest.

"Are you Commander Post?" asked one of the SEALs pulling Torres off him.

"Yes. Yes, I am," he said, trying hard to see a face in the black wet suit, night goggles, and camouflage paint.

"Where's the rest of the crew?" said Jaskula, a dark figure standing in the entrance.

"They're in a corner room at the end of the hall, on the left. The left!"

"Got it. Glenn, they're on your side. On the left!"

"Those flashes," said Mashari, approaching the radar room's lone window. "This is an air raid!"

When the shock waves hit the control tower, they shook the entire building, cracking or shattering most of its windows, including the radar rooms. Mashari and Sampras leaped away from it, then found they had to hold onto something solid if they didn't want to end up on the floor.

"My God, what are they dropping?" Sampras asked, as the heavier explosions shook the tower to its foundation.

"Contact Captain Walid! At once!" said Mashari, shouting at the operators whose console he was holding onto. "I want to know how many planes are attacking us!"

"Voodoo One, this is Backshot One. We're coming up on your four o'clock," said Hatch, retarding his throttles to slow his speed. "Have you heard from Backshot Seven? Over."

Northeast of Mahé the Prowler and the lead A-6E rejoined their formation. Miles behind them, the explosions were still going off at Seychelles International. They illuminated the airport, as well as the eastern side of Mahé. If the fires they ignited were still burning in thirty minutes they would be a beacon for the approaching helicopters.

"Backshot One, this is Backshot Seven. I'm right behind you guys, in your six o'clock," Hartmann answered, his Intruder just clearing the island's northern shore. "I have two airborne targets. One of 'em looks like a helo."

"This is Voodoo One, we're tracking them," said Sumner. "One's a helo all right, and the other is fixedwing. Neither is a threat to us, they don't have airborne intercept radars. And since we have no guns or air-to-air missiles, we're not a threat to them. Backshot One, you better alert the carriers that our raid has been successful. Over."

"Roger that. Switching to secure command channel Whiskey One," said Hatch. The moment he flipped a toggle next to his throttle levers, the plane-to-plane chatter in his headphones was replaced by the soft static hiss of a frequency set aside for scrambled, secure voice communications.

"I think it's over," said Julie, cautiously moving back the bed sheet covering her and glancing up at the windows. "But something sure is happening outside."

The flashes of light and staccato booming the astronauts had seen and heard ended as quickly as a tropical thunderstorm. After Julie, the others began peeking out, only to hit the floor again as heavier explosions shook the building. Then the door splintered and fell off its hinges. The charges had scarcely finished detonating, and the door was still falling, when a trio of figures dressed completely in black charged into the room.

"Americans, get down!" shouted the first one to enter. He and the others repeatedly swept the room with their submachine guns. "Americans, down. Navy SEALs!"

"There's no one here but us astronauts," said Reynolds, looking over the side of a bed.

"Stand up and identify yourselves."

One by one the shuttle crew rose from behind their makeshift barricade and read off their names to the increasing number of SEALs who came into their room.

"Commander Reynolds, I'm Chief Petty Officer John Landham," said the first SEAL. "You and your crew have just been rescued by the United States Navy."

"Everyone but my pilot," said Reynolds. "Walter Post's been taken to the interrogation room on this floor."

"We know," advised another SEAL. "My exec just

rescued him. John, go tell the assault teams this is now a hunt, and for the demo teams to lay their charges. Commander Reynolds, I'm Commander Glenn Allard. Is anyone in your crew unable to move?"

"No, they only gave us the third degree. Not torture."

"Good. With your rescue, half of our objective has been reached. Now we must rescue the *Phoenix*. Do you know if they planted any explosives on it?"

"We haven't heard but I doubt it," said Reynolds. "What we did hear is the Libyans are planning to take the Keyhole and fly it off the island."

"That would explain a lot of the activity my men saw," said Allard. "Better collect your gear and be ready to move with us. We'll 'blow this place' once we clear it."

"Christ, what an air show," Belford gasped, watching the fireballs blossom in the distance and rise off the ground. Nearly half a minute later the air strike's muted thunder rolled up the mountain to the reconnaissance squad's observation post.

"Keep your minds on your target," said Hassler. "Ty, is it in range yet?"

"You bet it is," Hall replied, still training his rifle on the helicopter. "It's a 212 model Huey. It's got door gunners and a searchlight."

Even with the strike going on behind it, the People's Defense Force helicopter continued to approach the mountains. It was now close enough for the popping of its rotor blades to be heard. When he raised his PSG-1 back to his shoulder, Belford could see its pilots and the rest of the crew moving behind them. When he touched a button on the side of his scope, a red dot appeared in the middle of its cross hairs. It would remain activated for thirty seconds, though it was unlikely he would need it for that long.

"You're cleared to fire," said Hassler, raising his binoculars and focusing them. "Keep firing until you either bring it down or it turns away."

As before, Hall and Belford fired their first rounds almost simultaneously. The rifles scarcely jumped in their hands, scarcely drew off-target in spite of the high-powered cartridges used. At nearly six hundred yards, the tungsten carbide slugs were nearing the limit of their effective range. However, the first two still managed to penetrate the helicopter's sloped, Plexiglas windshield.

One cracked the pilot's helmet, causing his head to snap back. The other hit him in the chest, puncturing his left lung and heart. The 212 swayed and pitched as the pilot died at its controls. Three more bullets came through the windshield; none hit the copilot though one struck the door gunner behind him.

To avoid the fire, he pushed the helicopter's nose down and banked it to the right. The last strikes were along its port side, especially in the prominent engine housing above the main cabin. Damage to one of the twin turbines was critical enough to cause a power loss and create a thin stream of smoke. The 212 dove away from the mountains and set a shaky course for the airport, where explosions were still lighting up the night sky.

"I'm sorry, Colonel. I cannot reach your tanks," said a console operator. "No one can! Security reports your entire flight line was destroyed."

"Is that possible?" Sampras asked.

"They must have used an entire squadron of their

attack jets," said Mashari, his face draining of color even though he was still angry.

"Colonel, security is now receiving reports of small arms fire," said the console operator. "In the area of the detention building. They think it's being attacked and are trying to reach it."

"Attacked? Someone must be trying to free the astronauts."

"Who, Colonel?" Aubin questioned sarcastically. "American commandos? I thought we were hunting their commando submarine off Frégate Island? Isn't their rescue operation failing?"

"Shut up, Aubin. I have to think," said Mashari, giving the airport manager a hateful stare. "We're dealing with either an insurgent or commando attack to free the astronauts and the shuttle. Have the helicopter and the remaining aircraft return at once, we'll need them. I'm going down to the flight line. Since no one can tell me what happened, I'll find out myself."

"Artie, look. It's the other trainer," said DeBrandt, stopping and pointing through a break in the jungle canopy. "Can I fire on him?"

Running since they had downed the first SF.260, Chen's squad had only just stopped to rest when the familiar drone of a Lycoming engine filtered through the trees. Briefly visible as a collection of lights moving against the night sky, its appearance caused the squad members to shoulder their weapons. Among them the Stinger missile launcher.

"Don't bother. It's out of range," Chen observed. "And it's heading west over the mountains."

"So what do we do?" asked DeBrandt. "Sit the rest of this operation out?"

"No, we got a better target of opportunity." Chen

pulled out one of his maps and shone a flashlight on the section he had unfolded. It showed the base of Mahé's north peninsula, and marked on it were several locations. After studying the section for a moment, he pointed to a mark which he estimated was closest to his squad's position. "This is a police station. It's about five hundred yards away. And if I were a local guerrilla, this would sure be a target I'd like to hit. Pack away your Stinger, we need the Armbrusts again. We'll hit both the station and the vehicles outside it. I'll give you guys another couple of minutes and then we'll move out."

"Colonel, we just got word from the A-6s," said the CH-46 pilot, looking up at the figure standing in the cockpit's entrance. "They've hit the airport; the defenses and most of the bombers have been knocked out. We can go in at your discretion."

"Most of the bombers?" Colonel Harris repeated. "Only most? I was hoping for all."

"Do you want to hold off and let the Navy take 'em all out?"

"No, it'll take us forty to forty-five minutes to reach Mahé." Harris pulled back his sleeve and glanced at his wristwatch to recheck the time. "By then the Navy should've finished its job, or we'll have to do it for them. Alert the Cobras, we're going in."

By now there were ten helicopters circling the *Belleau Wood,* all that had originally been on its flight deck. The half-dozen CH-46 Sea Knights were arrayed in two three-ship vees and flanking them were the pairs of AH-1W Sea Cobras. They orbited the carrier at an altitude scarcely higher than its island's top decks; when the formation swung due west it maintained the relatively low altitude to avoid any

402

possible radar detection. The helicopters accelerated to the Sea Knight's maximum speed, a hundred and sixty-six miles an hour. If they maintained it, they would reach Mahé in approximately forty minutes.

Mashari stumbled onto the tarmac at the control tower's base in stunned silence. The fire burning on the other side of the airport illuminated the terminal and its flight line with their surreal, unearthly glare. The Tupolevs and Ilyushins unlucky enough to be caught on the taxiway were fiercely burning wrecks, as were the fuel trucks and support vehicles around them.

Above the inferno's roar the sounds of munitions still going off could be heard. The cluster bombs on delayed-action banged sporadically; the deeper, sharper booms came from the ordnance the Libyans had brought along. Occasionally there was an explosive hiss as the heat ignited the solid-fuel booster to an Otomat missile.

"Colonel, our ZSU tanks are gone. Destroyed," said one of the ground crew for the surviving Tu-22 and Il-76. "They were hit by rockets before the bombs came."

"My God, the destruction is so complete," Sampras added, stepping up to Mashari. "They must've used an entire squadron of bombers to achieve this."

"No, sir. We only saw two planes. They fired all the rockets and dropped all the bombs."

"Two planes! Two planes and your vaunted Viper Force is destroyed!" said Aubin, his shouting caused both Mashari and Sampras to turn around. "And this won't be the end of it! The Americans have more planes and Marines! You came here, you dictated to us in our own country, and this is the result! You did to us what we accused the Americans of doing, and now the Americans will destroy us! Annihilation, Colonel, annihilation!"

The explosion was deafening and, to Mashari, unexpected. It made him jump, and for a moment he wondered why Aubin's heavy stomach was rippling. Then he saw the hole torn in his shirt and the blood spreading out from it. The look on Aubin's face was more of surprise than pain; not until he examined the blood did he realize he had been shot.

"Minister Sampras," he said, both he and Mashari turning to face the security chief.

The Beretta automatic in Sampras's hand barked again, and more tears were ripped in Aubin's shirt. He was hit three more times in the stomach and once in the left arm, causing it to go limp. He spun away from Sampras and tried to run for the door he had just stepped through, but the numbing pain and shock of being hit so many times caused his legs to buckle. Aubin sank to his knees, toppling onto the asphalt, where he would bleed to death.

"You just killed one of your own heroes," said Mashari, impressed at the ruthlessness and a little intimidated by it.

"Now he'll be one of our martyrs," Sampras replied, bending down and scooping up the spent shell casings from his gun. "Who's to say who killed him? We'll let the Americans take the blame for it. As they will for everything else."

"Very good, you've been trained well. Sergeant, has the bomber and the transport been refueled?"

"Yes, Colonel," answered the mechanic. "And the Tupolev has been armed with Otomats."

"Then we can still surprise the Americans," said Mashari. "Who's the highest-ranking officer here?"

"Major el-Jabr. He just brought in most of his

404

paratroopers when the air raid sirens started."

"Then find him quickly. I need his troops. There may already be American commandos on the base."

"Hello, hello! You must send us reinforcements at once!" Esparza shouted into the telephone receiver. Then he started hitting the buttons on its cradle when he no longer heard a voice on the other end. "Hello! What's going on?"

"There was an explosion outside," said Ebo Dorson, standing at one of the office's windows. "I think they destroyed the power and phone lines."

"Get away from there you id—"

A burst of machine gun fire shattered every pane of glass in the window Dorson had stopped at. The bullets that missed him peppered the ceiling; those that didn't lifted him off his feet and dropped him on the floor. His body was still convulsing when the office's lone door splintered from a concussion charge.

The wood chips it created were further disintegrated by more automatic weapons fire and shotgun blasts. The Ithacas used were fitted with muzzle brakes which produced instantaneous pellet spreads. For a few seconds the office became filled with clouds of thirty-caliber-sized buckshot. Esparza was hit by pellets in the face and neck. He staggered, then slumped against the back wall, and died.

"This is the last of them?" said Allard, standing at the door and sweeping the room with his MP5.

"Yes, sir. All other rooms have been swept and neutralized," said the team leader standing beside him. "Where to next?"

"The *Phoenix*. And we better move it. The demo teams found a kitchen on the first floor, and they're wiring their charges to its propane tanks. When this place blows, it's going to blow big time."

* * *

At first the knocking seemed part of the dream, and Cochran chose to ignore it. But it persisted, causing him to stir and lose his hold on the sleep so recently won. When the room lights snapped on, they washed away the last remnants of his dream; he scarcely needed the hand shaking his shoulder to finish waking up.

"Ed, it's time to get up," said Brenner. "It's begun."

"What? You mean the rescue?" Cochran mumbled, rubbing his eyes until they adjusted to the light.

"We got word from the *Eisenhower* about five minutes ago. Their strike team got called in by the SEALs and they just finished blasting their targets, so the SEALs are probably rescuing our friends. C'mon, this place is starting to jump."

It was only when Brenner turned for the room's open door that Cochran realized he was now wearing a bright blue NASA flightsuit. Out in the operations center, Cochran found the rest of his crew also in uniform, though precious few military officers. The highest-ranking ones were on Diego Garcia's flight line.

"Sorry to cut your nap short, Ed!" Nicolson said loudly, so he could be heard above the whine of auxiliary power motors. "But you told us you wanted to be awakened if we got any news!"

"Yes, but did you hear any good news?" Cochran asked. "Have the SEALs rescued my crew, Admiral?"

"We don't know yet! The *Belleau Wood* has sent in the Marines, so the Army's decided they better get moving now!" Nicolson waved a hand at the quartet of grey-green Starlifters. Under the flight line's sodium-vapor floods they were being preflighted and rapidly filled with columns of Eighty Second Air-

406

borne paratroopers. "It'll take them two hours to reach Mahé! We should know long before then if Terry Carver and his boys are successful!"

"I guess my people better get our planes ready!" Cochran glanced down the other side of the crowded flight line, where the 747 and C-5B towered above VP-44's P-3C Orions.

"And you better get moving, Ed! As soon as we secure the airport your jets are going to be the first ones to land on it!"

"Control, this is the TASCO Room. We got confirmation," advised Gregory Burks. "The *Belleau Wood* has launched its helos."

"Almost exactly on time," said Carver, checking his watch and the control center's digital clock. "Have you picked up any more of those local air-to-ground transmissions?"

"A few more," answered the voice on the speakers. "It's difficult to do so while submerged. And I think at least one of the planes is flying back to the airport."

"That's it, time for us to get more directly involved. Clarence, take us up and maneuver us as close to the shoreline as you can. Mr. Doran, activate air defense systems and Harpoon missiles. Control to Sonar, retract the BQR. Radio Room, retract ELF antenna and prepare to interface with the JTIDS. Radar, prepare to raise all masts. Captain to crew. Captain to crew, rig for surface running."

Circling like an aircraft in a holding pattern, the *Marshall* had remained in deep water and just outside the reef. It retracted both its towed sonar array and trailing wire antenna before expelling the water from its ballast tanks. As it grew buoyant, the diving planes on its conning tower pitched up, increasing its ascent angle. The submarine would be on the surface in minutes and just close enough for its antiaircraft weapons to cover the airport.

"Major, I want you to split your force into two groups," said Mashari, talking with el-Jabr and the other Army officers. "One will surround the spaceship. The second will reinforce the staff at the detention center. Down! Get down!"

Silently, a fireball blossomed into the night sky, rising above the buildings behind the military hangars. Because of the distance involved, Mashari was able to shout a warning to the people around him before the shock wave hit. The thunderclap startled those unprepared for it. Others, thinking it was part of a new air attack, fired weapons into the air wildly until Mashari stopped them.

"My God, that *was* the detention building," said Sampras, watching the glow of a fire continue after the initial eruption had burned itself out. "I fear something seriously wrong has happened."

"The rescue attempt has failed," Mashari concluded. For the first time since before the air raid began, he smiled slightly. "The Americans have killed their own astronauts. Major, a change in plans. Take *all* your forces to the center. Capture the survivors. And if you can't capture anyone alive then bring me the bodies. Especially of the astronauts."

"Colonel, I have a report from our helicopter!" said an excited People's Defense Force lieutenant. "It was fired on by counterrevolutionaries! It's making an emergency landing!"

"Calm yourself. Get your rescue crews ready for them. What about the attack trainers?"

"Three are returning, Colonel. One from the south and two from the east. The jamming has ended, the control tower is in touch with them and is tracking them on radar."

"Good. If the Americans have indeed blown themselves up then we still have a chance," said Mashari, turning away from the lieutenant and searching for another face in the crowd. "Sergeant . . . Sergeant Hamad, find the bomber crew and bring them here. They must get their aircraft ready to fly as soon as possible."

"Christ, when you said blow the place I didn't know you meant sky-high," Reynolds commented, glancing up at the debris still raining down from the explosion.

"That should keep them distracted," said Allard. "At least until we get your ship back. Mike, gather the demolition and assault teams, and clear out the hangars. I'll take the sniper and fire support teams. Anti-armor will be our backup. Mr. Reynolds, keep your people with the communications team. After freeing you, I'm not about to lose any of you."

Reynolds had barely acknowledged the orders for his crew when Allard melted into the night. He turned to where the SEALs' executive officer had been standing, and found that Jaskula had disappeared as well. In seconds the only men who were left with the astronauts were the communications team.

"God, it's spooky the way they do that," said Post, shifting his gaze to catch any movement of the SEALs. "It gives me the creeps."

"Don't you go saying spook around me, white boy," Julie humorously warned.

"Okay. How about, tar baby?"

409

"Knock it off, you two," said Reynolds, the irritation apparent in his voice. "Save your comedy for later. Right now let's keep our fingers crossed that these guys can rescue our Lady in one piece."

"Snipers, forward. We'll begin our attack when you open fire," Allard whispered.

The two snipers responded to their orders by clicking the bolts back on their PSG-1 rifles. Together with their team leader, who was more conventionally armed with an MP5, they crept along the hangar's side until they reached its front end. Barely fifty yards ahead of them stood the *Phoenix*.

The yellow lifting frame seemed to cocoon its fuselage, and the frame's power winches were still positioned directly over its torn open payload bay. Only now their heavy cables reached down into the bay itself, where they had since been attached to the KH-12's transport pallet.

Several dozen feet in front of the shuttle, exactly where the lifting frame ended, sat a flatbed trailer and truck cab. The air raid had caught the work crew just before they were going to raise the satellite. Now, they were cautiously moving back to the spaceplane and reactivating the floodlights.

While one sniper stood, the other crouched. Strung out behind them were Allard, the four fire support teams, and much farther back were several assault teams preparing to enter the hangar through a side door. The moment they whispered to their leader that they had their targets, he tapped them on their shoulders—their signal to open fire.

The first man to die was a Libyan Air Force officer standing high above the *Phoenix* in a cherry picker. A tungsten carbide slug exploded through the bullhorn he'd been using to direct his crew; it exploded out the back of his head a fraction of a second later. No one below realized he had been killed until his shattered bullhorn landed on the tarmac.

At the same instant, a concussion grenade detonated in one of the hangars. Screams from the personnel inside it blended with the scream of the second sniper victim; his body tumbling off the lifting frame and onto the shuttle's port wing as the rest of the crew scattered.

More concussion grenades exploded in the hangars and around the *Phoenix*. The fire support teams fired more than a half dozen from the grenade launchers attached to their M16s. The barks of the sniper rifles were replaced by the chatter of their automatic weapons.

"Keep moving!" Allard shouted, racing up to the *Phoenix*. "Check for demolition charges! Cover me, I'm going up!"

The fire support team charging across the tarmac with Allard stopped at the foot of the boarding stairs while he ran up them. At the top he halted briefly at the hatch opening and swept the mid deck with his submachine gun. Finding it empty, he stepped inside the shuttle and immediately pointed his weapon at the ladder leading to the flight deck.

"Who are you? What's happening?" demanded a uniformed figure standing in the roof hatch.

Allard trained his MP5 a little more accurately and squeezed the trigger. The burst of fire walked up the Libyan Air Force sergeant's chest and into his neck. The Glaser rounds impacted with enough force to lift him off his feet. He spun away from the hatch and crashed against the payload bay control station on the starboard side. By the time Allard climbed to the flight deck to check it further the sergeant was dead.

411

"The shuttle is clear!" said Allard, stepping out onto the boarding stairs. "Finish securing the area and bring the astronauts in! We need them to check the ship out."

"What's happening down there?" Mashari asked, walking out from behind the Tupolev and looking in the direction of the gunfire. "Those are automatic weapons and grenades."

"It's happening by the spacecraft," said Sampras. "Some of those American commandos may still be trying to carry out their mission."

"Or some of their counterrevolutionary friends. Find out what's happening, send a convoy down there. And send along what armored cars you can. Clear them from around the bomber, it will start its engines soon."

"We're ninety feet from the surface," Jefferson warned. "Half a minute to go."

"Thanks, Clarence," said Carver, as he finished adjusting the straps on his Kevlar vest. "Davies, open the roof hatch."

"Terry, are you sure you should go?" asked Doran, turning away from the weapons station.

"Who else would you suggest? Greg's running the TASCO center. You're in charge of weapons, and Dom will take my place here. Besides, if there's anyone on this boat who can order himself to take risks, it's me."

"We're forty feet from the surface," said Jefferson. "Diving planes, five degrees."

In the final moments of running submerged, the *Marshall* rocked gently in the wave action, and the motion scarcely increased when its nose-high attitude levelled off. The four-hundred-and-ten-foot-long submarine broached the surface quietly. Apart from the water sheeting off its hull, the loudest noise it made was the clank of a hatch opening in its flying bridge.

"Davies, get on the bitch box," said Carver, ending his climb up the conning tower's access tunnel. "Tell Mr. Doran to raise the anti-air weapons. Morlan, you're joining me on lookout watch."

Less than a minute later, with the *Marshall* stabilized and running at twelve knots, a trio of hatch covers popped open on its missile casing. Immediately behind the conning tower a modified Phalanx cannon and a lightweight, twin-arm missile launcher rose out of the first two hatches. At the casing's aft end, near the point where it sloped back down to meet the hull, a second Phalanx mount appeared and snapped its six-barrelled Vulcan cannon into a horizontal firing position. In minutes, after a forest of masts had been raised on the conning tower and Stinger missile packs attached to the launcher arms, the submarine was ready to defend itself.

"Apart from opening the emergency hatch and damaging the aft station, this looks pretty much the way we last saw it," said Reynolds, surveying the flight deck with Allard. "Though someone's been eating his lunch in my seat."

"Maybe it was him," said Allard, nodding to the dead Libyan. "Was all that damage on the lower deck done earlier?"

"That's more ransacking than damage. What I'm worried about is the way the payload bay doors were torn open. The orbiter may not be ferryable in this condition."

"Glenn, we got trouble," Jaskula warned, his head appearing in the floor hatch. "A convoy's moving down the flight line."

Both Reynolds and Allard immediately glanced forward, and through the cockpit windows caught sight of a string of headlights moving down the flight line. They had just finished weaving past the two largest aircraft at the far end and were forming into an orderly column.

"Judging from their speed they'll be here in about a minute," said Allard, before turning to the floor hatch. "Mike, get the anti-armor team. And tell everyone with shotguns to load sabot rounds."

Jaskula clambered off the ladder and bolted through the side hatch, shouting orders to the SEAL teams around the *Phoenix* while he was still coming down the stairs. Allard appeared seconds later, stopping briefly to tell the astronauts on the mid deck to stay put.

"John, what do we have?" he asked, reaching the bottom of the stairs.

"One, two BRDM armored cars," said Landham, still training his binoculars on the string of headlights. "A couple, no, three jeeps and a truck at the end. Distance, three hundred yards."

"Just in range. Where's the anti-armor team?"

"Coming, coming!" said a man running up to the shuttle with an Armbrust launcher in his arms; a dark green missile tube and a night scope already attached to it. "What's our targets?"

"The BRDMs," said Allard. "Nobody will fire until you do. M16 gunners, reload your 203s with AP grenades!"

The anti-armor team ran past the *Phoenix,* stopping when they reached the abandoned towing mule in front of it. They crouched behind the low-slung vehicle, the two gunners balancing their weapons on its flat hood. For a few more seconds they waited, until the rest of the SEALs had moved into position and the convoy was moving past a parked SF.260 trainer.

On the flight line's open ground the Armbrusts did not thunder as loudly, and their clouds of plastic flakes were carried off by the omnipresent sea breeze. The lead armored car suffered only a glancing blow to its pan-shaped turret, which caused the missile to deflect and explode harmlessly near the runway. It was the second BRDM that erupted in the expected ball of fire when hit amidships.

"Concentrate on the lead car!" Allard shouted. "Don't let it get away!"

The BRDM swerved to the right and gunned its engine; its turret firing both heavy and light machine guns simultaneously. The twin streams of tracers raked across the shuttle's nose; the lighter bullets spalling off pieces of its ceramic tiles, the heavier bullets shattering them.

Most of the return fire bounced off the car's half-inch thick armor plate, except for the tungsten slugs and antitank grenades. Exactly like the tank-fired APFSDS shells, the slugs discarded their encasing sabots the instant they left the shotgun barrels. The size of fifty-caliber bullets, the slugs needed fins to stabilize them because of their velocity, which they scarcely lost as they penetrated the BRDM's side.

One of them hit just below a driver's observation window, and continued on through his neck. A 40-mm grenade ruptured the turret's shell, killing the gunner and blowing his body out of his seat. In the final moments before he lost consciousness, the driver wrapped both hands around his neck to stop the fountain of blood. The BRDM stopped turning and drove straight into a hangar.

"Get out of there!" said Allard, when he noticed the vehicle's direction. "Evacuate! Evacuate!"

The armored car had barely entered the hangar when it rammed a Bell Jet Ranger. The fifteen-hundred-pound helicopter was easily crushed by the fifteen-thousand-pound car; but won back its revenge when its fuel tanks exploded. Flames rolled out the hangar's front and through holes torn in its roof by the blast. At the same moment a bullet-riddled jeep hit the parked SF.260, igniting another fire while the convoy's survivors scattered across the airport grounds.

"This is what we get when an *Air Force* officer orders ground forces," said a Cuban advisor, pointing to the distant explosions and flashes of gunfire.

"Shut up, Carreno!" Sampras commanded, deliberately putting his hand on his holster. "We don't need any more arguing!"

"We must not allow this 'setback' to paralyze us," Mashari, intoned soberly. "Send an emergency order to el-Jabr. All available military and security forces are to retake the shuttle. Tell Victoria to send reinforcements at once. We must act decisively if we're to continue stalling the Americans."

"I'm sorry, Glenn. One of our men was trapped in the hangar," said Jaskula, returning to the *Phoenix*. "Steve Powers. I'm afraid he's dead. The rest of his team only just escaped."

"All the shooting that's going on and I have to lose someone this way," Allard observed. "Keep the men away from the hangar. There's ammunition still going off in it."

"Commander, we're going to get more company. Real soon!" said Glassner, appearing at the shuttle's side hatch. "Clay spotted a helicopter from the flight deck!"

Standing at the top of the stairs, Glassner pointed south over the hangars and support building. In the night sky was a wobbling set of aircraft lights. Moments later the popping sound of rotor blades could be heard.

"If that's the helo Gordo told us about, then it's armed," warned Jaskula.

"I know," said Allard. "Fire support teams, hurry your reloading. Prepare to open up on my orders."

"This is Black Parrot Three to tower. We can see the emergency vehicles," said the helicopter's copilot. "Do you have an ambulance ready? Over."

Once the dead pilot had been removed from its cockpit, the 212 was easier to control. Though its port engine had to be shut down, the remaining PT6 turbine was just able to keep it in the air. From the mountains to Seychelles International the helicopter had been continually descending, a controlled crash landing. At five hundred feet it was over the airport's flight line, heading straight for a section of ground staked out by its remaining rescue vehicles — until flashes of gunfire sparkled along the military side.

"Tower! Tower! This is Black Parrot!" shouted the copilot. "Tell them to stop!"

At full automatic the M16s quickly exhausted their thirty-round clips; however, the M249 light machine guns carried two-hundred-round magazines. They put up continuous streams of tracer fire, and caught the helicopter in the curtain they raised. A few grenades were launched, but they fell far short of the stricken machine, which began to twist in a final effort to escape.

Its remaining engine hit, its fuselage and even its rotor blades getting shot apart, the 212 spiraled lazily into the ground. It landed on top of an Air Seychelles Islander, chopping the small airliner in two. The fire and explosion that followed scattered debris as far away as the Ilyushin transport and the Tu-22.

"Cool it *fucking now!* That's an order!" said Allard, quieting the cheer going up from the men around him. "This battle's not over yet. We've still got another twenty to twenty-five minutes before the Marines arrive."

"Glenn, you want the Com team brought up?" said Jaskula.

"Yes, and tell Willis to start raising the *Marshall.* We may need its air defenses if there are any more enemy planes out there."

"They shot it down!" Sampras stormed, watching yet another fire illuminate the airport. "They shot down a crippled aircraft! This is criminal! An outrage! Destroy them, Colonel, destroy them! Or I'll take charge and order it myself!"

"We must wait for Major el-Jabr's assault," said Mashari. "And not act rashly."

"What? A minute ago you told us we can't become paralyzed. Now you're telling us not to react?"

"We must act rationally and decisively. We should use the remaining aircraft you have airborne to support the assault. Get one of your officers to find out how many planes we can rely on and coordinate them with our ground forces. If necessary, we'll use them to destroy our prize."

"Artie, we planted charges on every car except the one in front of the door," said the demolition team leader, when he crept back to Chen's location.

"Yes, that would've been pushing it," Chen answered, giving the police station another look before turning the Starlight scope to the approach road.

"We set 'em all on the same frequencies. When do you want us to blow them?"

"Not just yet. Someone else is coming."

An irregular string of headlights slowly moved down the road to the police station. As it got closer, it became apparent that not every vehicle in the convoy had a complete set of headlights and many showed obvious battle damage.

"These guys look familiar," DeBrandt whispered. "I think we last saw them at the bridge."

"You're right," said Chen. "This just ain't going to be their night. Everyone hold off until they've arrived."

The convoy's lead vehicle, a battered Suzuki jeep, had barely rolled to a stop in the station's parking lot when most of the cars and trucks already there exploded simultaneously. The few ounces of C-4 attached to their gas tanks completely demolished them, and rained fire and debris on the personnel exiting the station.

"Mad minute! Mad minute!" Chen shouted, levelling his MP5 at one of the convoy's trucks.

Muzzle blasts flared brightly in the jungle that encroached on the parking lot. Scarcely a dozen yards inside it, the SEALs could hardly miss what they fired at. For sixty seconds they laced the convoy and the station behind it with automatic weapons fire and shotgun blasts. Since there were no armored vehicles they held off using their Armbrust missiles. When the noisemakers that Chen had set started going off, his squad melted deeper into the jungle. There they would wait until either another target presented itself or they received orders to cease operations.

"What the hell? As if the fires aren't doing enough to illuminate us," said Jaskula, running back up the boarding stairs. "Glenn, someone's turning the lights on."

Allard reemerged from the shuttle's side hatch with Post and Reynolds in tow. For a moment they watched as more of the tarmac lights came on at the airport's military side.

"Well I damn well know who it is," said Allard. "Shoot'em out! Now! All of them! All teams, prepare for attack! You guys better get back inside."

M16s and MP5s chattered again, and at first the response to them was the pop and tinkle of breaking glass. The sodium-vapor lamps on poles and hangar roofs flashed and emitted showers of sparks when hit. A few continued to short and burn afterwards, but the night retook the flight line. Except for the areas around the burning hangar and vehicles.

"Commander, the sniper team reports a large force is approaching us from the detention center," Willis advised, his backpack's handset still pressed to his ear. "You want to talk to them?"

"No. Order them to fall back," said Allard, arriving at the foot of the stairs. "Fire support teams one, two, and three, prepare to move forward. I'll command. Mike, you stay here with support team four and Landham's team. Don't leave the shuttle unless I order it."

Three of his unit's three-man fire support teams quickly gathered around Allard and ran across the tarmac to the hangars. Of the two, the one that the armored car had crashed into was now completely ablaze, its roof caving in and the BRDM's ammunition still detonating. The other was still intact, and bordered the road that led from the detention building.

As they rounded its corner, the group Allard commanded picked up their anti-armor team and several assault teams. By the time they reached the sniper team at the hangar's far end, they could easily see the dark shapes of an approaching convoy.

"These guys learned from the last attempt," Allard observed, studying the force with his binoculars. "They're not using their headlights or racing their engines. And there are no armored vehicles. Armbrust gunners, aim only for the trucks. Snipers, target the drivers."

"Commander, you think you should call in a little air support?" said the anti-armor team leader.

"Even if I did so now it would still take'em about ten minutes to reach us. And we're going to be in a firefight long before then."

"Roger, Tower. We have the spacecraft in sight," said Captain Sori Azziz, for the moment his gaze fixed out the left side of his cockpit. "Tell the major we'll be dropping flares in three minutes. Over."

The senior Libyan instructor pilot banked the Marchetti trainer to the left, heading it inland after circuiting Mahé's southern and eastern shorelines. After changing its course, Azziz pushed it into a dive to increase its speed and reduce its altitude to a hundred feet by the time it reached the airport.

"Arm fuselage flare dispenser," he added. "Set for one second release interval."

"Dispenser, armed," said the observer, a People's Defense Force lieutenant. The moment the aircraft levelled its wings, he looked past the starboard tip tank and caught sight of a strange silhouette lying beyond it. "Captain, there's something lying down there in the water!"

"Bridge, TASCO Room."

"Bridge, aye. What do you have, Greg?" Carver requested, then he released the transmit switch on the bitch box.

"Aircraft is not squawking any IFF signal. It's heading for the airport and is within Stinger range. Based on its radio traffic, it's a hostile."

"That's good enough for us. Launch Stingers. Now, now, now. Everyone, down!"

The lookouts with Carver ducked below the flying bridge's rim as a shrill firing alert tone sounded. Aft of the conning tower, the missile launcher snapped its arms down and tracked the SF.260, at the moment less than two miles behind the *Marshall*'s stern. In seconds the fire control system had a lock and fired the first of two FIM-92B Stingers.

"Activating searchlight," said the observer, as a beam from the starboard tip tank melted through the darkness and started sparkling off a distant patch of ocean. "There! Do you see?"

"I don't believe it," said Azziz. "We're supposed to be hunting that thing off Frégate Island. Tower, this is Kestrel Three. We've just spotted a submarine lying off the eastern shore. It's almost at the end of the runway."

The two flashes that illuminated the *Marshall*'s

conning tower and part of its hull died out too quickly for Azziz and his observer to understand what they saw. The tail fires of the ascending missiles were nearly invisible to them. Their first, and only, indication they were being intercepted was the dazzling burst of light which filled the cockpit.

Still banked high in a starboard turn, the first Stinger detonated less than twenty feet in front of the trainer. The shock wave caused it to tumble and filled the cockpit with shrapnel. The second Stinger exploded above its port wing, igniting the fuel in its tip tank. For almost half a minute the SF.260 cartwheeled lazily. The searchlight in one wingtip and the plume of fire tailing from the other creating an eerie display until it hit the water and broke up.

"What's going on?" el-Jabr questioned, glancing at the light dancing in the eastern sky. "I hope that's not our air support. Give me the radio."

He had just turned to his driver when a hole was punched in the jeep's windshield. It made no more noise than a light bulb shattering; the sound of the driver's head getting its back blown off was louder. Covered with blood and brain tissue, el-Jabr tried to grab the steering wheel away from the dead man, only to crash the jeep against a building.

The truck behind the jeep had its cab obliterated by an Armbrust missile. Automatic weapons fire cut down the men, who tried jumping from its load bed, and ripped through the troops who came forward to rescue them. Only el-Jabr managed to escape, just before his jeep was hit by 40-mm grenades.

"Cease firing!" said Allard. "Check and see if anyone's been hit."

"They'll be back," said the anti-armor team leader, pulling an empty clip out of his MP5. "We just surprised them."

"I know. We got about eighteen minutes before the Marines arrive, they'll try something else before then. Collect your men and come with me. I'll have to redistribute our forces if we're to be ready for another attack."

"Inside! Inside!" Mashari shouted, pointing to the control tower's entrance. "They're starting engines!"

After its auxiliary power unit had been whining for several minutes, a much deeper rumble now shook the Tupolev bomber. Its two Kolesov turbojets came to life, supplanting the whine with an earsplitting roar that forced everyone on the flight line to move away from the needle-nosed giant. Mashari, Sampras, and the officials around them retreated back inside the control tower's ground floor. There, the noise was muted enough to allow them to talk, and the tower crew could inform them of the latest developments.

"Colonel, those lights we saw in the distance?" said Sampras. "They were Captain Azziz's aircraft. The controllers say he was shot down, just as he spotted a submarine."

"What? A submarine?" Mashari repeated. "You mean . . ."

"Yes, the one we *thought* we were hunting off Frégate Island. It's on the surface, about a mile off our runway's eastern end!"

"On the surface? What a brazen insult!"

"Or they're desperate," said Sampras. "Perhaps the commandos have asked to be rescued? Maybe we've hurt them more than we can see."

"Hurt them?" said Carreno, incredulous. "They just shot down two of our aircraft, attacked a convoy, and stopped our assault cold."

"Desperate men always fight harder," said Mashari. "And I never told anyone the Americans don't fight hard. If we can capture or kill their SEALs, and sink their submarine, we can still claim victory. Do we still have two Marchettis inbound?"

"Yes. They'll be here in minutes," Sampras answered.

"Divert them to attack the sub. Get me el-Jabr, he has to try again. When can we expect our reinforcements from Victoria?"

"A police station was attacked on the island's western side," said a nervous Security Force lieutenant. "Forces are being sent to rescue it."

"Our prize is here!" Mashari stormed. "Not on the other side of this island! Tell your Defense Minister if we don't have reinforcements everything will be lost!"

"Clay, come take a look at this," said Julie, standing at the side hatch. "They're moving the trucks around."

Stepping onto the stairs, the astronauts found the SEALs were busily moving the vehicles scattered around the *Phoenix* into a series of barricades. Whether pushing them or driving them, they arrayed the trucks and jeeps in rows at either end of the shuttle and along the side facing the hangars.

"The demolition team is setting Claymores on the approach road," Allard told Jaskula. "When they return, tell them to set whatever they have left outside the vehicle perimeter. This will be our fall back area."

"Commander, what's going on?" said Reynolds, loud enough for those on the tarmac to hear him.

"The Marines are still about eighteen minutes away. And in spite of our success, we can expect more attacks. Our Recon Squad says there are convoys moving all over the island, including one heading here. We're in touch with the *Marshall,* and its anti-air weapons will defend us, but we'll have to defend ourselves from ground attack."

"What should we do?" asked Post.

"Stay out of trouble," said Allard. "We didn't come here to rescue dead astronauts, and we're not going to lose any of you now."

"Yes, Major. I understand they surprised you," Mashari replied impatiently, a telephone receiver pressed to his ear. "I understand you took losses. That's the nature of military operations. You must attack again, there's more activity around the spacecraft. If you can retake it, we can hold off their main forces."

"When I attack again, will I be given air or armor support?" said el-Jabr.

"We lost all our armored vehicles in a reconnaissance probe, and our remaining aircraft are being diverted to attack an American submarine. You'll have to do it on your own."

"But they have antitank weapons and who knows what else. We don't even know how many there are."

"Excuses, Major. You're giving me nothing but excuses!" said Mashari. "Their numbers can't be large. It's just a commando force! Either retake the shuttle or destroy it. Those are your orders, now carry them out!"

"Congratulations, gentlemen. We are now the first

U.S. submarine to down an enemy aircraft since World War Two," Carver announced, finally turning his attention away from the burning debris floating behind the *Marshall*.

"Bridge, TASCO Room. We're not through yet," said Burks. "Radar has two more aircraft inbound, from the northeast."

"Northeast? Could they be some of the Marine helos?"

"Definitely not, Terry. They're not squawking any IFF signals, and the Marine helicopters are at least sixteen minutes away. These guys will arrive in four."

"Rearm the missile launcher," said Carver. "Warn the crew, prepare for air attack. Morlan. Davies. If we're attacked, be ready to abandon the bridge *fast*."

For a few seconds, the *Marshall's* launcher swung back to its original position and rotated its arms until they were vertical. The empty Stinger pack, still smoking slightly from firing its weapons, was unlocked from its arm and slid back inside the hull. Moments later a fresh pack replaced it, and the launcher was again active.

"Kestrel One to Kestrel Two, the target has just come on radar," said the lead Marchetti's pilot, as a new blip appeared on his scope. "Do you have it? Over."

"Roger, Kestrel One. We have it as well."

"We cannot allow this intruder to submerge and escape. We must attack it simultaneously from two directions. Only then can we be assured of crippling it on the first pass. I'll attack from the north, you from the south. Break away, now."

The second SF.260 dipped its left wing and dove away while the leader changed his course a few degrees to the right. While the second fighter-trainer picked up speed, the leader reduced his; so both aircraft would arrive over the still distant target at the same time.

"Colonel, do you approve?" Sampras asked, once the latest transmissions from the aircraft ended. "If you want them to change their plans we should contact them now."

"No. Their tactics are sound," said Mashari. "And will allow them to overcome whatever defenses this 'commando' submarine has. It got lucky with Captain Azziz. What do you think, Major?"

"A submarine can't defend itself from air attacks in two directions," said Carreno, surprised that Mashari was interested in what he thought. "Perhaps you are right. We can still defeat the Americans on the verge of their victory."

"Commander, the snipers are reporting troop movements in two areas," Willis advised. "Someone's trying to sneak back up the road. And there's infiltration in the eastern tree line."

The communications team leader first pointed to the hangars, then to the palm and takamaka trees a few dozen feet beyond the tarmac's eastern end. Virtually a forest, they had a heavy scrub undergrowth and cut off nearly a third of the runway from view.

"Hand me the receiver," said Allard, and the moment he got it he was pressing it against his ear. "Joey, which do you think is the larger force?"

"The one sneaking through the trees," replied the sniper team leader. "I think the other may be a diversion."

428

"Then open fire on it. You and the assault team. Tell the fire support team with you to fall back here."

"What about the guys in the trees?" said Jaskula.

"They can't be bringing up heavy weapons," said Allard, glancing involuntarily at the forest on the tarmac's eastern end. "They'll probably try a direct attack, and we'll wait for them. Pass the word to the assault teams, reload with buckshot and Glaser rounds. And find out if the demo team has finished setting its Claymores."

"Major, do you hear? Your trick is working."

The lieutenant's remark caused el-Jabr and the rest of the men with him to come to a halt. When the soft rustling stopped, the crack and chatter of gunfire became more apparent, so to did its direction, from the west and behind el-Jabr's force.

"Yes. Now we must act fast," he whispered. "Squad leaders forward. We must rush them while they still think the feint is our main force."

Crouching, and even crawling, the Libyan and Seychelles Defense Force units still under el-Jabr's command moved up to the tree line's edge. There they all waited a few moments longer, until the firing in the distance grew more constant.

Screaming at the top of their lungs, el-Jabr and the other Libyan officers rose and charged out onto the tarmac. The enlisted men followed them, firing their AKM and AK-47 rifles. In the flickering light from the hangar fires, they could see personnel diving for cover around the *Phoenix* and the nearby trucks.

They received no return fire in the first few seconds of their attack; not until they closed to within a dozen yards of the trucks guarding the shuttle's tail. Placed against the vehicle tires to stabilize them, the half-

429

dozen Claymore mines detonated simultaneously. They unleashed a single wave of steel darts, hitting virtually everyone in the front rows of the attack.

The last thing el-Jabr saw were the bursts of light from the Claymores. The last sensations he felt were the darts ripping into his body . . . and flight. He was sailing backwards; the Kalashnikov blown from his hands and clattering to the ground ahead of him. The last sounds he heard were the cries from his men and new gunfire. The soft chatter of silenced MP5s and bangs of shotguns replaced the heavier barking from Soviet assault rifles by the time el-Jabr crashed back onto the tarmac and died there a few seconds later.

"Bridge, TASCO Room. The aircraft are approaching our starboard bow and directly astern. Distance, six miles and closing. ESM is not detecting any fire control radar, just surface search. How do you want them engaged, Terry?"

"Use the Stingers on the bow target," Carver ordered. "And the aft Phalanx on the stern one. Keep the forward Phalanx in reserve. Fire as soon as they're in range. Bridge, out. Davies, you spotted him yet?"

"No, Captain," said the forward lookout. "After that first one I think these guys got smart and turned off their lights."

"They must also be hugging the waves, from the way our people are playing with the radar."

Carver looked up as he spoke, the heavy whirring which attracted his attention stopped when the radar mast had been raised an additional eight feet. It was now the tallest among the conning tower's forest of such antennas and did give slightly better coverage.

Seconds later, the firing alert horn started blaring. Carver and the lookouts just barely had time to dive for cover before two of the slender missiles ripped through the air on the conning tower's starboard side. This time the tower and its flying bridge were covered with the acrid, choking smoke from the solid-fuel motors.

"Range, three miles. Rocket pods are armed," said the observer, his attention focused on his radarscope.

"Gun sight, set," the pilot responded, before he hit the microphone button on his throttle. "Kestrel Two, this is Kes—"

The first Stinger shot by the lead SF.260 without detonating, its seeker head unable to properly lock-on to so low-flying a target. In the last moments of its flight, the second Stinger dove on the fighter-trainer and exploded directly over its cockpit. The shock wave and shrapnel blew the canopy apart, killing both the observer and pilot instantly.

Fires were started, but they burned only until the aircraft dug its starboard wingtip into the water. Breaking up as it cartwheeled, its second contact was on its back and plowing tail-first into the ocean. Both of its wings were torn off, its tail plane crushed, and everything forward of the firewall broke off and sank immediately. The tall fountain of spray it sent up was the only part of its crash visible from the *Marshall's* conning tower.

The second SF.260 closed to within a mile of the submarine before it seemingly ran into a brick wall. A stream of 20-mm shells from the aft Vulcan-Phalanx mount chopped their way through it like a buzzsaw. The depleted uranium and incendiary rounds shredded the light aircraft, ignited its internal fuel tanks, and even caused its weapons to fire.

As its wings crumpled, the rocket pods under them

started launching their ordnance. The unguided rockets spiralled wildly through the night sky, like streamers from a fireworks air burst. A few splashed into the water several hundred yards from the *Marshall*. The Marchetti's remains went down almost exactly at the point where it had been intercepted. They were the closest any attacker would get to the submarine.

"Impossible! Both?" said Mashari. "Both were shot down?"

"The controllers saw both aircraft get hit and crash," Sampras answered, still holding the telephone receiver to his ear. "Obviously this submarine has some kind of missile defense system. The controllers want to know if they should stop the Tupolev from taking off."

"Yes, tell them to hold it on the flight line." Mashari turned, and, through the exit door's tiny window, he could still see the Tu-22's engine pods and highly swept tail surfaces. "Yes, what is it now?"

"The controllers just got a report from the radar room. They have a formation of aircraft inbound."

"Is it the carrier jets we've been watching?"

"No. They're moving closer but are still circling to the west," said Sampras. "The inbound formation is coming from the northeast. It's at low altitude, and from its speed the radar team believes the formation is made up of helicopters."

"It's their Marines," said Carreno. "The reinforcements these SEALs have been waiting for. How long before they arrive?"

"Radar says ten minutes. Do you want us to organize antiaircraft defenses? We can still shoot down helicopters with small arms fire."

"Yes. Order it done," Mashari replied, glancing

briefly out the exit door's window again. "And have the controllers order the bomber crew to disembark but leave the aircraft running. I will take command."

"Of course, Colonel," said Sampras, before he realized what he had been told. "What? Colonel, what do you mean? Colonel, wait!"

Mashari went through the door without offering an explanation to his orders. Because he had to relay them, Sampras would not catch up to him until he was out on the flight line, marching calmly and deliberately to where the Tupolev had stopped after taxiing away from its spot.

"Colonel, what are you doing? Why are you taking command?" Sampras demanded, once he caught up to him.

"All our attempts to retake the spacecraft have failed," said Mashari. "We don't have the time or the men to try it again. So I will destroy it!"

"How? By bombing it? That submarine has missiles; it'll shoot you down if you try to takeoff!"

"I know! I'll ram the *Phoenix!*"

Even at idle, the Blinder's turbojets emitted a deafening scream when one got close enough to it. Mashari circled around its port wing and was approaching its nose wheel when a ladder extended from the well. At the top rung a pair of boots appeared. By the time the pilot stepped onto the tarmac, Mashari and Sampras were there to greet him.

"Give me your helmet and parachute!" said Mashari. "And have the rest of your crew disembark!"

"This is insane!" Sampras protested. "Colonel, you're committing suicide!"

"I will risk death, like all the other men under my command have risked death! Once I have set the air-

433

craft on course, I will eject! This is not suicide, Minister!"

"Colonel, what are you planning to do with the aircraft?" said the pilot, as he handed his parachute over.

"All our attempts to retake or destroy the shuttle have failed!" said Mashari. "American Marines are only minutes away from landing! We have one last chance! I'll ram the bomber into the *Phoenix* and destroy them both!"

"But Colonel, there are trucks in front of the shuttle! And the armored car is still burning out there!"

"I know, I see them!" Mashari glanced down the flight line while he slipped the parachute straps over his shoulders. The BRDM-2 still sat where it had rolled to a stop, burning furiously like the nearby hangar. Between them, and illuminated by their fires, stood the *Phoenix*. "They're not tall enough to catch a Tupolev's wings! And by the time I reach the shuttle I'll almost be at takeoff speed! Wish me luck, this is our last chance to defeat the Americans!"

By the time the radar navigator climbed down the boarding stairs, Mashari had finished buckling up his parachute harness. He mounted the stairs, then retracted them after him, and climbed the narrow access tunnel to the cockpit. When he strapped himself into the pilot's seat, he was some thirty feet above the ground.

The scream of the Kolesov turbojets was now a muted roar, and the cramped surroundings of the Blinder's cockpit were familiar to him. Mashari though could only spend a fleeting moment on his memories. He glanced out the side windows to make sure the crew had moved away from the aircraft, released the brakes, and advanced the throttles. Moving slowly from the second that the brakes were unlocked, the Tu-22 accelerated smoothly as power was applied. Instead of taking one of the exit ramps to a taxiway, it rolled straight down the tarmac to the distant spaceplane.

"Commander, is it all over?" Reynolds asked, when he and Post reached the bottom of the stairs.

"Just about," said Allard. "The *Marshall* reports Marine helicopters are six minutes away. And that means all those carrier jets are inbound as well. They'll certainly find a target-rich environment when they get here. And they'll be welcome to it."

"Well it looks like the fucking rats are abandoning the ship," said Post, glancing up the flight line. "I wonder how far he thinks he's going to get."

The distant rumble grew steadily louder, and a dark, swept-wing giant loomed steadily larger. It had to weave by some of the airliners parked on the civilian side, slowing until it cleared the last one.

"It's not taking any of the taxiways," said Reynolds. "What the hell's going on?"

"I don't like this," Allard replied soberly. In spite of the strain and exhaustion apparent on his face, his eyes came to life as he watched the needle-nosed giant continue to approach the shuttle. "I think it's coming after us."

"What, you mean it's going to ram my ship?"

"I damn well think so. Hell, if they can do it to two-hundred-and forty Marines in Beirut, they can damn well do it to a space shuttle. Anti-armor team, forward! Get those launchers up here now!"

Mashari looked out his starboard window and watched the last airliner, a Britten-Norman Tri-Islander, slide by his right wing. Ahead of him were only the burning remnants of vehicles and aircraft . . . and the *Phoenix*. He could see muzzle flashes around it and the trucks in front of it, and could hear the occasional impact. The gunfire was too sporadic though to cause any major damage.

He glanced between his legs, and pulled the ejector seat lever to the "armed" position. Then he tightened the friction knob on his throttles, locking them at the two-thirds mark. It was the highest possible setting he knew he could use for taxiing, and it allowed him to keep one hand on the control wheel, the other on the ejection lever.

"Sorry, Commander. I can't penetrate the canopy glass," said a machine gunner from a fire support team. "You want us to use the grenade launchers?"

"No. I don't want to wait for this thing to close to a few hundred feet," said Allard. "All right, you guys. Make your shots count, you'll have no time for reloads."

Allard moved away from the anti-armor team, and waved for everyone else to do the same. While a few SEALs continued to fire on the needle-nosed giant, it became even more sporadic. What once had been a distant rumble was growing to an earsplitting scream, and the Blinder now appeared to be as large as the spaceplane it was bearing down on.

"I know those weapons can stop an armored car," said Post, pointing to the diminutive Armbrust launchers the anti-armor team were shouldering. "But that's a ninety-ton airplane out there."

"The Germans claim those things can stop a tank at close range," Allard responded. "I've come to rely on German engineering. And I have yet to find a plane covered with reactive armor plate."

The two gunners fired their weapons simultaneously. The showers of flakes they sprayed out were more of a surprise to the astronauts than their barks. With no flash or tail fire to see, the missiles were swallowed up by the night; for a few eternal seconds, there was no change in the oncoming bomber.

Mashari never saw the missiles either. His first inkling that something was wrong was the tremor he felt in the aircraft, unlike anything he had ever sensed before in a Tu-22. He instantly released the control wheel and pulled the ejection handle. Explosive bolts fired, blasting the angular canopy into the sky. The ejection rocket ignited next, and Mashari felt a searing wave of heat boil up from behind him. At first he thought the rocket motor was causing it until he saw the flames envelop him. Then the seat broke loose from its mounts and followed the canopy into the sky.

Both antitank missiles struck the Tupolev. The first hit it low on the fuselage, just in front of the wing's leading edge. The second was farther back and higher up, near the spine that ran from cockpit to rudder. Designed to penetrate several inches of armor plate with an explosive jet of gases, they easily punched through the external skin to detonate deep inside the aircraft, inside two of its main fuel tanks.

Thousands of gallons of JP-4 ignited instantaneously. The bomber's entire nose section was blown off, the largest section to survive intact. It pitched down and to the right just as the pilot's seat left the cockpit, sending Mashari on a trajectory over the hangars. The rest of the doomed aircraft was consumed by a fireball the size of a miniature sun.

The shock wave created by its birth knocked down

anyone who was standing near the shuttle. The heat it produced made them feel as if their skin were on fire, or that their wet suits were melting. Immediately after the shock wave there was a rush of air toward the explosion as it sucked in oxygen to sustain itself. The boiling mass of flames rose off the ground, carrying with it some of the lighter debris and leaving the heavier wreckage burning furiously on the tarmac.

What had been only seconds earlier a sleek, supersonic bomber as large and as heavy as the space shuttle had become a pile of twisted and melting scrap metal. Lying just outside the inferno were its only recognizable pieces: its needlelike nose and cockpit section, and the outer wing panels. All else was gone, either consumed by the flames or falling back to earth.

"Watch for debris! Watch for debris!" Allard warned as he moved among his men. "And stop cheering! There'll be time enough for that when the Marines arrive!"

"Someone just caught the express ride to paradise," said Post, after being helped to his feet by Julie and Rebecca. "Thanks, girls."

"Don't be too sure," said Reynolds. "Look!"

Stiffly, Reynolds pointed skyward, tracing the descent of a man under a parachute. He pulled weakly on the control cords, steering himself away from the fire and landing heavily in the grass just beyond the tarmac. He collapsed on touchdown and rolled, but managed to stagger to his feet by the time the astronauts and SEALs reached him.

"You . . . you're alive?" said Mashari, when he recognized the men and women in blue flightsuits standing in front of him. "Your prison was blown up!"

438

"We got carried away with redesigning," said Reynolds.

"Clay, he's the bastard who stopped Rebecca and me from being released," Julie informed. "He's a colonel or something in the Libyan Air Force."

"I'm Colonel Hazem Mashari." Mashari reached for his holster and undid the strap holding the Makarov automatic in it. "Of the Libyan People's Republic Air Force."

"Hold it right there, mister!" said Allard, levelling his MP5 at the officer. "I'll cut you in half before you can put your finger on that trigger."

"I'm surrendering, American. I'm declaring myself a prisoner of war, and I demand that you treat me in accordance with the Geneva conventions for prisoners."

"What? I don't believe this. You've got the arrogance to quote me international law after getting these people to trash it for the last few days?"

"Of course," Mashari answered, holding his pistol by its barrel and handing it to Allard. "You are an American soldier, the world's policeman, and you have to obey international law. So arrest me, American, and the final victory will be mine."

"Trust a fucking Arab to take a total fucking defeat and call it a victory," said Reynolds.

"One day, spaceman, it will be *our* time. And you will allow it to happen. You *have* to obey international law, the Geneva Rules of War. And that will be your downfall, American."

"Thank you, Colonel. For pointing this out to me," said Allard, smiling malevolently. "I want all military personnel *not* to harm Colonel Mashari. I'm afraid that includes you, Commander Post and Major Glassner."

"Why us?" Post asked. "What did we do?"

"You're U.S. military officers, and as such you fall under my control. However, civilians do not. You see, Colonel, I'm not as much of a policeman as you'd like me to be. I can't order civilians around like real police can. And since Congress has not seen fit to declare this a war, I can't use any of the special powers granted to me in a combat zone. All I can do is make 'suggestions' to civilians. And Commander, I suggest that you hold this down when you fire it. It kicks up and to the right."

Allard safetied his MP5 and handed it over to Reynolds. The moment he received it, he was flicking the safety off and advancing toward Mashari, whose expression was changing from confusion to one of fear.

"No, wait! Stop him!" he shouted, and instinctively his hand flashed down to his holster, only to find it empty. When Mashari looked up again, he caught sight of Allard, still smiling malevolently and waving his Makarov pistol tauntingly.

"This is going to be a religious experience for me," said Reynolds, before he squeezed the trigger.

With its safety lever on "auto," the silenced submachine gun started chattering immediately. The first Glaser rounds struck Mashari in the left leg and groin; then they walked up the rest of his body. More than a dozen bullets hit him, just as the wind caused his parachute to billow open.

The straps tugged at the collapsing body, snapping it upright before pulling it off its feet. Between the impacts and the windgust, Mashari was carried over fifty feet. He landed on his back, his arms and legs flopping lifelessly; his eyes open but sightless.

"How are we going to explain this?" said Julie, finally breaking the silence. "You know the Libyans will call it murder."

"He was resisting arrest," Allard explained. "Sometimes it does pay to be a policeman."

The silence continued to be broken by the distant popping and heavy rattle everyone had been waiting to hear: the sounds of helicopter rotor blades. First to appear were the AH-1W Sea Cobras. The pairs of slim-bodied gunships darted around the airport like dragonflies. One came to an abrupt stop and turned almost sideways. A TOW missile flashed off its stub wing and arced down on one of the few remaining BRDM-2 armored cars.

By then the CH-46 Sea Knights were landing, settling onto the grass strip next to the shuttle. The first squads of Marines poured off their tail ramps; in minutes they were setting up their machine guns, mortars, and TOW-firing units. As they expanded the perimeter established by the SEALs, a deep roar swept across the airport; a flight of F-18 Hornets wheeled high overhead while more fighters rolled in on a convoy approaching it. The rescue was over except for the fighting that was about to take place around the field. The *Phoenix* and her crew were once again in American hands. For them, the crisis was over.

Epilogue

TIME   FEBRUARY 12, 1993
Department: ESSAY.
Section: Cover Stories.
Headline: TROUBLED FUTURES.

> Will the newest space crisis set the
> Third World against the West?

Fate can be fickle, even for spacecraft. Less than a year ago the shuttle *Phoenix* and its French and American astronauts were hailed worldwide as heroes for their daring rescue of Soviet cosmonauts stranded in orbit. Last week to be sure most Americans cheered the departure of the *Phoenix* on the back of a NASA 747 and are preparing for its triumphant return. But around the well-earned fanfare can be heard the protests, demonstrations, and the ominous threats of revenge.

It begins on Mahé Island itself. From Revolution House in Victoria, the government-in-exile of Albert René has declared the impending "liberation" of the American-occupied zone following the shuttle's departure. Of course they will wait for the Marines and the Eighty Second Airborne to vacate the Green Line before completing their liberation. And their so-called "government-in-exile" is the most unique in history, not having been forced from its capital city by the invading Americans or even from its offices.

All this reality has little play among the Oppressed Nations of the World, the new Politically Correct label for the Third World. Here the phrase "Space Invaders" does not mean a video game but American astronauts. The new oppressions they now suffer from are Space Hegemony and Space Imperialism. Many such nations are already cancelling satellite launch contracts with NASA, France's CNES, and even Russia's Glavkosmos agency. They're talking about forming their own multinational space agency, with either China or India at its head.

Unlike the Gulf War, where Iraq's invasion of Kuwait threatened the oil supplies of many Third World nations, this crisis and its swift military response are seen in many quarters as an arrogant display of American power. The fact that Washington was unable to secure a vote in the U.N. Security Council against the Seychelles Republic's actions, chiefly because of China's vetoes, is seen as proof that the shuttle's emergency landing was a carefully planned pretext to an illegal invasion. It is not looked upon as a coincidence that America's elite commando submarine, the *John Marshall,* was stationed only a thousand miles away at Diego Garcia.

In addition to losing satellite launches, NASA is also losing its tracking stations and emergency landing sites in many countries. Senegal, Botswana, and Chile are all renouncing their agreements with NASA and ordering facilities vacated. One ironic result of this is closer cooperation between NASA, CNES, and Glavkosmos. The French are offering to build tracking stations on Reunion and Tahiti; the British will do the same on Tristan da Cunha; and the Russians may offer Baikonur as an emergency landing field for the shuttle.

As the *Phoenix* lifted off from what will soon be called Benoit Aubin International Airport, after the airport manager killed in the invasion, the final irony is that the future missions of it and its sisterships will no longer be looked upon as being done "for all mankind." The Space Race is changing and not for the better. Nations that can ill afford it may soon be wasting billions of dollars in space programs. The potential for trouble will increase and, if the threats from some quarters are to be taken seriously, the race will grow hostile.

Credits: Written by Victor Saban.

Origin: Time & Life Building, Rockefeller Center, New York.

END TRANSMISSION

FOLLOW THE SEVENTH CARRIER

TRIAL OF THE SEVENTH CARRIER　　　　(3213, $3.95)
The enemies of freedom are on the verge of dominating the world with oil blackmail and the threat of poison gas attack. *Yonaga*'s officers lay desperate plans to strike back. Leading a ragtag fleet of revamped destroyers and a single antique WWII submarine, the great carrier must charge into a sea of blood and death in what becomes the greatest trial of the Seventh Carrier.

REVENGE OF THE SEVENTH CARRIER　　　(3631, $3.99)
With the help of an American carrier, *Yonaga* sails vast distances to launch a desperate surprise attack on the enemy's poison gas works. But a spy is at work. The enemy seems to know too much and a bloody battle is fought. Filled with murderous rage, *Yonaga*'s officers exact a terrible revenge.

ORDEAL OF THE SEVENTH CARRIER　　　(3932, $3.99)
Even as the Libyan madman calls for peaceful negotiations, an Arab battle group steams toward the shores of Japan. With good men from all over the world flocking to her colors, *Yonaga* prepares to give battle. The two forces clash off the island of Iwo Jima where it is carrier against carrier in a duel to the death—and *Yonaga*, sustaining severe damage, endures its bloodiest ordeal in the fight for freedom's cause.

*

Other Zebra Books by Peter Albano

THE YOUNG DRAGONS　　　　　　　(3904, $4.99)
It is June 25, 1944. American forces attack the island of Saipan. Two young fighting men on opposite sides, Michael Carpelli and Takeo Nakamura, meet in the flaming hell of battle that will inevitably bring them face-to-face in a final fight to the death. Here is the epic battle that decided the war against Japan as told by a man who was there.

THE ONLY ALTERNATIVE IS ANNIHILATION . . .

RICHARD P. HENRICK

BENEATH THE SILENT SEA (3167, $4.50)

The Red Dragon, Communist China's advanced ballistic missile-carrying submarine embarks on the most sinister mission in human history: to attack the U.S. and Soviet Union simultaneously. Soon, the Russian *Barkal,* with its planned attack on a single U.S. submarine is about unwittingly to aid in the destruction of all mankind!

COUNTERFORCE (3025, $4.50)

In the silent deep, the chase is on to save a world from destruction. A single Russian submarine moves on a silent and sinister course for American shores. The men aboard the U.S.S. *Triton* must search for and destroy the Soviet killer submarine as an unsuspecting world races for the apocalypse.

THE GOLDEN U-BOAT (3386, $4.95)

In the closing hours of World War II, a German U-boat sank below the North Sea carrying the Nazis' last hope to win the war. Now, a fugitive SS officer has salvaged the deadly cargo in an attempt to resurrect the Third Reich. As the USS *Cheyenne* passed through, its sonar picked up the hostile presence and another threat in the form of a Russian sub!

THE PHOENIX ODYSSEY (2858, $4.50)

All communications to the USS *Phoenix* suddenly and mysteriously vanish. Even the urgent message from the president cancelling the War Alert is not received and in six short hours the *Phoenix* will unleash its nuclear arsenal against the Russian mainland. . . .

SILENT WARRIORS (3026, $4.50)

The Red Star, Russia's newest, most technologically advanced submarine, outclasses anything in the U.S. fleet. But when the captain opens his sealed orders 24 hours early, he's staggered to read that he's to spearhead a massive nuclear first strike against the Americans!